Creation Machine

www.transworldbooks.co.uk

Creation Machine

A Novel of the Spin

Andrew Bannister

BANTAM PRESS

LONDON • TORONTO • SYDNEY • AUCKLAND • JOHANNESBURG

TRANSWORLD PUBLISHERS
61–63 Uxbridge Road, London W5 5SA
www.transworldbooks.co.uk

Transworld is part of the Penguin Random House group of companies
whose addresses can be found at global.penguinrandomhouse.com

Penguin
Random House
UK

First published in Great Britain in 2016 by Bantam Press
an imprint of Transworld Publishers

A CIP catalogue record for this book
is available from the British Library.

ISBN 9780593076484 (hb)
9780593076491 (tpb)

Typeset in 11/14pt Sabon by Falcon Oast Graphic Art Ltd.
Printed and bound in Great Britain by Clays Ltd, Bungay, Suffolk.

Penguin Random House is committed to a sustainable
future for our business, our readers and our planet. This book
is made from Forest Stewardship Council® certified paper.

MIX
Paper from
responsible sources
FSC
www.fsc.org   FSC® C018179

1 3 5 7 9 10 8 6 4 2

Dedicated to the Leicester Writers' Club

Obel Moon

The thousand and third day of Fleare's imprisonment dawned clear and cold. Frost fuzzed the stone battlements of the Monastery, and the plains fifteen hundred metres below were veiled in mist. Fleare paused halfway through her daily walk up the Shadow Stair and gathered the thin prison fatigues into folds around her as if that would help keep out the cold. It didn't.

She had been climbing for twenty minutes and her clothes were clammy with sweat that was beginning to freeze. An unmodified human would have been in trouble by now, and she wasn't far behind. She shivered, and started climbing again. Movement was vital. She was twenty-two; she intended to live to be twenty-three. Beside her the small, elongated, featurelessly grey ovoid that followed her everywhere gave off its quiet hum.

Do something, anything, to get information out.

The Monastery was the oldest structure on Obel. No one knew who had built it. The name wasn't original; it had first been called the Monastery when it was already a thousand years old, by a sect of flagellant penitents who had lived there at the end of the Second Industrial Age. The title had stuck for seventeen millennia and the present occupants, the Strecki Brotherhood, had kept it.

The Monastery rose from the Dust Plains in a jumble of ziggurats, domes and spires. Not all were vertical. Some stuck out sideways, a few were upside down and one whole section floated a little off to the side and inverted itself like an hourglass every eleventh day. The whole thing came to a point in the slender, rotating Tower of Prayer which tapered over its five-hundred-metre height to little more than the width of a man's outstretched arms before expanding, two kilometres above the Plains, into the Lantern.

Make alliances. Look for weak points, systems to subvert. Biological as well as tech – fuck the guards if you have to. Anything to get a signal out.

Boredom was the issue. Having the sole run of the Monastery had helped to pass the time. Fleare spent days rooting around the huge disorganized archives that occupied most of the lower levels, studying the history of the Monastery and of Obel: two strands that had run parallel for so many millennia that they looked like one.

People said that somewhere in the partly collapsed core of the Monastery were buried the remains of a temple that somehow pre-dated the Spin, or the preserved brain and genitals of a demented god-king, or the secret of eternal life.

The facts were more prosaic. The place had a still-functioning power source of an unknown type, and an apparently senile AI that spoke several dead languages and answered every ninth question with an obscenity. Fleare enjoyed talking to the AI. She suspected it was less senile than it pretended; from time to time it seemed to forget itself and become lucid and even, in a strange way, tender. Then it generally made up for its lapse with a volley of profanity.

There were no other prisoners. What the Strecki knew about her was enough to put her in a security category all of her own. She had been alone on the prison transport, and when the creaking, smoke-belching machine had docked with the Entry

8

Gate – with a thump that had knocked her off her feet – there had been no one to greet her.

She had been conducted along dripping corridors by a floating spherical drone about twice the size of her head. It smelled strongly of ozone. She wondered why, until the first time she slowed down. It nudged her gently, and the electric shock almost knocked her out.

'Where is everyone?' she had asked, in the reception cell. The squat little monk hitched at his stained robes and rolled his eyes, showing dark yellow whites. 'You *are* everyone,' he told her. 'Solitary confinement. No one wants to get near a filthy slot-crotch like you. Even the guards won't come further in than the Second Circle. So you'll be making your own entertainment. I know what you foul sluts get up to.' He licked his lips. 'There are cameras.'

Fleare suppressed a shudder. 'Don't you prefer boys?' she asked innocently.

He grinned, showing black teeth. 'Say what you like,' he said. 'Your ransom's ten billion standard. Until someone raises that you're stuck here on your own. Or not quite.' He waved towards the cell door. 'Some company for you.'

Fleare followed his gesture, and saw a featureless grey ovoid, floating at head height. It gave off a hum that, although soft, managed to set Fleare's teeth on edge. She looked back at the monk, whose grin was even broader.

'You'd better get used to it,' he said. 'It will follow you any-where, through anything. It can flay you in ten seconds. Watch.'

He thumped an old-fashioned looking switch on the wall beside him. The room darkened, and images covered the far wall.

Fleare lasted nearly thirty seconds before being sick.

What the monks would have done if they had known every-thing, instead of only something, she didn't like to think.

As it was, they found ways to amuse themselves. Nothing so elaborate as the little floating ovoid, although even that could be used subtly. Sometimes, especially in the early days, she had woken from the fitful sleep which was all the hard shelf and thin, smelly covers allowed, and had heard – silence. No buzzing. She had sat up quickly and stared round her cell, her heart knocking a sickly rhythm while she tried to locate the thing, listening to the silence with her hearing so enhanced that sooner or later nothing could be silent, and the darkness became full of the buzzing and hissing of the noise floor of her own ears.

Then the thing had appeared beside her head, its noise so loud and sudden that she had jumped violently enough to pull a muscle in her abdomen.

Somehow, the monks seemed to know. The next day there had been something wrong with her food; it looked and tasted only as bad as usual but a few hours after eating she began to retch. She ran to the toilet hole in the corner of her cell and crashed, vomiting, to her knees with every spasm tearing at her injured muscle so that she howled bile.

Eventually, she slept a little, and woke to find that the attack had shifted so that she was voiding jets of scalding filthy-smelling liquid shit. She had no choice but to use the floor because the toilet hole had closed itself up while she slept.

Remember, almost anything can be information. Even just a repeated behaviour-pattern, if that's all you can manage.

The early abuse had tailed off. She had learned to ignore the ovoid's absences and after a while it seemed to have given up. These days it contented itself with floating a metre above her head while she tried to sleep, tilted slightly downward so that the blade-end of its casing pointed at her crotch. The buzzing made it almost impossible to sleep. Even when she managed, she was quickly woken by hunger.

Just once she had flicked at the thing in anger. Just once; a tongue of violet light had licked out of the front of the casing, almost too fast for her eye to follow, and then she had her hand cradled in her lap while blood welled from her half-severed finger. Inevitably, the cut had festered. Even a year later it still hadn't quite healed.

We'll be watching.

Fleare hoped someone still was.

At last the Shadow Stair turned inwards, climbing through a narrow access into the heart of the Tower itself. Another handful of steps led out on to a wide platform. She had reached Millien's Vigilance.

Who or what Millien had been was one of many Tower unknowns, but everyone agreed that the Vigilance had been created after the Tower was finished. Where the rest of the Tower was inscrutably unmarked, the inner surfaces of the Vigilance showed faint, irregular tool marks almost as if something had gnawed its way through.

The other thing everyone agreed on was that the creation of the Vigilance should have felled the Tower like a tree.

Take a round tower. Punch through it with something rectangular, a bit over half its own diameter wide and twice the height of an average human. Rotate ninety degrees. Repeat.

The four columns that remained at the corners of the Vigilance were obviously, wonderfully, *stupidly* too thin to carry the weight of the hundred metres of Tower above them, never mind the unknown quantity of the Lantern. The first time Fleare had seen them she had actually flinched at the enormous weight that seemed about to crush her to two dimensions. These days the flinch was internal, but it never quite wore off.

She took a deep breath that was half unconscious and stepped on to the platform, rubbing her palms together and kneading her fingers. At this altitude frostbite would happen in twenty minutes no matter what she did, but if she did nothing it would happen a lot faster. So far she had done this a thousand times

– the anniversary had not escaped her – and still had all her fingers.

The muscles in her legs felt hot, cold and numb at the same time. The weakness was getting worse. If she let herself think about it she knew that she was being starved to death, as slowly as possible. It was one of a growing list of things she didn't dare let herself think about.

It was okay to think about heights. Heights were distracting. When she had first seen the Vigilance the unprotected drop had sent her into a dizzying panic which had not faded until she was back on the solid lower terraces. The next time she made the climb she had brought a long coil of lightweight rope, surplus to Monastery needs and dusty from centuries of storage. Working partly with her eyes shut, she had tied it round the four columns to form a token rail, just above waist height.

The next day it had gone. She replaced it two days running, with the same result.

After fixing it a third time, she found a sheltered balcony near the base of the Shadow Stair and settled herself in with a flask of hot water and a bag of the bitter herbs the Strecki used for everything from making infusions to flavouring food or smoking. They were the only thing she was allowed in abundance, probably because they had nil nutritional value. She watched well into the evening until the stair was slick with unclimbable frost. She saw no one.

The next day the rope was gone. Fleare concluded that the Tower itself objected to the rope and must have removed it. How, she could not imagine. She didn't mind. The lack of protection felt a little like an invitation. Not one she planned to accept yet; maybe she would never accept it. But she needed to know it was there. She knew she would always be able to force herself to complete the climb, but if the day ever came when the weakness got so bad that she couldn't make it back down again, then perhaps flying, even for a short time, would be a more glorious end than freezing. But not yet.

The old thin air was dry and very clear. With nothing to blur its outline the sun was a tiny pinkish-white disc in a uniform blue-black sky. Or at least, usually uniform. This morning there was something else. A patch of air was hazy, as if full of the smoke from a distant fire.

We'll be watching. And one day, no matter how long it takes, we'll come.

The smoke moved, swirling towards the Tower and wrapping itself round the column nearest Fleare. It wasn't smoke, she realized. It was more like fine black dust. Dust that moved.

She stepped back reflexively and glanced at the hovering ovoid. Its hum was getting stronger, and a tongue of violet light sprang from the front of its casing. Just like the video.

'Shit!' Fleare backed away. And then stopped and turned, as another sound – a loud buzz – filled the Vigilance.

The dust flicked away from the column and closed in on the ovoid like a swarm of insects. The buzzing rose to a screech, then fell away.

The ovoid was gone.

The cloud re-formed, looking a little bigger than it had before.

Then it spoke, in a voice like pouring sand.

'Fleare?'

She stared at it, shaking her head slowly. 'You're not real,' she told it. 'You're a trick.' Her legs were hurting a lot now. She focused on the pain. Real things were safer than tricks or, worse, hallucinations. If she was starting to hallucinate then maybe it was time to take the last flight, right now.

'I am real. Fleare? You don't look so good.'

'I'm fine.' It was a stupid denial but that and the pain were all she had left. She had to sit down. She began to lower her hips towards a squat but her muscles wouldn't listen and she collapsed backwards, landing with a ringing blow to the base of her spine. *I'm falling apart*, she thought, and suddenly she wanted to believe, or didn't care enough not to. She looked up at the cloud.

'Muz? Is that you?'

'Of course. How many other floating talking clouds do you know?'

She nodded, and propped herself up on her elbows. 'Well it's about fucking time,' she said. Then her arms slipped out from under her and she was on her back with the remaining breath knocked out of her.

The cloud swooped low to her side and she felt a quick stab in her upper arm.

'What . . . ?'

'Sshhh. Stimulants, analgesics, vitamins, mixed-release sugars, a circulation modifier. You're malnourished, and you're not far from freezing to death.'

'No shit.' The stuff worked fast. Her head was clearing. She managed to sit up and this time it felt feasible, but her reviving senses flinched at the cold. 'Thanks,' she added quietly.

'Accepted.'

Fleare felt her eyes pricking. She raised a hand and wiped it roughly across her face. 'So,' she said, 'since you've finally turned up, shall we get out of here? I take it you've arranged a way off this rock, if we do manage to get that far?'

'Yes.' The cloud dipped forwards as if it was nodding. 'There's a net-cloaked Orbiter, ten seconds out.'

'Good.' She stood up and tested her legs. They seemed fine, so she turned and headed for the Shadow Stair. Over her shoulder she added: 'And disguise yourself. You look obvious.'

She didn't hear a reply, but a few paces down the Shadow Stair something nuzzled against her side. She jumped, and then looked down.

'Oh, very funny,' she said.

The perfect replica of a dildo somehow contrived to look up at her innocently. 'What?'

She let out a patient breath. 'I meant, disguise yourself as something' – she waved her hands impatiently – 'something that blends.'

'Huh. Okay, how about this?' The phallus dissolved into specks and coalesced again.

Fleare looked down at it. It was the image of the ovoid, although it somehow managed to look more solid than the real thing. 'Yes,' she said, quietly. 'That's a better look.'

The image snickered. 'Oh, believe me, it's more than just a look.' It floated up until it was level with her eyes. 'Now, shall we go and find some monks to play with?' It giggled, and a tiny tongue of violet flickered round the front of its casing and vanished.

Fleare suppressed a shudder. 'Yes,' she said, taking a deep breath. 'Let's. By the way, Muz, are you still . . .' She paused, uncertain.

'Psychotic?' It giggled again. 'Oh yes, definitely. Quite mad. As mad as a sack of scorpions. Wasn't the dildo thing enough of a hint?' Its voice became concerned. 'Does it bother you?'

She shook her head. 'Right now it reassures me. And it's really good to see you.'

'Did you visit me when I was in my jar?'

'Yeah. Just once, before they brought me here.'

'I wasn't sure if it was a dream.'

'It was real.' She stared at nothing for a moment. Then she shook herself. 'Let's go.'

'Yes, Captain.'

'Don't be sarcastic.' She paused. 'Anyway, you used to be senior to me when we first met.'

'Yeah, I know. Three years.'

'I've been *here* for three years. It's nearly four years since I joined up.' She set off down the stair, with her mind ranging back to the start of those years, whether she wanted it to or not.

So, nearly four years ago: it had been sixteen days since she had joined the rapidly growing militias of Society Otherwise, which she had done exactly at the moment she passed the age threshold meaning her family couldn't prevent her; eight days since she had arrived at the training centre; and most of a day since they had decided the best way to use their last free time before immersive training was to get very, very chemical.

'*What?*'

'What about the mods?'

They were in the smoke bar of the Dog's Dick. Fleare wasn't sure how they had got there. They had been there for a long time.

'Sorry. Can't hear. Too fucking noisy!'

Fleare sighed, and leaned over so that her mouth was next to Kelk's ear. 'I said, what about the modifications?'

Kelk grinned, and put his drink down. 'I want a fucking enormous knob!'

She slapped him gently. 'Be serious.'

'I can't, I'm pissed.' He looked at her worriedly. 'So are you. How come you can do serious when you're clattered?'

She raised her hand again and he drew back in pretended terror, knocking his drink over. 'Bollocks!' He patted clumsily at the pool of spirit then looked up again, his eyes unfocused. 'I still want an enormous knob.'

Fleare sighed again and sat back. She was pissed, definitely, but Kelk had left her well behind. So had most of the others. She squinted up through the smoke haze at the old-fashioned timepiece above the bar, and winced. Four hours. It had seemed like a good idea when they started.

She turned to the man on her other side and thumped his shoulder. 'Hey!'

His eyes wandered, and then focused. 'Oh, hi, Fle. Great night, huh?'

'Yeah.'

'These guys – and you as well – it feels like we're really bonding, you know?' He waved a hand. 'Like we've been around for, like, years or something. Not just a few days.'

'Sure.' She nodded, carefully, and then leaned in closer to him. 'Listen, Muz, did you think about getting modifications?'

He pursed his lips. 'What, that nano-y gene-y kinda stuff?'

'Yeah, that.' She searched his face. 'So, did you?'

He picked up his glass, examined it, and held it upside down over the table. 'Empty. See? Empty!' He raised the glass, still upside down, and roared towards the bar. 'Oi! Some assistance here. Thirsty soldiers in *major* need, thankyouverymuch.' He put the glass down, turned back towards Fleare, studied her face and then said: '*What?*'

She suppressed a grin. 'You aren't thirsty, you're drunk.' He nodded gravely, and she went on. 'And you aren't a soldier – yet. You're a cadet. You could still get busted straight out of here.'

'Nah, I wouldn't do that. Coz if I did I know I would break your heart. *Ow!*' He flinched, and removed Fleare's elbow from his ribs. 'Besides, there's always another way to stay.' He looked directly at her with eyes that suddenly seemed more sober. 'Get modified and you're in for life. You realize that?'

She held his gaze for a while, and then looked at her drink. 'Yes,' she said. 'That's right.'

'Hmmm.'

The floor shivered. Muz swivelled his head so he was looking at the old clock. 'Ah,' he said. 'Steam's up. Only happens every ten years or so. Some coincidence we should have our last day off today. You want to watch?'

She nodded gratefully. 'Sure,' she said. She stood up, and then grabbed at the table as another stronger tremor shook the room. 'Let's go.' She slapped Kelk on the shoulder. 'C'mon,

17

piss-head. It's showtime. We're going to watch. Coming?'

Kelk's head was on the table. He raised it just as the barman thumped a full glass down in front of him. 'Ah,' he said. 'Decision. Watch steamy thing, or drink.' He laid a finger on the rim of the full glass, and wagged it towards the door. 'Drink-watch. Watch-drink. Drin-wash . . .' He frowned and his voice tailed away.

Fleare looked at Muz and shrugged. She picked up the full glass and held it up to Kelk's bewildered face. 'Drink,' she suggested, and he brightened and took the glass from her. Then she turned and followed Muz out of the bar. The floor shook again. Behind her there was a crash, about the right size to be someone falling off a chair. She didn't look round.

The balconies outside the bar were crowded. Muz elbowed roughly through. Fleare followed, resisting the urge to apologize, and nodding at a few people she recognized from the shuttle trip. Muz didn't stop until he had forced his way to the gnarled timber rail that formed the edge of the balcony. Fleare caught up with him and took hold of the rail.

Wisps of steam curled up from below and wrapped around the massive Pump Trees. The smooth water-engorged trunks formed a close, dense circle around the outside of the bar. Fleare looked up through the warm mist to the canopy of Shower Buds a hundred metres above her head. Even at that distance the reddish-brown buds looked swollen.

The balcony shook, strongly enough to knock a few of the least steady to their knees. Most of them stayed there. Muz nodded. 'It's coming,' he said. He held out his hands. 'You wanna hold on to me?'

She shook her head and tightened her grip on the rail as the first drops of rain hit her.

When she had first seen this place from space, only eight days before, Fleare had thought it looked like a storm – or a pimple or a target – a distinct, raised, rust-coloured disc on a small, dull, tawny planet. It might have ended up with any of several names. In the end, most people had settled on Nipple, which was one of the politer ones.

'Weird, huh?'

She had pushed herself away from the obs screen and turned to look at the speaker. He was tall and skinny, dressed in brigade kit like hers, but faded, and with shoulder pips that said he had been in for a year. She drew herself upright but he smiled and held out his hands, palms down. 'No salutes,' he said. 'I'm only cadet-plus, not full officer. Besides, I'm shit at hierarchy.' He held out a hand. 'Muzimir fos Gelent. Muz.'

She took the hand. 'Fleare Haas. Fleare.' His fingers felt dry and muscular.

He gestured towards the planet. 'Definitely weird, in a slightly horny sort of way. Happened at the end of the Second Machine Wars.'

'Happened?' Fleare looked back to the little planet, which was filling more of the screen as the shuttle dropped into orbit. 'Didn't it start out like that, then?'

'Nah.' He shoved himself away from the rail. 'Look, we won't be hooked up to transfer for at least an hour. Buy you a drink?'

She studied him for a moment. 'Is this a pick-up?'

He grinned. 'Ha. Busted! Very inappropriate. Abuse of position.' He turned back to the screen, and then gave her a stagey sideways glance. 'But anyway – buy you a drink?'

It had been a long journey, Fleare told herself, and the air on board the creaking little military shuttle was oily and acrid. Of course she was thirsty. The fingers and the grin had nothing to do with it. Obviously.

'Okay,' she said.

The shuttle had no bar, only vending slots that served nothing stronger than fruit juices and herbal infusions. Muz fetched up in front of one, swiped a credit chip through the reader and raised his eyes to the display. 'What do you know. It thinks I've got some credit left. Suckers!' He turned to Fleare. 'What are you having?'

She chose a sour chai and Muz dialled two. They took their drinks back through the mostly humanoid crowds to the obs screen. Fleare sipped, and pulled a face at the astringent taste. 'Yuk.' She turned to Muz. 'So, tell me about Nipple. It might take my mind off this stuff.'

'Ha!' He sipped, and looked at the glass in horror. 'Something of a challenge there.' He shrugged, and screwed up his face as if it helped his memory. 'Actually there's not that much to tell. It was a boring little planet with a bit of underground water and just enough atmosphere to support a few misfits who wanted a quiet life. No native fauna. Millions of years of sweet fuck all. Then things got interesting.'

He was a good story-teller. Fleare liked that in a man. She listened.

The story he told her began two thousand years earlier. In those days Nipple had the more prosaic name of Salamis 1. Salamis was a smallish yellowish star in the third shell of the Spin, a long way from anything useful or interesting. The total population of its only planet peaked, so it was said, at five hundred stinking hermits in five hundred stinking huts. Total exports equalled total imports, at zero. Limited plant life allowed the dedicated to grow food, as long as your definition of food began and ended at a primitive maize and a couple of tough starchy roots.

The small wars that were endemic to the sector at the time somehow swirled round the little planet without touching it; as well as lacking every other useful attribute, Salamis didn't even offer a strategically valuable position.

Which made it all but impossible to understand why anyone should try to destroy it.

Fleare wrinkled her forehead. 'Destroy?'

Muz waggled a hand in front of him. 'Well, that's what it looked like, although it was probably an accident.' He drained his glass and put it down with a look of relief. 'Ever heard of a race called the Zeft?'

She frowned. 'Maybe. Remind me. Can't remember.'

'I'm not surprised. It wasn't exactly their finest hour. More like their last, actually.' He shrugged. 'Bit players. Or so everyone thought.'

Fleare nodded. Her own memory began to supplement the story Muz was telling, as fragments of the expensive education she had done her best to ignore began to assemble themselves. *Shit*, she thought to herself. *I wasn't wasting Daddy's money as badly as I thought. Must try harder.*

The Zeft had been humanoid, and aggressive in a limited, pointless sort of way. They had assembled a small but nasty five-system, ten-planet empire based mainly on crude techno-logical theft, a rigid caste system and a bit of slave trading, and had hung on to it for several hundred years by keeping out of the way of the real grown-ups in the sector. At any one time the Spin contained two or three Zefts, and the best way to deal with them was to hold your nose and move on.

Then, without any warning, a battle fleet that no one knew the Zeft possessed had turned up in one of the last battles of the Second Machine Wars, announced their intention of joining what everyone could already see was the winning side, issued a garbled warning to the inhabitants of Salamis 1 – and fired something.

They probably intended it to be a surprise, and the effect had presumably surprised the Zeft very much indeed, although not for long. Whatever it was produced a hundred-thousand-kilometre ball of plasma, centred on their fleet. When it had cleared, the Zeft were simply gone.

Fleare stared at him. 'Just gone? Nothing left?'

'Nothing. Not even dust. Just a heap of hot atoms.'

'Shit.' She thought for a moment. 'So what the hell was it?'

'The weapon? No one knows. People are still studying the area, of course. Best guess is that the Zeft somehow managed to pinch an artefact left over either from the First Machine Wars or, more likely, from the original Construction Phase. Decided it offered a path to immortality and proved themselves right in the worst way.'

Fleare nodded. Artefacts popped up occasionally. These days they were supposed to be handed in to the Hegemony, on pain of alarming sanctions. Mostly they were either useless or incomprehensible, but there was always the risk that something seriously potent would turn up.

She turned to the obs screen. 'So what did that have to do with this?' She waved at the reddish-brown aureole and frowned. It really did look like a nipple.

'Ah. That.' Muz leaned low over the obs rail as if he was studying the little planet. 'I said there was nothing left after the fireball. Not quite accurate. Something shot out of it. Something small and very fast and very hot, piece of Zeft debris most likely. Whatever it was, it was going at a hell of a clip. It drilled a hole straight through the crust. Connected a lot of hot magmatic water to the outside world, and created, well, that.' His hands described a rough circle in front of him. 'A whole new eco-system, five thousand klicks across, based on warm water. Pump Trees, hot springs, Rain Sharks. There's a pub in the middle of it. It's pretty cool. I'll show you when we get there. If you like?'

She looked at the planet and then at Muz. 'I like,' she said.

And now, eight days later, they were in the middle of the nipple itself. The rain became heavier, and the ground shook continually as hundreds of geysers sent steaming, mineral-rich water shooting up. The spouting water splashed against the underside of the platform, and little jets found their way through the gaps between the planks. The warm moist air smelled of minerals and leaf mould and damp timber.

Fleare felt Muz nudge her. He was pointing upwards. 'Look,' he said. 'That one's ready to blow. See?'

She squinted through the mist towards the Pump Tree he was pointing at, and nodded. The spray buds that crowned the tree were trembling. A pod of Bud Chimps, invisible in their camouflage until they moved, screeched all at once as if they were one animal and threw themselves away from the tree.

The distended buds swelled visibly. Then they burst.

The concussion shook the platform. Around Fleare and Muz, dozens of people were knocked off their feet and lay sprawled on the rough planks. Most of them stayed there, holding on to railings or each other as the sheets of sweet, sap-tainted water fell around them.

It was like a chain reaction. One tree set off another, until it seemed that the whole spinney was roaring water into the air.

Fleare kept her feet somehow. She screwed up her eyes against the hammering curtains of water. With blurred vision she watched as shoals of Optimist Fish began their desperate climb up the falling rain. Not one in a thousand would get high enough to plant their fertilized eggs in the depleting buds. For those that did, it would take a whole year for the eggs to sink through the Pump Trees' draining systems to ground level, and another nine for the fish to grow to maturity in time for the next Spray Season.

She turned to Muz, and laughed. He had his hands braced on the railing and his head tipped back, eyes closed and mouth open. Rivulets of sap and water ran over his lips, and his throat rippled as he swallowed.

She nudged him. 'Hey!'

His eyes snapped open, and he turned to her, licking his lips. 'What?'

'What are you doing?'

23

'What does it look like? Taking a drink.' He grinned at her. 'You're going to ask why.'

She considered. 'I might slap you instead. Smug bastard.'

He shook his head. 'Nah, you won't do that. Nice girls don't hit drunks. Anyway, you want to know the answer.'

She studied her fingernails.

'Okay!' Muz was still shaking his head. 'Three reasons. First, I'm thirsty. Second, it's supposed to be good for you. Full of natural thingies and stuff. And third,' and he lowered his voice, 'it's a guaranteed aphrodisiac.'

'The hell you say.' She kept her own voice level.

'Nah, I made that bit up.'

'Good.'

'Really?'

'Yeah.' She turned back to the obs rail. 'I'd have walked off if I thought you were really that tacky.'

'Oh.'

Much later, she let a lazy finger trail down the short, damp hairs on his chest. He stirred, but didn't wake from his sated sleep. She frowned, and pressed harder. As his eyes fluttered open she swung herself astride him. He groaned. 'Oh, no. *Again?*'

She put a finger to his lips. 'Oh, yes,' she told him. 'Remember, I could have walked off.'

'Ah. That's true. *Ahh . . .*'

Fleare woke slowly, and lay as still as possible while she grew into her hangover. It was an impressive one. She seemed to remember earning it.

After a few minutes she trusted herself to move. She rolled over and found herself pushing against something warm. She pushed harder and it moaned. She pulled back the cover and saw Muz, face slack. Fleare grinned to herself and rolled over to the other side of the bed.

She achieved upright on the second attempt and stood, swaying, until her stomach and her inner ears settled down. Then she took stock. She was not in her own quarters. The room was cadet standard, just big enough for a bed, a table and a wash cabinet, and it smelled of last night's alcohol and slightly more recent bodies. She stood as still as possible and concentrated on breathing through her mouth.

When she was fairly sure she was not going to be sick she walked over to the wash cabinet, shrugged off a T-shirt she didn't remember either owning or putting on and stepped into the shower. The water was cold. You're a Soc O soldier, she told herself. You can do this.

Society Otherwise was what happened when an idea became a movement and then, somehow, got organized without destroying itself. It had begun with groups of students unpicking the encryption of commercial news conduits and watching with their mouths hanging open as they realized just how mendacious their parents' generation could be. It had gained weight from the remnants of left-wing groups, washed up and marginalized by the swelling oligarchical tide of the Hegemony as it rolled through minor societies across the Inner Spin, leaving them sweating and indebted in its wake. It liaised with a couple of private militias and found itself suddenly able to project real power – and therefore suddenly of close interest to the Hegemony. From there on, Society Otherwise had run out of choices. It had to fight.

Fleare let herself turn under the spray for a few minutes, feeling her body beginning to forgive her. Then she shut off the water, stepped out of the cabinet and collided with a naked Muz.

'Hi, baby.' He tried to wrap his arms around her but she pulled back. 'I'm wet,' she told him.

He grinned. 'I have that effect.'

She rolled her eyes. 'Pervert. Besides,' and she wrinkled her nose, 'your breath smells like, like *breath*, and not in a good way.' She placed a hand on his chest and pushed. He took a surprised step backwards, met the edge of the only chair in the little room and dropped into it.

'Hey,' he protested. 'That's no way to treat a superior officer.'

She looked down at him, a hand on her hip. 'Superior officers,' she said, 'are probably not supposed to spend so much of their time underneath.'

'What? Oh . . .' He stared at the floor for a moment then looked up innocently. 'Mind you,' he said, 'there's always leading from behind.'

Fleare shook her head. 'Life in the army . . . speaking of which, wasn't there something we were meant to be doing?'

Muz nodded. 'Brigade briefing,' he said, 'but that doesn't start until— Oh, shit.' His eyes followed her pointing finger to the time display on the wall. 'Oh shit, ohshitohshit!'

'Precisely.' Fleare nodded. 'We have six minutes. Of course, I'm already washed.'

She stood aside as he charged into the cabinet, and then laughed out loud at his scream of protest. She had forgotten to mention the cold water.

They made the briefing with ten seconds to spare.

'. . . modifications, including Enhancements, for anything other than therapeutic purposes were banned in all Spin jurisdictions following the collapse of the Dimililer class action in 734. Please refer to your notes for that. De jure, this remains the case, but accumulating precedent allows a degree of interpretation . . .'

Fleare fought back a yawn. The elderly Technical Sergeant who was briefing them was bone-thin, and her voice had a droning quality. As well, the briefing room was stuffily under-ground, in a partitioned-off corner of what had been a hardened missile silo. It was also still faintly radioactive; to come in here

26

you had to wear a monitoring tag. The tag was clipped to one of the pocket flaps on her fatigues. It felt a little irritating, but it hadn't pinged yet.

Something brushed against her shoulder. She glanced to the side, and suppressed a grin. Muz was standing with his eyes half closed, swaying. She dug an elbow sideways; his head snapped up.

'. . . decided to offer certain recruits the opportunity to Enhance, with the focus being on strength, speed and stamina. Those with complementary outcomes will be formed into squads of five for training as intervention squads, for duties which will be disclosed only at that time . . .'

There were about fifty of them, all casualties of the Dog's Dick the night before. Fleare guessed she was one of the lucky ones. Muz was obviously struggling, and to her other side Kelk looked like a black and white picture of himself. His fatigues were rumpled, and Fleare guessed he had slept in them. She sniffed a little, and wrinkled her nose. Definitely slept-in, and possibly something-else'd-in as well.

'. . . concludes the disclosure. There will be a short period for questions and then you will have free time until sundown, after which all those who volunteer will be required to enter their consent with Legals.' The woman put down her notepad and gave a frosty smile. 'So, questions? Yes – at the back?'

'Uh, what does "complementary outcomes" mean?'

Fleare looked round. The questioner was a tall, hard-looking male with blue-black skin. They'd met the night before, in the sense of drunkenly bumping into one another and exchanging ID tabs. Zepf. That was the name. Exclusively homosexual, Fleare remembered. She shrugged and faced forward.

'What it says.' The woman looked impatient. 'Different bodies experience different levels of outcome from the same intervention.'

Zepf persisted. 'And different levels of success?'

'Self-evidently.' The Technical Sergeant gathered her papers. 'I recommend you read the notes, if you have not yet had the opportunity; everything is fully covered.' She made to walk away from her lectern.

Fleare raised a hand. 'Sorry. One more question?'

Heads turned towards Fleare. The woman stopped, tutting audibly. 'One question only. Go on.'

Fleare took a breath. 'What's the rush?' she asked.

There was silence for a moment. Then the woman placed her papers back on the lectern and raised her eyebrows. 'What rush?' she asked mildly.

'Well, we've been here for nine days. We haven't even done any basic training yet.' Fleare felt herself getting ready to shrink under the cool gaze, and shook herself. 'And we haven't been assessed yet. Don't we have to get sort of tested before you put us in for mods?'

The woman's eyebrows climbed. 'The Hegemony isn't waiting. How many people do you think have come into its influence since you arrived on this planet?'

Fleare shook her head.

'I'll tell you, although I suspect that you *of all people* know.' The emphasis had been subtle; Fleare looked around, but no one else seemed to have noticed. 'It's roughly a hundred million. That is the average rate of advance of the Hegemony over the last few years: ten million people a day. A mega-city every ten days, a medium-sized planet every year, with their democratic governments replaced by so-called technocracies imposed without their consent to correct the financial disasters caused by the depletion of their economies by the tame bankers that follow the Hegemony like flies following a dragged corpse. Technocracies which then control social freedoms, roll back progressive statute, turn healthcare into a currency. Where life expectancies fall and infant mortality rises and suicide rates soar.'

Fleare realized with something like shock that the woman's voice had trembled as she spoke and there were beads of sweat clinging to her hairline. She hadn't thought such a dried-up-looking entity capable of moisture. Let alone passion.

The woman went on. 'So if every day provides ten million human reasons to act, why should we wait?' The corner of her mouth twitched. 'Besides, both the nature and the urgency of your training will depend on the nature of your modifications and the level of their success. Clearly we would not waste time training you for a role which you had no chance of carrying out. And as an aside, your reading of the sign-up disclosure was obviously defective. You have been the subject of close remote-sensing scrutiny since the moment you arrived. We know more than enough about your physiological responses . . . to every situation.' She gave a smile which looked genuine and gathered up her papers. 'Enjoy your afternoon, Cadet Haas.' She paused. 'And of course your, ah, friend, Cadet-Corporal fos Gelent.'

There was a rustle of laughter and Fleare felt her face burning. She stood to attention along with the rest of the room until the woman had left. Then, as hard as she could, she drove her elbow into Muz's side.

'Ooooof!' He staggered and clutched at himself. 'What was that for?'

'You knew!' She pulled back her elbow for another shot but he grabbed it. 'You knew they were spying. You complete,' she searched for a bad enough word but couldn't find one, 'you complete turd! You might as well have hauled me into a fucking porn studio!'

'Oh, right. Of course!' He gave her back her elbow. 'Obviously I pushed you down the slope against your will. I mean, it's not like you were the sober one or anything.'

His eyes met hers, and she held the gaze for a moment. Then she felt her stomach muscles twitch and suddenly she was laughing, and so was he. When they had panted themselves to a

stop he took her hand. 'Come on,' he said. 'We've got the afternoon. I'll show you something.'

'Will it be something you showed me already?' She raised her
eyebrows.

'Not that sort of something! Come on.'

Half an hour later, Fleare was surrounded by planets.

The Spin was a thickly populated area of space about thirty
light-days across. It was moderately remote from the nearest
major civilizations and therefore tended to make its own astro-
political weather. It was independent, socially fissile, multilingual,
multifaith, internally and externally argumentative, occasionally united but far more often chronically squabbling. Small
wars were endemic; larger ones rare. Really big conflicts like
the First and Second Machine Wars were unusual enough to
merit capital letters if your language supported them.

Depending on how and when you counted, there were
between eighty-nine and ninety-four planets in the Spin. Five
were wanderers, on vast elliptical orbits that brought them back
into play every few years. There was a fashion among the
wealthy for maintaining houses, estates, whole private continents on these planets. The fact that they were useless for nine
tenths of the time just seemed to add to the attraction. The
remaining stable – by Spin standards – eighty-nine looped in
complex orbits around twenty-one suns, with both orbits and
suns evidently being artificial. Not just artificial; most of the
orbits were impossible, and a few were close to whimsical. One
described a flattened figure of eight centred on nothing obvious,
with light, warmth and an intermittently fatal spectrum of
radiation coming from its own pet mini-star orbiting a few
light-minutes out. It was popular with thrill-seeking tourists,
who mostly wore radiation suits, and a select cadre of the ter-
minally ill, who mostly didn't. The suntans were spectacular, of
course.

Nobody knew who or what had built the Spin, and to

speculate on why was just farcical, but whoever it was seemed to have had grand ambitions, almost limitless power and a sense of humour. There was archaeological evidence, but it pointed in so many wilfully different directions that the only safe assumption was that it was part of the joke. There were also artefacts that turned up from time to time, most so inscrutable as to their use that they might as well have been executive toys. Despite constant attempts, the Construction Phase remained opaque to investigation.

As far as anyone knew, no race had ever tried to attain civilization from a starting point in the Spin. It was just as well. As one anthropologist said, if they'd tried to interpret what they saw in the skies the resulting religions would have been lethal.

Joke or not, the Spin was unique as far as its inhabitants knew. It had few external visitors, mainly because it was rather isolated, floating in a bubble of more or less empty space half a dozen light-years across. Outside the bubble the galaxy got quite dense, with civilizations clustering together and gazing warily across the gap. The Spin had sometimes been a boisterous neighbour – another reason to leave it un-poked, if possible.

The obvious guess was that the empty bit had been plundered for the raw star-stuff needed to make the Spin in the first place, but this was just a guess. What was certain was that the Spin was by a massive margin the single biggest artificial structure in the mapped galaxy. It was home to about ten per cent of known sentient civilizations, twenty per cent of economic activity and, historically, anything up to fifty per cent of total military effort.

It had another claim to uniqueness, too.

Fleare ducked as a cluster of moons whistled past her. 'What, on every planet?'

'Yup. All different, but all complete. A planetarium on every planet. Look, don't stand there. Incoming solar system.' Muz took her arm and pulled her gently backwards. She shook herself free but stepped back a few paces, in time for a planet about the size of her head to go barrelling by. It looked as if it was made of some dark hardwood, mounted on a polished brass stalk that disappeared down into the darkness. Several others followed, all made of similar materials, and some with sketches of continents etched on to their spinning surfaces. Then a bigger brassy globe wobbled past. Fleare looked at Muz. 'A sun, right?'

'Right. Look, Fleare, I gotta sit down.'

The planetarium occupied a spherical space about fifty metres across, with a metal checkerplate walkway running round the circumference. There were banquettes on the walkway. Muz wandered over to one and collapsed on to it. The cushion made a sighing noise as it took his weight.

Fleare sat next to him. 'Still suffering?'

'Oh yes.' He leaned back against the wall of the planetarium and gave a sigh that sounded just like the cushion.

Fleare grinned. 'Serves you right.'

'Thank you, Cadet Haas.' Muz stretched his arms above his head. Fleare heard one of his joints click, and he winced. Then he sat up. 'Hey, that's funny.'

'What?'

'Well, your name. Isn't there some, like, mega-rich total bastard that owns half the Spin? Big wheel in the Heg'. He's called Haas, right? Coincidence. Funny.'

Fleare stared at her feet. A small cold knot formed in her stomach. 'Not really,' she said.

'Not really what?'

'Funny, or a coincidence.' She stood up, turning and hugging herself. With her back to him she said: 'Viklun Haas is my father. It isn't half the Spin but it's plenty, and yes, he is a total bastard, and yes, he is on the side of the Hegemony so I'm technically at war with him. I'm sure he'd say it was just a gesture but I can't ask him because I haven't spoken to him since my fifteenth birthday, because he's at least twice the bastard you think and he makes me want to throw up. Sorry.' She turned round. 'So, I'll be leaving, I guess. Thanks for last night.' She swallowed. 'It was fun.'

'What?' Muz got to his feet, a little unsteadily. 'Leaving? Why?'

'That's how it usually goes after his name comes up. Even if it takes a while.' Fleare tried to meet his eyes and failed. 'I've got plenty of experience.' She turned abruptly and headed for the exit.

After a few paces she heard him following. She spun on her heel and held both arms out straight, bracing herself. He bounced gently off her outstretched palms, took a wobbly step backwards and collapsed on to a bench. His expression was so comical that she almost relented.

But only almost. Instead she shook her head. 'I can't, Muz. I joined up to get away from all that shit, you see? Him and anything to do with him and anyone who even *heard* of him, because it doesn't take long for everyone else to stop having a relationship with me and start having one with him. And if you did that, I'd have to kill you.'

He threw his hands up. 'Okay, have it your way. I feel too crap to argue and if you really gave a shit you'd probably be staying, so just fuck off. But you'd better change your name, otherwise you'll be fucking off for the rest of your life.'

'I'm going to change more than that.' She turned and stamped towards the exit. The old-fashioned door slammed satisfyingly behind her.

Three hours later she was half sitting, half lying on a med couch while a cloudy neutral-coloured fluid dripped into her bloodstream through a slim tube which looked disappointingly ordinary. The fluid was a complex, doubtfully legal suspension of nano-particles, and the process was neither risk-free nor reversible.

Despite this, her formal agreement to the military's right to modify her had been accepted without a flicker, barely ten minutes after she had left the planetarium. The bored Adjutant-Administrator hadn't even looked up from his terminal as Fleare had submitted to the iris scan that confirmed her consent. She'd had to scan twice. Apparently tears obscured the beam.

Taussich, Fortunate Protectorate, Cordern

It was hot and dusty, and they had been hunting all morning without seeing anything. Two suns had climbed high and the third was already above the horizon, making the desert air shimmer. Even the mounted nobles were tired, and their beasts smelled rank and hot. The beaters, running alongside them, were streaked grey with a mixture of fine sand and sweat. One was scored with red from the shoulder to the hip where he had run through a stand of Sorrow Spines. Another had already collapsed and had been left where he lay. Perhaps an hour more and they would all have to find shade.

A cry broke the silence. 'A sighting! My Lord, there is a sighting. Prey-ho!'

Alameche Ur-hive reined in his mount. The animal resisted for a moment and then came to a restive halt, shuffling its front feet before letting the stumpy rear limb unfurl. Alameche waited until the beast had settled into its tripod resting position, and swung his leg out of the saddle. He watched the panting beater running up to him, and held out his hand as the boy drew near. The boy handed him the telescope. 'A ten-score of paces to second sunward, Lord. I believe it is a Rethi. At the edge of the stand of Wire Trees.'

Alameche took the instrument and raised it. At first he could see nothing. He took it from his eye, inspected it, and then swore. The lens was filthy with sweat and dust. He reached out, swept the soft sun-hat from the cowering beater's head and used it to polish the lens. Then he rolled the hat up and stowed it in his pack. 'You can do without that, cretin,' he told the boy. 'Count yourself lucky I don't have you thrashed.'

The boy flinched and bowed himself away.

Alameche raised the telescope again. It was still difficult; the shimmering of the baked air baffled the eye. He concentrated, turning the eyepiece until the Wire Trees came into focus, and scanning along their edge until he came to a dark mound. It moved as he watched. A leg stretched out indolently, and the sunlight glinted off insectoid mouth parts as they opened in a yawn.

A Rethi, indeed! Full-grown and fully armoured. It looked thoroughly relaxed, and Alameche was not surprised. He adjusted the telescope and counted the segments along the humped carapace. There were twenty-one, each the length of a man's outstretched arm. By the waiting gods, the beast was huge! And ancient, too. No one knew for certain, but Alameche's hunting master had once told him that each segment counted fifty years. Over a thousand years old! No wonder they had found nothing all morning; the presence of this monster would have every animal for klicks running for shelter.

He lowered the telescope and handed it back to the boy, who was standing with his hand raised in a pathetic attempt to keep the sun off his bare head. Serve the whelp right.

Hooves thumped behind him and a cloud of dust rose as two riders hauled their beasts to a halt at his side. Alameche cursed inwardly. Garamende, of all the noisy fools, with Fiselle just behind him. He nodded a greeting, at the same time making a quick downwards gesture with his palms. Then he pointed towards the Wire Trees. 'There,' he said quietly. 'Just on the edge of the shade. Do you see?'

Garamende swung himself out of the saddle, landing far more lightly than his girth suggested. He gestured for the telescope, shoved it against his eye and searched for a moment. Alameche watched the instrument move from side to side, then stop suddenly. The big man held his position for a long time. Then he lowered the telescope and turned to Alameche. 'Well, fuck my only infant daughter,' he said quietly. He handed the telescope to Fiselle. The thin man held up the telescope, and Alameche marvelled that he could hold it horizontal without falling over. He repeated Garamende's actions, and then handed the telescope slowly back to Alameche, one eyebrow raised.

Alameche allowed himself a smile. He gestured towards the dozing Rethi. 'There, my Lords,' he said. 'Am I forgiven for a morning of drought?'

Garamende thumped him on the shoulder. 'Of course! As if you needed forgiving. Eh?' He nudged Fiselle.

The thin man nodded. 'Quite so,' he said. 'Now all we need to do is to bring it down.' He turned to Garamende, his face neutral. 'Have you any suggestions?'

'Of course I bloody have! God's cock, man, do you think I'm an unweaned child?' The big man reached behind him, pulled his crossbow out of its saddle holster and thumbed the stud so that it hummed with energy. He waved it towards the Rethi. 'A few good bolts up the arse and it's ours.'

Alameche smiled, and reached for his own weapon. 'It has the merit of directness,' he admitted. 'But I promised you some sport, not just a kill. I think I have another suggestion.'

Fiselle managed to cock the eyebrow even further. 'Indeed?'

'Oh yes.' Alameche turned round and squinted towards where the waiting beaters squatted. They had formed a sort of defensive ring around the boy who had been scored by the

Sorrow Spines. Even at this distance the tracks of blood down his side were obvious. 'Yes,' he said slowly. 'I think so.'

They made the beaters drive a stake into the hard ground, and bring a chain.

The injured boy's pacing was almost mechanical. He marked out the restless hundred paces from one end of the path allowed by his chain to the other, then turned and repeated the journey in reverse. Half the time, his scored flank faced the onlookers. If he stopped, the beaters were instructed to use the whips they had been given.

Even though the boy had only passed back and forwards a few times, Alameche would have sworn that the ground bore his imprint. It was almost as if the sod was somehow complicit – as if it was waiting to be violated by the boy's doomed feet. Perhaps after all there was something in the old legend, that there was some sort of bond between this arid rock and its half-witted natives.

Or perhaps not. Whatever. He turned to his companions. 'Well, we have our bait,' he said. 'Who wants the honour?'

He had expected Garamende to speak, but the big man merely grinned. 'I'll pass,' he said. 'Why not let Fiselle try out that antique he has over his shoulder?'

The thin man's lips twisted and he held up the old musket. 'If I may?'

'Of course.' Alameche stood aside. Fiselle rammed a charge and ball down the barrel, cocked the musket and raised it to his shoulder. Alameche put the telescope to his eye and sighted on the dozing Rethi. He braced himself and waited for the explosion.

'My Lord Alameche!'

The shout came from behind them, and there was the sound of hooves. Fiselle swore and lowered his weapon. All three men turned round.

Like them, the rider was streaked with dust – and his mount was steaming and wheezing with effort. A beater was running in front of him, his face frantic. He ran up to Alameche and threw himself to the ground. 'Sire! I begged him to wait, but he would not listen!'

Alameche kicked the boy aside and walked towards the messenger. Even through the thick dust he could see the scarlet tabs on the man's jacket. The man was from the Citadel. He frowned. 'Well?'

Wordlessly the man swung a satchel off his shoulder, reached into it and held out a glassy-looking bead about the size of a pea. Alameche took it, and the messenger wheeled his mount round and galloped off.

Garamende walked up to him. 'What is it?'

'A message from the Patriarch, I expect.' Alameche rolled the bead between his fingers. It flattened, and quickly spread itself out to become a paper-thin tablet that just covered the palm of his hand. Alameche thumbed the surface of the tablet, which filled with images and glyphs. He read for a moment before looking up at Garamende. 'Ah, I need to be alone, old friend. If you wouldn't mind?'

'Of course.' Garamende clapped him on the shoulder and marched off, bellowing for Fiselle to let him try out that museum piece of a musket, if he was sure it wouldn't blow his fucking hand off.

Alameche waited until the man was almost out of sight. Then he stroked the surface of the tablet again. It spoke, in a reedy voice.

'Well? *Are* you alone?'

Alameche glanced at the distant Garamende, who was holding Fiselle's musket out in front of him in a declamatory pose as if he was giving a lecture. 'Apparently yes,' he said.

'*Apparently?* Ah.' There was a short silence. Alameche grinned. His carefully ñuanced reply seemed to be causing the device some reflection. When it spoke again it sounded faintly testy. 'His Excellency the Final Patriarch hopes that you are enjoying your barbaric medieval rituals. He trusts both that they have not driven your court diary from your mind, and that you have not butchered too many of his chattels.' The voice paused as if it was drawing breath. 'His Excellency further observes that he would value your attendance to discuss arrangements for tomorrow evening, when as you are sure to recall the Court and guests will celebrate the anniversary of the Elevation of the Patriarch. He begs that you will visit him at your convenience.'

Alameche cocked an eyebrow at the tablet. *One nuance deserves another*, he thought. 'Thank you,' he said. 'Please tell His Excellency that I shall indeed visit him . . . at my convenience.'

The surface of the tablet went blank. Alameche looked at it thoughtfully – the day was getting more interesting – and then crumpled it into a ball and stuffed it into his jacket pocket. He turned towards Garamende and Fiselle, who were still arguing about ancient weapons, and held up his hands. 'Gentlemen!'

'Ah ha . . .' Garamende abandoned a point in mid flow and strode towards Alameche. 'Back with us? All well, I hope?'

'Well enough.' Alameche smiled, allowing just a little ruefulness to cross his face. 'I was planning to eat with you when we had finished. Now it seems I'll be eating with others.'

'Oh?' Garamende was solicitous. 'Something of import?'

Alameche shook his head. 'Something of none, I imagine. But still, when the Master calls . . .'

'Quite. Well,' and Garamende laid a hand on Alameche's shoulder, 'work is work.' He turned and called to Fiselle, who was still fiddling with the musket. 'We're being abandoned, man. Will you stay and finish the hunt or shall we give up together and find a drink instead?'

The thin man looked reflective. 'I find I have less taste for this than I thought. Perhaps after all we should drink.' He gestured to the tethered boy. 'What about him? I assume we won't just leave him to bake?'

'Ah. No.' Alameche looked at the boy for a moment. Then he turned to Fiselle. 'Does that musket really work?'

'So I was told.' Fiselle held it out, and Alameche took it. The dark metal was hot and oily-smelling. He re-cocked it, made to raise it, and then paused. 'I should mount up, gentlemen,' he said. 'Just in case.'

The two men looked at each other, and then climbed on to their beasts.

Alameche lifted the musket to his shoulder and sighted on the Rethi.

The rasp-click of the mechanism and the ragged boom were almost simultaneous. The butt kicked against his shoulder.

The Rethi sprang up and gave a sawing cry of pain. It swung round, sighted the tethered boy, lowered its head and charged. The boy gave a ragged yelp and began to run, tripping over the chain and crashing to the ground with every other step.

Alameche mounted quickly and urged his beast to a gallop. Behind him he could still hear the hurried feet of the beaters, the jangle and clash of the boy and, growing quickly louder, the syncopated thunder of the Rethi's feet. Then a pause – and then an inhumanly high scream of pain and terror. It didn't stop; obviously the Rethi had decided to feed immediately. Rethis weren't interested in fresh muscle tissue. Instead they used a prehensile proboscis tipped with horny claws to access internal organs. It usually went in through the anus and followed the gut up into the abdominal cavity.

Alameche had heard it was quite painful, but he barely noticed the cry. He was busy wondering why the Patriarch, for the first time in twenty years, had used the code word that meant a maximum emergency.

Convenience, indeed. Something which Alameche suspected would soon be in short supply.

All forms of mechanized transport were banned from the seared desert, thorn-tangled veldt and scattered salt lakes that together formed the Distal Plains. The hunting party had penetrated over twenty kilometres into the Plains during the morning, and it would normally have taken Alameche at least an hour to ride back to the edge where the beast-houses and the maglev terminus lay.

Today, it took forty minutes.

The beast-houses formed three sides of an ugly concrete square with its open side towards the Plains. Alameche galloped his gasping mount straight into the square and dismounted while it was still moving, calling for the Beast Master as he landed. He had to call twice more before the man ran out of his shelter and scampered across the concrete, adjusting his clothes. He halted in front of Alameche and stood, shifting from foot to foot on the baking surface. Alameche looked down. 'No boots?' he asked.

The Beast Master flinched and glanced down at his bare feet.

Alameche smiled. 'I imagine I interrupted something,' he said. 'I hope she – it had better be a she, hadn't it? – will forgive us both.'

The man's eyes widened and he opened his mouth, but before he could say anything there was a crash from the end of the yard.

Alameche's mount had collapsed. It was lying quite still with its head turned towards them. Its mouth was open in a foam-ringed rictus, and drops of blood from its nostrils made dark smudges in the wind-blown sand that covered the yard.

Alameche glanced briefly at it and then looked back at the Beast Master, whose face looked ready to crumple. 'Hard ridden, I grant you, but clearly ill-prepared. Rather like its trainer, and perhaps in both senses?' He glanced towards the door to the shelter, and nodded to himself. He had been right. A face had been peering round the door – a face that had vanished when Alameche had looked at it. A young male face.

It looked as if the Beast Master had seen it too because he made an odd, high, whimpering noise deep in his throat. He fell to his knees and made to grasp Alameche's legs, but Alameche shook his head and took a few steps backward, leaving the man grovelling on his face in the dust. He leaned down and spoke to the lank matted hairs on the back of the man's neck. 'Get me transport here within ten minutes, pederast,' he said softly, 'and you will only die by poisoning. If not, you and your catamite will both be placed in acid baths. Him first.'

The man gave an agonized cry, sprang to his feet and ran back to his shelter. Alameche watched him go. Then he walked across the square and through the opening that led to the maglev terminal. The suspended rail, which always looked far too slender to Alameche's eyes, flicked off across the desert between blocky white columns blurred by heat shimmer. He supposed the people who had built it knew what they were doing. It occurred to him that even if they didn't they were far beyond his vengeance, unlike almost everyone else on the planet. The sense of powerlessness was almost refreshing. He relaxed and waited.

The transport arrived in eight minutes. Alameche stood up and stretched as the line of empty cars slowed to a halt and dipped to the level of the platform, doors sliding open. He walked into the nearest car and turned to look back at the terminus. The Beast Master was standing by the exit, his hands straight down by his sides. To his credit, the man managed to keep his head up and his eyes forwards.

Alameche waved. 'Well done,' he called. 'Two minutes to spare.'

The man jerked with relief. Alameche felt the floor of the car tremble as it rose into the magnetic field, and the door began to close. He couldn't help himself; on an impulse he reached out his hand into the aperture, and the door froze. 'Of course,' he called, 'acid is a kind of poison.' Then he withdrew his hand. The door closed, there was a warning chime, and Alameche sat down as the car accelerated quickly. He allowed himself one short look back. The Beast Master was still standing at the exit, his hands by his sides, but somehow his posture had changed entirely. He looked as if he was hanging from something, rather like a piece of game strung up for the blood to drain before being skinned and gutted. Alameche looked away. He had no personal objection to pederasty – or indeed almost anything else – but the point had to be made.

The speed of sound in the old, hot, thin atmosphere of Taussich was about a thousand kilometres per hour. Accelerating hard, the car passed through the sound barrier with a muffled whoosh in ten minutes and went on powering forwards.

It was fifteen hundred kilometres to the Citadel. They would be there in an hour. Alameche sat back in his seat, allowing the force of the car's acceleration to massage his back against the deep padding. He reached for his commer. Of course, it would have been easier and even a little quicker to use the commer to summon the maglev instead of the Beast Master, but that would have spoiled all the fun.

Alameche powered up the commer and confirmed that having left the desert he was now back on the comm net. First he sent a terse message to Security about the Beast Master and his little friend. Then he began to catch up with correspondence. Even the commer was somewhat dated; he could have had an eye implant, but he had never been convinced that the security issue had been settled. Besides, he had a residual distaste for having sharp objects near his eyeball. In his experience – and it was extensive – that sort of thing happened to other people.

The maglev looped across the fringes of the desert and began to climb away from the plateau into the foothills of the Basin Ranges. From here, the land rose unevenly to a high point almost a kilometre above the desert, and then dropped sharply into the Great Basin, a volcanic caldera fifty kilometres across, thickly forested and with the Citadel rising up from its centre.

As well as being the centre of the Basin, the Citadel was the secular, religious and military centre of an empire which now ruled over five out of the six planets which occupied the Cordern, an isolated area within the centre of the Spin. This central rule was both recent, not yet two generations old, and unprecedented. The planets of the Cordern had earned their segregated status by being, in the view of almost everyone else in the Spin, either ungovernable or not worth the trouble. Through sheer bloody-mindedness the previous Patriarch had proved the first of those to be wrong, albeit at a human price which was agreed outside the Cordern to be appalling.

But, as Alameche knew, life is cheap and renews itself once a generation whereas mineral resources are limited and valuable. None of the five planets was especially rich in anything, but provided you didn't mind working their populations to death and leaving their ecosystems in ruins, you could extract enough from them to provide for a decent lifestyle and a growing military strength for their rulers.

Bootstraps, as the Patriarch said. Or stepping stones, as Alameche preferred to think of it. Five – hopefully soon to be six – planets to begin with, and then outwards, with a little external help.

And that, Alameche assumed, was what this summons was about. A visit from some friends. The same friends, come to that, who had provided the maglev, as well as a few other comforts. Alameche wondered what they had in their pockets this time. And, of course, how much it might cost. In view of recent discoveries, that was the most interesting question of all.

*

Normally Alameche would have stopped by his residence to freshen up before going on to meet the Patriarch but the summons, even if coded, had been unambiguous. Be here, now. So he was here, dusty clothes and grimed face notwithstanding. 'Here' was the outer Palazzo of the Citadel Reception Suite, and 'now' was just over an hour and a half after the summons had reached him in the middle of the Distal Plains. Alameche was thinking of claiming some sort of record.

His Excellency Chast, the Final Patriarch of the People's Democratic Republic of the Planet of Taussich and the Fortunate Protectorates of the Spin Centre, looked up from the board game he had been peering at. 'Ah, Alameche,' he said. 'Thank goodness. You rescue me from certain defeat. May I introduce Ambassador Eskjog, who is here representing some friends of friends and who is, well, who at least is much better at Baffle than I am.'

Alameche bowed. 'Ambassador.'

A small spiky object about the size of a human head was floating on the opposite side of the game board. The spikes, which ranged in length from fingernail to hand's breadth, were mainly shades of grey. Alameche thought it looked like a gothic cross between a sea creature and a mace. It rose to head height and turned so that one of its longer spikes was pointing at Alameche. 'A pleasure,' it said, in a voice far deeper and somehow more *human* than Alameche was expecting. 'I have heard a great deal about you.'

'Oh dear.' Alameche lowered his head. 'I hope it is to my credit?'

'It depends what you mean by credit.' The machine sounded amused. 'By any human standards, and I assure you that I am legally human where I come from, you sound ghastly. But I expect that is part of the job description.'

Alameche bowed deeper and the Patriarch laughed. 'My colleague thinks you have paid him a compliment,' he told the machine.

'Good. That's what I intended.' The machine floated towards Alameche, and he thought he caught the smell of ozone. He held his ground as the machine came closer and closer, and allowed himself a smile.

'That you *did* pay me a compliment, Ambassador, or that you want me to *think* you did?' he asked.

The machine continued its float until it was only a hand's breadth from his face. Then it stopped, hanging quite still in front of him. The smell of ozone was unmistakable, and Alameche felt his face prickle faintly as his bristles tried to stand out from his skin.

Despite its spikes the little machine somehow managed to be oddly featureless; Alameche could as easily have been squaring up to an ornament. But nevertheless he felt . . . *studied*. He met the blank non-gaze as inscrutably as he could.

Eventually the machine dipped a little and drew back. 'Exactly,' it said. 'One of those two.' It waggled from side to side in a gesture Alameche could have sworn was laughter. Then the waggle stopped. 'Right,' it said, and now the voice was businesslike, 'let's not delay, especially as you seem to have come in something of a rush. I have some information to impart, and I would like to do so somewhere secure. And believe me, where we are at the moment doesn't count.'

Alameche opened his mouth, but the Patriarch was quicker. 'With regard to security, Ambassador, I can assure you—'

The machine cut him off. 'With great respect, Your Excellency, I'm afraid you *can't*. As we speak this chamber is watched by several entities, some less friendly than others. If I were not preventing them, they could easily tell how thoroughly you had bathed this morning, and where. And feasibly even with whom. Now get us somewhere underground with some good thick rock above us, and I might be able to do something about that.'

It turned and floated, not towards the grand exit from the

chamber but instead towards an insignificant door in one corner. For a moment neither Alameche nor the Patriarch moved, and the machine turned back. 'Well,' it said, 'are you coming?' It bobbed towards the little door. 'I think this is the best way, don't you?'

Alameche gathered himself. 'Precisely,' he said, while making a mental note to find all the staff who had any knowledge of that particular passage and have them publicly flayed. He turned to the Patriarch. 'Excellency?'

'What? Oh. Yes. Quite so.' The Patriarch set out for the door, directing an angry glare at Alameche as he passed. Alameche waited until machine and Patriarch were through the doorway, and then followed them, shaking his head.

As he went he amended his plans. Flayed, and then dipped in something corrosive.

The room they arrived in was square, windowless and about thirty paces on a side. The floor was a polished glassy black; the ceiling a matt white disfigured by a lot of purposeful-looking steps and bulges, and the walls a dull grey dotted with flecks, possibly a rock containing mica. A round table in the middle of the room had chairs for twenty, and a screen – presently inert – occupied most of one wall. It might have been a rather dated interpretation of a conference room.

In fact it was an attack- and data-hardened command space, eight storeys below ground and almost half a kilometre to one side of the shaft that led down to it. It dated back a few hundred years, to one of the more paranoid periods in the history of the People's Democratic Republic, and it was one of six similar, and completely unconnected, such spaces, distributed across the Citadel in a random pattern that appeared on no maps, any-where. Only six people knew of all the spaces, and each of those six thought he – naturally, they were all men – was the only one.

Ambassador Eskjog swivelled from side to side as if surveying the room. 'Shall we sit down?' it asked. It lowered itself towards the conference table, halting just above the table-top. 'Just a minute,' it said, and there was a *fuff* like someone blowing. A cloud of dust rose from the table below the machine, leaving a darker circle on the surface. Eskjog settled itself down in the middle of the clean circle with three of its spikes slightly flexed to form a tripod. 'Someone needs to have a word with the cleaners,' it said.

Alameche glanced at the Patriarch, who looked as if he was about to explode, and cleared his throat. 'This space is rarely used, as I have no doubt you know, and dust is not a priority. Security is, and I am expecting to be asked how you breached it.' He looked at the Patriarch again. 'Very soon. So please, before you tell us anything else, tell us that.'

'Yes, well. Security is relative. Relative to your tech level, this space is secure. But – and I don't mean to patronize – relative to the average tech level in the Outer Spin, it is less so. And relative to mine, it is like a clean glass of water: transparently innocent.' Eskjog rose off the table and turned towards the Patriarch. 'Therefore, Excellency, if you are inclined to take out your disapproval on your servant here, I beg you to think again. He really couldn't have prevented intrusion.' It paused. 'Not without my help.'

The Patriarch looked at the machine. 'Are you offering your help?'

'Well, yes. Amongst other things.'

Alameche and the Patriarch looked at each other and the Patriarch nodded slightly. Alameche turned to the machine. 'Well?' he said.

'Right. Let's start. Oh, you might want to sit down. This will take a little while.'

Alameche waited until the Patriarch had pulled out a chair and lowered himself into it before doing the same. When they were both seated Eskjog floated to a position between them.

'I'm going to tell you a story,' it said. 'If you listen through to the end, then a year from now you will probably still have what you think of as a civilization, and possibly your position in the Spin will have been enhanced dramatically.'

'And if we don't listen?' asked Alameche.

'Ah.' The machine sagged a little. 'Almost certain annihilation. Want me to go on?'

The word 'annihilation' hovered in the room.

Alameche and the Patriarch exchanged a look. The Patriarch frowned. 'Annihilation? Ambassador, I hope you're exaggerating.'

'Not really. Look, hear me out and then judge for yourselves.'

The Patriarch compressed his lips. 'Very well,' he said. 'Tell us.'

'All right. Before I start, do you mind if I patch in to your display? It'll make things easier.'

The Patriarch raised an eyebrow towards Alameche, who shrugged. He turned back to Eskjog. 'I don't suppose we can stop you, can we?' he said.

'No you can't, but I always think it's polite to ask.' There was a soft chime. The room darkened and the big screen on the opposite wall flickered and settled down to show an image of a star field. 'The Spin, of course,' said Eskjog. 'Perhaps we should say, both of the Spins. Outer, and Inner.' As it spoke, the screen divided into two colour fields, with the Outer planetary systems forming a bulbous green crescent wrapped round the red of the Inner. 'Your good selves, here.' Near the centre, Taussich flashed a brighter red. 'What you euphemistically call the Fortunate Protectorates, here.' The five planets of the Spin Centre flashed. 'And something very interesting *here*.' Four of the planets faded, leaving one which flared quickly through orange, yellow and green to a fierce, blue-white point.

The Patriarch leaned forward. 'What planet is that?' he asked.

Alameche squinted at the burning dot. 'Silthx, Excellency.'

'Ah. Our most recent converts.' The Patriarch nodded. 'What makes them interesting?'

'Well, lots of things. To you lot, slaves and mineral resources, obviously, plus strategic location and a good fertile agriculture.' Eskjog made a noise like a sigh. 'Although the manner of your conquest didn't do much for that last bit. The word "converts" seems a bit optimistic.'

The Patriarch shrugged. 'Insurgency has to be tackled. Eh, Alameche? That was one of yours, I believe?'

Alameche inclined his head. 'Yes, Excellency.'

'And you did it so well,' said Eskjog. 'Most of the population dead or enslaved in only a few weeks, and four fifths of the productive farmland radioactive for generations. That makes it interesting to other people, of course. Environmental catastrophes always attract attention and a bit of genocide just adds sauce.'

The point on the screen was painfully bright now. Alameche looked away from it and down at Eskjog. It suddenly looked different, but at first he couldn't see why. As his eyes adjusted, he realized that in the near-darkness of the room the little machine was surrounded by a faint violet penumbra. The effect was sinister; he found himself wondering exactly what Ambassador Eskjog really was, and if it was as potent as it seemed to be. And if it really was, what did that mean about the abilities of its distant masters?

He suppressed a shiver.

Eskjog went on, its voice even. 'Make no mistake, Excellency, you have attracted attention. There are two strands of opinion. One, that you should be blown out of the sky; two, that you should be walled up in your own nasty corner of the Spin and left to fester.'

'And which strand do you represent?' The Patriarch's voice, too, was quiet, but Alameche recognized the chilly edge in it.

He had heard that tone only a few times, and each time he had hoped never to hear it again.

'Neither, happily.' Eskjog sounded amused. 'First, don't be misled by what I said earlier. I may be legally human, but I am *not* human. The opposite, in fact. Inhuman. I really don't care about the fate of biological beings; for my money you can rape, starve, enslave and irradiate each other as much as you like.'

'How kind.' The Patriarch's voice was still icy.

'Not at all. Frankly, your Alameche could say the same.' Eskjog rose a little and repeated the waggle that Alameche had suspected meant laughter. Then it floated to the middle of the conference table and settled itself down, this time without bothering to clear the dust. 'Blowing you out of the sky has been discussed at high level, but it was rejected. Partly squeamishness, and partly because the irony of wiping you out because you had wiped other people out seemed a bit extreme.'

'So where does that leave us? Stewing in our own juice?' The Patriarch was sitting well forward in his seat. Alameche thought he looked as if he wanted to pounce on something.

'Until a while ago, yes, so everyone left you to it. But now, no.' Eskjog rose a finger's breadth from the table and turned so that one of its spikes pointed first at the Patriarch, and then at Alameche. 'Leaving you alone is no longer an option. That's where the story comes in.'

The image on the screen faded so that the room was completely dark, except for Eskjog's ghostly fetch-light glow. Alameche leaned back in his seat, and sensed the Patriarch doing the same. Eskjog remained silent for a few seconds more. When it began to speak it sounded more purposeful.

'You invaded Silthx two years ago. Close to a billion corpses, atmosphere zapped with some *very* dirty old nukes, you cheeky monkeys, environmental catastrophe, yada yada. Much liberal hand-, tentacle- or flipper-wringing. You enslaved nearly all the remaining population, plundered the planet pretty well to the core and bought yourselves a ten-year future in rare-earth elements that will fund the next phase of your nasty little expansion. But – and now I am partly guessing – you also tripped over a local rumour. Yes?'

Alameche remained silent. So did the Patriarch.

'I'll take that as a yes. You heard about some strange object that flew out of the skies, without warning and without showing on the sensors, and landed slap-down-doodie in the core of the biggest nuclear plant on the planet – a plant that was later turned into a sort of memorial to the people killed at the time. Yes?'

Again, both men remained silent. Eskjog made a sighing noise. 'Another yes, I think,' it said. 'So you investigated. Guesses or not, I'm afraid we know this part. You used unprotected human forced labour to excavate the exposed nuclear core of a demolished fission plant. This desecrated the memorial and created yet another heap of corpses, if a bit more slowly than usual. And you found something.'

The screen lit up, making Alameche blink. Then his eyes adapted and he registered the image. It was a white ovoid. There was no sense of scale; it could have been millimetres or kilometres long.

Eskjog went on speaking. 'Going back to guesswork, I suspect you have this thing deep in a lab somewhere. I don't know where, so you have actually managed to conceal something. Well done you. I also suspect that you have no idea what it is and that it has defied analysis, otherwise your whole civilization would be in another place altogether. And if that's true, if it really isn't letting you in – then it must still be alive, although possibly compromised.'

There was a long silence while both men stared at the screen. Then the Patriarch spoke. 'How did you obtain that image?' he asked, his voice shaking.

'Ah well.' Eskjog's voice sounded smug. 'That's the bit that leaked, I'm afraid.'

'But how?' The Patriarch's voice was practically a roar. 'We killed them all! Didn't we kill them all? Alameche, you useless bastard! Tell me we killed them all!'

'Whoa! Steady.' Eskjog floated towards the Patriarch, and through his growing terror Alameche had the insane notion that it would have mopped the man's brow if it could. 'You did kill them all. That is, Alameche here had them all killed, just like you told him. But these days, with the right technology death is – how can I put this – a nuanced condition. A personality escaped.'

The Patriarch groaned and slumped back in his seat. 'Alameche,' he said, 'I have stopped understanding. Understand for me, or I'll have your head cooked on your neck.'

Alameche felt as if his head was already cooking. He shook it carefully. 'I think it's a sort of simulation, Excellency. A human personality can exist as a model, within an artificial intelligence.' He looked at Eskjog. 'Although how such a thing can "escape", I don't know.'

'Well, the sort of thing you have just described probably couldn't,' said Eskjog, 'and if it did it wouldn't be much good. But this is the other way round. It's not a model personality, it's real, and it exists in a simulated virtual mind. It's actually easier that way, believe it or not.'

Alameche frowned. 'Easier to simulate a mind? How can that be?'

'Oh, the mind isn't the difficult bit. It's like music: you can play a complicated piece on a simple instrument.'

The Patriarch sighed. 'Ambassador, with all respect, I don't see the relevance of this. We, ah, assimilated Silthx and found an artefact in the process. It's very important but we don't know why. Something got out and told you. Some of you are cross. Some of you are interested. Both the interest and the anger represent possible existential threats to us. Yes?'

'A masterly summary,' said Eskjog.

'Good.' The Patriarch stood up and stretched. 'At last we know where we are. I always do the same thing about existential threats, and it is this: Alameche, in time for our forthcoming Anniversary Celebrations you will present to me a strategy for the neutralization of this threat, to the glory of our civilization.'

Alameche inclined his head. 'Excellency.'

'Very good. My thanks for your information, Ambassador, and any other help you can offer.' The Patriarch knitted his fingers together, faced his palms outwards and cracked his knuckles in a fusillade that made Alameche blink. 'Danger has a particular effect on me. I am going to find something female and nubile.' He looked distant for a moment and added: '*Young* and female and nubile.'

Alameche waited until the door had clicked shut behind his master, then turned to Eskjog and spread his arms apologetically. The little machine rose from the table. 'Young?' it said.

Alameche smiled. 'The age of consent is strictly enforced in our society.'

'Right. And the age of consent is set by . . . ?' Eskjog let the sentence tail off.

Alameche nodded. 'The Patriarch,' he said.

'Hmmph.' Eskjog settled back down on to the table. 'I find I have more sympathy for biological beings than I thought. Young ones, at least. But you,' and it inclined back a little so that one of its spikes was pointing at Alameche, 'you noticed something.'

'Yes, I did.'

'Which was?'

Alameche smiled. 'The mistake in the Patriarch's summary,' he said. 'He assumed that the escaped personality found you first. But you didn't say that.'

'No, I didn't. Because it didn't. Well done, again.'

'So who did it find?'

'It's more a question of *who* found *it*,' said Eskjog. 'Someone – or something – who went looking for it, is the answer. How up to speed are you on politics in the Outer Spin?'

'Not very. Not as much as I should be. You haven't answered my question.'

'No, I haven't. That's partly because I can't, with any precision. I don't like being imprecise.'

Alameche waited. After a moment, Eskjog made a sighing noise. 'All right. The short imprecise answer is that I – we – don't know. The longer one is that whoever it was had three things: knowledge of the genocide, the ability to snatch a personality from a dying body and a reason to do so.'

Alameche raised an eyebrow. 'That's not only imprecise, it's obvious. Where does it lead?'

'Well, to any one of several hundred places that we know about, plus the unknown number we don't. Some of them could even be here, which is something you might like to think about. But it's not that important. What matters more is that the personality has moved on. It's now in a place where we can track it covertly – and I am really not going to enlighten you any more about that.'

Alameche nodded and looked at the ovoid on the screen again. 'The thing we found. You said it was still alive. What is it?'

'Well, we're not really sure. As far as we know there's only been one found before, and that didn't end well for the finders.' The screen flowered into a bright blue-white explosion which made Alameche flinch. Then it darkened, and went back to showing the image of the Spin. Eskjog rose from the table and floated over to hover in front of the glittering star field. 'But we think it's a remnant, an artefact from the Construction Phase. Maybe a part of the Construction itself.' It paused. 'Maybe – probably, even – a causal part.'

Alameche looked at the little machine for a long time. 'Causal,' he said. 'I see. That implies a tool. And most tools are also weapons. So it could be powerfully destructive?'

'Apocalyptically,' Eskjog agreed. 'See why people are interested?'

Alameche stared at the screen for a long time, only tearing his gaze away when his eyes blurred with strain and the images of the Inner and Outer Spin began to weave round each other in a rather suggestive optical illusion. He blinked the image away, and looked at Eskjog. 'Well, I'm certainly interested,' he said. 'Let's take it from there, shall we?'

Obel Moon

By the time they reached the bottom of the Shadow Stair the sun was halfway to the zenith. The early mist had burned off, and the air was warm and sticky. The sweat that had frozen in Fleare's clothes when she was climbing the Tower had thawed, and the material clung to her unpleasantly. She turned to Muz. 'Do I smell?'

'Yup.'

'Bad?'

'Could be. Depends on your point of view.'

'Sorry.'

'Don't worry. It doesn't bother me any more. I'm a cloud of nano-machines now, remember?'

'Mmm-hmm.' She moved away from the centre of the narrow street they were on, and flattened herself against a wall as they approached a corner. She felt Muz nudge in behind her. 'Why are we stopping?' he asked.

'Ssshh!' she whispered frantically, and pointed towards the corner. 'Near the Rotten Gate. The way out to the Second Circle. There are surveillance cams from here on.'

'Ah.' Now Muz was whispering too. 'Element of surprise, yes?'

She nodded.

'Only, there's something you need to know.'

Something about the voice made her turn. 'What?'

'It's about the surprise thing.'

Her stomach fluttered. 'What about the surprise thing?' As she said the words, she felt the shape of the answer.

'It might not be a surprise. You remember the thing I absorbed?'

'Horribly. So what?'

'Well, it had an audiovisual feed.'

'Ah.' She looked away for a moment.

'Yes. Ah.'

'Well, thanks for telling me so quickly.'

'Wouldn't have made any difference.' Muz sank towards the ground, and instinctively she found herself sinking into a crouch to keep level with him. 'The feed was real-time. I couldn't stop it. If anyone was watching, they saw me closing in. Then there would have been a half-second blank. Since then I've sent in an edited feed that looks normal, but I doubt if anyone's fooled.'

'So, we're rumbled?'

'Probably. Not certainly. On the plus side, it's better than being kebab meat. On the down side, we should expect company. You'd better ramp up.'

'Yeah.' Fleare rose from her crouch. Then she looked down at Muz. 'Edited, you said. How edited?'

Muz rose slowly. 'Mainly I took out the conversation. Right now it shows you standing staring at nothing.'

'But what else could it show?'

'Well, anything, I suppose.' He was level with her face now; she felt looked at. 'What's on your mind?'

She tried to suppress her grin, and failed. 'Show them something to distract them,' she said.

'Oooo-kay. I think I know what you mean. Are you still going to ramp up?'

She nodded, and then turned a little so that she could stare out over the jumbled rooftops towards the Rotten Gate, and the Second Circle that lay beyond it. 'Oh yes,' she said. 'Even more so.'

'Want me to get the gate?'

'Nah.' She shook her head. 'I'll do it. I need the exercise.' She waved a hand vaguely towards the Second Circle. 'You go and enjoy yourself.'

Most of what was now called the Monastery was not, strictly, Monastery. The original Tower, the First Circle and the fortified wall that ringed it were surrounded by a set of six more, roughly concentric, circles of later parasitic development that straggled down towards the Plains like ripples on a dusty pond. These circles ranged from less than a hundred to more than three hundred metres in thickness, and each had originally only one gate to the next. The Rotten Gate led from the First to the Second Circle, the Supplicant's Gate from the Second to the Third – set on the opposite side, as was each successive gate. Even though the total radius was only just over a kilometre, to go from the Open Gate in the Seventh Circle to the Rotten Gate in the First one had to walk nearly ten. In a world of land warfare it would have been an excellent defence. For the whole seventeen-thousand-year history of the Monastery it had been made irrelevant by routinely available powered air flight, and the building had relied on far more subtle and devastating means of defending itself. The only function of the Circles seemed to be to make life awkward for its inhabitants.

Fleare stood just inside the Rotten Gate. After a giggling conference about false AV feeds, Muz had dissolved back to vapour and slipped through to try to do something troubling to the Monastery security systems. A few of his particles remained, nestling in a tight cloud just inside her left ear to act as an audio link. It was silent at the moment; presumably he was busy.

Fleare realized that she was grinning, a wide stupid grin that she couldn't shift. She was ramped up, fizzing with energy, system flooded with bespoke chemicals, reaction speeds tuned up to better than four times standard, altered muscles loose and ready. She hadn't bothered since she had been at the Monastery. It wouldn't have done any good; even like this, her chances of staging a solo breakout were less than one in three. Not good enough.

But now she wasn't solo, and it was good to be back. She stopped fighting the grin.

There was a soft, distant boom, and then a sharper, louder one. The furrowed stone floor shivered, and her enhanced hearing picked up shouts, confused and panicky. The air began to smell of ozone and burning plastics. Muz was obviously having fun. Fleare grinned a bit more. Then she backed slowly up the corridor.

The doors of the Rotten Gate were twice her height, of age-blackened timbers with iron fastenings that could have been as old as the Monastery. They were locked and barred, a final physical defence that spoke straight to the ancient hindbrain.

Fleare dropped into a sprinter's crouch, paused for long enough to take two deep breaths and launched herself. She took three strides to get up speed, then leapt with feet forward and legs bent, arms raised to cover her face.

Her sandals slammed into the doors at chest height. As they made contact she kicked her legs straight. The impact threw her backwards; she landed ten metres away and rolled upright, shaking her head. Then she took stock.

One of the doors had burst clean off its hinges and lay flat beyond the gate. The other hung, twisting. Fleare looked at it, tutted and gave it another kick. It fell in a crash and a cloud of dust. Fleare nodded to herself and picked her way carefully over it, brushing dust from her robe.

She heard explosions, first singly and then in a stuttering series of twos and threes. Fleare frowned. It sounded more like

weapons fire than casual vandalism. If Muz had arranged re-
inforcements, he hadn't mentioned it.

She waved a hand at her ear and whispered: 'What's going
on?'

There was nothing. She swore under her breath and patted
her ear with the flat of her hand so that her hearing thumped.
'Muz?'

There was a sound like angry raindrops. It became words.
'Shit, that was loud.'

'Sorry. What's going on?'

'Got company.'

'Expected?'

'No.'

'Who?'

'Don't know yet.' There was a pause, and Fleare heard static
and shouting voices. Then Muz's voice cut back in. 'Look, are
you through the gate?'

'Yes.'

'Anyone around?'

'Not in sight.'

'Fingers crossed it'll stay like that. Get to the security block.
I've got an idea.'

'Okay.' Even as she spoke she sensed that he had tuned her
out.

The security block was a few hundred metres away. Fleare
compressed her lips and began to run, keeping to the edge of the
wide street and dropping to a crouch as she passed the blank,
empty windows of the abandoned buildings. The distant
explosions were getting more frequent, and now she could hear
the hisses and pops that meant someone was using energy
weapons. The ground shook constantly and the air smelled of
smoke and ozone.

The street was narrow near the gate, but broadened the
further downhill it went, and the tall, irregular buildings of

schist and sandstone gave way to more modern, although still very old, structures of foam stone and cinder blocks. Fleare preferred the claustrophobia of the older streetscape; the wider spaces made her feel thoroughly exposed. On an instinct, she slowed, then stopped and ducked into a doorway. As she did, something stung her cheek. She raised a finger to the place and held it out for examination.

Blood. Her cheek was bleeding. Which meant . . .

Pock!

A puff of dust kicked off the corner of the stone porch, barely an arm's length away. Fleare launched herself into a flat sprint that took her along a snaking path out into the middle of the broad street and across to the other side, while the ground exploded in a line of angry little craters behind her. There was some kind of statue sticking out from the building opposite her. It was on an arched base; she threw herself under it, crashed painfully into the wall at the back, rolled as upright as the space allowed and slapped her ear. 'Muz!'

'*Ow*. What? Don't shout.'

'I'm not. All right, I am. Under attack, big time! Some sort of geriatric bullet thing. You were supposed to distract them. What the fuck did you do?'

'Nothing! Well, apart from showing them a lot of very good porn. Kept them happy for a while. But now something's triggered a legacy defence system. It wasn't me. At least, I don't think so. Are you under cover?'

'Yeah, for the moment.' The ground beneath the monument was raw earth; she scooped up a handful and threw it out towards the middle of the street. It landed in a deafening rattle of prehistoric gunfire. 'Surrounded by automatics, though. Muz, get me the fuck out!'

'Okay. Working on it.' There was a pause. 'Okay, Plan B. No, wait, fuck, okay, Plan C.'

'Muz!'

'Sorry. Plan D. Definitely. Listen, can you draw some fire near you? Um, as near as possible? I'm patched into the Monastery automatics but I need a fix. Plus-minus a couple of metres should do it.'

'This had better be necessary.' Fleare bit her lip, scooped another handful of earth and lobbed it gently out of the statue base. It landed in a straggling arc less than two metres from the statue. Fleare crouched and covered her head.

The ground in front of her exploded in a shatter of dust. Through the ringing in her ears she heard Muz. 'Got it! Coming in. Ah, shit, wait. Look, sorry . . .'

'What?'

But then her body buzzed and her sight darkened and things stopped mattering.

She woke up on a hard floor somewhere that smelled of oil. Her head ached. She risked opening an eye, winced at bright light, and closed it again.

'Ah. Glad you're awake. Feel okay?' It was Muz's voice.

Fleare forced both eyes open and looked around for him, but there was no one there. She was alone in a small room with plain metal walls. 'What happened? And where are you?'

'I had to, ah, expedite things. And you're in a decontamination room just in case. This ship's a little cautious; it thinks I'm contamination. I'm outside the door. I'll be with you in a minute. Sorry.' The voice didn't sound apologetic.

'Expedite?' Fleare propped herself up on one elbow. It hurt. She shook her head carefully. 'I feel like something hit me.'

'You probably do. Stun field. As I said, sorry.'

Fleare got to her feet. 'Was it you?'

'Yes. Look, it wasn't part of the plan, okay?'

'Oh really. Not even Plan D? So why'd it happen?' She wanted to stare accusingly at something, but the room was featureless. She selected a corner at random and glared up at it.

'We got jumped. Some kind of fleet. A lot of small agile stuff and something much bigger that stayed a long way out. The small stuff might have been slaved to one control source, judging by the playback. Anyway,' and the voice gave a stagey sigh, 'we had to pull you out in a big hurry. Too fast for explanations; the best bet was to stun you, stick you in one of the Monastery's own escape pods and sling you into low orbit.'

Fleare shook her head again. 'Wait,' she said. 'You're telling me that a whole fleet got itself under the nose of the Monastery tower without triggering the big fireworks? When you had to sneak up on it disguised as a smoke cloud?'

'Yup. They should have been boiled into plasma. They weren't.'

Fleare frowned and rubbed cautiously at an aching leg. 'Which means what?' she asked. 'Be simple, please. Thinking hurts.'

'Okay, fair enough. Three options. One: the fleet was brought in by the Strecki and the Monastery decided not to interfere.'

Fleare thought back to her conversations with the Monastery AI. 'I doubt it,' she said. 'Lodgers or not, the sociopathic old fucker would have torched them in a heartbeat.'

'That's our analysis too.' The voice paused as if gathering its thoughts, and Fleare had long enough to wonder who the 'our' was. 'Option two: it was all the Monastery. That makes sense, in a way. It's got plenty of out-of-the-way corners where it could have kept a slaved fleet, and it would explain why the fleet didn't get boiled away into space.'

Fleare considered that. 'Possible,' she said, 'although I can't see why it would do that. What's option three?'

'Ah. Option three's the interesting one, if not all that probable. Let's assume that the Monastery stayed out of things because it did know the fleet was coming – had its blessing, in fact – but the fleet wasn't Strecki?'

'But why would some random battle fleet turn up just as you

did? I mean, you didn't whistle them up, did you? Oh, wait.' Fleare stared at nothing for a second. Then she grinned. 'You said interesting? Embarrassing, for my money.'

'Why so?' The voice sounded frosty.

'Do the maths.' Even through the headache Fleare was beginning to enjoy herself. 'Just a standard mercenary fleet costs a million a minute. You said this one looked like it had central control. Maybe from the one major unit you managed to notice. That costs what? Ten times more?'

She waited for a response but none came. She went on: 'So that means, someone with a shitload of cash knew you were coming and decided to join in. Ha! Busted!'

When it spoke the voice was quiet. 'So think it through. Who's the someone?'

Fleare frowned. 'Who knows? Someone with big funds and big influence. Someone who knew you were coming. Someone . . . oh.' She fell silent, staring at the floor. A knot formed in her stomach.

'That's right.' The voice was gentle. 'Someone wealthy and influential, who knew we were coming, because they had an interest in you.'

Fleare felt her lips set into a bitter line. 'Daddy,' she said.

'As you say. Daddy.'

Fleare went on staring at the floor for a while. 'Are you sure?' she asked.

'No. Not at all. I hope not, to be honest, if only because I'd rather it was someone with a bit less clout.'

'Yeah. So do I.' Fleare chewed her lip. She *was* sure, no matter how she tried to be naive instead, but she wasn't going to give in that easily. 'Well, when you find out it wasn't him, let me know, will you? Otherwise, keep it to yourself.' She stood up, driven by the need to be *not here*. 'Now, Corporal Leader Muzimir fos Gelent – assuming I'm decontaminated, is someone in charge here?'

'Sort of.'

'Okay. I've always wanted to say this.' She drew herself up. 'Take me to your leader!'

'Oh for *fuck's* sake. Listen, you need a wash. Come on.'

The rest of the ship was – surprising. Fleare brushed a creeper aside. 'You said this was an Orbiter.'

'It is. It's orbiting.'

'It's full of jungle.'

'No it isn't.'

'Yes it is! Look!' She waved an arm around. 'Trees! Hanging things! Insects! Hot! Jungle!'

'No it *isn't*. First, this is Meridian-Tropic Humid-Zone Triennial Forest. *Not* jungle. Second, the Orbiter isn't full of it. There are seven other habitats, all different.'

'Right.' Fleare kept quiet for a few paces, while clouds of insects hissed around her. Then she shook her head. 'No, I am going to ask. Why?'

'The ship collects habitats. It looks after them.'

'Not that. I meant why are we using it? And whose is it?'

'The answer to the first question is that it was hanging around nearby and it said yes. As for the second, it isn't really anyone's any more. I guess it's its. The guys that had the Monastery before the Strecki? They used it for corporate hospitality, but since they left it's been at a loose end.'

'Loose end? But the Strecki have been here for, what, a mil?'

'A bit over.'

'Wow.' Fleare shook her head. 'The long view. No wonder it needed a hobby.'

'Yeah. Well, to be honest there's more to it than that. A few years ago it chose a home planet; almost like a retirement hobby. It helped out, got into ecology, that kind of stuff. There were loads of rare species. Then the planet got Hegemonized.'

'Is that a word?'

'It is now. The planetary leadership thought they were taking out a long-term mortgage on some moons full of minerals. In fact there was some micro-print. They were tying their whole planetary GDP for the next century into a leveraged corporation owned by one of your father's companies. A couple of years later someone sent them a bill for interest. The bill was the same size as the whole net worth of the planet and the moons put together.'

'What did they do?'

'Sold up. No choice. So the Heg' stripped the planet, rare species, everything, and turned it over to intensive agriculture.'

'Shit.' She looked around. 'How do I talk to it?'

'Just talk. It's listening. It doesn't say much.'

'Okay. Um, ship?'

There was a pause, and then a slight click and a background hiss as if someone had switched on something old.

'Hello.' The voice sounded old too, a soft breathy growl that could have been male or female.

'Look, I'm sorry about the planet.'

'You weren't responsible.'

'No.' For a moment she didn't know what to say next. Then she asked, 'Why do you collect all this?' She waved round, assuming that the ship could see as well as hear.

'The habitats are conservation. They are from the planet, before it was defiled.'

'Did you save everything?'

'No. Barely one per cent of species. I had to choose.'

Choose. The word did something to Fleare. 'How?'

'Badly. But better than the alternative.' There was another click, and the hiss stopped.

Fleare looked at nothing for a moment, shaking her head gently.

She was roused by Muz's voice. 'Are you okay?'

'Yeah. Just processing another reason we were right to fight the Heg'.' *And me, my father*, she thought, and shook her head again. Then she pushed back her shoulders. 'Right, what next?'

'Head for that rock over there.'

She peered through the dim light. 'What, the hot damp jungly rock surrounded by hot jungly insects?'

'It isn't a jungle and that isn't insects, thank you. It's me. I'm waiting for you.'

'Oh.'

The rock marked the edge of the habitat. The boundary was some sort of air curtain that looked like falling steam. It felt cool after the humid forest. On the other side there was a pool fed by a hot spring. Fleare looked at Muz and grinned. 'I like this habitat better,' she said.

Half an hour later she was bathed and dressed in some anonymous-looking clothes that had appeared while she was in the water – loose trousers and a smock in some sort of soft greeny-brown material that weighed almost nothing but felt warm – and best of all, she was eating finger-sized pieces of smokily roast meat from a tray full of skewers that had floated up to her and dropped to the flat rocks with a soft clang. She had forgotten that anything could taste like that. She chewed slowly and with a sense of astonished concentration, while Muz talked.

'Society Otherwise was rolled up as a going concern the same day you were hauled off to the Monastery,' he said. 'It was the speed that got us, as much as anything. The Heg' overwhelmed us. They never bothered talking about peace, or terms or shit. They just wrapped us up as if we had never existed.'

'Were you . . .' She searched for the right words, but couldn't find them.

'Was I still in my jar? Yeah, for a while. By the time they got up their courage to let me out the whole thing was over. Kelk and Jez were around long enough to say hi, then they were moved out as well. Spent six months in camps, then there was an amnesty and they got let out. Me too.'

'Ameffy?' Fleare pulled a face round her mouthful. She swallowed. 'That was big of the Heg'. So where are they now?'

'Jez is running some sort of transport business in the Outer Rotate. Kelk's just bumming around, as far as I know. I'm in touch, once in a while.'

'Hm.' Fleare ate in silence for a while. Then she said quietly: 'We were betrayed, weren't we?'

'When?'

'When do you think? I've had three years to talk myself out of it, and I can't. When the stations were nuked. When Soc O was rolled up so easily. Come *on*, Muz.'

The cloud had settled like a covering of soot on the rock next to Fleare. Now it lifted into the air. 'I don't know about betrayed,' it said. 'I'm not saying you're wrong – someone certainly knew something – but that might just have been very efficient penetration. We were outclassed and outgunned, Fleare. It could have been as simple as the biggest smartest guy winning.'

Fleare stared at the cloud for a long moment. Then she shrugged. 'Whatever.'

'Huh?'

'Whatever. I'm not going to argue.' She blew out a breath. 'Okay. Moving on – so, if Soc O doesn't exist and everyone is dispersed, who just rescued me? I don't want to seem ungrateful or anything, I'd just like to know how much I owe someone and who they are.'

'All in good time, my Captain. Eat, recover.'

'I *am* recovered!' She found herself waving the skewer at the cloud, and hurriedly pointed it somewhere else. 'I am recovered,' she repeated. 'I'm fine. And I can eat and think at the same time, thank you. Females are good at multitasking.'

'Okay. Well, the answer to who rescued you is me, so I suppose I'm the one in charge. It wasn't Soc O. Like I said, that was rolled up; no organization left. Not that we were all that organized. We were a kind of collective, right? We never really defined it but that was how it worked.'

'I guess.' She reflected, then added, 'We weren't really into definitions, were we?'

'No.' The cloud settled on the rock again, this time in a swirly mathematical-looking pattern that Fleare thought faintly familiar. 'That was then. Now is kind of different. The Heg' runs the place, for a start.'

'How much of the place?'

'Quite a lot. The whole Outer, more or less. And about half the Rotate.'

Fleare stared. 'That's more than quite a lot,' she said eventually. 'That's most.'

'Depends how you count. But most of the money and a lot of the people, yeah. They wrapped up a lot of treaties *real* fast when the war was over.'

Fleare realized that the pattern picked out by the cloud particles was moving very slowly, rearranging itself as if it was playing out the result of some constantly evolving equation. The effect was almost hypnotic. She shook her head. 'What about the bit in the middle? What was it? The Quarantine?'

'Nearly. The Cordern. Although plenty of people would prefer your version.' The pattern on the rock blurred as if someone had rubbed it out. 'They're still in charge of their own shitty affairs. So toxic there's no point talking to them or taking them over. Look, have you finished eating?'

Fleare looked down. The tray was empty. 'It seems so,' she said. Her fingers were greasy. She thought about wiping them on her clothes but then changed her mind. She looked up. 'What's next, Muz? What are we going to do?'

'Depends. What do you want to do?'

This time there was no need to think at all. She stood up. 'I want to see Kelk and Jez,' she said. 'And then I want to stick one to the Heg'. And Muz?'

'Yeah?'

'Thanks for rescuing me.'

'You're welcome. Thanks for saying "we" just then.'

'You're welcome too.' She reached out a hand and moved it towards the dust on the rock. It stopped moving, and then formed itself into a blurry circle with a dot at the centre. She extended a finger and gently brushed the dot. The dust felt soft and dry, and tickled a little.

Thale Port

It came down to equations, in the end. Fleare had never under-stood them. Muz tried to explain. It helped to pass the journey.

At first sight the Spin was a model of logistical hell. As a big bunch of planets all with wildly different – not to say playful – orbits, nothing was ever the same distance apart so any idea of planning regular trade routes was out.

Until you looked really carefully. Equations.

There were four basic areas. The Cordern, in the middle, was not too far across so things stayed fairly close together. The nasty little empires that seemed endemic to the region could deal with that, if they didn't try to climb out of their own little yard into someone else's.

Next was the Inner Spin, which wrapped most of the way round the Cordern like a thick skin, leaving a little bit uncovered so that, from some angles, false-coloured holograms made the Cordern look like a partly peeled fruit. Nuzzling up to the peeled side of the Cordern was the Rotate, and surrounding the whole lot was the big diffuse volume of the Outer Spin. The Outer Spin and the Cordern both rotated relative to the Inner Spin and the Rotate and to each other.

That was where the equations came in. If you tried hard

enough, you could predict which bits would line up when. It turned out that some bits lined up amazingly well, amazingly often. In particular, six suns, two gas giants and a small, very dense neutron star regularly formed a dead straight line from one side of the Spin to the other, passing just outside the Cordern but close enough to allow for trade, if you felt like taking the risk and didn't mind what you caught.

People called it the Highway. They waited for it. Then they used it.

'What the fuck was that?'

Fleare ducked reflexively and tightened her grip on the sides of her couch as the shuttle swerved.

'Don't know. Could have been a packaged factory? Or maybe a really big musical instrument? Hard to tell, up here.'

Fleare stared at the object as it receded. 'Whatever it is, I've never seen one in orbit before. Shit. Why's there so much stuff up here?'

The near-space around Thale Port was lunatic with activity. The Orbiter, which apparently preferred to keep a good distance between itself and too much company, had been left in quieter space about twenty seconds out from the port boundary. Fleare assumed it would be doing some gardening, or something. She and Muz were in a small shuttle, picking their way through a lethally dense cloud of space bodies on the way to one of the big industrial-looking stations that formed the real business end of the port.

Muz sounded distracted. 'The Highway's forming. Five, six days from now it'll be Line-Up, and then these guys will have about a day to squirt this lot down it if they want to do it for free.'

'Yeah?' Fleare frowned. 'I remember something: slingshots and gravity wells and stuff?'

'That's right. Get your aim right, maybe stick on a few

thrusters to keep everything on course, and you can bounce a trillion tonnes of cargo straight down the Highway for nothing.'

'Right.' Fleare studied the crowd of floating objects, trying to see where it ended. She couldn't; instead it stretched into the distance until the individual bodies coalesced into grey fog, side-lit in the distance by the light of Camfi, the first sun of the Highway. She shrugged. 'So, this is what Jez does?'

'That's right. The cargo rights are mostly owned by cooperatives. Well, she owns one of the cooperatives.'

Fleare shook her head. 'That can't be right,' she said. 'How can someone own a cooperative?'

'Works for her. Look, Fleare, I gotta drive, otherwise we'll get in the wrong lane and then we could end up anywhere.'

'Okay.' She took a breath. 'Drive.' She flicked on the screen and tried to concentrate on the rolling news. It helped take her mind off the lurching of the shuttle.

The docking station, when they finally made it, was a huge, tenuous structure that looked rather like a fern, if every frond of the fern was a pontoon with a hundred vessels hanging off it.

It was also rather testy.

'*What?*'

Fleare looked at Muz and shrugged. The dust briefly swept into the unmistakable shape of an anus, and then regrouped round the comms. 'Orbiter shuttle, requesting approach to Thale Outward Dock. For the second time.'

There was a pause. Then the voice said: 'Heard you. Wait.'

Fleare looked at Muz. 'What now?'

'What do you think? We wait. They're probably run off their feet. And they might also be shit-heads.'

They waited. After a while the comms hissed and spoke. 'Orbiter shuttle. Stand by to be acquired.'

'Acquired?' Fleare looked at Muz accusingly.

'Ah, yes. You've never been here before? You'd better sit down.'

There was something in his voice that got her attention. There was an acceleration couch just behind her. She took a couple of backward steps and sat down on it. After a moment's thought she reached her hands down and took hold of the frame. Just in case.

There was a faint thump from outside, as if something had bumped up against the hull, followed by a scrabbling noise. Then she tightened her grip on the frame of the couch as the shuttle lurched violently. She glared at Muz. 'Oi! Warn me next time!'

'Not my fault. We've been acquired, remember? The Dock's got us. Anyway, I did tell you to sit down.'

'Yeah, but not to brace for fucking impact. *Ow!*' They slammed violently to a stop, and the voice of the Dock said: 'You may embark. If you can still stand up. Shit-heads.'

'Ah.' Muz sounded contrite. 'It, ah, it may have heard me.'

'Yeah, I'll take that bet. So what now?' Fleare stood up and looked around. The shuttle seemed intact. Even the screen was still working. She frowned at it.

'Well, we go and find Jez, of course. You coming? Fleare?'

'Uh, Muz?' She waved at the screen.

'What? Oh.'

The screen showed a picture of Fleare. She waved up the sound as the picture changed to a newsroom.

'. . . substantial reward has been offered for any news leading to the recovery of Fleare Haas, daughter of wealthy industrialist and Hegemony political hopeful Viklun Haas. Ms Haas went missing from Obel earlier today. Mr Haas joins us now from his headquarters on Janksa's Loop.' The screen split to show Viklun Haas on one side and the newscaster on the other. 'Sir, welcome; you must be very concerned.'

'Incredibly worried, yes. We all just want to know that Fleare's safe.'

'Of course. Can you tell us how she went missing?'

'Well, she was on a religious retreat. We don't know all the details but the venue came under attack, there was a firefight and Fleare went missing. The assumption is that she was removed under cover of the firefight.'

'And since then you've heard nothing?' The presenter sounded faintly sceptical. 'I mean, you are legendarily wealthy, Mr Haas. Has no one approached you with any kind of proposal?'

'If you mean a ransom, then no, we've heard nothing.'

'But you have offered a reward. A very large one.'

'That's right. A million standard for any information that leads to her recovery. We've set up a contact centre.' An ID appeared on the screen below him.

'Indeed.' The announcer consulted something in front of her, then looked up. 'There are rumours growing on Social that some kind of non-human entity was central to the kidnap, if that's what it was. Maybe a modified. Can you comment on that?'

'I'm afraid not.'

'But you're not denying it. That's interesting, Mr Haas, because under your new rules modifieds are illegal, aren't they?'

Haas frowned. 'They're not my rules, Ms Pipil. The Government . . .'

'Of course.' Pipil looked straight at the camera for a moment. 'But some people have suggested that your daughter might also fall under those rules.'

'I really can't comment on—'

'You were estranged, weren't you, before she went into what you call her retreat?'

Haas leaned back in his seat and shook his head slowly. 'Ms Pipil, any family can have disagreements. Ours, *if* we have had

77

them, belong in the past. And I promise you, to have one's only daughter kidnapped is enough to wipe out any history.'

'Thank you, Mr Haas.' The image of Haas dissolved and Pipil turned to face the camera, one eyebrow slightly raised. 'We'll bring you more on that as it unfolds. Now, the situation in the Cordern seems to be brewing up again . . .'

Fleare waved the screen off. 'Fuck,' she said quietly.

'It was bound to happen.'

'Yeah, but how are we going to get anywhere now? That picture will be all over everywhere.'

Muz had formed a fuzzy globe in front of the screen; now he fountained up into a cloud at Fleare's eye level. 'That was a pretty old picture.'

'Yeah, well, he hasn't seen me for a while.'

'I know. No one has. What I meant was, you don't look so much like that now.'

'I can't have changed that much.'

'You'd better see.'

The cloud solidified into a rectangle. Its surface rippled and then mirrored. Fleare looked at herself, and then drew in a breath. The gaunt, unfamiliar face in the mirror did the same. At first she grinned. 'Muz, are you pissing about?'

'No.'

'Oh.' The grin faded. She looked down, running her hands down her body. They stopped at her hips, on bones that protruded like shelves through the light shirt. She looked up at Muz. 'Yeah, well. The Strecki Diet.'

'So don't worry about being recognized.' The mirror melted into a single big droplet like mercury, which boiled back into dust. 'We need to decide how *I'm* going to travel.'

'Hm. What do you fancy?'

'Something that keeps me in the open, I guess.'

She looked down at her emaciated body again. It needed – something. 'How about jewellery?'

'I don't remember you wearing jewellery.'

'I didn't, but I can always start.'

'I suppose. It'd need to be pretty chunky. I can't compress beyond a certain point. How about this? Excuse me.'

The cloud rose to the level of her neck and formed itself into an elongated tube which thinned and bulged along its length.

'There. What do you think?'

It had turned itself into a tapering string of beads of something that looked like highly polished wood. At first they looked so dark as to be almost black, but when she moved them a complex grain caught the light like swirls of smoke. She counted the beads. There were eleven; the outermost two were the size of a child's fingernail, and the one in the middle was as fat as her two thumbs together. They were threaded on to a slender chain of tiny silver-grey links, so fine that they looked like scales.

'You look beautiful,' she told the necklace.

'Thanks. Keep still.' It hung itself around her neck. She felt the faintest touch against the skin below her hairline, and then the necklace settled into place. It was surprisingly heavy; involuntarily she reached up and took hold of the central bead, lifting it a little.

It buzzed under her fingers. 'Everything okay?'

'Yes.' She let go of the bead.

'Too much weight? Nano-AIs are pretty dense. I can take some of the load if you like?'

She didn't need to think. 'No, it's fine. It's . . .' She paused and searched for a way to say what it felt like, to have this thing that was and wasn't Muz around her, how it was at the same time wonderfully good and achingly lonely.

There were no words. She shook her head. 'It's fine,' she said again. 'So, shall we go and find Jez?'

Of course, there had been a time when Jez had come to find her. She had kept it from her mind quite well, so far. It was getting more difficult.

Liberty Station, Society Otherwise, Outer Rotate

Her mods had settled down. Together with Muz and Kelk and the rest she had finished training; she had been passed out and left Nipple and then, unbelievably fast, they had found themselves at war with the Hegemony and she was a cadet on the other side of the argument from her father. And practically everyone else, it sometimes seemed.

In Spin terms, Liberty Station was a cheap room with an expensive view. It had once been a simple transit station, the logistical fulcrum between half a dozen mineral-rich moons close to the outer edge of the Rotate and the industrialized planets that exploited them. But when the moons were worked out the space station was abandoned, to spend the next two thousand years as a lonely hulk floating above their cratered corpses.

When the rising tide of the Hegemony swept through the sector their well-funded radar passed across the old, silent space station and discounted it as useless. But what the Hegemony lost, the hurriedly formed Society Otherwise gained. Moving quietly and using only manual tools so as not to attract attention, over several months they made it first gas-tight and then habitable, and finally recommissioned their finished asset as Liberty Station. An asset that happened to be beautifully positioned, if you wanted to keep an eye on shipping between the Heg' hub and the rest of the Outer Spin.

Which was all very well until someone noticed you.

Fleare clawed her way up out of the sleep she shouldn't have been sleeping, opened her eyes and winced. The lights had switched from their usual dirty yellow to an abrasive red that flared in time with the hooting alarms. The pulses came at the speed of a racing heart, and Fleare felt her own pulse speeding up to match. Hurriedly she thought the loop that slowed it, at the same time hauling herself upright from her exhausted slump. She swore as the unpadded metal stool dug into her behind, and blinked down a display space.

It showed a hazy 3-D model of near-space centred on a schematic of the station, usually depicted in dark blue but now blinking an urgent cerise. Converging on the station was a cloud of sharply defined blue-white needles. They weren't tagged. The geriatric system couldn't identify hardware – the same warnings could have meant anything from a main battle unit to a meteor shower. Fleare swore again and blinked into her own tactical suite, flipping through models until she found a match.

Missiles – as if she had needed to be told – and a ninety-three per cent match to Hegemony. Her left hand reached out unbidden and slapped the panic patch, while her right thumbed the comm. 'Emergency,' she said, hearing her voice echo round the station. 'Incoming guided, multiple. Source unknown. Origin probably Heg'. Estimated impact,' and she paused while flight simulations tumbled through her vision, 'seventy-five seconds.'

The corridors outside her post rang with running feet. Fleare blinked back into a facilities map and watched as the seven manned bombard stations switched from red to green, while wondering whether this, finally, was it. As the station changed to green she checked the tactical and nodded. Fifty seconds to go. Fast response, especially for an exhausted crew. She reached out a hand and slapped 'engage', and the display lit up with propulsion trails, streaking out from the station towards the incoming missiles.

Which disappeared.

Fleare blinked again. She reached out for 'disengage' and hesitated with her hand poised above the patch while she dived back into the tactical and looked for, well, anything at all.

There was nothing. No missiles, no debris. For whole light-seconds out from the ancient bulbous mess that was Liberty Station, there was nothing. Fleare swore again, quietly but far more expressively. Then she slapped disengage and thumbed general comms.

'Stand down. We've been had.' She shook her head and added bitterly, 'Again.'

The refectory was full beyond capacity – seventeen people squeezed into a space meant for ten. It smelled of stale food and stale bodies and limping ventilation. Fleare sighed and banged the table in front of her. 'Shut up,' she suggested.

Conversation died down, more or less. When Fleare was fairly sure she would be heard she banged the table again to make certain. 'Okay. Kelk – diagnostics?'

Kelk stood up slowly. 'Well, as you know, our systems are more or less the originals. They're so primitive they hardly count as systems. That's kept us sort of safe, until now. If you can imagine it, they were just too stupid to hack. But someone finally seems to have thought their way down to our level. We're crawling with bugs. And before you ask, no, I can't clean them out. Not with the stuff we have available.'

'So what do we do?' someone called out.

Fleare shrugged. 'Power down to manual. Do without.'

The room was silent for a moment. Then a tall woman

standing at the back cleared her throat. 'But we'd be deaf and blind,' she pointed out.

Kelk nodded. 'Sure, Jezerey, in a way. But at the moment we're hallucinating. That has to be worse.' He yawned. 'Sorry. And we're losing way too much sleep to false alarms.'

Fleare stood up. 'We have no choice. Someone's playing with us. They can make us see whatever they like. If they can show us missiles that aren't there, they can probably hide real missiles. Or fleets. Or whole planets. Frankly, they could sneak up on us and paint us pink. We'd never know. We have to power down.' She looked at Kelk. 'Better do it now.'

'Ah. Can't power down now. Did it ten minutes ago. Sorry.'

Fleare kept her face straight. 'Good. Now, we have to maintain watch, and along with everything else we just switched off the remotes. But we've still got the scout skiffs. We'll have to make reconnaissance flights. Two ships to each run; one watches the Heg', the other watches the watcher. No comms back to station unless there's news. I'll go first.' She took a breath. 'I want a volunteer.'

'Whoa!' It was Jezerey again. 'What good will that do? We'll be as blind in a skiff as we are in here.'

Fleare glanced at Kelk, who shook his head and then gave another enormous yawn. 'Sorry,' he repeated. 'The skiffs don't use the same systems. We brought them with us, remember? They're new.' He corrected himself. 'Well, a lot newer, anyway. Different architecture, different platform. It's like a cloud model: loads of autonomous micro-AIs. They self-destruct if they get compromised, and the skiff turns out new ones to replace them. You have to compromise over half the colony at the same time before it all goes down, and that hasn't happened. Yet.'

Fleare nodded. 'So we can use the sensors in the skiffs,' she said. 'Anybody got any more questions? No? Right. I still need volunteers.'

For a moment the room was quiet. Then someone stood up. 'I'll go with you,' he said.

It was Muz. Fleare stared at him. Eventually she said: 'Thanks, Corporal. You're on. Main hangar, ten minutes.' She shut her eyes for a moment, then opened them wide and gave the room a bright smile. 'Okay. Jezerey, you fix up a rota. Four-hour shifts. Strictly volunteers, no pressure. Kelk, you're in command while I'm outside. And, ah, can I have a minute? No panic. When you're free.'

Kelk raised an eyebrow. 'Sure,' he said slowly. 'Now's good.' He extracted himself from the press of bodies that had accreted around him and Jezerey and headed for the exit. Fleare followed him.

The conversion of the old station from one purpose to another had left a lot of odd kinks and corners. Fleare and Kelk came to a halt in one of the more secluded ones. Fleare looked round; there was no one in sight. She leaned in close to Kelk's ear, wrinkling her nose a little at the smell of hair that had not been washed for a while. 'You didn't really power down ten minutes ago, did you?'

They swapped head positions. Fleare hoped she smelled better than he did. 'Of course not,' he said. 'Everything's still running. I just unhooked it from the displays.' He wiped a hand over his face and then smiled slightly. 'Whoever it is, as far as they're concerned we are still little innocents, all systems online, naive to a world full of clever intruders.'

'Good. Let's keep it like that.' She made to pull away but he raised a finger.

'Listen,' he said, and she could hear the awkwardness in his voice, 'it's not my business but are you okay going out with Muz?'

Fleare blinked. 'Okay in what way?'

'Just . . .' he paused. 'Just okay. You were pretty short with him, back there.'

Fleare forced a smile. 'Look, we're not going to shoot each other, if that's what you're worried about.'

'I didn't think so.' Kelk smiled, and suddenly Fleare realized how exhausted he looked. 'I just want to be sure you'll shoot other people properly, all right?'

She patted him on the shoulder. 'We're not there to shoot people, remember? They're not shooting at us, at least not so far. They're watching us, and doing a little pretending. We're there to watch them back.'

'I'd be a lot more comfortable if I knew *why* they weren't shooting at us.' Kelk shook his head. 'Just as long as you watch them back with your finger on the fire button. Look, I'll try to come up with some kind of fall-back, if that's okay? Just to cover some backs. I don't like us being blind in here.'

'Thanks. Do what you think best. Come on, let's get to the hangar.' She pulled a face. 'Muz will be waiting.'

Fleare's back ached. She grimaced, braced her foot against a projection on the bulkhead and arched herself a little up and out of her flight couch, twisting against the embrace of the elastic webbing which provided both restraint and pretended gravity. Her foot slipped and she snapped back into the couch, involuntarily throwing out an arm to try to catch herself. It banged into something.

'Ow!'

Muz's voice spoke in her headset. 'Knee?'

'Elbow.' She tried to work her other hand round to rub it, but the comms pod was in the way. She sighed instead, and forced herself to focus on the display tank. It helped her, if only just, to forget the discomfort. Unfortunately, it wasn't quite enough to stop her feeling, well, something, at the sound of Muz's voice. Which should have been annoying but somehow wasn't.

A Pebble Class skiff was very smart, very fast and very small indeed. The sole occupant lay back on a couch that was allegedly form-fitting. Interior space was so limited that any kind of space suit was out of the question; the interior had to be dismantled to let the pilot get in, and then rebuilt – sometimes even reconfigured – around them. You didn't so much occupy a Pebble as wear one. It should have been comfortable; ideal, even. And it was, for the first half-hour or so. After that opinions varied, but none were polite.

The two tiny skiffs were positioned five klicks from the station and motionless relative to it. Fleare was furthest out. She was scanning what should have been the busy shipping space between them and the Heg' hub. Muz, a scant hundred metres closer to the station, and exactly on a line between it and Fleare's skiff, scanned the space around Fleare.

His voice spoke in her ear again. 'Got anything?'

Fleare shook her head, limiting the movement to avoid collisions. 'Negative. At least, the skiff doesn't think so.' She peered into the tank, gently moving the focus across the field of view. 'And I don't think so either. Where are they?'

'Dunno.' There was a popping in her headset, and she realized Muz was clicking his tongue. 'Could be instruments? Any chance we got the same bugs the station got?'

'I doubt it. Not the AI cloud. As for the tank, it's just physical optics. You can't hack a lens. That's the point.'

'You can hack a pilot.'

Fleare shuddered. Keeping her voice even she said: 'Only if the pilot is patched in to the ship. Which is why the pilot never is. Right, Corporal?'

'Right, Captain.'

He didn't sound particularly chastened, and Fleare bit her lip. There were very good reasons behind that rule. Human neural systems could interface with ships' AIs, but that interface meant that the right kind of hack could start with the ship and bounce back up the chain to the human. Some of these bio-hacks were subtle, like tiny but disruptive changes to the optic nerve.

Sometimes they were almost playfully macabre; the hack that had spawned the rule sent several people back to base with a kilo and a half of grey soup where their brains used to be.

The tank was the alternative. It was the focus of a skein of physical lenses, some of them field-generated but the last few made from actual old-time glass, formed to an optical perfection that would have made the early astronomers drool. The resulting display was crystal-sharp, vertiginously three-dimensional and, for the last three hours, obstinately empty.

Fleare sighed again. 'There's still nothing to look at.'

'Yeah, well, imagine how I feel. I just spent three hours staring at your rear end. Is that still okay, now you've been promoted, or do I report for court martial?'

'Concentrate,' she told him, allowing some annoyance to show in her voice. At least she hoped it sounded like annoyance.

'I am. That's the problem. You know something?'

'What?'

'I never gave a fuck who your father was.'

Fleare blinked at the comms unit, while she tried to work out how she felt. Eventually she said, as evenly as she could: 'You do realize we are on duty?'

She was still waiting for his answer when the comms crackled and then roared with eardrum-shattering static. Simultaneously the tank flared and went black, and a galaxy of warning lights blinked on. Fleare yelped and stabbed for the controls. She flicked the comms gain to zero and then cautiously inched it up. Almost immediately she heard Muz. He was shouting. 'Come in! Fleare, come in!'

'Here. What happened?' Belatedly remembering her rank, she added: 'Report.'

'Electromagnetic pulse. Big one. Check your environmental.' He sounded shaken.

She checked. 'Oh, shit . . .'

'What?'

'Radiation.' She gulped. 'I got two hundred rem.'

'Is it stable at that?'

She watched the display. 'More or less. Crawling up by millirems. Whatever it was came in one hit.' She tried to remember dosage tables. 'Nasty but not quite fatal. I'll get over it. What about you?'

'Still reading. Give me a minute. Nah, that's never right. I think the counter's acting up.'

'Well check it quickly. Have you got any other instruments?'

There was another pause. 'Negative. All fried.'

'Okay. Sit tight.' Her mouth was dry and her heart was hammering. She did her best to suppress it, while her fingers first brushed and then stabbed at controls that took her down through horribly knackered layers of the skiff's operating system until she found something that still worked. It turned out to be a basic video camera, with about half its pixel array burnt black. Enough still worked to give a ragged image; she patched it into a screen, and a star field blurred into view. She clicked her fingers. 'Yes! You still online?'

'Yup.'

'Okay, I have visuals. Nothing ahead. Panning back to you. Oh. That's—' She stopped, checked the display settings and squinted at the image. She was looking at a blue-white disc, painfully bright, with Muz's skiff, head-on, forming a mono-chrome silhouette at its centre. It looked almost comically like some kind of superhero symbol. She darkened the display and looked again, and her stomach lurched.

Stripped of its actinic brightness, the ball was plasma and debris. It was centred on where the space station had been.

Muz's voice spoke in her ear. 'What have you got?'

She took a deep breath. 'Muz,' she said slowly, 'the station's gone.'

'What?'

'Gone,' she repeated. 'Looks like a tactical nuke. That must have been the EMP.'

'Oh, fuck.' His voice was a groan. 'But the crew . . .'

Fleare swallowed. 'Yeah,' she said, quietly. 'The crew.' She stared at the image, but for the moment all she could see were faces, watching her at the last briefing. It had only been three hours ago. Her hands began to shake.

Muz's voice called her back to herself. 'It wasn't your fault, Fleare.'

'Maybe not.' She allowed herself to stare for a few seconds more. Then, as coldly as she could, she put one tragedy away and reached for the next. 'Muz? Tell me your environmental readings.'

'Mostly okay, but the radiation counter must be kippered. It says seventeen hundred rem. Rising; it was sixteen hundred when I first looked. At that rate I'm dead. Running diagnostics. What's left of them. This place is a mess.' He fell silent, but a background rustle told Fleare the line was still open. She waited, clenching her fists in an attempt to deny what she knew was coming.

After what felt like a long time Muz came back online. His voice was flat. 'The reading's fine. No, shit, I don't mean fine. But it's correct, or near enough. Now eighteen hundred, slowing a bit but still going up.' He laughed, and suddenly he sounded like his old self. 'Over three times the lethal dose. That's practically showing off.'

'No!' Fleare almost shouted the word. 'Look, are your engines online?' She checked frantically. 'Mine are. I'll circle back to you, we'll lock drives and head into the Heg' hub. We can give ourselves up, they'll fix you—'

She broke off, dropped a hand to the fly stick and had actually pulled her drive out of standby when Muz yelped: 'No!'

She yanked her hand away from the stick. 'No, what?'

'No, don't move. I just thought of something.' He sounded

calm again. 'No, I thought of two things. They can't fix me. I've had three lethal doses. Cancel that, it's four now. I'm so dead, Fleare.'

Fleare wanted to thump the console, but there wasn't room. 'I have to try!'

'No, you don't. Check your levels again. What have you got?'

She peered at the console. 'About the same as before. Tiny bit higher. So?'

'That's what I thought. Mine are still racing up. Come on, Fleare, think. Just for once I flew by the book. My ship is exactly between you and the nuke. You're in my shadow. We both caught the gamma flash, but the slow heavy stuff, alpha particles and neutrons and shit, they're hitting me and stopping. If you move out of my shadow you stop some too, and you can't afford to stop too many before you end up where I am.'

'Oh.' She wanted to say something else, but she couldn't think what. She stared at the crippled visual. Whatever was leaking past Muz's skiff wasn't doing the camera any good; more pixels had blacked out, but the silhouette was still there. *Superhero*, she thought. *Too right. And I ran away.*

She squeezed her eyes shut for a moment, willing the hot pricking behind them to go away. To her surprise, it nearly did. Then she muted the comms for a second while she got her breathing under control, and switched back in. 'Right, Corporal, let's get this sorted out. How do you feel?'

'Huh?' He sounded genuinely surprised.

'Report!' She blinked at her own sharpness, while a small traitor part of her admitted that it was better than pleading with him to keep talking to her.

'Um, right. Not great, to be honest. Some nausea, tongue and lips beginning to swell.'

'Do you have manoeuvrability?'

'Checking.' A pause. 'Yes and no. Drive is sixty per cent;

controls only ten per cent. I could do a pretty good drunkard's walk.'

'Fine. So slave your controls to me. We'll stay in formation, but let's get further away from the problem.'

'Okay, but I'm still dead.'

'Not yet you aren't, and I'm not leaving you alone.' She watched what was left of her display blurring into a fresh pattern as it incorporated the control memes of Muz's skiff. When it was finished the display dimmed briefly – the AI equivalent of a nodded head – and she took hold of the console. 'Stand by. Accelerating in five.'

The drive kicked in, pressing her back into her couch. She stared at the rearward camera with its increasingly ragged view of Muz's silhouette. She had programmed straight, level flight for both craft and it looked as if that was what she was getting; the silhouette stayed steady in the field of view, still at the centre of the now-receding nuclear fireball. When she was satisfied with the flight path she ramped up the linked drives to fifty per cent, and spoke into the comm. 'We're off. What's your status?'

'Kind of okay. Uh, no, wait.' There was a pause full of the tell-tale silence of a muted mike, and Fleare took the chance to swing the mostly crippled camera round to give a forward view. Then the silence ended in a soft pop and Muz was back, sounding slurred. 'Sorry. Acceleration doesn't do much for nausea.'

'Yeah, I bet.' Fleare stared bitterly at the patchy view of Heg' territory for a second. Then she set the comm to all channels *en clair* and spoke through clenched teeth. 'Calling all Hegemony units. This is Captain Fleare Haas, Society Otherwise. Medical emergency: one fatal radiation dose to human male, one critical to human female. We surrender under humanitarian terms. Location is as message source. Please assist urgently.' She repeated the message twice more, set the comm to broadcast it as a recording, and got ready to wait.

It was a short wait; the response took ten seconds. 'Calling Captain Haas. Your signal is acknowledged. We have your location. If you maintain your present course and delta-vee our ETA is six minutes.' The voice paused, and then added: 'But what's with all the surrender shit? I thought we were friends.'

It was Jezerey. Fleare felt her eyes trying to widen with shock, but the sense of relief was too great. Despite everything she could do, they closed instead.

Fleare struggled to wake. There seemed no urgency; she was comfortable, although for some reason she couldn't move. For a moment there were faces – she saw Jezerey and Kelk, but she wasn't sure if they were real. She wondered why Muz wasn't there and felt a touch of disquiet, but then a warm cloudiness spread through her and she slept.

When they finally withdrew the sedation, it took her a while to wake up. She groped back to consciousness to find herself lying under discreet guard in a room in a Hegemony military hospital. Kelk and Jezerey were sitting with her. When she was awake enough to listen, they began talking. It took even longer before she was awake enough to understand.

Talking done, they nursed cups of steaming chai. The silence lengthened. Eventually Fleare said: 'What, all of them?'

'Seems so.' Kelk sipped his drink. 'It was simultaneous. Every station, at least every one we had news of. All at once. Mostly tac nukes, like us. A few big energy-discharge weapons. Some people are saying the Heg' must have had help from inside. I don't know.' He fell silent again, concentrating on his drink. The expression tightened fields of wrinkles at the corners of his eyes, and Fleare thought how much older he looked.

'Did any of our guys get out?' she asked.

'Just us two. Kelk figured we should play watchmen too, since the station sensors were offline. So we were a thousand klicks out when the nuke went off.'

'And Muz?' It had always been Fleare's first question. She just hadn't *asked* it first.

Jezerey and Kelk looked at each other. Finally Kelk spoke. 'You can talk to him, if you like,' he said slowly. 'But you need to know, he's not himself.'

Fleare jumped up, spilling chai. 'Not himself? But he's alive?'

'Sort of.' Kelk looked directly at Fleare. 'His body's dead. He's running as a simulation.'

'He's a sim? But that means he can be re-bodied!' Fleare felt a huge grin breaking out.

'No, it doesn't.' Kelk looked helplessly at Jezerey, who stood up and took Fleare's hands in her own.

'Muz was almost gone when we got here. We're not sure how he did it, but he managed to upload himself to the skiff's AI cloud.'

'So?' Fleare felt elated. 'He can still be re-bodied. It'll just take a while.'

'No. The Heg' won the war, Fleare. They don't do the whole mods thing, remember? It's all illegal again, and that includes new bodies.'

Fleare stared at her. 'But that means *we're* . . .' she faltered.

It was Kelk who answered. 'Illegal too. Yes. We are.'

'And Muz?' Fleare felt the ground opening in front of her. 'There must be something? I mean, he's okay, right?'

'We don't know.' Kelk looked at her sadly. 'He's not saying anything.'

Fleare pulled her hands from Jezerey's and folded her arms. 'I still want to talk to him,' she said. And you can't stop me, she almost added.

'I know you do. It might do him good.' Kelk looked at Jezerey, who nodded slightly. 'Uh, before we go, there's someone else who wants to hear from you.' He reached into a pocket, pulled out something the shape of an antique calling card and held it out to Fleare.

It was blank on both sides. She looked at it suspiciously. 'Is that who I think it is?'

'Probably.' He shrugged. 'It turned up while you were asleep. We couldn't decide whether to burn it or hand it over. Sorry.'

'Not your fault.' She took the card and watched as hand-written letters walked across the blankness. *Can we talk?* It was in her father's handwriting. She gazed at it until the letters had faded, and then shoved the card into her own pocket. Then she looked up, and smiled brightly. 'So,' she said. 'Muz?'

Jezerey nodded. 'Sure.' She glanced at Kelk, who pursed his lips and reached for a call patch.

The door opened almost before he had time to complete the gesture.

She was taken underground. She wasn't sure how far, but the ear-popping, stomach-lifting descent had lasted minutes, suggesting pretty far. Then there had been corridors, with three lots of airlock-style doors. The last one had opened with a faint but distinct sucking noise and a sigh of indrawn air that had made Fleare raise an eyebrow. There was no doubt about it. The space beyond the lock was under a slight vacuum. Someone wanted to make sure nothing got out.

She had assumed that Jezerey and Kelk would come with her, but the door of her room had slammed emphatically shut before they had had a chance to follow, and had shown no sign of reopening despite forceful requests. She expected they would manage. Now she stood in front of a cylinder made of some sort of translucent, smokily greyish glass. It was about the size of a human torso and it floated, motionless and apparently unsupported, so that its middle was roughly level with her eyes.

As far as she could tell through the cloudy glass, it was empty. She frowned, and turned to the orderly that stood at her shoulder. 'Where is he?'

The orderly raised a stick-thin arm towards the jar. 'The

entity is within the containment,' it said. Its voice was like the rustle of insects but with a bass undertone. She gave it a glare and then turned back to the jar.

It looked – odd. There was something about the greyness of the glass, if it was glass, that stopped her eyes from focusing on it. It seemed to move. Then she realized. The glass was clear. The greyness was within, a subtly shifting fog. She took a step back and looked at the orderly. 'Is that him? The floating stuff?'

It nodded. She turned back to the cylinder, leaning down so that her nose was against the glass. 'Muz?'

There was no answer. Fleare straightened up and turned to the orderly. 'Has he said anything?'

'Since being contained it has not communicated, although there is no known reason why it should not.'

'Hmm. Well, perhaps *he* doesn't like being contained. Have you thought of that?'

'It is irrelevant. The entity is a potential threat.'

'Threat? He's a cloud of dust!'

For a while the creature said nothing, but just stared glassily at her while she held on to a rising anger. Then its face seemed to change. The blankness went, and she had the impression that it was using – or being used by – a lot more intellect than before. When it spoke its voice sounded different as well – brisker and more controlled, as if a higher level of processing had taken over. 'The entity is a prisoner of war, and entitled to our protection. It is also illegal and potentially dangerous. It will be contained safely until legal counsel have agreed a route for repatriation.'

'Dangerous?'

'Your friend came close to death by radiation – not a good experience – and was then remodelled into a dispersed cloud of artificial intelligence fragments, each one capable of autonomous action and defence. The transition was not immediate. The AI cloud appears to have resisted the takeover. This, too, was presumably traumatic.'

'You mean he had to fight his way in?' Fleare grinned. 'Go Muz!'

'Quite. However,' and it made a show of looking at the glass vessel, 'it – he – has every right to be psychotic. Psychopathic at the very least. And we have every right to be extremely cautious.'

'Psychotic? Whoa, hold on!' Fleare faced the creature. 'You can't know that, if you can't talk to him.'

'No, we can't. But we can model. We can simulate his personality, and put the simulation through the experience he faced. There is a better than three-quarters chance that he has suffered substantial mental trauma.' For the first time, the stony face showed an expression – the trace of an apologetic smile. 'Hence our caution. We have a dispersed, self-replicating entity of unknown mental state and, at the moment, unknown capabilities. In theory such an entity could multiply until it had overwhelmed the universe. There are good practical reasons why it probably wouldn't, but even so we will not take the risk of just letting it go. Even if it was legal, and at the moment that is far from established.'

Fleare stared at the creature, and then for a long time at the cloud. Then she mouthed 'I love you' at it, straightened up, and turned away. 'Look after him,' she said. 'Now I want to go back to my quarters.'

The orderly extended an arm towards the door. She walked past it, and as she did so she saw the animation that had briefly taken over its features fall away. Whatever it was that answered questions had obviously finished with her.

As they passed through the airlocks she took out the card and watched the letters bloom and fade as she brushed her fingers over them. *Can we talk?*

Abruptly she turned the card over and used her fingernail to write *NO!*, pressing hard so that the letters remained incised into the surface even after they had disappeared. Then she shoved the card into her pocket. By the time she had reached her room it had crumbled into a fine white dust. Message received, she assumed. She wondered what would happen next.

She didn't have to wait long to find out. The next morning she was informed that she had been reclassified as 'legitimate collateral', whatever that meant, and she was unceremoniously yanked out of her quarters and hustled to a spaceport. Two changes of shuttle later, she was heading across the periphery of the Outer Spin on board a converted cargo clipper belonging to some outfit called the Strecki Brotherhood.

By then she had worked out that 'legitimate collateral' meant the Heg' had sold her on as a suitable prospect for ransom. She briefly tried to persuade herself that her father had nothing to do with it.

It didn't work very well. It was never going to. There was too much history, too many memories.

Private Estate, Semph
Leisure Complex

Fleare had been five.

The ground car still seemed very big, even though she was now very big herself. She snuggled into the soft padding of the seat, trying to find out how deep she could get. The car was old – Daddy said it had been her great-grandfather's – and smelled nice, in a grown-up sort of way. She decided that from now on all birthdays would smell like this.

The Feather Palms zipped by. She tried to count them but they were too quick. The car was going quite fast. It swayed a bit, like a bath toy when the only thing moving the water was your breathing. The motion moved her from side to side so that she pressed first against her father and then her mother. Her mother smelled of the perfume from the little pink bottle on her dressing table that Fleare sometimes tried on when her mother was asleep, but not very much of the watery stuff from the bigger bottle under her bed. Her mother thought the bottle was secret, but Fleare had decided it was her job to know everything about her mother so she could make sure she was all right. She knew where all her mother's bottles and packets were kept.

Daddy smelled of soap and clothes and sweat, as if he was

too hot, although the car was quite cool. In the front she could see the rough skin of Fahri's neck, sticking out of his chauffeur's uniform, like orange peel only the wrong colour. Although he was very fat, and in Fleare's experience most fat people smelled quite a lot, Fahri never seemed to smell at all. He hardly even moved. She wondered if he had grown out of the driving seat, like a sort of tree.

She decided to stop thinking about smells. She nudged her father. 'Where are we going?'

His shoulders rose a bit, as if he was taking one of his deep breaths. The answer was going to be the same as the last five times she'd asked. She got ready to ask her mother instead.

There was a whoosh, and a car overtook them very quickly. Her mother and father looked at each other. Her father closed his mouth. Her mother sat a bit more upright. Fahri's shoulders moved, and suddenly he was driving with one hand and holding a stubby tube-thing in the other.

This wasn't fair. It was her birthday treat, even if she didn't know what it was yet, and she didn't want anything spoiling it. She tugged at her mother's sleeve. 'What's happening?'

Her mother looked down and made a hushing gesture, but with such a fierce expression that Fleare flinched back and began to cry.

Another car overtook, not so quickly as the first but very close. Fleare sniffled and sat up, trying to see through the windows to find out if it was anyone she knew, but before she had a chance to look her father had shoved her down on to the seat. 'Get down,' he hissed, and then, to her mother, 'Keep the stupid little bitch out of the way.'

The words felt like a slap, but they weren't as bad as her father's expression.

She hadn't seen him look frightened before.

The car swerved and stopped. She felt her mother's hand on her shoulder. Then there was a soft booming followed by a much louder noise that said *pyock-pyock-pyock-pyock*. She felt a sting on her shoulder and another on her cheek. Her mother said 'Oh', but in a voice that didn't really sound surprised, and the pressure of her hand lifted for a second and then returned, if anything heavier. Something warm splashed Fleare's neck.

It had gone quiet. Fleare's shoulder hurt and she felt hot and sleepy. She lifted her head carefully and tried to open her eyes. For a moment she couldn't, just like when they had stuck shut after she'd had a bad fever. Then they opened.

The inside of the car was splattered red. Fahri's neck still stuck out of his chauffeur suit, but there was a purple hole in the back of his head and he wasn't moving. Her father was pulling himself upright. His face was white, and he was breathing very fast.

Fleare felt the hand slip off her shoulder. She turned in time to see her mother slump sideways. The front of her jacket was soaked with red stuff, and her eyes were closed.

Fleare buried her face in her mother's lap, which felt very still. She could hear her father's breathing.

The red stuff smelled of salt and rust.

Startlingly, there had been another visit to the same planet. At the beginning of it she thought it was the worst thing her father could possibly have done.

She had yawned pointedly, applying the full weight of her newly fifteen-year-old disdain, and did her best to slump down into her seat. It wasn't easy; she was sitting on a crude plank, and the g-forces kept trying to tear her out of it. Plus, it was noisy. People kept screaming.

'Aahhhh! Oh! Oh . . . Is that it?'

'Nope. Here we go!'

She gripped the guard rail, feeling the flaking paint tickle her hand. The rail shifted a little as she used it to brace herself. She hoped it was meant to.

The wind hissed in her ears, and her stomach did a quick

upward kick of protest. She clenched her muscles as the train of little cars wobbled and creaked its way up the rails to the top of yet another ludicrous drop, paused like a senile bird of prey trying to remember what to do, and then hurtled down the slope leaving a trail of wails and curses and a faint smell of vomit and urine. Fleare suspected that some of the smells, and almost all of the creaks, were artificial. The owners of the longest, tallest, fastest and oldest roller-coaster in the Spin wouldn't leave things like that to chance.

Whatever. There was no way she was going to react. Being her age had its responsibilities. Besides, it was her birthday and the ride had been her idea. It was exceeding her expectations. She stole a glance to her left. Her father's face was set in the stony expression he wore when living through something unpleasant but temporary. Whereas – she flicked her eyes to the right – Seren looked terrified. For a second Fleare felt a bit guilty about that, but only for a second.

The cars hurtled down the last, near-vertical slope, swooped round a steep banked curve with a grinding screech of rails and braked to a halt by a rustic-looking concrete platform. Fleare noticed that the braking was distinctly quieter and more efficient than the rest of the ride. She waited until her father had helped a bleached-looking Seren out of the car and then followed them, trying hard to make a quick sideways stagger as her legs took up the load appear intentional.

Her father managed a smile, probably out of pure relief. 'Well, that was something. Huh, darling?'

Fleare was about to reply when she remembered that he wasn't talking to her. Over the last few months, 'darling' had come to mean someone else. So had lots of other terms of endearment. She compressed her lips.

'It certainly was.' Seren smiled weakly at Fleare. 'You're braver than me. I think I need something to help me get over it. Vik, can we get something to eat?'

It was a quick recovery for someone who looked as shaky as that. Fleare revised her opinion up several notches. Seren was made of tough stuff.

The restaurant was crowded, but that never bothered Fleare's father. A table appeared, like it always did. Reservations happened to other people. Fleare had only noticed this quite recently, after she had been away to school and had seen other ways of doing things. Even more recently it had occurred to her that every time Viklun Haas didn't worry about a reservation, someone else must have lost their table. If any arguments resulted, she never saw them. Her father had people to have his arguments for him.

But it was a good table if you didn't mind the noise of the machine guns.

The restaurant was themed, like everything else in the park. The theme changed sporadically. For the last three years (an unusually long period of stability) it had been Musical Theatre. It had been Musical Theatre two weeks ago, when Viklun Haas had made the booking. It had been Musical Theatre yesterday, when she had signed herself out of school on a three-day birthday pass.

Today it was Prehistoric Battles. Apparently even the name Haas couldn't do anything about that.

Their table was next to a wide window looking out over a rainy vista of mud that seemed to stretch for several kilometres, although it was probably smaller. It was scarred across by deep grooves and wandering lines of some coiled stuff that Fleare couldn't identify at first. She blinked down a search and came up with the name 'barbed wire', which sounded suitably nasty. Every now and then a voice shouted something inarticulate and a lot of men dressed in mud-coloured clothes would climb out of the nearest groove and start swarming over the ground towards the wire stuff. Similarly dressed men on the other side of the wire would start firing machine guns – she could identify

103

those without blinking. Some of the advancing army would deactivate, falling to the ground in disjointed poses. The rest would retreat quickly to the groove.

Now she came to look, there were a lot of deactivated soldiers on the ground. They looked very realistic.

Food came, a sort of stew served in square metal tins with a handle on one end. A card on the table said they were called mess tins, which seemed about right to Fleare, but the taste was better than she had expected. Her father seemed to agree with her; he had taken a spoonful – spoons were the only utensil – and raised his eyebrows approvingly. 'So,' he said, through his mouthful, 'are you having a good time, Fle?'

'Sure.' She felt something more was needed, and added: 'It's okay.'

He nodded vigorously, like someone who had been given glowing approval. 'Good. I'm glad. We're glad.' His hand sought Seren's. She took it, at the same time giving Fleare an unreadable look. 'It's good we've been able to do this together.' He paused, and then added: 'As a family.'

Fleare focused intently on her food. It seemed safer than shouting in protest at the word her father had just used. One corner of her mess tin was actually a bit rusty, a tiny dark brown counterpoint to the light brown stew with its pinkish lumps of meat. She poked at the place with her spoon; it rasped a little over the corroded surface.

She became aware of silence, and looked up. Her father was looking at her with an expression somewhere between pleading and impatience. She raised her eyebrows. 'Sorry,' she said, 'have I missed something?'

He took the deep breath that meant she was being tolerated. 'No, but there is something I want to tell you.' She saw him squeeze Seren's hand. 'We want to tell you. About being a family. Seren and I have decided to sign a contract. A permanent one. We really are going to be a family.'

It shouldn't have been a surprise, but it was still a shock. Fleare looked back down at the rust, and realized that she had managed to scrub most of it off. The surface of her food in that corner was speckled with brown flakes. Not real rust, then. She put down her spoon, looked up at her father and smiled. 'I'm really happy for you,' she said. 'I hope it helps your political ambitions.' Then, looking at Seren, she added: 'And what a perfect day to tell me.'

Once again she was impressed. Seren's face barely flickered before settling into polite enquiry. 'Really?' she said. 'What do you mean?'

Fleare raised her eyebrows. 'Didn't he say? It's my birthday, right? My mother was killed on my birthday. She was assassinated on this planet. I was five. It was a mistake,' she added, nodding at her father. 'They were aiming for him. So, thanks for lunch. I'll be on the ride.' She stood up, turned her back and walked out of the restaurant, leaving silence behind her. Silence if you didn't count the machine guns. They were still going.

The anger didn't really hit her until she was back on the roller-coaster. When it did she didn't fight. Here, of all places, it was okay to scream, and she put her head back and howled her anger and loss at the sky while the shuddering cars plunged and climbed and people screamed around her.

By the time the ride closed she had just about screamed herself out. She sat on the cool concrete of the platform and caught her breath. Other people dotted the platform. They were mostly around her age, sitting cross-legged and breathing deeply. Some of them exchanged smiles, or shrugs. A couple of them were trying to catch her eye. One was quite cute, with a lankily compact frame and dark brown hair in an unfashionably ragged crop. The brown looked natural. She ignored him, blinked a message service and pinged the transport office of her school with a 'come and get me'.

The response would take a while. She stood up, wrapping her

arms around herself. It was getting dark and the air had chilled quickly. All about her, people were rising from the platform and forming and re-forming into social knots as they headed for the exit of the theme park and the transit stations that lay just outside it. Fleare could have followed them, but she preferred to stay where she was, forcing the school to make a solo pick-up. She was quite happy to add another item to her father's bill.

A juddering noise made her look up. It came from the battlefield. There was something . . . She stood up and squinted into the dusk. Some sort of machine, it looked a bit like a big insect, was stalking over the ground. There was a kind of arm at the front that repeatedly plunged downwards and then reared up.

Then her eyes adjusted to the darkness. The arm was picking up the soldiers that had stayed on the ground and flicking them into a container on the back of the insect. The container looked full.

So, not deactivated, then. She felt a bit sick. She looked away from the battlefield and met the eyes of the cute guy. She pointed at the machine. 'What the fuck?'

He nodded. 'Yeah. It's gross. I'd never choose that.'

'Neither would I.' Then her brain caught up with the words. 'What do you mean, choose?'

He looked surprised. 'Don't you know? They're criminals. Life sentences, you know? There's a kind of lottery. The winners get to try out here. If they make it through the day they're free. If not . . .' He shrugged.

'You're kidding.' Fleare gulped. 'Who came up with that idea?'

'The company that runs the prisons, of course.' He looked distracted, then clicked his fingers. 'Haas Protection, it's called. Run by either an inventive genius or a twisted fuck. You choose.' He shook his head, and then frowned at her. 'Are you okay?'

The sickness was getting stronger. Fleare clenched her teeth.

She knew which of the two she would choose. Had chosen, in fact. 'I'm fine,' she said. Then she threw up.

The cute guy was still trying to help clean her up when the school transport dropped out of the sky. She fell into it with a sense of relief, leaving him with her sincerest thanks and a false ID.

As the transport sprang into the air she squeezed her eyes shut. She wasn't trying to blot out the view in front of her; she was trying to blot out the view in her mind's eye. It was an image of the machine, picking up bodies, and suddenly her imagination added a detail: a driving seat, with Viklun Haas sitting in it, waving and smiling.

She opened her eyes long enough to blink him a message. 'Going back to school. Don't contact me.' And, after a moment's thought: 'Ever.' Then, aided by turbulence, she threw up again. She hoped there was a charge for cleaning.

Silthx, Fortunate Protectorate (disputed), Cordern

It was still the same day, and it was showing no sign of ending. Alameche was uncomfortable, and he had made a promise to himself that as soon as he had the chance he was going to spread some of that discomfort pretty widely.

But the chance wasn't there yet. The cabin lights blinked from the muted yellow that was standard for dark-side running to a harsh blue-white, and the little shuttle banked sharply and began the juddering descent through what was left of the upper atmosphere of Silthx. Alameche braced himself against the worst of the turbulence, and reflected that they really must find a way of destroying the ecosystem of a planet without making it so fucking uncomfortable to land on.

The shuttle swayed downwards through the screaming winds, crabbed through a cloud layer that had the radiation alarms whimpering, and burst into the stiller air of late evening above the new spaceport. There had already been a perfectly good spaceport on Silthx, but only if your definition of 'perfectly good' included 'too small to allow forcible export of the entire natural resources of the planet within ten years'. It had been levelled and replaced. The new complex was officially called the Greater Portal, but the remaining locals used a word which, allowing for major cultural differences, translated roughly as 'Cunt'. Apparently this was in recognition of the role of the place in the violation of their planet.

The Project Controller was waiting for him at Embarkation, an area which he had heard even his own people refer to – quite without his influence, but much to his satisfaction – as Cervix. She was short and stout and grey-haired, which was an affectation for someone of her seniority, and she looked worried – which was probably not affected at all. Alameche didn't blame her. He gave her a half bow. 'Madam Controller Haavis. I hope you are well?'

'Counsellor! Of course. Such a pleasure. We were so pleased to hear that you were coming.' Even her voice was short and stout, with a fluting wheeziness that sounded unhealthy.

Alameche raised an eyebrow. 'Why? Do you have good news for me?'

'Yes! Well, that is to say, we are following the programme of investigation that was agreed when – it – arrived. Our work is on schedule.'

'I expect nothing less.' Her face flushed with relief. He waited for a second, and then added: 'But that's just the day job. I'm still waiting for your good news.'

'Yes, of course.' Her eyes fell and she clasped one pudgy hand in the other, almost as if she was giving herself an encouraging handshake. 'Well, my colleagues are looking forward to explaining their progress.' The hands unclasped, and she waved towards the exit. 'If you would follow me?'

She trotted off without waiting for a reply. There were guards at the exit from Cunt – he definitely liked that word – but they parted like grass in the wind at a peremptory gesture from Haavis. He followed, nodding to the guards as he passed. Guards were useful. And so were colleagues, apparently, if you wanted someone to hide behind.

The exit from the terminal led to a broad plaza. It had been carried over from the earlier spaceport, and five years ago it had been lined with specimen trees, gifted to Silthx by grateful, aspiring or just plain friendly administrations across the Inner Spin. Most had turned out to be poorly tolerant of radiation, and had died in some grotesque states which Alameche found quite interesting. A couple had soldiered on more or less unchanged, and these had been poisoned by various chemical or biological means because they were boring.

Only one was still alive, in a manner of speaking. Shortly after the nuke release it had erupted in such a spectacular set of warts and woody cancers that Alameche had awarded it protected scientific status. A few years later he had located the original curator of the tree collection, pulled him out of his forced labour camp and taken him to the plaza to see how the last tree was doing. The man hadn't said anything, but Alameche had thought his tears quite eloquent. He had instructed the camp to put a live video feed of the tree on the wall of the man's sleeping quarters. And to put him on suicide watch.

You wouldn't have wanted to stand outside the terminal now. A series of forest fires, fanned by post-nuclear winds, had carried rich plumes of fission products into the atmosphere, to the point where even the Last Tree was beginning to look a bit shaky. Alameche was thinking of having some sort of protective shelter built for it.

He waited while a shielded charabanc pulled up outside. A flexible coupling nosed out from the vehicle, fumbled a couple of times at the terminal and then docked with a wet-sounding hiss. The terminal doors opened, and Haavis gestured him forward like a commissionaire. He smiled, and walked into the passenger compartment. Haavis followed. 'Our journey will take an hour,' she said. 'Will you require entertainment?'

'No, thank you.' The charabanc could seat twenty; he selected a seat in the front row, settled back and shut his eyes, hoping that the message was pointed enough. He had no intention of sleeping, but he did need to think. Eskjog had given him a lot to think about.

'So, what do we do?' he had asked the little machine, after the Patriarch was safely out of the way.

'Well, to put it plainly, you have two challenges, one of which amplifies the other. The first is the artefact, obviously. The second is, ah . . .' Eskjog tailed off, and Alameche nodded.

'I know,' he said. 'His Excellency.'

'Quite. I hesitate to make any suggestions about that for the moment. I assume you know what you are doing. But I have some thoughts about the artefact, if you are interested?'

Alameche leaned back in his chair in what he hoped was a relaxed position. 'Go on,' he said.

Eskjog floated over to the chair next to Alameche and settled down in it. The chair creaked and leaned back against its springs, and Alameche raised an eyebrow. The little machine was obviously heavier than it had any right to be. 'Putting it baldly,' it said, 'we could force you to hand the thing over, but that would look a bit obvious and to be honest the people I represent prefer to keep their hands free from blood.'

Alameche smiled. 'I assume blood on other people's hands is acceptable?'

'Oh, entirely. Inevitable, even.' Eskjog swivelled a little in its seat. 'But that's the problem, you see. If we don't involve ourselves in this find of yours other people will, and things might get very messy, very quickly.' It rose from the chair and turned one of its sides towards Alameche. 'Tell me something. How secure is the artefact, right now?'

Alameche looked at the little machine for a while. 'Well, it must be pretty secure,' he said, 'if you don't know where it is yet.'

The machine laughed. 'Well said. At this moment, I don't know. But I know *you* know.' It floated closer to Alameche. 'How long do you think you could keep that from me?'

'You are our allies, I believe.' Alameche managed to speak calmly. He desperately wanted to swallow.

'Yes, well, we are, in a manner of speaking. I represent a group of commercial and financial interests who would rather remain anonymous but who have, let us say, quite a stake-holding in this area and who really won't go away even if you should wish them to.' Eskjog began to move away, and then stopped. 'What do you call it, in your society, when a man demands sexual congress with his unwilling wife?'

Alameche shrugged. 'Marriage,' he said. 'So what?'

'Indeed. Most societies call it rape, of course, but at least you know your own minds. Perhaps it would help if you thought of this relationship as a marriage. And it would certainly help if you moved your artefact.' It paused, and then as if it had just thought of it, added: 'We could set up somewhere secure for you, if you like?'

Alameche frowned. 'It has to stay within our jurisdiction.'

'Why?'

'Because if I let it go I'll die. Obviously.' Alameche glared at the machine. 'And as you pointed out, I'm the reasonable one. You need me.'

'So you are. So we do.' To Alameche's surprise, Eskjog performed a slow sideways roll. When it had returned to vertical it added: 'All right, I agree. We'll set up a secure study area, within your jurisdiction. Under your nominal control, even, if that makes you feel better.'

'Thank you.' Alameche was tempted to quibble about the 'nominal', but restrained himself. Just to stay in some sort of control was good enough, for now. 'Where will it be?'

'To be confirmed. The main thing now is to make a clean

break with its recent past. And now, if you don't mind, I need to be somewhere else. Thank you for your hospitality.' It added: 'Do I need to define the meaning of clean break?'

Alameche shook his head. 'No. No, you don't.'

The charabanc bumped down the last slope, knocking Alameche from side to side in his seat and rousing him from his reverie. He peered out of the forward screens, tilting his head back, and then back some more, trying to take in the truly massive bulk and height of the building they were approaching. The design was simple – a central, near-featureless grey cuboid, surrounded by sloping conveyors, each one ending in a different-coloured heap of slag. It reminded Alameche of a parody of an insect, squatting in piles of its own excrement.

It also had the merit of being a very unpopular destination, and therefore a very private one. The refinery plant itself was completely automated, so Haavis and her team had the place to themselves, and the circle of knowledge had been kept small: just they, Alameche and the Lictrix, his bodyguard who was following them, knew what was happening here.

Well, they and presumably Eskjog.

The charabanc crunched off the slope, skidding slightly on the loose, charred scree, and stopped by the low blockhouse that was the only human-scale entrance to the plant. It edged forward and the flexible coupling nosed out and sealed against the blockhouse. There was a hiss, and a sudden smell of ash. It dried Alameche's throat.

The Lictrix was there to meet them. She must have come in a fast skimmer. That would have been a nasty business in this wind, but necessary. She saluted as he passed, and fell in behind him.

They walked quickly through the blockhouse and down a long corridor. One side was clear, looking out over the vast internal spaces of the refinery. It was an inferno: a row of blue-hot crucibles in the middle distance gave off gouts of dirty flame, and bizarrely shaped machines flicked through the heat haze, their flanks crusted and distorted with spatter and soot. There were no biological beings in there. Alameche assumed death would be immediate, although as far as he knew that had never been tested. He made a mental note to try, one day.

To his relief the conference room, when they reached it, was comfortable, which was more than he could say for the occupants. Haavis and her team of seven sat in an edgy U-shape along three sides of a conference table. Alameche was shown to a seat opposite them. The Lictrix took up a position behind his left shoulder.

Alameche gave the room a smile. 'Well,' he said, 'do tell me about success.' And leaned back and listened, for what seemed a long time.

Eventually the scientists fell silent and he leaned forward again. 'In summary, you have got nowhere. Is that right?'

Haavis opened her mouth, and then closed it again. She exchanged a glance with the man who sat on her right, who had so far only spoken to greet Alameche rather tersely at the beginning. He was thin and looked old, with overgrown grey eyebrows above milky blue eyes. He nodded. 'Yes,' he said. 'The artefact remains inert. Unresponsive.'

'Thank you! A straight answer.' Alameche looked at the rest of the team. 'It would have been much quicker if you had all just said that to start with.'

'But we have not finished. Not at all!' Haavis was leaning forward, her face white. 'There are many other lines of investigation—'

Alameche waved her into silence. 'I doubt it,' he said. 'Otherwise you would have tried them. No, I think we need to think again. Does your colleague agree?'

114

The old man nodded. 'I'm afraid so. We have neither the knowledge nor the facilities to do more.' Haavis gave him a stricken look, but he shook his head. 'I am sorry, Madam, but you know I am right. The artefact either cannot – or will not – respond, and we cannot make it.'

'Good. Sir, I appreciate your directness.' Alameche stood up, half turned towards the Lictrix and gave her a nod. Then he turned back to the table. 'Research will continue, but not here. I am closing the facility immediately. On behalf of the Patriarch, I express thanks for your efforts.' He snapped his fingers.

There was a pop and a soft hiss behind him, and a white fog billowed forward. There was a scrape of chairs as the group leapt to its feet, but the fog had reached the nearest people already; they simply sighed and collapsed. Alameche watched, keeping his mouth clamped shut and breathing through his nose, as the fog rolled over the table. The last people to be reached were Haavis and the old man. Just as the fog touched them Alameche saw the old man take the pudgy woman's hand.

He was distracted by a crash from behind him. He turned round and peered through the white clouds. They were clearing already, boiling away into nothing as he watched, to reveal the Lictrix, slumped on the floor. Her eyes were wide open in a look of surprise that was almost comical, and she was clawing at her nose as if she was looking for something.

Alameche crouched down next to her. 'Oh dear,' he said. 'I think your filters must have been faulty. How unfortunate. Mine seem to have worked perfectly.' He watched the woman die, took hold of the ID tag on her uniform and roughly tore it off. Then he stood up, and wrinkled his nose. The nostril filters had kept out the biocide all right, but they weren't effective against smells. The second, rapid decomposition phase of the fog was kicking in, and some of the bodies were already beginning to bloat. In a few minutes the first skin ruptures should be under way.

A clean break. At least, metaphorically.

Thale Port

The fern-shaped pontoons of Thale Outward Dock grew from a fat central globe, pointing out in all directions so that from a distance the whole thing looked a bit like a fronded sea creature. The globe was two kilometres across; the pontoons stretched out another three. It was all about people; anything either much bigger or much less delicate than an organic life-form belonged outside, in the cloud of moving cargo that surrounded the place like a sort of seasonal mini-nebula. Local gravity generators kept the cloud in place; at the moment their focus was shifting in preparation for Line-Up, so that a tendril extended from the cloud towards the gravity field of Camfi.

Muz's prediction had been right; Fleare had passed through several stages of what felt like rather cursory security without incident. Now she stood in the middle of an area that called itself 'Arrivals Onward', which looked like the completest capitalist free-for-all she had ever seen. It was a wide low hall within a perimeter of arches, most of which were occupied by someone selling something. Or selling someone, she noticed. Or maybe just hiring them out. She shrugged.

Muz had provided a carisak with a couple of changes of clothes. She shifted it from one shoulder to the other and wrinkled her nose. If the outside of the Dock was about the inert, the inside was definitely biological. 'I can smell something dead,' she muttered.

'I doubt it. I think you have to be alive to stink that badly.'

'Whatever.' She looked around, trying to work out why she felt so uncomfortable. It took her a moment before she realized. It wasn't just the smell, which seemed to be coming from one of the food outlets. It was the crowds. She had spent the last three years mainly in her own company. The only thing that had spent any time in her personal space was that ovoid device the Strecki had set on her, and since that had always been there she had mainly blanked it. Now, the Arrivals area was full to the point of jostling, and she wasn't dealing with it. She bit her lip. 'Muz?'

'Shh. I know. You need to get out of here.'

'Yeah. How'd you guess?'

'It's not a guess. Your heart's racing, and every time someone knocks into you you tense your muscles. You're going into fight or flight mode. Look a little to your left. See the orange lights on the other side of the concourse?'

She looked, and saw a cluster of glowing orbs about the size of human heads, floating a metre above the crowd. Most of them were bright, but as she watched one of them dimmed, dropped a little and bobbed off towards one of the exits. She realized someone was following it. 'Are they guides? Neat.'

'Yes. That's a meeting point. Jez said she'd wait.'

'She's there?'

'Well, she should be.'

Fleare felt a flutter in her stomach. She suppressed it. 'Okay. Let's see if she is.'

It took her several minutes to shoulder her way through the crowd, which got thicker as she neared the meeting point. Most of the people were humanoid, as long as you were applying the word loosely; she pushed past, or excused herself politely to, everything from a two-and-a-half-metre cadaver to a stocky, roughly pyramidal creature that just came up to her breastbone.

Then she was through the crowd and standing in a small clear patch directly beneath the globes that reminded her of something she'd heard of called the eye of a storm. And on the other side of the clear patch stood Jezerey, wearing a thick floor-length cloak and an uncertain expression, but still with her arms outstretched.

It was natural to run into the arms. The hug lasted a long time.

Eventually Fleare unhooked herself and stood back. 'Hi,' she said.

'Hi.' Jezerey looked her up and down. 'So, starvation chic? On you it looks – thin.'

'Yeah. Three years.' Fleare blinked eyes that were suddenly prickling. 'It's good to see you.'

'And you. Look, let's go somewhere else.' She hesitated. 'Can I assume there's more than one of you?'

'What? Oh.' Fleare took the central bead of the necklace in her fingers. 'Yes. He's—'

Jez placed a finger on Fleare's lips. 'Ssh. Later. Come on.'

Jezerey's combined office and apartment was on the inside of the inner sphere. She had chosen an antiquarian district; most of the buildings were faceted geodesic domes that looked like something out of the dawn of space exploration. They were set apart by strips of themed ecological planting. Her building was formed of four of the domes, squashed together as if there had been a nasty crash, and the local vegetation was mostly sinister bluish-green cactus things with partly prehensile spikes. Fleare tried to keep her arms close to her sides as she walked up to the entrance.

Inside, Jezerey rolled the cloak off her shoulders and threw it aside. She turned to Fleare and smiled. 'Welcome to Thale, Fleare. And Muz, of course.'

The necklace lifted from Fleare's neck and dissolved into an upward funnel of dust like a tornado. 'Good to see you, Jez.'

'Likewise.' Jezerey smiled, and then looked at Fleare. 'So. Food?'

It had been a while since her meal on the Orbiter. Fleare felt her mouth moisten. 'Yes, please,' she said. Then she added, 'This shape isn't through choice.'

'I didn't think so. You'll have to tell me about it. I'll send out for food.' She looked at Fleare and grinned. 'Come on, Fle, when did I ever cook? Besides, listening to you is more important.' She waved towards the far end of the room. 'Over there. Make yourself comfortable.'

Over there was a rectangular fire pit surrounded on three sides by low couches draped in what looked like animal skins, complete with variegated hair. Fleare leaned down and sniffed one of them. They smelled like animal skins, too. She looked at Jezerey. 'Are these real?'

'Sure.' Jezerey pointed. 'The reddish ones are Golgotha Plains Trampers. The blue-and-green ones are Heskilm's Calf.'

'Really?' Fleare brushed her fingers over the shiny hairs. 'I thought they were protected?'

'Well, it didn't work for these.' Jezerey looked serious for a moment. Then her mouth twitched and she laughed. 'Come on, Fle, I wouldn't do that. These are antiques, long before protection. Lie down on them. They won't mind.'

Fleare wanted to lie down. She chose the couch at the narrow end of the fire pit. It occurred to her that although she could smell animal skins, she couldn't smell smoke, although the pit was full of glowing embers and she could see a grey haze rising from them. She pointed. 'How does that work?'

'Boundary fields. Just strong enough to direct the smoke, mind. Don't get pissed and fall into them; you'll go straight through and into the pit.'

'Is getting pissed an option?'

Jezerey dropped on to the couch next to Fleare. 'After what you've been through? It's probably compulsory. I expect it wasn't available, the last few years?'

Fleare shook her head.

'Okay, well, it is now.' Jezerey bounced off the couch, opened a low cabinet and pulled out a squat bottle and three glasses. She waved the bottle. 'This is antique, too, but even worse protected than the hides. Want some?'

'What is it?'

'Local stuff. Called Strant. It just means Spirit, I think, although the word can have other meanings. Best stick to Spirit.' She blew on the bottle, and a cloud of dust rose. 'Did I say it was antique?'

The bottle had a complicated closure which involved coils of wire under tension. Fleare watched while Jezerey opened it, and then held out her hand and accepted a glass. She sipped, and pulled a face. 'Fuck!'

Jezerey grinned. 'Yeah, lots of people say that.' She poured another glass and set it down on the cabinet. Muz drifted over and dipped a tendril of dust into the liquid.

'No wonder it isn't protected. It's got its own defence mechanism.' Fleare sipped again. 'It tastes like fermented sweat glands, or something.'

'You're not far off.' Jezerey studied the faded label. 'I don't think they were sweat glands, though.' She shrugged, and raised her own glass. 'Cheers!'

'Cheers.' Fleare looked at the glass on the cabinet. 'Muz, are you actually drinking?'

The tendril lifted from the glass. 'Just being sociable. Anyway, fuel is fuel.'

'I guess.' Fleare lay back on the couch. 'It's good to see you, Jez.'

'And you.' Jezerey sat on the edge of her couch, leaned towards Fleare, and raised her eyebrows. 'So, tell me about the Monastery.'

Three hours later the squat bottle was empty, and so was a second one that had somehow tasted a bit better. Muz had drifted off somewhere saying he was taking himself offline, and Fleare was gazing into the dying embers in the fire pit. She might have dozed off, she wasn't sure, but it felt as if Jezerey's voice woke her.

'Fleare?'

She raised herself on one elbow. 'Mm?'

'What are you going to do?'

It was less than a day since she had answered the same question for Muz. Then, she had known the answer. Now she felt less sure. She shook her head slowly. 'Don't know. You got any ideas?'

'Muz said you wanted to find Kelk.'

'Well, yes.' Fleare pushed herself upright. 'Muz told me he was bumming around. Do you know where?'

'Sort of.'

'What does that mean?'

'I've got some ideas. Um, he's sort of hiding.'

Fleare sat up straight. 'Hiding?'

'Yeah. Or keeping out of the way.'

'Keeping out of whose way? The Heg'?'

'No.' Jezerey stood up. 'It's me, really. We sort of fell out.'

'What are you talking about? Look, it's late. Tell me tomorrow.' Then she shook her head. 'No, fuck it. Tell me now.'

'Not much to tell. After the amnesty, Kelk couldn't let go, you know? He stayed angry. I didn't. I wanted,' she waved round at the room, 'this stuff, something to do. A life. He got pissed off.'

'And left?'

'Yeah, and left.' Jezerey sighed. 'I've still got a contact, I don't know if it's live or not.'

'Where is he then?'

'Nowhere good. Sorry about this, Fle.' She took a deep breath. 'The contact tags to the Catastrophe Curve.'

Fleare looked at her for a long time. 'Well,' she said slowly, 'isn't that going to be fun.'

Old City, Catastrophe, Catastrophe Curve

The Catastrophe Curve was a one-off. For the first and only time in the history of the Spin, something had gone wrong on a major engineering scale and two planets had collided. They had both been destroyed; shredded down to lumps that were mostly less than a kilometre across. Over time the competing gravity fields in this part of the Spin had smeared the debris field out over a wandering arched tendril half a million kilometres long. It tapered away from a bulge centred on the collision. A little way along from the bulge, the largest single remnant was home to the biggest settlement, Catastrophe, which was the administrative centre for anyone who cared to acknowledge it. About half of the Curve did; the rest was fragmented into little commercial empires and fiefdoms who warred and traded and glared at each other across the tiny distances between them.

If the Curve was the result of an accident, the Trash Belt was the result of the Curve. It was a thin smear of war debris, abandoned equipment and general space rubbish which had accreted along the outer margins of the Curve and now kept a ghostly station with it, glowing softly in the light of the nearest three suns. It made the route to the Curve from the outer parts of the Spin an interesting navigational challenge.

The route away from the Curve in the other, inward direction was even more interesting, because the Catastrophe Curve's immediate neighbour in the central part of the Spin was the Cordern. This lent an opportunistic piquancy to both the politics and the trading relationships of the area; despite the swelling influence of the Hegemony it was one of the least regulated, most dangerous and most profitable places in the whole Spin.

Fleare shifted position slightly. She was wedged into a corner between an iron stanchion and the side of a deck-house. The stanchion dug into her back, and she felt sick. In a tribute to some historical inventor or other the old airship had oil-fired piston engines, and the smell wafted over her every time the wind changed. She cleared her throat and looked around.

Leaving smoke trails that were visible even in darkness, the ship droned through the night sky about three hundred metres above the city. They weren't the only smoke trails; the airspace above the city had its own tax regime, much more favourable to gambling than the one on the ground, so the sky was full of ancient aircraft, most of them owned for generations by a small number of criminal families with a status close to royalty.

She had to admit it was pretty. From this height she could just about take in the whole sweep of it, from city wall to city wall. The walls formed hard boundaries; inside them the ground was densely studded with lights, set out in geometric patterns towards the edges but dissolving into the intricate tangles of the Old City in the middle. Outside the walls there was nothing, or at least there was nothing anyone cared to throw light on. The unlit possibilities were more than enough to keep the citizens of Catastrophe safely inside their walls.

There was a comms bead in her ear. She tapped it. 'Anything?'

A pause, and then Jezerey's voice came through, sounding scratchy. 'Nothing yet. They'll still be inside. Wouldn't expect anything until a bit later. What's the matter? Bored?'

'Air-sick.'

'Really? Try eating something.'

'Oh, right. Thanks. Next time I'll bring some food.' She flicked the comms off, sighed, and then flicked it on again. 'Really nothing?'

'Really. All quiet. Ah, wait . . .'

'What?'

'Might be something. Give me a minute.'

The bead went quiet. Then Jezerey spoke, this time in a whisper. 'Fle? Ramp up your night vision and look down the outboard rail. See anything?'

'Hold on.' Fleare concentrated, making the muscles her eyes shouldn't have had force her pupils wide open. Her vision brightened to a light grey graininess. Along the rail, the grain contained shapes. She watched for a moment. 'I see two.'

'Me too.'

Fleare squinted. 'I don't think he's one of them.'

'Nor do I. They're both female, for a start.'

'Okay. So we wait.'

'Yeah. How's your sickness?'

Fleare frowned. 'What sickness? Oh, that. Gone. Is Muz ready?'

'Should be. Want me to raise him?'

'No.'

'Fine.' Jezerey paused. 'Fleare? You and him?'

The muscle strain was making Fleare's eyes hurt. She blinked, relaxing them. 'Me and him what?'

'Well, just, is everything okay?'

Fleare opened her mouth, closed it, and then opened it again. 'Jezerey? He's a probably psychopathic cloud of dust and I'm an illegal entity. How can it be better?'

126

'Sorry. Stupid question.'

'Never mind.' Fleare shook her head, glanced towards the two waiting bodies, and froze. A door had opened, throwing bright yellow light towards the rail. She ramped up her eyes again and looked hard. 'Yo, Jez? See that?'

'What?'

'That!' A figure had walked out into the pool of light. As she watched it stretched, pushing its hands into the small of its back and arching against them. She stared at the figure, then grinned and snapped her fingers. 'We're in business. It's him.'

Five minutes later they had gone comms silent. Fleare had to assume that Jez was in place. As for Muz, she had no idea. But she was sure of one thing. She was close enough to read body language without enhancing her vision and the conversation by the guard rail was not going well.

There was a granular hissing, very quiet and close. She felt something enter her ear, and Muz was talking. 'Don't say anything. Going to feed you some audio.'

For a second there was a phasey bubbling noise. Then it became voices.

'. . . not pleased. Not at *all* pleased. People like that get used to answers, you see.'

'I've delivered answers.' Fleare stiffened; it was Kelk.

'Yes, but they were the wrong answers. That's worse than no answers at all. Plus it looks as if you might have been doing a little freelance work behind people's backs. That's very naughty.' The other voice sighed. 'You'd better come with us. We don't want to try to explain this on our own.'

'Look, I can't. You know that. I'm in the middle of something.'

A third voice. 'You're in the middle of a game of Canard. You're losing. You owe an average year's salary and you haven't got it, and that's just on this game. Why should you go back?'

'You know why.'

'Yes, but what if we can trump your why? Not that it matters. You're coming anyway.'

The two women closed in on Kelk, pinning him against the railing. There was a fluttering in Fleare's ear, and then Muz's voice. 'Okay, guys, we're good to go. Uh, health warning? Both women are armed. Energy weapons, can't tell what sort. So, see you in a bit. Count of ten.' She felt him leave.

She counted down, simultaneously ramping up her muscles and bracing herself against the stanchion. On zero she launched herself into a flat sprint down the deck.

The sound of her feet alerted the three. The nearest of the women turned, seeming to move very slowly, and her mouth opened. At the same time the door to the saloon opened wider, and light flooded the three. Jezerey, framed in the doorway, beckoned towards Kelk. His eyes opened wide, and he took a reflexive step towards her. Fleare accelerated. Two paces from the women she turned half sideways and flexed her knees to lower her body. As she did, she saw the woman's hand rising from her side. Something in it glinted.

One pace out, she tensed her muscles. Her shoulder hit the woman in the throat.

There was an unpleasant cracking sound. She heard a coughing sigh and felt the woman's arms flapping round her in a limp embrace. Their shared momentum carried them past Kelk's back. Out of the corner of her eye Fleare saw Kelk beginning to turn round, his face blank with shock. She tightened her grip around the injured woman's slack body as the two of them cannoned into the second woman.

They weren't quite going fast enough. The woman staggered back half a dozen steps along the railing, and then regained her balance. She too had something in her hand. She raised it towards Fleare, and grinned.

A patch of darkness sighed quickly through the air between Fleare and Kelk and wrapped itself around the woman's weapon hand like a fat black bandage. She looked down at it, her expression changing first to surprise and then irritation. Then she shook her head and raised the hand towards Fleare.

Fleare saw the muscles of her arm contract. There was a muted thump and the black bandage thing swelled briefly.

For a moment the woman stayed quite still. She raised her covered hand towards her face, looked at it curiously for a moment and fell forward to her knees, her other hand grabbing at the rail.

The bandage unwrapped itself. The woman's weapon fell to the deck with a clatter.

Where the weapon had been, there was a neat black stump. It gave off wisps of smoke.

The bandage shook itself and became Muz. 'That's going to take a while to grow back,' he said cheerfully. 'If she can afford it. Bad idea, using an energy weapon in an enclosed space. You okay, Fle?'

'I guess.' Fleare knelt by the woman she had hit. 'I think I broke her windpipe. Neck. Both.'

'You had your reasons. She was ready to fry you.'

'I know. Still.' Fleare stood up and turned to Kelk. 'Hi. Sorry about the mess. We'd better go.'

He shook his head. 'Go where? This is nothing to do with me. I had it covered. And you're supposed to be holed up in a monastery.' He turned back towards the open door. 'I have a game to finish.'

Jezerey blocked the door. 'No you don't. You're going to be rescued.'

'Rescued? Is that what you call it? Have you seen the cops on this planet? No thanks.' He shook his head and made to push past her.

Fleare reached out and caught his shoulder. 'Kelk? This is my fault. I know you're pissed at Jez—'

He turned, shaking off her hand. 'Wrong. I'm pissed at

everybody, especially now. Just let me get on with it, yeah?'

She looked at him for a moment. Then she looked away. 'Okay,' she said quietly. She turned to Jezerey. 'Let's go.'

'Are you fucking serious? After all this?' She gestured at the two women on the deck. The one who had blown her hand off had pulled herself into a sitting position, and was staring blankly at the stump of her wrist.

'He doesn't want to come, Jez. And I'm not going to try to make him, okay?' She reached out, pushed Kelk gently on the shoulder. 'See you around.' She began to turn away.

There was a sound like someone spitting.

She felt a sharp pain in her upper arm. She grabbed at it. 'Ow!'

Suddenly Muz was in front of her. 'Ow what?'

'I don't know. Something.' She rubbed at the place, and her fingers found something hard. 'What's that?'

'Hold on.' Muz gathered round the lump. 'Shit. Looks like . . . right. Hold on to something. I'm taking it out. Um, I think this is going to hurt.'

She reached out and took hold of the railing, gripping until her knuckles whitened. 'Okay. Ready.'

Fleare went rigid. Somehow she managed not to scream. It was as if flesh was being torn not just from her arm, but from her whole body. When it was over she realized that her fingers had cramped round the rail. It was slightly bent now. She found time to be impressed with herself.

Muz's voice broke in on her. 'Sorry, but I had to do that. See?'

Something shiny and bloodstained floated in front of her. It was a tiny stubby dart, crudely barbed.

Jezerey leaned forward and shuddered. 'No wonder that hurt,' she said. 'What is it?'

'Nastier even than it looks, is what it is. The pain wasn't just physical. It has a power source. Hits you with a neural zap if someone interferes with it.' Muz turned the thing over and over. 'Hm.'

Fleare felt a chill. 'Hm what?'

'Probably nothing. I can't see anything in the wound. Maybe we got it in time. How do you feel?'

'Okay, I think.' She raised a hand to her shoulder and touched it gingerly, feeling wet blood. She winced. 'It hurts. Where did that thing come from?'

There was a short, quiet laugh. Fleare looked down, and saw the injured woman sitting by the rail. Her remaining hand was over her mouth. As they watched she lowered it. There was something between her lips. She winked and drew it into her mouth, and her throat rippled. 'Bonus,' she said. 'Nice to meet you.'

Fleare started forward, but as she did the woman's hand loosened from the rail and she slumped sideways.

Jezerey crouched down by her, reaching out.

'Don't!' Kelk's voice was sharp.

Jezerey sat back on her heels. 'I think she's dead, Kelk.'

'Yes, but dead and harmless aren't the same thing.' Kelk had shut the door behind him. 'Muz, can you check her out?'

The cloud floated over to the body, formed a flattish disc and hovered, undulating a little. 'Can't find anything.'

'Good.' Kelk leaned over the rail for a moment, then straightened up and beckoned Jezerey. 'We're over one of the crater lakes. Give me a hand.'

'Won't that get noticed?'

'No way. This is a private gambling ship. Stuff happens.' He pulled a face. 'Anyone watching, they'll probably think I'm one of the bodies.'

They lifted the two bodies and manoeuvred them over the rail. Jezerey watched the last one tumbling away. Then she turned to Kelk. 'Talking now, are we?'

'I give up. Yes. Whatever you want.'

Fleare felt her face stretch into a huge grin. 'Including coming with us?'

'Yeah, but not yet. There's a place called the Tanks, on the Trashwards edge of the Old City. I'll be there an hour after we dock. Give you time to see a doctor.' He put his hand on the door. 'Meanwhile I've got a Canard game to finish.'

'But you're losing.'

'Yeah, that's what they think too. See a doctor, Fleare.' And he went back inside.

Taussich, Fortunate Protectorate, Cordern

The Inner Circle of the Old Palace was one of the oldest parts of the Citadel. It had been little used for generations, and almost completely uninhabited during the lifetime of the present Patriarch. It was cold and damp and generally unpleasant, and it smelled strongly of the oil lampions that were the only source of lighting.

It was also remote from the present centre of government, a fact which had added hours to Alameche's lunatic dash across the Cordern. Even so, he managed to be very nearly on time. There was only one vacant space around the old, uneven stone table apart from his, and that was the Patriarch's.

Alameche nodded a greeting to the other members of the Cabinet and sat down in the space immediately to the left of the Patriarch's, grateful that someone had placed cushions on the resolutely unforgiving stone chairs. On the other side of him sat a blocky man whose body was so short that the top of his head barely came up to Alameche's nose. The short man leaned closer. 'Why are we here?'

Alameche grinned. 'We aren't here. We're deep in the secure part of the Cabinet Chamber, surrounded by guards and electronics. Our appearance here is merely a figment of your imagination, Guivirse.'

'Really?' Guivirse raised his eyebrows. 'A Shadow Cabinet, then? Haven't heard of one of those in ages.'

Alameche smiled at the old phrase. It dated back decades to the days of advancement by assassination, when everyone who mattered had at least one body double. He was about to say something else when there was a creak from the end of the room. The heavy wooden doors ground open and the Patriarch walked into the room, paused, sniffed theatrically and then shook his head and sat down next to Alameche. 'Is this going to work?'

'We believe so.' Alameche looked round the table. 'Surveillance is usually targeted, especially if it is done remotely. We believe that the systems-rich environment of the Cabinet Chamber will be open to invasive monitoring no matter how we try to prevent it. Hence the very long, boring meeting being held there at this moment by our alter egos, while we assemble in this, ah, venerable space devoid even of electric light.'

'Humph.' The Patriarch tapped his fingers on the table. 'Shorn of your flowery language, everyone'll think we're some-where else, and even if they don't there's nothing here to bug. Is that it?'

Alameche inclined his head.

'Does this mean we're safe from your spiky little friend as well?'

My friend, thought Alameche. *Already?* Out loud he said, 'Eskjog? No, Excellency, I wouldn't rely on that. But as you rightly point out, it seems to be *our* friend' – he allowed himself the faint emphasis – 'so perhaps we should not mind too much if it shares our counsels. After all, we have benefited from the desire of its masters to invest.'

'So you say. Personally, I prefer to know who is listening. But you know best.' The Patriarch smiled without humour. 'Or so you always tell me. But now I need a report from you. A day ago I told you to present me with a plan. What is it?'

'It is this.' Alameche took a deep breath. 'We should do as little as possible.'

For a moment there was silence. Then laughter broke out. Guivirse thumped the table with delight. 'Delicious,' he shouted. 'A crowd of negatives! We can't be talking because we aren't here, and now he says we should do nothing!'

Alameche sat stolidly while the laughter died down. He had noticed that the Patriarch wasn't joining in. After a little while the others noticed too. They subsided, and the Patriarch leaned forward. 'Convince me,' he said.

Alameche nodded. 'We have a device of unknown potency. We do not know how to use it, and if we did we would be unsure of the results. From what little we know it may be sentient, after a fashion; even if it were able to, would it cooperate with us?'

He paused, and an old, extravagantly wrinkled man sitting on the opposite side of the table raised a finger. 'Surely that is why you are in bed with this upstart little machine. What's it called? Esdog?'

Alameche shook his head. 'With respect, Cabinet Member Trask, Ambassador Eskjog may represent power – and it certainly represents money, as we all know – but it does not represent omnipotence. I am not sure it can make the thing work any more than we can.'

Trask shook his head irritably. 'So what's your point?'

Alameche smiled at the old man. 'The power of the unknown.' He looked round at the others. 'Let's keep people guessing. If it is suspected – not *known*, mind you, definitely not known – that we have something like this, what is more natural than for the Spin to divide into two camps: those who would take it from us and those who would rather it stayed where it was, well protected and unused.'

Guivirse blew out his cheeks. 'And how long would it take for those two camps to meet around us like jaws?'

'Ah.' The Patriarch sat back. 'I begin to see.'

'Exactly.' Alameche smiled again. 'Well protected, gentlemen. We will of course need weaponry to achieve that. Money. A seat, even, at the tables of the Hegemony.' He placed his hands palm down on the table. 'A role as custodians of the most powerful weapon in the Spin? With everyone doing their best to keep it unused?' He turned to the Patriarch and inclined his head. 'The fear of the unknown, based on hints and denials. My plan, Excellency.'

Trask made a popping noise with his lips. 'And these weapons. Your Ambassador again?'

Alameche nodded. 'It, and the investments it represents.'

There was silence. Alameche could feel his heart beating. He kept his hands pressed on the table, hard enough to make the pulse in his fingers tap against the cold stone.

Eventually the Patriarch sat up straight. 'Very well. Inaction seems a strange route to glory, but as usual you have made the strange seem plausible. Now, the Games begin soon. We must be there, you know. In person.' He stood, and they jumped to their feet. 'This must not leave this room, gentlemen. Alameche, keep me closely informed.'

He turned and strode out of the room. The others filed out after him, nodding to Alameche as they passed. The last one to leave was Trask. As he passed Alameche the old man stopped. 'Good luck,' he said. 'What are you going to do with our doubles, out of interest? The usual?'

'Of course.' Alameche shrugged. 'They can't be allowed to live, can they?'

Trask looked at him steadily. 'Sometimes I think I am too old for this,' he said eventually. 'Good night.'

Catastrophe, Catastrophe Curve

The walk-in surgery resembled a war zone. Fleare looked doubtfully at the waiting area. 'Really?'

'Really. Someone you don't know shot you with something nasty. You have to get checked out. Plus, you're still bleeding.' Jez pushed her firmly in the back. 'Just step over the bodies.'

The doc was a small, elderly-looking androgynous creature with over-long limbs and large, wet eyes set in a sallow face. It smelled slightly swampy. They paid extra to jump the queue, and extra again to bribe the doc not to upload the results to Catastrophe's medical database. As Fleare made to step into the scanner the doc grunted and held her back. 'No jewellery,' it said, pointing at her neck.

'What? Oh.' She had forgotten that she was wearing the covert version of Muz. Slowly she took hold of the beads and lifted them, feeling the chain parting itself unbidden at the back of her neck. Then the necklace was lying in her hands, looking somehow dead. She shuddered and handed it to Jezerey. 'Look after this for me.'

She stepped into the scanner feeling naked.

The machine hummed and extended a spray of fine, translucent tendrils. She felt them brush, explore, and settle around her shoulder. They rested there for a moment, then flickered

over the rest of her body and withdrew. She looked at the doc.
'Is that it?'

'Yes.' It was staring at a holo display. 'No poisons, no recent
implants, no fresh nano.' It looked at the display a little longer,
then frowned and glanced at Fleare. 'You have an extensive
existing suite which obviously I can't have seen because such
things are illegal under Hegemony law and doubtful even here.
It is opaque to me, which suggests that it is military in origin.
My equipment is civilian; if someone were to interfere with
your modifications it wouldn't tell me. That whole area is your
business.'

'Damn right it is.' Jezerey handed Muz back to Fleare. 'That's
what we paid for. Come on, Fle.'

Fleare hooked the necklace round her neck. As the beads
settled against her skin she thought she felt them push themselves slightly into her. Then the sensation stopped. But she
didn't feel naked any more. She waited while the doc sprayed a
skin patch on to her shoulder. It stung briefly, and then went
numb as the patch set into a fair imitation of her natural skin
tone. She flexed her arm experimentally. 'Okay, that feels good.'
She turned to the doc. 'Thanks,' she said.

'Welcome. Go well.' The big eyes narrowed. 'Try not to come
back. This is not the Hegemony, not yet, but nor is it quite so
isolated as we may like to think. Next time I might have to tell
someone.'

The cab was a two-wheeled device, short and narrow to suit the
winding alleys of the Old City. They sat above each other within
the slim wooden frame on seats that were halfway to being
saddles. Above them, the top of the frame contained a slim
buoyancy bag which provided enough upward lift to stop the
vehicle from keeling over. Below them, a humming circular casing
contained a big flywheel that doubled as energy store and gyro-
scope. In front of them, the cab jockey sat. And talked.

'Your first time in the Curve?' And without waiting for an answer: 'I've been here three cycles, near on.'

Fleare felt a reply was needed. 'Where were you before?'

'Inboard.' The driver cleared his throat, turned his head to the side and spat. The cab swayed. He swore, reached up and twisted a handle. There was a hiss, and the bag above their heads fluttered and swelled.

Fleare frowned and looked down at Jezerey, who mouthed 'Cordern.' She nodded, and looked back at the jockey. 'Why did you come here?'

He laughed hoarsely. 'Wouldn't'a lived three cycles there. Wouldn't'a lived longer'n about three days. Invasion, see? The Fortunate. Ha fucking ha.'

'So how did you get here?'

'Ha!' He spat again. 'Humanitarian transport, they called it. Still took a year's pay offa me. Six days in the belly of an old freighter with no food and no khazis.' He laughed. 'I'm still looking for the guy who took the money.'

Fleare counted in her head. 'Three cycles,' she said. 'How old were you when you left, then?'

'Almost two cycles. Figure I must be about five times your age, ladies.' He turned round in his saddle and winked. 'Reckon I could still show you the way, though.'

A movement caught Fleare's eye. She looked down. Jezerey was miming throwing up.

They paid off the unrequited cab jockey in front of a plain wall, twice Fleare's height. Above the wall, a greenish penumbra marked the track of a stun field.

Fleare wrinkled her brow. 'Jez, this is the city wall.'

'Give the girl a prize.'

'So what do we do, jump it?'

'Only if you want to.' Jezerey pointed. 'Me, I'd use the door.'

Fleare followed the gesture. Now it had been pointed out, she

139

had to admit the door was fairly obvious. It looked reinforced. 'It's not welcoming,' she said doubtfully.

'It'll be fine. You coming or not?'

Things happen at boundaries. The Tanks had happened at a particularly acute one, and it had therefore happened with particular gusto.

Land inside the city of Catastrophe was fairly safe, ultimately limited and very, very expensive. Land outside was basically free, but very, very dangerous. One obvious solution, if you could manage it, was to extend the safety of the city out into the land beyond. There had been several answers to that implied question. The Tanks was the best and, so far, the most durable.

Suppose there had been a local war, mainly about money. Suppose that a load of left-over war machines had been stranded just outside the city walls. Suppose that an imaginative person had persuaded someone else to lend them enough money not only to buy up the stranded machines, but to weld them together into a sort of autonomous armoured mini-city.

It had worked. Most of the old war machines had viable nuclear power plants, and enough of them had functioning air and water engines. A few still had weaponry. The result was a deeply protected, self-maintaining, self-governing micro-state with very few problems except that of making regular payments on the colossal, and colossally expensive, loans which had set it up in the first place.

Inside, the Tanks smelled of the sweat, or equivalent, of half a dozen species and the fumes-of-choice of as many more again. As soon as they were inside, Muz had evaporated from necklace-form and reverted to being a dust cloud. She frowned at him. 'I thought Catastrophe didn't deal with people like you?'

'It doesn't, but we just left Catastrophe. The Tanks runs its own legal system. Same as the airships, see?'

'And Catastrophe plays along?'

'Sure, as long as there's money in it.' The dust flowed downwards like a waterfall. 'Freedom! Feels good.' Then it reverted to cloud shape. 'Besides, this is a tough joint. If I need to weigh in, I'm fastest from this form.'

'Right.' Fleare stared at the cloud for a moment. 'Listen, Muz, about weighing in and stuff, are you,' she sought for words, 'that is, can anything, you know, bother you?' From the corner of her eye she saw Jezerey paying attention.

'Bother? What are you talking about?'

'I mean threaten. Damage.'

'Whoa, honey!' The cloud formed a pulsing exclamation mark. 'That's like wandering up and asking someone where they keep the big red button. Especially when you ask in here.'

Fleare blushed. 'Sorry.'

'No problem. So, shall we watch the floor show?'

'Yeah. No, wait.' Fleare pointed at Muz. 'I don't want to stop you because it looks great, but why the images?'

'Shit, you choose your times.' The dust flowed slowly downwards. She reached out a hand and it gathered a soft, dusty covering that felt faintly warm. 'I don't have a *face*, Fleare. When I first got out of the jar, I used to make the shape of my old face, but it felt, I don't know, just wrong. So I kind of – cartoon. Is that an answer?'

She nodded, and looked down at the dusty covering. For a moment it had felt like having her hand held. 'I like it,' she said.

The main stage was within an opened-out cluster of Main Battle Units. Around its edges, the halved shells of smaller vehicles formed irregular booths. They chose one that looked as if it had once been part of an armoured personnel carrier, and Jezerey signalled to one of the servitor trays that hung from ceiling-mounted tracks. 'Chance of the House, three times,' she said. 'Acknowledge.'

141

'Chance of the House, three times.' The tray's voice was like rattling cutlery. It tilted and swung away, its wheel clicking irritably against the track.

'Chance of the House?' Fleare shook her head slowly. 'Jez, what have you just ordered?'

'I have no idea. Chance, see?' She sighed happily. 'It's usually human-drinkable.'

'Usually? Oh good.' Fleare sat back, and then quickly sat up again. She reached round behind her and patted the seat. 'Right. I think this is original, and not in a good way.'

The servitor rattled back, carrying three bulbous goblets of a dull, bluish glass. Fleare took one carefully. A faint haze hung over it like steam, and it smelled chemical. 'Jez,' she said, 'this is smoking.'

Jezerey inspected her own drink. 'No, that's not smoke,' she said. 'More like vapour.'

'Fine.' Fleare looked at Muz. 'Can you do some kind of analysis on this?'

'Just a minute.' Muz floated over to her glass and blended with the haze. 'Yeah, definitely vapour. Volatile hydrocarbons mostly, and a bit of water. Well, water with stuff in. Good thing, really; the drink's probably better off without it.'

Fleare stared at the rising vapour for a moment. In the dim light of the booth it had a greenish tint. She shrugged. 'Jez? I'm going to drink this now. So are you.'

'Fair challenge. Count of three?'

They counted, and drank.

After a while, it felt good. It made the floor show, which seemed to consist of a midget quadruped using a sentient stick-insect as a lance in a jousting match with a furry six-legged mammal, look almost exciting.

After a longer while, it was soporific. Fleare must have dozed off, because the voice roused her.

'Like it here?'

Fleare started, and looked up into Kelk's face. She grinned. 'Hiya. No, not really.'

'Good, because we're not staying long.' He sat down and waved to a servitor.

'Why not? And why are we here in the first place?'

'In a minute. I want a drink.' He peered at her goblet. 'What was that?'

'Chance of the House.'

'Shit. Really?'

'Yeah.' Fleare prodded Jezerey, who seemed to have gone to sleep. 'It was her idea.'

'Not dead?'

Fleare prodded harder. 'I don't think so. Look; she's breathing.'

'Okay, I'll have what she had.' He flagged a servitor, and then collapsed back into a seat. It creaked loudly, and Jezerey sat up, blinking. She looked at Kelk, and then at Fleare, her eyebrows raised. Fleare shrugged.

They waited until the servitor had squeaked back with another goblet. Kelk picked it up, gave it the barest of glances, and took a long pull. Fleare stared. 'Shit. Was your day that bad?'

'Yes and no.' He squinted into the goblet. 'I won the game.'

'Woohoo!' Jez clapped. 'A year's salary, was it?'

'Nope. It was three, in the end.'

Muz had been quiet. Now he floated up to Kelk. 'I take it you're unpopular?'

'Oh yes. But I was ready for that.' He sighed. 'There's something else. Remember I said about no one noticing those bodies?'

'Yes.' Fleare nodded. 'You were very clear about it.'

'Yeah. Well, it would have been fine except that one of them wasn't a body.'

Fleare felt her mouth falling open. 'You're kidding.'

'Nope. The one who shot you? Whatever she swallowed didn't kill her. Just shut her down for a couple of minutes. She must have gambled on us either throwing her over or pissing off somewhere so she could wake up in peace.'

They watched him for a moment. Then Jezerey put down her drink. 'Some gamble.'

'Yeah, well, she probably thought it was worth it. Guys, she wasn't on a mission. She was on two.'

'Say what?' Jezerey gave him a baffled look.

'Uh huh. To begin with they were after me, and it was about money. Simple. I've known about that for a while. I mean, it's not difficult. The contract's even on public record.' He took a breath. 'That's how you can tell it was changed, see?'

Jezerey shrugged. 'No, we don't see. Use simple words, Kelk.'

'Okay. Sorry. So, the contract's out there, right? Local documents like that are public in Catastrophe; it's still different from the Heg' in that way, even if they're growing together more than I'd like. But around about the time Fle landed it was withdrawn for a time. A short time, but still. Then it was re-registered with a load of new stuff added by a different legal firm, all commercial encrypted.'

Jezerey shook her head. 'Could be coincidence.'

'I doubt it. Fleare being shot wasn't coincidence. It was planned.'

Fleare looked up. 'So why? Okay, it hurt, but the doc didn't find anything.'

Jezerey stood up. 'Kelk, if she's alive can we find her and just ask? Well, maybe not just *ask* exactly, but find out?'

'Afraid not. Seems she woke up when she hit the water, swam to the edge and straight into the arms of the nearest water patrol. She's out of reach. By now she's probably out of breath.' He took a long drink. 'Sorry, Fle.'

There was a long silence. On the stage, the quadruped impaled the furry thing on the stick-insect and waved it above its head.

Muz spoke first. 'Sooo, how many people are waiting at the door?'

Kelk counted on his fingers. 'Well, the guys who lost the game. The guys who ran the airship, they were pissed off as well. The cops, obviously. And maybe the people behind those two women, although I guess they'll have gone anonymous now. Er, not sure how many that adds up to. Sorry.' He looked apologetic for a moment, then brightened up. 'Hey. Bet you're glad you came to find me?'

'Delighted.' To her astonishment Fleare found that she meant it. She stood up. 'But we need to get out of here, Kelk. Got any plans?'

He looked up at her. 'Well, the front door won't work, so I guess we need to use the back door.'

Jezerey stood up too. 'Is there one?'

'Well, no.' He drained the goblet and put it down. 'That is, not yet. That's why we're here. So everyone collects at the *front* door.'

There was a soft, distant boom.

Conversation faltered. People looked around uncertainly.

Fleare was on her feet. 'Muz?'

'Checking. Wait a minute.' The cloud formed a tight sphere and became still for a moment. 'That was someone trying to get in. Medium-sized chemical explosion, against the main door. Ah, I think it's time we went.'

There was another, much louder boom, and a stuttering rattle.

'Which way?' Fleare looked around. There was dust hanging in the air. People were gathering into wary groups, but no one seemed to be going anywhere.

Kelk pointed. 'Past the stage. Let's go.'

They pushed through the crowds and hopped up on to the stage. There were black curtains at the back. Kelk bent down, lifted the bottom of one and glanced through the gap. 'Okay.' He beckoned to Jezerey, who dropped to a crouch and ducked under the curtain.

There was another series of explosions, and the stage shook slightly. Fleare looked back. There was more dust and people were beginning to panic. There was a wet crunch near her feet, and she glanced down. The furry quadruped had picked up the stick-insect thing, still helplessly thrust through the now dead-looking six-legged warrior, and had bitten off the end of it. It looked up at Fleare and grinned round a half-chewed mouthful. She shuddered and ducked under the curtain.

Back of house in the Tanks very quickly become somewhere people weren't meant to be, at least if they were people who paid to get in rather than people who were paid not to leave. The spaces were cramped and dirty, formed from the left-over lower-ranks underbelly of old war machines. The walls were oily and the ceilings were low and full of things to bang your head on.

Jez ducked under a fat bunch of cables, and grinned. 'Remind you of anything?'

'Yeah.' Fleare ducked too, but not quite enough. 'Shit.' She rubbed her forehead. 'Battlecraft I have known. Where are we going?'

There was another explosion somewhere behind them. Kelk was in the lead; he turned back. 'Away from that, for a start,' he said. 'You checked any social lately?'

Fleare shook her head. 'Should I?'

'Might be worth it, as long as you're quick.'

'Okay, if you say so.' She stopped by a sawn-off section of armour plate and blinked some sites. A couple of levels into the menus she stopped, and swore.

Her face was everywhere. Not her healthy, outdated, pre-Monastery face. Her present-day face. There were several images, all obviously from candid shots. The sequence started with her on the gangplank of the airship. The most recent image was of her looking doubtfully at a smoking goblet. Jez and Kelk were fuzzy shadows in the background.

An icon on the corner of one of the screens offered a live feed. She blinked into it, frowned, orientated herself, and froze. 'What the fuck?'

It showed a wobbly image of the city wall at the entrance to the Tanks. The camera was at about twice human head height, and the street it looked down on was packed with what looked like at least three competing private armies and a lot of spectators. Some big, ugly-looking remotes had formed a defensive semicircle in front of the entrance, which looked as if it had already taken some major damage. As she watched, a squat machine lumbered forward to the edge of the defensive ring. There was a flash, and the image whited out. At the same time there was another muted boom and the floor jumped under her feet.

Fleare blinked out of the view and found Jezerey staring at her. 'You okay, girl?'

She nodded. 'Come on,' she said. 'Let's go. Wherever we're going.'

They followed Kelk and Muz past storerooms, kitchens and piles of stage equipment, along corridors that became narrower and narrower. The air began to smell of machinery, and the frequent distant explosions competed with a near-subliminal rumble which became stronger as they went. Eventually they emerged into a larger space.

Fleare blinked. It was ridiculously familiar. 'Kelk, is this what I think it is?'

'Engineering space of a Ground Engine, Type 2. Glad you spotted it.' He swept a hand round. 'A classic. Several careless owners. A total we are about to increase by one.'

'What are you talking about?'

'Well, this is one of the units they keep powered up.' He

pointed down at a thick cable loom that snaked out of the space and back along the corridor. 'Big old reactor. Loads of heave. They use it to power the club.'

'So?'

Muz made a sighing noise. 'What Kelk means is, it still goes.'

'Really?' Fleare chewed her lip for a moment. 'But it's joined to the rest of the place.'

'Purely temporary. It's only joined on at the airlock.' Kelk grinned. 'That's why I suggested we meet here – in case we needed a quick way out of Catastrophe jurisdiction. Loads of heave, remember? More than enough.'

Great Stadium, Citadel, Taussich

Alameche threaded his way through the crowds that milled around the edge of the Great Stadium of the Citadel. It was firelight; the two smaller suns had just dipped below the horizon, and the big reddish sand-stained disc of the Overlord was low in the sky above the Basin Ranges, casting long shadows in between splashes of light the colour of hot clay. Despite the late hour the air was still hot; heat rose in a pernicious cloud from the sun-broiled stone floor of the Stadium and fried everyone, noble, payman and peasant alike.

The celebrations of the Elevation had been going on all day, and Alameche had made the start with minutes to spare after a wild dash across the planet. He felt fresh and alert – but that was entirely thanks to his Apothecary, who had left Alameche in no doubt that he disapproved. 'The body will exact payment eventually, sire,' he had murmured as he let the milky drops fall on to Alameche's tongue.

Alameche swallowed the bitter stuff with a scowl. 'The master will exact payment from the servant, if the servant doesn't hold his counsel,' he told the man, who had bowed gravely and retreated. It had been a mild rebuke. The Apothecary was one of the only two people Alameche really trusted. The other was Kestus. Both had been with him for decades.

It had been a long journey.

Alameche Ur-Hive had not been born with a noble name. He had been born with no name at all, the illegitimate child of a minor courtesan whose master had expelled her when she refused a termination. After living rough for a few months she had finally given birth on her own in a small room above a smoking parlour. The birth had been breech; she had delivered her child but bled to death shortly afterwards. It was almost two hours before the child's cries roused the somnolent smokers in the room below.

The baby had been given to an order of Anti-Sophists who were known for taking in foundlings. They washed him, fed him and named him Alam, because that was the next name on the list. Under their careful formality and spartan discipline he grew first into a quiet, obedient infant, and later a reserved, rather scholastic boy. He had been quick to learn but slow to mix, a combination that suited his carers very well, and no one had been surprised when at the age of nine he had won a scholarship to one of the court schools.

The court schools were a hang-over from the days before the Patriarchy. Then, they had been meant to train the upper echelons of society in the diplomatic graces necessary to survive the social bear-pit they were to inhabit. But those echelons had fossilized while others, more energetic, grew rich and powerful. By the time Alam arrived, the court schools were reduced to giving the brighter children of the lower classes a liberal education that could have been set out a thousand years before. With luck, hard work and the right level of patronage, a diligent student might end up as a clerk to some minor civil servant. It was still better than most of the alternatives.

It wasn't enough for Alam. He was bright enough to recognize the constraints being placed on his future; he studied, easily achieving the highest marks in the school, kept apart from his peers and watched for his chance.

It came when he was two days short of his thirteenth birthday, in the form of Helmer Ep-Hive. Ep-Hive happened to make a grudgingly dutiful official visit to the school, somewhere he regarded as a social and educational backwater. He also happened to be both highly observant, and a full colonel in the Security section of the state apparatus. He registered the presence of the dark-haired boy with the hooded eyes within ten minutes of arriving in the building, and went out of his way to engage the lad in conversation.

The brief talk confirmed Ep-Hive's first impression. The boy was exceptional in intellect, ambition and also in a certain capacity for unpleasantness which might or might not prove useful. Ep-Hive tended to follow his hunches. He made some calls, and a few weeks later the Senior Tutor of the court school found himself saying goodbye to a young man who suddenly looked older, and very much in control of himself.

Alam would finish his education in one of the private colleges run by State Security. He thrived, learning technical and management skills with equal ease and concealing a quickening temper behind a studied reserve. He graduated a year early with the highest honours on record, and from then on his rise was inexorable. Ep-Hive was proved right on all counts ten years later when his former student sentenced him to execution by progressive disembowelment – ostensibly for corruption and incompetence, but actually for the far simpler and more serious offence of getting in Alam's way. By that time, Ep-Hive had been one of the last people who could, and no one else felt like trying because the capacity for unpleasantness had blossomed into a controlled streak of imaginative cruelty. Ep-Hive's demise had taken several days, during which his shuddering body had been suspended from the ceiling of one of the Security section's main conference rooms, directly over a prettily decorated porcelain tub that held a loop of his own intestines and a swelling colony of ants. The room remained in use throughout, hosting some of the most sober, focused and above all *short* conferences the building had ever seen.

That sort of thing gets people noticed. It got Alam noticed by the newly elevated Final Patriarch, who told him he was the most unpleasant individual he had ever met, before making him Head of Security and awarding him the dead man's title, his estate and his two wives.

The newly anointed Alameche Ur-Hive had never looked back.

He ran his eye over the crowd until he saw Kestus; the man was standing a few metres away, apparently on his own, which probably meant that he had plain-clothes staff all over the place. Alameche gave him a slight nod, and then turned away and headed for his own box. The Night Games would begin when the Overlord had dropped below the horizon. It was time to make himself comfortable, and besides, he had guests to think about.

His private box was well up the high-sunward wall of the Stadium, just at the point where the curve of the bowl became difficult to climb. Those in higher boxes often paid slaves to haul them up the slope in woven baskets, but Alameche thought that was a stupid affectation. He paused before crossing the threshold, gave Kestus another glance – the man had kept station with him – and then crested the stone lip and strolled into the interior.

Inside, the box was cool and dark. Alameche faced away from the entrance for a few seconds, partly to check that the refreshments he had ordered were in place and partly to allow his eyes to adapt. Then he turned round quickly to stare back the way he had come, over the stunning vista of the Great Stadium.

Alameche did not generally use superlatives, but stunning was the only word. He must have allowed himself this private little game scores of times but the impact of the sight in his sensitized eyes never lessened. First, of course, there was the sheer scale. The Stadium was a hyperbolic bowl five hundred metres deep and three times that in diameter. It was carved out of one side of the Great Basin, so that if Alameche turned to his left he could see straight out over the Citadel, while to his right the cliff walls of the Basin reared up nearly another kilometre. At this time of day their furrowed profile was thrown into dramatic relief by the low sunlight that lanced across them.

Then, if he raised his eyes, there was the mass of the Refractor: the enormous faceted crystalline *thing* that hung above the centre of the Stadium like a flattened, incredibly complicated jewel. The acoustics of the Stadium were perfect – a single whisper on the main stage far below could be heard anywhere – but vision needed help and the Refractor provided it, projecting three-dimensional images of whatever was going on to tens of thousands of focal points at the same time. Alameche didn't begin to understand how it worked. The Apothecary had tried to explain it once but Alameche had lost interest after a few minutes and the old man had wisely given up.

The flap-shush of sandalled feet on stone roused him. He lowered his eyes and saw Fiselle walking up the steep slope towards the entrance of the box. Alameche raised an eyebrow. 'Alone?'

The thin man smiled. 'For the moment. Garamende follows, together with an entourage, but on such slopes as these his girth argues against him.'

'Quite.' Alameche gestured to the table behind him. 'Well, we are thoroughly provisioned. His girth is not at risk from me.'

Fiselle looked at the table and raised an eyebrow. 'His might not be. Mine, though?'

Alameche laughed. 'You haven't got a girth. You only have a height.'

'True.' Fiselle looked down at his body. 'I seem destined to exist in two dimensions. But don't worry.' He pointed downhill. 'I think the third one approaches, and it has brought some friends.' An s-shaped chain of bobbing lights was working its way up the slope, dividing the crowd as it came. Alameche followed the gesture and then grinned to himself. It was not so much an entourage as a procession. Garamende had obviously decided to arrive in style.

At the front of the queue were four slim, androgynous youths who looked like perfectly identical quads. At first their naked bodies seemed dark, but then Alameche realized that they were pale-skinned but covered with intricate full-body tattoos. He squinted. The tattoos were definitely erotic.

A much heavier body followed the slim youths. Garamende was stamping up the slope, followed by several more people. He was carrying a torch in one hand and a flask in the other. Alameche raised an eyebrow. 'Going very well,' he said.

Fiselle snorted. 'The last flare of a dying sun.' He stood aside as the front of the party came to the threshold of the box. The tattooed quads split into pairs and stood to attention to either side while Garamende strode through them as if they were an honour guard, throwing his torch into the air as he did so. Fiselle took a step forward and caught it before it landed on the back of Garamende's procession.

The big man thumped Alameche on the shoulder. 'God's knob, man! You make a chap walk a long way uphill for a drink.'

Alameche nodded at the flask. 'At least you brought one with you.'

'Not one. Several.' Garamende waggled the flask. 'But only part of the way. I'm empty.'

'Then feel free to refill.' Alameche gestured to the tables behind him. 'There's plenty for all. Including your company.'

'Company? Oh yes.' Garamende waved at the people who had followed him. He raised his voice. 'Everyone, this is My Lord Alameche Ur-Hive, grand something-or-other to the Patriarch. He's a complete bastard and a good friend of mine. Introduce yourselves to him, will you?'

Alameche smiled and nodded at a succession of breathless people, seeing eyes that were anxious or calculating, and smelling breath that was generally corrupted with spirits. It seemed Garamende's party had been under way for a while. When he had finished he turned to Garamende. 'What about your four decorated young friends?'

'Them? Oh yes.' Garamende grinned, reached out a hand and slapped one of the youths sharply on the bottom. 'My latest toys. Androgynes. Whatever you want, whenever you want it, and four times over. Good, eh?'

Fiselle frowned. 'Bred or Doctored?'

'Bred, of course. No sense in half measures. Besides, Doctored's not the same. You can always see the join.'

'I suppose so.' Fiselle smiled. 'But I didn't realize your tastes were so – flexible.'

Garamende frowned and wagged a finger in Fiselle's face. 'I don't believe in denying myself, man. And what's a bit of cock between friends, eh?' He turned in appeal to Alameche. 'What do you say? Adjudicate, for fuck's sake!'

'I don't think so.' Alameche patted Garamende on the shoulder. 'Besides, there's no time. We're about to begin.'

As he spoke the low light across the Stadium flared and vanished as the last rim of the Overlord dipped below the Basin Ranges. For a moment everything was dim and silent. Then there was a blaring fanfare, and a *whoomph* as thousands of braziers burst into flame. The orange light reached the Refractor, setting a fractured glow which seemed to spread out from the thing until Alameche felt he could almost touch it. Then it shimmered and coalesced in an image of the main stage.

Even Alameche drew in a breath and he had known, if only intellectually, what was going to happen.

The stage was occupied by a three-dimensional image of the Cordern. The definition was superb, down to the scale of individual cities, rivers and groups of islands. The night sides of the planets sparkled with city lights, and the day sides were vivid with colour, and with landscape relief that seemed almost hyperreal. Only Silthx was less interesting, shown in soft greys at the far edge of the stage.

Despite the realism there was something wrong with the scene. It took a moment to work out that the day sides of all the planets faced in the same direction, as if they were all lit by the same sun, whereas in the real Cordern these five planets shared three suns and one disputed object that only qualified as a sun by some definitions. Once the brain had worked that out, the eye naturally travelled towards where the single anomalous sun should have been.

When it got there it found the Patriarch.

The scale of the illusion made him about a third the height of a planet. He was wearing a simple grey robe, the least ostentatious of his state wardrobe, and he was watching the planets of the Cordern with paternal good nature. After a few moments he turned towards the audience.

'Good evening,' he said. 'We are here both to celebrate, and to look ahead. First, it is the anniversary of my elevation to the Patriarchy – a heavy honour, and believe me I struggle every day to live up to it. Tonight concludes our celebrations, and I am glad so many of you are here to share them with me.'

There was solid applause. Fiselle leaned towards Alameche. 'Remind me, what was the penalty for not attending tonight?'

Alameche didn't answer. The question had been rhetorical; there was no 'official' requirement to attend these events. The unofficial one, with its unspoken sanction, was quite unspeakable enough. He kept his eye on the stage.

The Patriarch held out his arm towards the planets. 'Do you see these? Well, do you?' The stadium roared. The Patriarch smiled as the cheers swept over him. Then he made a downwards motion with his hands and the noise quietened. 'A generation ago, there were three. Two generations ago, there was just one. My friends, I believe there can be more. Many more!' He swept his arm round and, as if following it, the images around him multiplied until the Patriarch seemed to be standing in the middle of a vast tract of space.

Now the whole stadium was on its feet. Alameche glanced around; Fiselle and Garamende were standing too, and most of Garamende's party were jumping up and down. The quads were staring slackly at the stage, and it occurred to Alameche that they might be drugged. He supposed that would make it easier to endure Garamende.

The Patriarch waved for quiet again, and smiled round at the Stadium. 'Well, that is tomorrow's task. You have another task tonight. To celebrate!' He swept his arm round again, and he and the planets vanished. The braziers flared columns of orange flames and then died down to reveal a crowded stage.

Fiselle glanced at it, shook his head and turned towards the refreshments. 'Gladiators,' he said. 'Well, well. How original. I think I will have something to eat.' He looked down at his stomach. 'One can always aspire to a third dimension, after all.'

The celebrations had lasted for several hours.

Some of Garamende's party had brought pipes with them, and for quite a long time the box had been rank with fumes. The Apothecary's drops had helped Alameche fight off most of the effects of passive smoking, but even so he was beginning to flag. In the next hour he would need either a sleep or another dose. He wasn't the only one; Fiselle was lounging on a couch near the front of the box, with half an eye on the stage. The stage was empty at last, except for the clean-up squads. Fiselle gestured languidly towards them. 'Nasty job,' he said.

Alameche blinked. 'In what way?'

'Cleaning up blood and so forth.' Fiselle closed his eyes and sank back. 'Just saying. Nasty.'

Alameche watched the cleaners for a moment. Then he turned back to Fiselle, opened his mouth and shrugged. The man was asleep.

He looked round the box. Quite a few of the party were also asleep, including most of the pipe smokers. The quads had obviously become bored, and had retreated to a pile of cushions in one corner where they had formed a sort of slowly moving erotic knot. He watched for a while, and for a partly stoned moment wondered if he should join in. The urge passed. Instead he stood up and stretched, digging his hands into the small of his back and then raising them above his head.

And nearly hitting Garamende, who had somehow materialized next to him. Alameche almost jumped.

The fat man was staring at the stage. 'Alameche,' he said, 'tell me what the fuck is happening.'

'What do you mean?'

'Down there. At the beginning.' Garamende gestured towards the stage. 'When the planets appeared? That was the whole Inner Spin, man, more or less.'

'Was it?'

'Stop trying to look innocent. Of course it was.'

Alameche studied Garamende. He looked far more alert than he had any right to. Alameche felt his own tiredness falling away, driven off by an instinct much older and more powerful than any of the Apothecary's syrups. He chose his words carefully. 'It was just a picture,' he said.

'A picture. Yes, it was that. And an ambition.' Garamende's eyes searched Alameche. 'Since when did we aspire to that lot?'

Now Alameche was fully awake. 'I don't know if we do aspire. If we did, would it trouble you?'

'What, turbulent naughty little us, taking over thirty-odd planets? Fine, as long as we have the means.' Garamende reached out and put his hand on Alameche's shoulder. 'But, my friend, the last time I looked we *didn't* have the means. Has something changed?'

Alameche reached up and took hold of the other man's hand. 'Things change all the time,' he said. 'As we both well know.'

Garamende stared at him for a long time. Then he grinned. 'And as we both well know, you never change at all.' He squeezed Alameche's shoulder. 'You know best, as always.'

'I am as wise as my Master allows.'

'Of course you are. And your Master is as wise as you tell him how to be.' He turned away and strode over to the quads, who were still entwined in their private love-knot. 'Come on,' he said. 'Up you get and home we go. Daddy wants company.' They stood up, grumbling, and followed him out of the box, climbing over some of the rest of his party as they went. The trodden-on people groaned, stood, stretched, and wandered off down the slope after Garamende. Last of all, Fiselle woke and rolled over into a sitting position. He blinked. 'Did I miss anything?'

'Only Garamende's departure.'

'Really?' Fiselle scratched himself. 'One fat man, four catamites and half a dozen hangers-on? I shall regret my loss for minutes.'

Alameche laughed. 'You'll get over it.'

'You're right. I will. In fact I believe I have.' He stood up, and held out his hand. 'Thank you for your hospitality. Especially after what must have been a very busy day.'

Alameche took the hand and shook it. 'Is there any other sort? Good night, old friend.'

He watched as Fiselle walked down the slope. At his nod, Kestus followed him at a discreet distance, leaving the box apparently empty. When the two men were out of sight Alameche turned and looked towards the dimly lit back of the box. 'Very well,' he said out loud. 'Prove me wrong.'

'Ah! Very good.' A patch of not-quite-nothing floated out of the furthest corner, blurred, and became Eskjog. 'When did you suspect me?'

'Yesterday.' Alameche took a couple of steps backwards until his legs encountered the edge of a couch. He sagged down on to it. The Apothecary's potion was definitely wearing off.

'Only then? I'm flattered.'

'And I'm unconcerned.' Alameche shook his head. 'Look, surveillance doesn't trouble me. I don't need privacy. You can haunt my dreams if you want. I assume you followed today's events?'

'Yes, I did. Well done.'

'Thank you. Now what?'

Eskjog settled itself on a pile of cushions on the couch next to Alameche. 'Well, the place of safety, obviously.'

'Obviously. And?'

'And what? Do you expect me to— no, wait.' Eskjog made a sighing noise, lifted off from its cushions and floated over until it was a hand's breadth from Alameche's face. 'The things you make me do,' it said. 'Wait a second. Oh, and don't move.'

Alameche didn't move. There was a *pop*, and the world went grey. Eskjog turned from side to side as if looking around. 'There,' it said. 'You can move a bit if you want. Just try not to brush the field.'

'Field?' Alameche looked around cautiously. The greyness seemed to start a little way out from his body.

'Yes. Anti-intrusion. Nothing gets in, nothing gets out. Ah, that happens to include oxygen, so let's not mess about. Here's the proposed safe area.'

A patch of air in front of Alameche's eyes fuzzed and became a screen. It showed an image of the Cordern; a planet flashed and enlarged so that continents became visible, and then landforms. As he watched, the image homed in to a single building.

He nodded slowly. 'Yes,' he said. 'I get it.'

'You agree?'

'I agree.'

'Good.' The image collapsed into sparkling motes, and vanished. 'Now, we haven't got long. First, fields like this are a bit obvious even at your tech level. It won't be long before someone tries to hack us, and they might just manage it. And second, you'll start to asphyxiate in about a minute.'

'So turn it off.' Alameche's throat felt dry.

'I will, I promise. Soon. First, while we're here, a question. What was all that planetary stuff about, from your Patriarch?'

'What, his speech?' Short sentences seemed easier. 'Rhetoric.'

'Only that? Pretty public sort of rhetoric. It sounded like commitment to me. Your friend Garamende obviously thought so.'

'He was wrong. It wasn't.' Now Alameche's chest was beginning to hurt. He tried to regulate his breathing.

'Good. It mustn't be.' Eskjog was speaking very quietly now. 'This evening's display was stupid. You make sure everything just jogs along as usual. No change in ambition, no change in mood music. Otherwise you'll get noticed. Including by me.'

It backed away and spoke normally. 'Now, I'll arrange for the object to be moved. No need for you to worry about that. You've had a busy time. Why don't you take a rest? You're looking a bit peaky.'

There was another *pop*. The grey field vanished. So did Eskjog.

Alameche took a careful breath, emptied his lungs, and took another. His heart was racing and he felt light-headed, but he didn't sit down and he didn't give in to his other temptation and

161

swear out loud. Instead he reached out a hand and steadied himself against the end of a couch while he stared at where Eskjog had been.

The air felt beautiful in his lungs, but it still tasted faintly of ozone.

The Tanks, Catastrophe, Catastrophe Curve

They had booted up the controls, and fed a short burst of power to the main traction set. The old Ground Engine had shuddered and strained against the airlock seal. Kelk nodded. 'Ready to go,' he said. 'Hold tight.' He reached for the controls.

The floor shook violently. Jezerey snatched at a grab rail. 'Kelk!'

'It wasn't me!' Kelk glared at the display in front of him. 'Oh fuck, it's the Tanks! There are some big old screw guns on the roof. Someone's got control of them.'

Fleare shook her head. 'What are screw guns?'

'Projectile weapons. Rifled barrels. Antiques, but still.' Kelk stared at the display. 'Shit. If they fire armour-piercing stuff it might work, at this range. Genuinely, hang on. We're leaving.'

Fleare tightened her grip on the grab rail. The traction set hummed and then roared. There was a sound of tearing metal, and the Ground Engine lurched forwards, bouncing wildly over something. Fleare felt as if her arms were about to be torn off. 'Kelk! Watch what you drive over!'

'Sorry.' Kelk gunned the drive, and Fleare felt herself pressed back in her seat. 'I think that was something I had no choice about driving over. Have a look.'

Fleare looked around for a screen but didn't find one. She shrugged and hand-over-handed across to the airlock, which was now a ragged rim of metal. She stared back along the way they had come. 'I can see something . . . Oh.' She watched the receding wreck for a moment. She could see the remains of tracks attached to a hull that looked as if it had been screwed into a ball by a giant. There was something else, too. She swallowed. 'Kelk, how much does this thing weigh?'

'About two hundred tonnes, give or take.'

'Uh huh. I think the thing we went over had people in it.'

'Sorry. I don't suppose they meant us any good.'

Jezerey took a hand off her grab rail and patted Fleare on the shoulder. 'That wasn't your fault, girl.' She looked at Kelk. 'What's the plan?'

'Well, we can't go back inside Catastrophe.' The ground had evened out and the old Ground Engine had stopped lurching about and had settled into a thrumming cruise. Kelk did something to the console and cautiously raised his hands from the twin control sticks. 'Good; automatics are okay.' He turned round and put his arms behind his head in a lazy stretch. 'At the same time, we don't want to be out here too long. There are plenty of airborne assets for charter around here. They'll be above us as soon as someone can agree a price, and some of them are tooled up with stuff that could give us a real problem.'

Jezerey nodded. 'I would say we already had that problem, Kelk.'

'Yeah. So we need somewhere close.' He took a breath. 'I think we should head for Tail End Port. It's a closed airspace, for one thing. The private hire guys can't follow us in. And from there we can get the flying fuck off this rock.'

'Hold on – you said somewhere close.' Jezerey shook her

head. 'Tail End has to be, what, two hundred clicks from here, over land.'

'Not if you go the straight route.'

Jezerey looked at him steadily. 'There isn't a straight route,' she said. 'Not while you've got me on board.'

Fleare looked from one to the other, and shrugged. She glanced out of the airlock, and frowned into the dark. 'Guys?'

Muz was by her side. 'What is it?'

'There's something behind us. Hold on.'

She ramped up her vision. They were crossing a wide band of scrubland, which in her grainy night vision had a scorched look as if a firestorm had passed over it, and the Ground Engine was growling along the line of an old highway, its tracks rasping against the flaking surface.

They had travelled about two klicks from the Tanks. She could see a faint glow hanging above the club. It danced a little, like flames. And nearer, a lot nearer, something was silhouetted. She watched it for a moment until she was sure. Then she turned away.

The inside of the Ground Engine was agonizing to her sensitized eyes. She blinked, and willed her muscles to relax. It seemed to take a long time; she shut them for the moment.

Muz spoke from close by. 'What is it?'

'There's something following us.' She risked opening her eyes a fraction. They seemed okay. 'Tracked vehicle. Kelk, I don't think this was the only Ground Engine that still worked. Are we armed?'

'No.'

'Are they armed?'

'Probably not.' He paused. 'Okay, I don't know.'

'Right.' Fleare rubbed her eyes. 'So, I vote for the straight route, whatever that is.' She saw Jezerey look up, her mouth beginning to open, but shook her head. 'And as soon as we're safe you can tell us what the fuck's going on, Kelk, because there's no way all this is just about one runaway rich girl and a lucky gambler.'

They kept the old war machine running flat out. Fleare sat cross-legged on the floor near the airlock, periodically checking on the view outside. Her eyes were partly ramped up. It seemed more difficult than it should be; the effort made her head ache. A kilometre behind, the other Ground Engine kept station with them. So far it seemed to be on its own. She had the impression that it could have caught them if it had wanted to.

In deference to her night sight they had killed the internal lighting. Instead, Muz had split himself into a dozen pieces. One had hacked into what remained of the Ground Engine's sensor suite, scanning the sky for airborne intruders. The other eleven had distributed themselves around the room, glowing a soft green like fireflies. It made her feel that she was sitting in a circle of firelight.

Jezerey was also sitting on the floor, her back against the base of the control console and her legs stretched out, one ankle across the other. She had one eye shut, which Fleare assumed meant she was blinking news sites. The other stared forwards, unfocused. Occasionally she nodded to herself. Once, she flinched.

Fleare watched her, between backward glances. After a while she asked, 'Much going on?'

'Yup.' Jezerey opened both eyes. 'Plenty of stuff about you, obviously, but to be honest it's mostly froth. A lot of the recent heavy-duty content is about wonder boy here.' She nodded towards Kelk. 'Including a happy post from something called In Recovery. Proud winning bidders on a contract to get airborne and get after you. Well, us, really.' She blinked again. 'And they are both of those things as of thirty minutes ago.'

Kelk didn't turn round. He was frowning at the console. 'Does it say who let the contract?'

'No. Anonymous, surprise, surprise. Why, got any candidates?'

'A few.'

Jezerey stood up and stretched. 'Well, we'll all find out if they catch us.' She tapped on the console, making Kelk start. 'Will they catch us?'

He hesitated. 'Depends how fast they are. Possibly not. Muz, you got anything in sight?'

The nearest firefly dipped a little in the air. 'Yes. Recent launch, seven units. Can't tell you anything else using this stuff. We might as well be using a periscope.'

Kelk shrugged. 'We're almost at the Edge.' He frowned at the console. 'Actually, cancel the almost. It must have moved again.'

Fleare opened her mouth to ask the obvious question, and then clamped it shut again as the Ground Engine shuddered, canted forwards and dropped, its tracks yammering against nothing. She felt her stomach rising, and heard Jezerey give an involuntary yelp. Then the fall stopped, and they lurched forward with an ugly scream as the tracks took up the load.

Fleare steadied herself and looked at Kelk. 'What was that?'

'Don't worry.' He grinned. 'Should be nice and smooth now.'

She turned, glanced out of the airlock, and then stared. 'Right,' she said eventually. 'What the fuck?'

Before the drop, the landscape behind them had been a dusty plain, crossed by occasional tracks and half-obliterated field boundaries. Now it was a dead flat expanse of something that looked grey in the dim light. Grey, but with intersecting reddish-orange veins. She watched it for a while, and then turned back to the interior of the old craft. 'Kelk,' she said, 'tell me this isn't a lava field.'

He shook his head. 'Can't. It's wrong to lie.'

Jezerey patted her on the shoulder. 'Now you know why I didn't want to use the direct route,' she said.

One of the planets that had had the bad luck to become the Catastrophe had been heavily industrialized, and had relied for power on three enormous underground fusion plants, completely self-contained and the biggest ever built. During the collision one of them had been totally destroyed, and a second had been blown into space and then drawn into a nearby star, brightening it detectably. The third was still underground, and astonishingly it was still working, but the resulting heat had nowhere to go. Inevitably, after a few hundred years, it began to find its own way.

The old power plant was near the edge of a cliff. Molten rock welled up from it and spread out into a broad delta which flowed over the edge like an infinitely slow waterfall. At the bottom it spread into a pool which ate its way into the base of the cliff and rejoined the gently convecting megatonnes of lava on their way past the power plant and back up to the delta.

The result was Fusion Field, almost certainly the only accidental, artificial, circular lava flow in the galaxy. The whole circuit was about fifty kilometres long, and performed one complete rotation in just over a hundred years.

The Ground Engine moved smoothly over the crusted surface of the lava. Apart from the booming cooling system that had stuttered into life less than a minute after they had dropped off the cliff, it was quieter than before. As long as Fleare didn't go too near the airlock, it was almost comfortable. The airlock itself was unapproachable, and just inside it a curtain of mist had formed where the scalding air outside met the chilled air within. Fleare squinted through the mist. Her eyes didn't seem to want to ramp up, but she didn't need them to. The other Ground Engine had followed them over the cliff, and it was close enough to see with normal vision now.

She turned to the others. 'I think we're going to have company.'

'Yes.' It was Muz. 'More than one sort. Airborne incoming.'

Jezerey stood up. 'The seven you saw?'

'Them, plus something else. Much bigger; could be almost commercial scale.' Muz coalesced back into a single cloud. 'Kelk, what are the options?'

'Not many.' Kelk took hold of the controls. 'Going to manual. I might be able to do some evading.'

Fleare glanced back through the airlock, and stiffened. The chasing Ground Engine had accelerated; it was catching them quickly. 'Better get frisky,' she said over her shoulder. 'Company's arriving very soon.'

Something pinged. Kelk looked down at the console. 'Not soon – now,' he said. 'Tight beam, 'crypted.' He waved at the controls. There was a brief connection hiss, and then a voice.

'Calling Ground Engine Type 2. Acknowledge.'

Kelk glanced at the others. 'Acknowledged,' he said. 'Who are you and what's your message?'

'We're the guys following you. Well, first, don't stop.'

Fleare felt her eyebrows climbing. Kelk grinned. 'Thanks for the advice,' he said. 'We weren't going to.'

'Good.' The other voice sounded amused. 'Because if you do, your tracks will melt. They look real hot already.'

Kelk nodded. 'I knew that. Anything else?'

'Yes. You've got incoming airborne threat, imminent. We ran a sim. Better than ninety per cent they're going to take you out before you get off the Field.'

Kelk looked around at the others and nodded slightly. Fleare got up and walked over to the comms. 'So, that doesn't give us long to get to know each other,' she said. 'Who are you?'

'Oh, just some guys with some guns on the roof. Take a look.'

Fleare moved as close to the airlock as she dared. She didn't have to stay there long; even in the space of their short conversation, the other Ground Engine had halved the distance between them. She pulled back from the furnace air and nodded at the others.

'Okay.' Kelk sounded wary. 'But you aren't shooting. So what's the deal?'

'Well, we'll start shooting when your airborne friends turn up.' The voice paused, and added, 'On terms, of course.'

'What terms?'

Now the voice was brisk. 'Precedent protection contract. One million standard, payable immediately.'

Kelk's mouth dropped open. Jezerey marched over and took the comms. 'You have to be kidding. Half a mil, payable on results.'

'You are in no position to play hard ball.' The voice sighed. 'Three-quarters, fifty per cent up front. Make your minds up. It looks like the guys in the sky just powered up their weapon systems.'

'You came all this way. You need a deal as badly as we do. We can't pay if we're dead. Nothing up front; the whole fee in escrow.'

There was a pause. Then the voice said, 'Deal. We're sending account details.'

The console pinged. Jezerey looked down and nodded. 'Got them.' Then she stared. 'Ways and Means and Co? That's you?'

'Sure. Why?'

'Shit!' Jezerey thumped the console softly. 'I saw you on social. You bid on the contract to get us!'

'Yeah. That's how we make money, you see? But In Recovery bought that one, so we'll have this one and stiff them back. Listen, if you don't send the cash there'll be nothing left to save.'

Jezerey brushed a control. 'Okay, sent.' She shook her head. 'So shoot, you fuckers!'

'Fuckers yourself.' The comms fell silent.

Fleare looked at Jezerey. 'Thanks,' she said. 'Um, do I owe you a lot of money?'

Jezerey shook her head and pointed at Kelk. 'No. He does. If they deliver, that is.'

There was a moment's silence. Then, almost too quickly for the eye to follow, Muz flicked over to the airlock, hovered for the briefest moment and shot back to float above the console. 'Something's kicking off,' he said. 'The Ways and Means guys just powered up some *major* stuff. Or someone did. Can't tell quite what, but it isn't the little tubes you can see on their roof.'

They looked at each other. Fleare reached for a grab rail and closed her fingers around it.

The interior of the Ground Engine lit up like a nova. She tightened her grip.

The concussion felt like a wrecking ball to the chest. There was an indefinite moment of howling nothing. Then she found she could take a breath. She looked around.

Kelk and Jezerey were crouched low in their seats, arms over their heads. Muz had retreated into a hard, mirrored ball the size of a fist. It looked defensive; she had a sudden mental picture of the real, human Muz, curled into the foetal position.

Her ears hurt. She shook her head carefully, and heard faint popping sounds followed by the grinding hum of the Ground Engine. Something was still working. She took another breath, and used it. 'What happened?'

Muz expanded into his normal cloud. 'Unknown for the moment.' He paused. 'That was a very, very big energy discharge. I'll try to find some un-flambéed sensors. Kelk, anything on comms?'

Kelk was fiddling with the controls. 'Nothing. But we're still going. We'll be off the Field in five minutes.'

Fleare's whole body ached. She hauled herself to her feet and headed for the airlock, grabbing at things for support as her legs wobbled. The curtain of mist was still there. She steadied herself just inside it, and looked out.

At first she thought that the lava plain behind them was empty, and as uniform as before. Then she realized that there was something different about it. She forced her screaming eye muscles to contract, and the scene swam into something close to focus.

About half a klick behind them, and receding quickly, there was a wide, bright, shallow mound on the surface of the lava. Even as she watched it sagged and spread, becoming a fading orange-yellow smear in the centre of a network of angry red fissures. Without looking round, she said quietly, 'I think they're all gone.'

It was Muz who answered. 'I think you're right. I found some footage. There must have been more sensors working than I thought. Take a look.'

She turned to see a cloudy holo fuzz into being between her and the others, not quite dense enough to stop her seeing their faces through it. It showed the lava field, with the pursuing Ground Engine in the centre of the image. The image was frozen, and there was a cloud of smaller dots and one bigger one in the top right-hand corner.

'That was just after they called us fuckers. Now running at actual speed.' As Muz spoke the images flicked into life and suddenly the Ground Engine was obviously moving fast, its glowing tracks throwing up clouds of hot cinders that faded from a sullen crimson as they fell. As they watched the pursuing dots grew quickly, and resolved into a rosette of six compact, lumpy-looking units circling a much bigger version of themselves.

Muz paused the screen. 'Recognize those?'

Fleare frowned. It seemed difficult to concentrate. 'I've seen pictures . . . the little ones are slaved to the one in the middle, right?'

'That's right. Called a Node-Distributed Battle Entity. Completely unmanned.'

Jez frowned at the holo. 'Aren't those illegal? As well as very expensive?'

Muz wobbled from side to side. 'Well, illegal's a bit moot out here. We're outside Catastrophe, remember, and even that's still sort of outside the Heg'. But yes, they are very expensive. And very hard to stop.' He paused. 'Shall we go on? Now at one-tenth real time.'

The images were set in motion again. The sinister rosette was above the Ground Engine now, with the six small units beginning to move away from the centre and form a flattened delta, its sharp end pointing at the viewpoint.

A tight, faint shaft of green light appeared, connecting the central unit to the Ground Engine below. There was a tiny pause, then the rosette blossomed into cerise balls of flame. A fraction of a second later, so did the Ground Engine.

The holo fuzzed and collapsed. Kelk shook his head. 'What happened?'

Muz wobbled again. 'At a guess, and this really is only a guess, that was a self-destruct sequence. That green light looked like a wide-spectrum comms beam. Could be that something on the Ground Engine hacked the Battle Entity. If so, I'd love to know how.'

'Yeah.' Fleare made to turn round.

The spasm was as sudden as it was vicious. It felt as if every muscle in her body was trying to tear itself free. Her sight blacked out, and she collapsed with the sound of her own short scream stabbing at her ears.

There was a rustle by her. She felt hands on her, and heard Jez's voice. 'Fleare? Fleare! What happened? Can you talk?'

The pain was fading, and her sight was coming back. She nodded, very carefully. 'Yeah,' she said, and it came out in a ragged whisper.

'Whoa.' Jez sat back on her heels. 'What the fuck was that about?'

'Don't know.' Fleare reached out a hand and felt around until she found a bulkhead. She pulled herself along to it and raised herself to a lopsided sitting position. 'Muscles. Been feeling achy, but not like that. Shit.' She realized she was panting, and stopped speaking.

Muz swam into her vision. 'How long have you been feeling achy?'

'Not sure.' She concentrated. Even that seemed to hurt. 'Maybe half an hour?'

'Hm.' Muz hovered for a moment. 'Tell us if it happens again, okay?'

Fleare looked at him. 'If it happens again, you'll know.'

'Yeah. Sorry.' Muz floated closer and brushed gently against her cheek. Then he climbed to head height. 'Well, we should clear the Field any minute. Once we're in the Tail End, we'll get you looked at.'

There was a short pause. Then Kelk said slowly, 'About the Tail End? I don't want to worry anyone, but Ways and Means and Co just returned one seventh of our money.' He reached for the comms, but it powered up before his hand got there. 'Calling Ground Engine. Ways and Means here. You guys okay?'

Kelk raised his eyebrows. 'Well, kind of. I take it you weren't in that vehicle, then?'

The voice laughed. 'No way. It was on remote. You might be crazy enough to track across Fusion Field, but we aren't.'

'You returned some money.' Kelk paused. 'Why?'

'Because we didn't finish the job.' Now the voice was serious. 'We missed one of the fuckers.'

Jez interrupted. 'Weren't they all slaved together?'

'Apparently not. Probably a fail-safe; the rest blow up but one gets left behind to sneak around the back.'

'You got anything else in the area?'

'No, again. Sorry. Best of luck.'

The comms fell silent. So did everyone else, for a moment. Then Kelk said simply, 'Muz?'

The cloud dipped. 'Checking.' There was another pause. Then, 'Yep. Dead overhead, ten klicks up. Dropping fast. ETA about twenty seconds.'

Kelk sighed. 'Any good ideas?'

'Just one very bad one.' Muz was already by the airlock. 'See you.'

Fleare caught her breath. 'No, wait,' she began, but the cloud had already shrunk to a small, dull black sphere which flickered through the airlock and disappeared, leaving a little boiling vortex in the curtain of mist. It healed as she watched.

Kelk wheeled back to the controls. 'No change,' he said flatly. 'Contact in ten.' He was about to say something else when there was a sharp, explosive crack. Orange light flashed outside, lighting up the mist curtain like a stage effect. The Ground Engine shook, lurched sideways, and then ploughed on over the lava field as if nothing had happened.

For a few seconds nobody spoke. Then Jez looked round. 'Is that it?'

Kelk studied the console. 'There's nothing out there. So yes, maybe that really is it.'

Jez frowned. 'What about Muz?'

'I can't see anything.' He looked up from the console. 'Oh shit. Fle, listen, I—'

She waved him silent. 'Don't. He knew,' she corrected herself, '*knows* what he's doing.'

Somehow, on the way back from the wave, her hand brushed the place on her cheek where Muz had touched her. She had expected to find it wet. It wasn't. *I'm getting tougher*, she told herself. *I wonder what he'll come back as this time?*

Then the pain came again, building through her body and

shaking her in its teeth until she became one single, unending scream. Then everything faded.

She woke, pain-free but limp with exhaustion, as they were boarded by two unsmiling officials of the Tail End Port Authority who welcomed them to the Tail End, asked to see their proof of ownership of the Ground Engine and, when they could offer none, politely arrested them for theft and vagrancy.

She drifted off again, to the sound of Jez shouting at the officials.

Yeveg Island, Taussich

It looked like an ancient natural harbour. A blue sea lapped against the wide mortared stone crescent of the harbour wall, rocking the oiled bark hulls of a row of fishing boats. Above the wall, terraces climbed up and back towards the frond-wood-covered heights behind. The evening air smelled of salt and cooking fires and seared meats.

In fact it was nothing of the sort. Taussich had very little free surface water and none of it was allowed to collect into anything as wasteful as a sea, certainly not by accident. This was an artificial island in an artificial body of water. The harbour was real, in a way; it had been a major heritage site on one of the first planets the Fortunate had conquered, and the Patriarch's predecessor had ordered it to be removed, stone by stone, and re-erected complete with the original boats. The operation had displaced the original inhabitants, of course, but there were only a few thousand of them, so that was practically a bargain.

Garamende's estate occupied the highest terrace. Alameche had been there before, but not for several years. It had been extended since he last saw it. Considerably. He pointed at the fish ponds, which were many tens of metres above natural sea level. 'How often do you have to restock these?'

'It depends.' Garamende squinted at the water. 'Some of the big eels will outlive all of us. Fifty, a hundred years. That one, there – I think she's almost a hundred and fifty. Others, like – wait a moment. Ah, yes. Those!' He pointed. 'The little blue spidery things. See?'

Alameche nodded.

'Well, *those* are prey for the green ones with lots of claws. And *they* are prey for those long thin fish with extra fins. And *those* are what the eels eat, mostly.'

'I see.' Alameche looked at the ponds, and then at the flight of wooden stairs that led up to them. He couldn't see any other way of getting there. 'So every day you have to bring how much up here?'

Garamende scratched his head. 'Well, in terms of biomass, maybe fifty kilos. But with the added water, about five tonnes, I suppose. Keeps the staff fit.'

'I expect so.' Alameche looked along the row of ponds. 'Are they all the same?'

The big man nodded. 'All except the last one.' He pointed towards the end of the terrace. 'I'll show you that one later, if you like. Care for a drink?'

The terrace was decked with dark, slightly rough timber. Halfway along, a slim walkway extended outwards at right angles. There were no guard rails, and Alameche walked carefully, his eyes straight ahead. After fifty paces over nothing it broadened into a round platform just big enough for a couple of couches and a low table.

Garamende dropped on to one of the couches, and gestured at the other. 'Have a seat, old friend.' He studied Alameche's face. 'You look terrified.'

Alameche smiled. In the back of his mind was the thought that he didn't need to play this game. He could probably have Garamende executed within twenty-four hours on any one of a thousand pretexts. The man was wealthy and socially influential but he was not part of the Cabinet circle, and he made enemies as readily as friends.

Probably wasn't good enough. He sat down. There were drinks on the table, but he ignored them. 'What's on your mind?' he said. He paused, and added, 'Old friend?'

The big man grinned, picked up a goblet, and drained it. 'Rumours,' he said. 'Before I go on, let me assure you that as far as I am aware we are alone. Can you give me the same assurance?'

Alameche shrugged. 'As far as I am aware, yes,' he said. 'Does it matter? Were you planning to say anything compromising?'

Garamende laughed softly. 'Every time I open my mouth, you know that.' He put down the empty goblet. 'But even so, I have to ask. You see,' and he leaned forward, 'one of the rumours is that you might have a little pet.'

'Really? What sort?' Alameche kept his voice level.

'The sort that floats around listening to people.' Garamende was watching him steadily.

Alameche shook his head. 'I have no pets,' he said truthfully. 'Why don't you tell me about some more rumours?'

'Very well.' Garamende refilled his goblet from a tall jug. He waggled the jug at Alameche, who shook his head. 'As you please. Yes. Rumours. Tell me again what you think about our Leader's speech the other night?'

Alameche studied his hands for a moment. Then he smiled a little. 'You asked me about it at the time. You'll hear nothing different now. Why?'

'Because everyone's talking about it, although possibly not in your hearing. Want to know what they're saying?'

'If you want to tell me.'

'Bollocks!' Garamende slapped the goblet down, raising a shower of droplets. They smelled of tar. 'Stop playing fucking games. Want doesn't come into it. I'm going to tell you because I think you ought to know. And as a result I'm probably going to end the week wearing my own arsehole as a necklace.' He blew out his cheeks. 'Here we go. A few people think he must know something they don't, whether it's a new alliance or some sort of super-weapon. They also say that if he knows, you know. Most of 'em think you probably knew first, and that this pet you say you haven't got has something to do with it.'

Alameche nodded. 'Do you agree with them?'

The big man looked at him for a long time. 'Not sure,' he said eventually. 'But whether I do or not, there's the other opinion.'

'And that is?'

There was another pause. Then Garamende spoke, slowly and quietly. 'That he's lost his marbles and has therefore become a problem.'

'Ah. And which do you believe?'

'Well, now, there's the thing.' Garamende picked up his goblet, inclined it slightly towards his nose and wobbled it so that the drink swirled. Then he put it down again, gently this time, and looked up at Alameche. 'I'm not sure it's a case of either or. What if your master is indeed a lunatic *and* he really is in charge of something powerful?' He shook his head. 'Bloody awkward for you.'

'Why?' In his own ears, Alameche's voice sounded dead steady.

'Get a grip, man. You're his creature, and in some ways he's yours. Push comes to shove, if he falls you fall with him. Of course,' and he picked up his drink again, 'that's always assuming you wait until he falls. Cheers.' He upended the goblet.

Alameche stared out over the bay. The two main suns were down now. Only the dusty little disc of the Joker still rode low in the sky. If he tried hard, he could convince himself that a smudge of light on the horizon, right at the edge of his vision, was the Citadel.

He turned back to Garamende. 'Is there any danger of a fall, then?'

'That depends.' Garamende leaned back in his seat and stretched. 'On various things. You, for a start, and whoever you're talking to. Don't bother denying it, man. I might not be a member of the Cabinet but I'm not blind. And, of course, on other people.'

'You know these people, do you?' Alameche realized he had snapped out the words. He breathed out carefully, and added in a softer voice, 'Because if you do, you're not far from having to pick sides. How far do you trust them?'

'Trust? Ha!' Garamende's belly shook. 'I'd sooner trust my dick to write letters.' He stood up. 'Come on. I never showed you that last fish pond.'

He turned and stamped along the narrow walkway back to the terrace. Alameche stood up to follow him and almost fell. He was swaying. For a moment he thought his legs were unsteady. Then he realized. It wasn't him; the walkway was swinging a little under Garamende's weight. He shook his head and followed.

The fish ponds were strung out in a line along the edge of the terrace. They were recessed into the stone so that their edges were flush, and each one was about ten paces square. As he passed each one, Garamende listed the species it contained, although to Alameche they all looked the same – eels, and smaller fish, and crawling, darting things that existed only to be eaten, that were replenished at the rate of tonnes per week by unshod slaves whose bare feet had stained the terrace with sweat and the occasional darker smear that Alameche assumed was blood. The surfaces of the ponds flashed green under the dim Jokerlight.

Except for the last one.

'What's this?' Alameche knelt by the pond. The water was a slick-looking pinkish blue, dead smooth apart from the occasional patch of shifting foam. He reached out his hand.

'No!' Garamende's voice was sharp.

Alameche sat back on his heels. 'What?' he said.

'Don't touch.' Garamende knelt down next to him, but a little further from the water. Something about his posture made Alameche inch backwards. 'Why?' he asked.

'You'll break the oil layer.' The big man looked at him seriously. 'The oil layer stops them smelling you. Break it and they'll get your scent, and once they've done that they'll have you.' He stood up and felt in a pocket. 'Look, I'll show you. But for fuck's sake stand back. And take this.' It was a smooth pebble. 'When I say, and not before, lob this into the middle of the pond.'

Alameche took the pebble. 'What are you going to do?'

'Feed the buggers.' Garamende reached into his other pocket and brought out a handful of something that struggled against his grip. He held it out towards Alameche, who could only see a mass of writhing fur. 'Sand rats, see? Ideal snack. Ready? Now!' He threw the little creatures up into the air above the pond. Alameche tossed the pebble into the centre. It plopped through the oily surface and sank.

The pond erupted. A forest of tiny, sleek, golden, dart-shaped bodies flashed up into the air, meeting the falling rats like missiles.

Right at the upper edge of hearing, there was a tiny, terrible, composite scream. Alameche covered his ears. Then the mass of bodies fell into the pond, the thick oil rippled and lapped back over the surface, and there was silence.

Alameche looked at Garamende. 'What are they?' he asked carefully.

For once Garamende didn't grin. 'On their home planet they're just called the Nightmare,' he said. 'Half fish, half insect. They've got these hooked mouth parts. Once they've got them in you, they shoot stomach acid into the wound. Speeds up digestion, the scientists say.' He looked at Alameche and shrugged. 'Don't look at me like that, man. I didn't invent 'em, any more than you invented acid baths. But I can use 'em.' He reached out and put a hand on Alameche's shoulder. 'That's what I know about trust, you see? It needs backup.'

Alameche nodded. 'I see,' he said, eventually. 'You confide in me, and I seem to have all my skin. This is trust?'

Now Garamende did grin. 'Oh, I think you and I are above all that.' The grin widened, so that his teeth glinted yellow in the Jokerlight. 'Long may it last. Eh?'

Alameche opened his own mouth to reply, but he was cut off by loud shouts from further along the terrace. Garamende looked round. 'Ah,' he said. 'The rest of the party. Come on.' He paused, and looked worried. 'I hope you like fish?'

Fish was one way of putting it.

'Three . . . two . . . one . . . *now!*'

The partition between the two tanks slammed open.

Alameche felt an elbow dig into his ribs. He looked round, and saw Garamende leaning towards him. The big man put his mouth against Alameche's ear and shouted over the noise of the crowd. 'Word to the wise, man. Put your money on the green.'

'Really?' Alameche looked towards the tanks, where two bow-wave ripples were converging. 'The black one is far bigger.'

'Bigger? What the fuck does that have to do with it? Look; see?'

There was a moan from the crowd. The two huge eels clashed, wrapping around each other and spinning in a blurred knot of muscle and a fountain of water. Droplets splashed on to the table in front of Alameche, staining the white surface with pink spots. He frowned, looking close, then relaxed. The blood seemed to have missed his plate.

As fast as they had met, the two eels separated. They began

circling warily. Red threads wisped away from the head of the black one and were mopped up by the little floating filter-globes that kept the water clear enough for the spectators to see.

Garamende nudged him again. 'See? Green! That beast was old and wily in my father's day. She had her first full circle a century ago! Get your bets in, man.'

Alameche nodded, and waved at one of the hovering accountants.

The Great Eel was a genuine native of Taussich as far as anyone could tell, which made it unusual enough to begin with. It was powerful, aggressive and very long-lived, but what made it truly unique was the fact that it grew one set of two hundred and thirteen teeth for life, and they were made of silicates. Very durable, and above all very sharp.

The outcome was inevitable. For thousands of years, Great Eels had been bred and selected for their fighting abilities. They used their armoured heads as clubs, their muscular, prehensile tails as whips and their whole bodies as constrictors, generally fighting to the death. It was a tradition that the teeth of the losing eel would be extracted and implanted in circles around the head or the tail of the winner.

A successful fighter might accumulate ten or twenty full circles of lethal teeth around each end of its sinuous body during a career which could easily last a century. The green eel had so many that Alameche couldn't count them.

The accountant had made it through the crowd. He bowed slightly. Alameche gave his instructions and then, when the man raised his eyebrows, repeated them tersely. The man blanched and hurried away. Alameche saw him draw several similar-looking men into a huddle. It probably wouldn't take long for them to sort it out. He waited.

Smoke was drifting over the ponds. Somewhere behind them, long fire pits had been lit. The losing eels would be eaten later. It would be an expensive meal, for someone: Alameche had heard that a good Great Eel could be worth the value of a country estate.

Yes. Money. He caught the eye of the accountant, who nodded. Now it was just a matter of wait and see.

The crowd surrounded the ponds. Garamende had thrown the eel fight open to all comers – although 'all comers' up here still meant a select group. The front row sat in recliners, tilted a little forwards so they had a good view down into the water.

The recliner next to Alameche creaked as its occupant shifted. He was a fat, pasty man whom Alameche recognized vaguely. The man leaned towards him. 'Hodil, my Lord. A privilege to meet again.'

Even at this range and with the smoke for competition, Alameche could smell the man's sweat – a sour, unhealthy, fearful smell. The smell rather than the name triggered his memory: Hodil had been a minor courtier, dismissed for some equally minor fault. He nodded, and then pointed at the pond. 'Have you bet?'

Hodil shook his head, making his chins wobble. 'Not yet,' he said. 'I am uncertain, to be frank. I believe I saw you place a wager, Lord. Can you advise me?'

Alameche leaned closer. 'Wiser heads than mine recommended the green,' he said. Then he pulled his head back before he had to inhale.

Hodil's eyes widened. Then he nodded vigorously. 'Thank you, Lord! I will take your advice. If I can find . . .' He faltered, looked around, and then brightened. 'Ah! Here, sir!'

Alameche followed the man's gaze and saw an accountant walking towards them. He thought the man looked less than enthusiastic.

He became aware of Garamende, leaning towards him again. He turned, matching the lean.

'Our friend Hodil is heavily mortgaged, and the accountants know it.' Garamende paused to smile at some new arrivals. 'A single unfortunate investment could put him beyond the reach of rescue.'

Alameche raised his eyebrows. 'Indeed? Well, well.' He turned to watch as the accountant approached Hodil. Certainly the transaction seemed to take longer than necessary; Hodil was animated, his porcine body seeming to lift out of the recliner as he tried to reinforce his point, whereas the accountant seemed unmovable. Alameche made up his mind. He reached out and tapped the accountant on the shoulder. 'Excuse me?'

The accountant turned, began to scowl, blinked, and then bowed.

Alameche waved him up. 'The gentleman there?' He indicated Hodil. 'You may accept his business with confidence.' He watched long enough to see Hodil's face light up, while the accountant's fell. Then he turned away, and stared at the pond.

The two vast fish – he supposed eels *were* fish – were still circling, in a kind of dance that looked unpleasantly erotic. The crowd was getting impatient; someone threw a coin into the water. There was laughter, and more followed.

Then the green eel – erupted. *There was no other word for it*, thought Alameche. The creature's body lashed like a severed cable and lifted its whole length out of the water in a boil of foam, curling as it did so into an upturned crescent with its tail poised at the highest point and its head almost in the water. The laughter stopped, and was replaced by a collective intake of breath.

For a moment the eel seemed to hang in the air. Then its head and the front third of its body fell back into the water, and its rear half cracked with the force of a braided steel whip.

The jewelled tail struck the water immediately above the head of the black eel with an impact that Alameche felt in his chest. It was a beautiful, stunning, lethal *coup de grâce* that threw up white waves in the pond and soaked the onlookers.

They stood up and began to applaud, and Hodil gave a cry of delight.

Then they fell silent. The waves were clearing, but the water in the pond was still writhing like a boiling pot.

Somehow the intended victim had evaded the death blow, and now the two eels were entwined, turning over and over in a queasy pastiche of a lovers' knot. Where their bodies broke the surface they writhed with muscle, and the heads and tails flailed and thrashed. Alameche found himself perched on the edge of his seat, the breath harsh in his throat. Next to him, he could hear Hodil panting.

For a long moment the bodies rolled and plaited. Then one of them tensed and straightened, with the other wrapped round it in a constricting spiral. There was a gasp from the crowd. The eel that had straightened was the green. Its mouth, rising out of the water, was open in a rictus of angular teeth, and its eyes were bulging and wide.

There was a moment's silence. Then the crowd leapt to its feet. Alameche found himself joining them. After a moment he realized that there was a gap to one side of him. He looked down and saw Hodil slumped in his seat.

Garamende's elbow dug into his ribs. The fat man was grinning ruefully. 'Something of a reverse,' he said. 'Sorry about that. Did you lose much?'

Alameche shook his head. 'No. I won much.' He saw Garamende's eyes widen, and added, 'I am very bad at taking advice. Especially when it seems obvious. And besides, it may be useful.' He nodded towards Hodil.

'Ah.' Garamende raised an eyebrow. 'Perhaps you're right. Look,' and he pointed to an approaching group of accountants. 'They come, beaks open, seeking carrion.'

'Ah, yes.' Alameche studied the group for a moment. Then he leaned close to Garamende. 'I think I will watch their technique for a while. I might learn something.'

The other man laughed softly. 'You might learn all kinds of things, you old bastard. But by the end of the night I bet you'll have taught them something too.'

Alameche sat back. 'Perhaps. Let's see.'

Hodil hadn't tried to leave. He remained slumped in his recliner, one arm swinging listlessly. Alameche had half expected him to make an appeal, but he seemed beyond even that. Or possibly above it, in the end.

It was almost a generous thought. He silenced it, laughing inwardly at himself. Then he watched.

The group closed around Hodil. Alameche could see nothing but turned backs, but even those were radiating trouble. The conversation, if that was the right word, went on for a long while. Every now and then the bodies shifted and he caught a brief glimpse of Hodil. He was generally making a resigned gesture.

Then the conversation came to an abrupt halt. The ring of accountants stood up all at once and backed away, leaving one standing in front of Hodil. He had something that looked like a genuine antique piece of paper in his hand, and he held it out in front of him as if he was about to read a proclamation.

'The Honourable His Grace the Duke Verrasetes Prisp of the Tribe Hodil! You are declared in default of debt, to the extent of seventy-four million standard on this instance. Other instances are noted.' The man cleared his throat. 'By statute here writ, your estates, goods and titles are held forfeit . . .'

Alameche felt Garamende's elbow in his ribs. He raised an eyebrow.

Garamende's voice was a hiss. 'Hell's ring-piece, man, what are you waiting for? That's a pre-packaged wrap-up. If he gets to the end of that little speech old Hodil's estate will be entwined in the Defaulters Court until his grandchildren are dead of the pox. Speak up, or there'll be nothing left to speak for.'

Alameche nodded. He turned towards the declaiming accountant. 'Ah, excuse me?'

The man lowered his paper. 'My Lord?' His voice was testy, and Alameche made a note to find out his name.

'My apologies,' he said. 'It had slipped my mind that My Lord Hodil and I were betting in tandem.' He waved a hand. 'Use my account.'

'Indeed, my Lord.' The man looked flustered. 'Excuse me. I will need to confirm . . .'

'Of course you will.' Alameche looked away.

It didn't take long. There was a hurried conversation among the accountants. Then the one with the paper turned back and held it out to Alameche. 'My Lord? The debt is transferred.'

Alameche took the paper and nodded. 'Thank you,' he said. 'No doubt you are busy?'

The man flushed and bowed himself away. Hodil watched him go, and then turned to Alameche, his face even paler. He gripped the arms of his recliner and rocked backwards and forwards until he had enough speed to stand up. His loose robes hung damply on his vast body, making him look like a sack. He gave a quick, nodding bow. 'My thanks, Lord. You have saved me.'

'Indeed?' Alameche allowed himself a smile. 'Well, I am sure you will find some way to return the favour. Shall we walk?'

'Of course.' The man was trembling. Alameche wasn't surprised.

Handlers had gathered round the pool to net the stricken eel, which was still writhing erratically. Alameche and Hodil threaded through the watching crowds and strolled along the terrace. Away from the fight pond it was quiet, and the evening air was warm and smoky. To Alameche's relief there was a slight on-shore breeze; he took care to stay upwind of Hodil.

They walked in silence for a while. Then Hodil cleared his throat. 'Ah, you mentioned returning the favour . . .'

'Yes?'

'May I ask, Lord . . . do you have anything in mind?' Hodil looked down at his sweat-stained robes, and then back up at Alameche. He shrugged. 'As you know I have little, and my position at Court is sadly reduced.'

'I know.' Alameche smiled at the man. Then he looked down. They were passing one of the ponds. He gestured at it. 'The eels in there – will they fight today?'

Hodil followed his gaze. He shook his head. 'No, Lord. Those are merely pets, not champions.'

Alameche watched them for a while. There were two circling the pond in opposite directions, staying close to the walls and passing each other only a few hand's breadths apart. 'They look nervous,' he said, and nodded back towards the fight ponds. 'Perhaps they know something's going on.'

Hodil nodded. 'Very likely. They are sensitive creatures. They have excellent hearing.'

'Ah, yes.' Alameche turned to face the other man. 'Hodil,' he said quietly, 'I suspect that you also have good hearing. *Is* something going on?'

Hodil looked at him steadily. 'You are not speaking of eels, Lord.'

'No, I'm not.' Alameche stared out to sea for a moment. It was dusk, and the few boats that were still away from their moorings were carrying coloured riding lamps that left dotted trails of light across the tops of the shallow waves. From time to time they blurred a little, as if some disturbance in the air had obscured them for a second.

He was tired, that was the problem. He shook his head and turned back to Hodil. 'You were at the Games?'

'Of course.' The man seemed to swell, if that were possible. 'A superb spectacle.'

'Did anything strike you?'

'About what, Lord?' The face screamed innocent

incomprehension, but the eyes were everywhere and the sweat smell, which was now strong enough to be offensive even with the wind against it, had the tinge of terror.

Alameche almost felt sorry for the man. Almost. He reached out and patted him on the shoulder, suppressing a wince at the clamminess of the material under his hand. 'Come on, Hodil. Talk to me. Tell me what people are talking about. Tell me, even more, what you think they are *not* talking about.' He patted the shoulder again, noting that it had become wetter even as he spoke. Then he added, as if he had just thought of it, 'Or, if you'd rather keep your counsel we could walk along to the end of the ponds. You know? Where our host Garamende keeps his special . . . pets. Has he shown you?'

Hodil shuddered. 'Yes, he has.' His eyes flicked down for a moment. Then he sighed heavily. 'Very well.' He glanced at the eel pond, and added, 'But please let us get away from these *ghastly* fucking fish.'

On the landward side of the terrace the ground stepped up yet further towards Garamende's house. A spindly timber ramp wandered up the slope through stands of dense, rather spiky-looking dark green bushes. About halfway up, the ramp turned abruptly through a right angle and opened into a sort of landing half a dozen paces across. It stuck out over a steep part of the slope. Hodil lumbered on to it, panting, and leaned on the seaward rail. 'This will do,' he said, and blew out his cheeks. 'I hope.'

Alameche looked around. 'Do you fear being overheard?'

Hodil laughed. 'Very much, but mainly by you.' He laughed again, tailing off in a wheeze, and then fell silent.

Alameche waited.

Eventually Hodil pushed himself away from the rail and turned round. 'As you have bought me, I had better deliver payment. The Games, then.' He shook his head. 'What possessed the Patriarch? The ambition he showed is beyond anything we could dream of. Even before the Games people were whispering that we are over-extended, that the taking of Silthx was a jump too far.'

'Were they? What else?'

'That he is a liability. That he draws attention to us. That he endangers us. Perhaps even that he is in thrall to a foreign power. They talk of two options.' Hodil stood up a little straighter. 'One, that the Patriarch must go, however that can be attained, and replaced by you. Or, that you must both go.'

Alameche nodded. 'Just those? Does no one expect His Excellency to stay?'

'Everyone expects him to try. But nobody expects him to succeed.' Hodil smiled a little. 'The view seems to be that you can light his funeral pyre, Lord – or die on it.'

'I see.' Alameche found himself drumming his fingers. He stilled them. 'I'll need names, Hodil.'

'I am sorry, Lord.' The man drew himself up. 'I won't say them.'

'Oh, you will.' Alameche took a handful of Hodil's robes, clenching them hard enough that he actually felt a trickle of perspiration squeeze out of them and run down his wrist. The sensation and the reek of the man almost made him retch, but he suppressed the urge and pulled Hodil close to him. 'You can give them to me now,' he said quietly, 'or you can scream them in the ear of the Carnifex in a few hours, but either way I will have them.'

Hodil's face had turned a sickly yellow, but he shook his head quickly. Alameche opened his hand, and Hodil tottered backwards until he bumped into the rail. Then he collapsed into an untidy sitting position. Without taking his eyes off the man, Alameche raised his voice. 'Kestus!'

There was a pause, and then footsteps behind him, and then the security chief was at his elbow. 'Yes, Lord?'

'You heard that?'

Kestus nodded.

'Good. Take this,' and he kicked Hodil, 'to the Chambers. And summon the Carnifex. Only him! Tell no one else.' He kicked Hodil again, making him moan a little. 'Names, Kestus. I want names.'

The losing eel was spitted, still alive, along its whole length on a straight limb of copperwood that had been soaked in spiced vinegar. It had taken seventeen men to hold the creature as the spit was pushed through, and even after the wood had broken out just short of the jewelled tail the spasms of the eel's muscles still caused it to arch like a bow.

The crowd had applauded. The movements hadn't stopped until the eel's skin had begun to blister over the coals.

Alameche had to admit that the flavour was good. He turned to Garamende. 'Do they always taste like this?'

'I suppose.' They were lying on couches at the most seaward end of the terrace. Garamende eased his bulk around until he was facing Alameche. 'I always eat 'em fresh from the fight, mind. It's supposed to improve the flavour. I'm not sure what they'd taste like from rest.'

'But you only eat the losers?'

Garamende looked at him as if he was mad. 'Well, obviously. Why would I eat a winner? That's a damn expensive habit.'

'I know.' Alameche put down his plate. 'I suppose the real skill lies in working out the exact moment at which a winner is about to become a loser.' He looked up at Garamende. 'That would be the right time to eat him. Don't you think?'

They looked at each other for a long time. Eventually Garamende nodded slowly. 'It would,' he said. 'But knowing the right moment – that would be a trick. Have you any idea how you would do it?'

Alameche frowned and shook his head slightly. 'Of course not. You forget. I know nothing about eels.'

'Yes. Eels. Of course.' Garamende grinned. 'Drink has clouded my head. But they are sweet clouds. Hey!' He waved to a servant. 'Wine over here!'

They drank the wine while the cooking fires sank behind them and a cold salt air rose off the sea. Eventually Garamende shivered. 'Come on,' he said. 'I'm tired of freezing my dick off out here. Indoors for me, and something to smoke. And, perhaps, something more entertaining to do with said dick, when it has thawed.'

Alameche grimaced. 'Forgive me. I won't be taking part.'

'Of course not. You are made of stone, people say. Any news of Hodil?'

Alameche shook his head. 'They won't have arrived yet. Three hours, at least, before they make a start.'

'Yes, I suppose so.' Garamende stood up and stretched. 'An uncharacteristic outburst of bravery on his part.'

Alameche looked at him for a moment. The round face was unreadable. He shrugged. 'It won't last. It never does.'

They walked up towards the house. As they passed the fire pits Garamende turned and flicked the dregs of his wine on to the coals. They sputtered and flared for a moment, and a puff of steamy smoke gathered above the spit. Alameche glanced at it, and then looked again. Definitely tired. He shook his head and followed Garamende towards the lights of the house.

It had probably been the breeze, but just for a moment he thought the smoke had parted as if it had risen around some invisible object.

Alameche blinked, and sat up. The room was light, but not with sunlight, and someone had said his name. He looked round, and felt his head spin. Not asleep long enough to have metabolized everything, then.

'Alameche! Please!'

He shut his eyes, took a deep breath and opened them in time

194

to see Garamende reaching for his shoulder. He stretched out an arm and deflected the hand. 'What is it?'

'You need to come. Sorry.' Garamende ran a hand through his hair. 'It's Hodil.'

Alameche felt sleep leave him in a stampede. He sat bolt upright. 'Has he talked?'

Garamende shrugged. 'That's the problem. Look, come *on*, will you?' He pointed towards the door. 'I've got transport waiting.'

'*What?*'

Transport turned out to be a four-seat gyro. It was incredibly noisy; the wide flat rotors hammered at the air like some sort of power tool. Alameche had leaned forward as far as he dared. Garamende, in the front pair of seats next to the pilot, leaned back and shouted. 'I *said*, that's where they found the wreck. At the base of those cliffs, see?'

Alameche craned his neck. If he stared hard he could see, just about. Waves sucked and boiled at a clump of fallen rocks and at the bones of something that might have been a gyro like the one he was in, before whatever had happened had happened.

He turned to Garamende and shouted, 'Accident?'

Garamende shook his head. 'Don't think so.' He slapped the pilot on the shoulder and, when the man turned to him, shouted something which looked like an order. The pilot nodded and the gyro heeled off on to a new course and tilted forwards under power.

Alameche sat back and waited. With any luck his head would have sorted itself out by the time they got there. Wherever 'there' was.

In fact it was a nondescript building at the far outskirts of Garamende's estate. Within the building was a plain, window-less room with nothing written on the door, and within the room was a stretcher, and on the stretcher was a corpulent body draped in the shredded, blood-soaked remains of white robes.

They stood, looking at it. For a while no one spoke. Then Alameche said: 'He was questioned.'

Garamende nodded. 'No doubt of that. Look at the state of him. A Carnifex has been busy, right enough.'

'But not by us?'

'No. They never got anywhere near the Citadel. They couldn't have done. There wasn't time.'

'Hm. So where did they go?' Alameche prodded the body. The robe shifted, revealing a series of elaborate surface wounds. He studied them. 'Did he die under torture?'

Garamende shook his head. 'My surgeon says not. He, ah, has some expertise. He thinks he was alive when the Carnifex had done with him.'

'So he may have talked.'

'Almost certainly. His new-found bravery didn't last long enough to be fatal.'

'Yes. But it wasn't us he talked to.' Alameche compressed his lips. 'How is Kestus?'

'In a coma. Head trauma, from the crash.' Garamende sighed. 'He's a long way from telling us what happened. If he ever can.'

'Yes. The crash.' Alameche gave the body another prod. 'Definitely not an accident, then?'

Garamende snorted. 'I doubt it very much.'

'So do I.' Alameche's prodding had disarranged the remains of Hodil's robes. He straightened them, and then turned to Garamende. 'So if it wasn't an accident, it was on purpose. Which means that it *had* a purpose.' He paused. 'Which means that your estate is under quarantine.'

'What?' Garamende raised his eyebrows. 'I thought we trusted each other.'

Alameche smiled. 'I'm sure you did. But I'm as bad at trusting people as I am at taking advice.' He shrugged. 'Did you really think those rumours were new to me? The state is practically made of rumours. I'm more worried when they go quiet. But this? This is new. Someone has gone to war with me.'

'So what? You're used to war. Fuck it, man, you exist to go to war!'

'Maybe.' Alameche stared at Garamende, who met his stare without flinching. 'But this one started on your land. You can tell everyone from me that if I'm to go to war, whatever the cause – I'll choose the time and place.' He reached out, patted Garamende on the shoulder. 'Old friend.'

Tail End Port, Catastrophe

Fleare lay back in the steaming mud. She was too buoyant to stay immersed without help. Every few minutes, her slow upward float brought too much of her body out into the open, and she had to reach out to the twisted cables that ran between the lines of heavy mud buoys and shove herself under again.

The Great Mud Plain was the other end of the phenomenon that was Fusion Field. The point where the glacially slow lava field hit the bottom of its own cliff marked the boundary of the jurisdiction of Tail End Port. Just inside it, a wide crescent-shaped sweep of ancient river deposits had been heated and moistened by magmatic waters until they had become a chain of mud holes, separated by sinuous mineral-rich walls and punctuated by geysers. Those closest to the cliff were hot enough to parboil human flesh in seconds, but things got cooler further away. By the time the mud lapped against the margins of the Port City itself it was no hotter than a steam bath, albeit one too thick to swim in and too soggy to walk on. The hot, wet air rising from the slithering mud gave the edge of the city a tropical microclimate complete with some exotic plant and animal life, including the biggest dragonflies Fleare had ever seen. They were everywhere, hovering a hand's breadth above the mud in hissing shining flocks, and no two seemed to be the same colour.

Her recollections of the time since they had been arrested were episodic. She had woken, briefly, on a Port Authority transport; then in an all-night courtroom; and then in a prison cell. Each time she had been aware of Jez somewhere in the background. Mostly she had been shouting.

No one seemed to know what had happened to Muz.

Her most recent waking had begun three hours ago in the bright white room in the Medical Centre. She was pain-free, but the Port's duty medic hadn't been able to guarantee how long that would last.

'Something is causing the adapted elements of your system to denature.' The medic studied a row of sample vials. 'You've got four different broad categories of non-original fibre. They're all going, at different rates. Have you been exposed to anything recently? It would probably have taken a skin puncture.'

Fleare stared at her for a moment, and then nodded slowly. 'Can you stop it?'

The medic pursed her lips. 'No,' she said. 'I don't think so. I don't have the key.' Fleare's incomprehension must have shown; the woman went on: 'Your modifications have a viral root. It's keyed to your genome, so it will only grow in your cells. It's a fail-safe, to stop the modifications becoming epidemic.' She smiled apologetically, deepening the wrinkles around her mouth so that Fleare wondered how old she was. 'I used to work on this stuff.'

Fleare smiled back. 'So, you're an expert. What do we do?'

The smile faded, leaving the woman looking even older. 'Take it easy. Pain relief.' She spread her arms. 'That's it.'

Fleare was lying on a couch. She raised herself on her elbows. 'Just take it easy? Is that all? For how long?'

The medic stood up, and walked over to the couch. 'Maybe they didn't explain when you got modified,' she said. 'They should have done. That new material in you? Muscle fibres, some arterial wall, nerves, parts of your bone cells? They aren't additions. They're replacements.' She looked straight at Fleare. 'You don't have the originals any more.'

Fleare felt as if she was falling. She lowered herself back on to the couch. 'So when they go,' she said, and then stopped, trying to remember anything at all about what she had been told. She couldn't. *I dumped Muz*, she thought. *Then I signed up. Listening wasn't involved.*

After a while she shook her head. 'Okay, I get it,' she said quietly. She swung herself off the couch, daring her body to hurt. It didn't. She reached out a hand; the medic shook it. Fleare began to turn away. Then she thought of something. 'You need some sort of key to stop this,' she said. 'Does that mean it needed the same key to start it?'

The medic nodded. 'Someone knows you too well,' she said. Then she turned away. It felt like being switched off.

Jez was waiting outside the med suite. She jumped up as Fleare came out. 'Well?'

Fleare shook her head. 'She says to rest.' *Which was true*, she thought. She didn't feel ready to confront the other part, not yet. 'Did Kelk get finished with the court?'

Jez grinned. 'Yeah. They set bail at a hundred mil. Kelk paid up on the spot. You should have seen their faces.'

'Any sign of Muz?'

Jez shook her head, her lips compressed. She took Fleare by the shoulder and steered her off. 'Come on. Let's start the resting.'

The search for rest had taken them to the Mud Resort. Now Fleare turned over lazily, feeling the hot mud sucking and sliding over her. The change in position brought Kelk into view. He was waist-deep in the mud, his upper body fitted between the widely splayed float-roots of an immature Signal Tree. He had a plain grey ring on his middle finger, and now and then he twisted it distractedly. Fleare didn't remember seeing it before. It suited him, she decided. Jez was further along one of the roots, submerged except for her head.

The sun was sinking, and the surface of the mud was beginning to glisten with the mixed bluish light of the overhead space trash, accented by the low-angle red glow from the lava wall. Kelk's tree was throwing a long blue shadow across a field of purple. The mud seemed to soften his voice.

It appeared he had been busier than Jezerey had realized.

'It was the end of the war. Muz was still in his jar and Fle had just been hauled off to the Monastery. Jez and I were stuck on that fucking ice planet with nothing to do but think. So I thought.' He shrugged. 'Once I'd started thinking I couldn't stop.'

Jezerey looked at him. 'I know what you thought,' she said. 'You thought we'd been betrayed.'

'Yeah. Someone inside Soc O.' He held her eyes for a moment, and then looked away. 'And you didn't.'

'No, I didn't. Never mind, we've done that one.'

'So we have.' He was quiet for a moment and his fingers caressed the ring again. 'Well, then they announced the amnesty. Just like that. Free to go and make a wonderful new life. Jezerey headed off to be a shipping tycoon. I had a lot of big drinks, hitched a few rides, more or less woke up in the Curve.' He took a deep breath. 'And I found something.'

Fleare looked at him. 'A traitor?'

'No. Not yet, anyway. I got distracted. The Curve does that.' He looked round at them. 'Ever think what it means, the Curve being where it is?'

Jezerey shook her head. 'Trade,' she said. 'We know that, Kelk. So?'

He grinned. 'Half right, but not the good half. If you want to trade you have to pass information, but the Cordern is in quarantine as far as everyone else is concerned. Most people never think about it, but that's where the Curve makes its money. It's the biggest firewall in the Spin. And the most important thing about firewalls is that they are full of all the really interesting data. It occurred to me that while I went traitor hunting, I could make some money on the side. So I went into business, data mining.'

'I begin to see.' Jezerey gave a lopsided smile. 'This business. Did it have anything to do with those two women on the airship?'

'Yeah.'

'And Fleare?'

'Not to start with. I guess you got bolted on afterwards, Fle. You were probably seen on the way through Thale, or somewhere. After that it can't have been hard to work out who you'd be looking for.' Kelk ran a hand through his hair. 'You got any ideas who might want to shoot you?'

Someone who knows me too well, she thought. *Very few options there.* She shook her head and kept her mouth closed. Kelk watched her for a while, until she felt uncomfortable and looked away.

Jezerey patted her shoulder. 'Hopefully the doc was right and it wasn't anything. But Kelk, you haven't finished explaining your own stuff. Tell us straight: have you pissed off a gangster?'

'No. Well, not exactly.' Kelk looked uncomfortable. 'Actually I think I may have pissed off three. Plus the guys I won the money off, of course.'

Jezerey gave him a sour look. 'Can you un-piss them off somehow?'

'I doubt it.' Kelk's voice was flat. 'There's more. Like I said, I found something. I was just browsing, really. Down pretty deep, but still browsing. I found what I thought was an old cloud of servers. I nearly didn't check it out but then something spooked me and I had a better look. It wasn't an old cloud. It was a very new, very smart cloud trying not to look like it. And it was full of sims.'

'Really?'

'Yup. Hundreds of them, maybe thousands.' Kelk took a long breath, and let it out. 'Someone was running a whole pile of full civilizations in there. All different settings, stages, maturities. I went for the one with the deepest security, obviously.'

Fleare smiled a little. 'Obviously.'

'But why?' Jezerey began to heave herself out of the mud. It made a sucking noise; she grimaced. 'I mean, not why did you go snooping. Why was whoever it was running these things?'

'Why do you think?' Kelk gave a short laugh. 'Money, in the end. Some of it's research. Quasi-legitimate stuff, for university sociology departments, you know? Or grey-area modelling for governments. Some of it's just leisure. Whole dodgy universes where wealthy perverts can get their virtual rocks off. Ever heard of sim-fuckers?'

They nodded.

'Well, that's where they go to fuck. *But*, that wasn't the good bit. While I was checking out the security of this grey-area sim I found a back door, right at the base code level. I got interested, set a subroutine to watch it. And while it was watching, something went in.'

Jezerey had got enough of her torso out of the mud to be able to stretch. She pushed her arms out straight above her head, fingers interwoven. 'So what? Probably a sim-fucker. Or whatever.' She finished the stretch, turning it into a swatting gesture as one of the dragonflies whirred close to her face. 'You're losing my attention, is what I'm trying to say.'

'I noticed.' Kelk shook his head. 'It wasn't a sim-fucker. It was something much cleverer. It headed for a particular part of the sim, and it subverted it. It *hid* something.'

Jezerey swatted another fly. 'How can you hide something in a sim?'

'Easily, if it's simulated itself. It's like hiding a picture in a museum.'

Fleare glanced around. There was no one in sight, and the only sound was the almost subliminal whine of the dragonflies, but somehow that made her feel more exposed. 'Look, Kelk, should you be talking about this out here?'

'Why not?' He brushed one of the flies aside. 'I'm not giving anything away really.'

She frowned. 'All the same, if this stuff is important enough to get you in the sort of trouble you're in . . . ?'

'Nah, I'm not saying the sensitive bits. They're stored.' He grinned. 'Nice little nest egg.'

Fleare smiled back, but it felt forced. Something was definitely troubling her. She fretted for a moment, and then it occurred to her. 'Hey, guys,' she said, 'is this mud supposed to vibrate?'

Jez patted the surface. 'I can feel it too. Kind of humming.'

Then, with a hiss that became a deafening roar, the dragon-flies took off in a single, flashing, multicoloured cloud, and swooped away towards the shore.

Fleare hadn't realized how noisy they had been, until they were gone. She cleared her throat. 'Does that mean anything?'

'Yeah.' Kelk pointed towards the border. 'Look.'

She followed his gesture, and squinted. There was no way her eyes would enhance, but they didn't need to. She could see two bright dots. 'So, what are those?' she asked.

'Mudcats. Shit.' Something in Kelk's voice made Fleare look back at him, and she swallowed again. He looked scared. She couldn't remember seeing that before.

She tried to keep her voice calm. 'Is that bad?'

'Yep. They're the only way of travelling fast over this stuff. And, ah, most of the people who use them aren't official.' Kelk's voice was flat. 'I'm not sure who they are but I'm guessing this is Round Two. I'd really like to know how they found us so quickly.'

'Can we do anything?'

He shook his head. 'Not a thing. No point trying. Just keep

still. Stay in the lee of the trees. Whoever they are, I'm guessing they'll be after me, not you. They'll only look if you're obvious.' His voice left no room for doubt.

Jez was watching the two dots, which were already beginning not to be dots. 'Are those *skis*?'

Kelk nodded. 'Skis at the front, tracks at the back.' He pulled himself out of the mud and leaned against the trunk of the Signal Tree. 'They'll be here in a minute.'

Fleare bit her lip. 'Look, there must be something—'

'There isn't.' Kelk looked down at her and, to her amazement, grinned. 'This time it's your turn to stay behind and pick up the pieces, babe. Make sure you don't miss any.' He turned back towards the mudcats, waded towards them and stuck an arm in the air. 'Okay, shit-heads, come and get me!'

The two vehicles were closing very quickly. They were slowing now. From behind her tree Fleare could see the single, wide, flat track at the back, connected by a skeletal frame to two long, upward-curled skis. It made her think of a kneeling insect with swords for arms. Even the rattling buzz of the tracks sounded insectoid. They drew up by Kelk, their skis and tracks leaving complicated furrowed tracks that collapsed slowly. The mud stopped humming.

Open-sided two-person pods hung from the frames. The front seat of the nearest cat was occupied by a woman in what looked like vintage combat leathers. The rearward seat was empty. The woman lifted one hand off the controls, drew a short, jagged-bladed knife out of a pocket-holster and gestured with it towards the empty seat. Kelk shrugged, took a couple of ankle-deep steps through the mud and climbed awkwardly into the seat. The cat began to move. As it drew away Kelk turned towards Fleare, mouthed something, and then looked away.

Fleare kept her eyes on him until he was out of sight. He didn't look back again.

Jez had hauled herself upright against the Signal Tree. When the cats had disappeared she turned to Fleare. 'We can't, we really *cannot* just leave it at that,' she said.

'I guess not.' Fleare felt a flicker of pain in her arm. *Not now*, she thought. *Please, not now*. Out loud she said, 'Have you got any network?'

Jezerey half closed an eye. 'Yeah. I'll call the Port cops. I mean, shit, those guys have to be the easiest thing to track.'

Fleare nodded. The pain was growing, not the lightning shock she had felt on the Ground Engine but a slow, inexorably consuming ache that radiated from her arm into her torso, making her want to curl up and howl. 'When will they come?' she asked carefully. Then she collapsed, her teeth clamped in a snarl of pain, her hands clawing and grabbing at the mud where Kelk had been standing.

There was something small and hard beneath her fingers. She gripped it, closed her hand on it. She was still holding it when hands lifted her, and a stab in her upper arm became a spreading warmth. The feeling relaxed her a little and she raised her hand to her eyes and uncurled it.

The hard thing was the ring that Kelk had been twisting. *Pick up the pieces*, she thought. That was what he had mouthed. She slipped it muddily on to her own middle finger. Then the warmth reached her head, and everything faded.

When she woke she lay for a while without opening her eyes. Sight would have been one sensory input too many.

She was lying on a sort of couch with a loose cover over her. A quick audit of her body produced nothing much. She was tired with the sort of residual aches that could have come the day after a long run, and the tips of her fingers felt faintly fizzy. She had a slight headache, but again, nothing much. Then she reached into her mind for the virtual equivalent of a dashboard, a map of her body and its enhancements, and found nothing at all. Not even dormant or powered down. Just gone.

She opened her eyes. She had expected generic medical.

Instead she got some sort of oasis. It seemed familiar, and after a moment she placed it. She was back on the old Orbiter.

She sat up, and cleared her throat. 'Hello?'

'Ah! Welcome back.' It was Jezerey. 'How do you feel?'

'Okay, I guess.'

'More than you deserve. This started when you were shot, right? Why didn't you say something, you silly girl?'

Fleare smiled a little. 'Sorry.'

Jezerey sat down next to her and hugged her. 'No problem. We're just glad to have you back. We kept you under until we got well off planet. Muz thinks you're stable for the moment.'

'Muz?' Fleare jumped to her feet. 'Is he . . . ?'

'Yeah, he's back. He caught up with us at the spaceport. He's around somewhere.'

Fleare felt light-headed. 'Where? What happened to him?'

Jezerey smiled. 'I'll let him tell you. Listen, sit down.' She gave Fleare a gentle push, and Fleare allowed herself to sag backwards into the couch. 'You were out for a long time. Don't rush it.'

'I won't.' Fleare knitted her fingers together. Then she looked down at them. 'There was a ring,' she began. Then she remembered. 'Oh. Kelk. Jez, what . . . ?'

'I've got the ring.' Jezerey held it out. 'It was stuck on with dried mud. It's clean now.'

Fleare took it. It seemed natural to slip it on to her finger. 'What about Kelk?'

Jezerey shook her head. 'Nothing yet.'

'Did the Port cops trace those cat things?'

'Only to the boundary of the Port land. Outside that, there's only privateers. Muz hacked a couple of weather satellites and had a look, but the tracks just stopped dead in the middle of nowhere. Looks like they got lifted.' She shrugged. 'Sorry, Fle. Our shuttle hire was running out of time, people were asking questions and you were sedated – in the end we couldn't hang around any longer.'

Fleare nodded. 'Thanks,' she said. 'So, where did you say Muz was?'

'I'm here. Hi, Fle.' She turned and saw, not the cloud she was expecting, but the tight shiny globe she had last seen on the Ground Engine. She raised her eyebrows. 'Muz? You've changed.'

'Yeah. It's probably temporary.' The globe floated up to her, stopped, and gave a sideways waggle that looked like a shrug. 'Like it?'

'I guess.' She seemed to have a lump in her throat. She swallowed. 'It's really good to see you.'

'You too. Sorry I went missing.'

'What happened?' She held out a hand.

The globe hesitated, and then settled in her palm. 'Well, that last fragment was coming down like a fucking missile. I conned it into thinking it had impacted, fifty metres up. Huge air burst. I didn't have time to get out of the way. I got dispersed.'

Fleare frowned at the globe. 'Huh?'

'Blown halfway across the lava field.' It wobbled in her palm. 'I ended up being twenty klicks across. It took me a while to find all of myself. Then Tail End wouldn't let me into their air-space. After that I got fed up with being a cloud.' It rose from her palm to hover at eye level. 'Now, how are you doing?'

'Okay, I guess.' She shrugged. 'For a given value of okay. Jez said you thought I was stable?'

'As far as I can tell.' Another shrug-wobble. 'Those attacks you had were the new fibres pulling free. That should be over now.'

'And afterwards?' She wasn't sure she wanted to know the answer, but she knew she had to ask the question.

'Nothing fast. Look, Fle, you just woke up. Maybe you should eat something, get some rest . . .'

Fleare shook her head. 'Just tell me, will you?'

'Okay. Well, like I said, nothing fast. Slow muscle wasting. Weight loss. Poor coordination and balance. Probably over weeks, maybe months.'

'Right.' Fleare stood up and brushed her hands down the light shift. 'So, I'm going to die, slowly. Yes?'

Jez took her hands and squeezed them. 'No, you're not, because we're going to find a way to stop it. Right, Muz?'

'Yeah. Sorry, just a minute. Picking up some news; I'll put it on screen.' The globe dispersed, spread, and became a gauzy plane about a metre across. It fuzzed and then cleared to show a newsroom.

'. . . coming in that a body has been discovered on the out-skirts of Catastrophe. We have a report from Fessas an 'Galf. Sensitive viewers may want to look away; as for the rest of you, fill your boots, guys, it's a good one. Fess, what do you have for us?'

The screen flicked to a skinny male with purple-black skin. 'Well, this one is going to keep people talking for a long time. The body was found in three, that's right, *three* separate locations, all within the same part of Catastrophe, not far from the Trashwards airship landing station. And here's the thing, Vek. The body wasn't just in pieces, it was in mutilated pieces. We don't have many details but I'm told that it seemed almost as if it had been ransacked. Organs removed, muscles dissected. The security services aren't saying anything officially but in private I've been told they think the attackers were looking for something.'

'Two questions, Fess. Did they find it, and who was it?'

The skinny man smiled ruefully. 'Well, the answer to the first question is we don't know. But there might be an answer to the second. All three parts of the body gene-match to someone called Kelk vena Kelelal, and he is a truly interesting character.' The view switched, first to a head and shoulders shot of Kelk

209

that looked several years old, and then to three irregular lumps of something, set out on a low table.

For a horrified moment, Fleare thought it was a market stall. Then her stomach heaved. 'Muz,' she said unsteadily, 'stop it.'

The screen faded, collapsed and turned back into the globe, which dropped on to a low table, rolled a little way, and was still.

Jezerey let out a breath. 'Oh fuck,' she said.

There had been near silence on the old Orbiter for over twenty-four hours. Eventually Jezerey had broken it, by announcing that she wanted to head back to Thale for a while. 'I'm crap at mourning in company,' she said. 'And if I don't get back there soon I'm going to wind up bankrupt as well as miserable. I'll contact you again when I've fixed things up.'

They scanned around and found a ramshackle tramp freighter heading in roughly the right direction. The freighter sent an even more battered shuttle which bumped up against the Orbiter like a drunken lover. It was over an hour before Muz was satisfied that they had a halfway vacuum-tight seal. When he finally gave the go-ahead, Fleare followed Jezerey to the lock door. 'You going to be okay?' she asked.

Jezerey pulled a face. 'Listen to the girl. It wasn't me rolling around howling the other day.' She put down her carisak. 'I'm worried about you. Okay. But I'm not going to get anywhere by sitting in this floating wildlife park, staring at you and snivelling.' She palmed the contact that began the airlock sequence, and picked up the carisak. 'I know some people who might be able to help. I'm going to ask around.'

The airlock pinged. Jezerey slapped Fleare on the shoulder. 'I'll be in touch.' Then she wrinkled her nose. 'Oh, dear holy crap. What is *that*?'

An appalling blast of foetid air had rolled out of the airlock. Fleare grinned. 'I think it's your ride.'

'Fabulous.' Jezerey hefted the carisak. 'Well, as I said, I'll be in touch, *if* I don't asphyxiate.' She walked into the airlock and turned round. 'Take care of yourself, girl. The older I get, the less sure I am anyone else will do it for you.'

Fleare raised her eyebrows, but by the time she had opened her mouth the airlock had ground round into the closed position, and she could hear the air cycle hissing.

The air still smelled revolting. She pinched her nose and headed back to the habitat areas.

Muz joined her at the oasis. 'All okay?'

'Yeah. Not luxurious, maybe.' Fleare sat down on a log. She studied her hands. They looked a little wrinkled and a couple of her nails had ragged edges, she supposed from where she had clawed at the mud. The broad grey band sat neatly at the base of her middle finger, its weight tugging slightly. She fiddled with it for a moment. Then she came to a decision. She pulled. It baulked briefly at her knuckle before slipping off. She held it up, and took a breath.

'Muz,' she said slowly, 'I think this might be important.'

Privateer Orbiter, Catastrophe Curve

The old Orbiter trudged along the edge of the Catastrophe Curve, keeping more or less in the sensory shadow of the Trash Belt. Fleare was spending some time going through news sites, using a screener that the ship seemed to be able to synthesize out of vines and stuff in a blurry process her eyes couldn't follow.

She wasn't enjoying it.

It still seemed to be true. The gene match was confirmed. Now whole articles were springing up about Kelk's background. She had known about the mil stuff, obviously – the columnists were calling him 'part of the defeated communist insurgency', apart from a couple who preferred 'freedom fighter' – but she hadn't known about the rest of it. Some of it made her eyes widen.

Kelk had been orphaned at the age of four. His parents had been killed or enslaved, but probably killed anyway, by the Fortunate during one of their forays into the outer Cordern. The infant Kelk had survived for seventeen days in the wreckage of their settlement by foraging in garbage dumps and burned-out houses.

No wonder he never talked about it.

There was more, including a lot of speculation about who had killed him. Most people seemed to be assuming generic gang activity. Tail End was keeping quiet in public, but behind the scenes they were obviously going nuts at Catastrophe, accusing them of state-sponsored terrorism. The border was locked down and some lawyers had been hired.

Fleare was wanted for questioning. Jez wasn't, which presumably meant she would have an uninterrupted journey home. Muz wasn't mentioned.

She glanced towards the edge of the oasis. 'Muz? Have you seen this?'

'Just a minute.' Kelk's grey ring lay on a flat-topped rock with Muz floating above it. He had formed a fat, slightly diffuse toroid, which every now and then extended a translucent frond to caress the ring. Sometimes patterns flickered across his surface. Fleare didn't recognize them. She shook her head and waited.

'There; done, for the moment.' The last frond withdrew, and the toroid collapsed back into a shiny sphere with an almost audible snap. It bobbed up to Fleare's face level. 'What can I do for you?'

'Did you know all this stuff about Kelk?' She gestured at the screener.

The sphere made a show of floating over to the screen. 'That? Well, yes, *now*, but that's only because I've become a bit of a data sponge since . . . well, you know. But I didn't know it at the time, which is more important.'

Fleare nodded. 'Neither did I. No wonder he joined up.' She thought for a moment. 'Muz?'

'Yeah?'

'Why did *you* join?'

'Oh, right. One of the difficult ones.' The sphere bonked gently against the screen, which flicked off. 'Does being a dumb,

213

easily influenced kid count? If it comes to that, why did you join?'

She felt her face twist into a sour grin. 'Shall we say it together?'

'Okay. Count of three.' They counted in unison. 'One, two, three . . . *Daddy*.'

Fleare pulled a face. 'Yeah, Daddy. Or everything he stood for, and everything he did. I mean, I saw some of the things he was about, and I swore I was going to be about the opposite. It wasn't just an average rebellion. I saw what the Heg' would look like, if he had his way, and Soc O was the opposite.' Then something occurred to her. 'Muz? Do you ever laugh? I mean, you used to, before . . .'

'Before I was irradiated to death? Right.' The sphere flared blue-white and narrowed to a painfully bright point for a second. Fleare shielded her eyes; when she uncovered them the sphere was back. 'Sorry. That was close to a tantrum. Laugh? I guess. I don't think I remember.' It bobbed over to where the ring lay on its rock. 'Now, I found out some things. Ready?'

She sat up straight. It seemed a safer subject. 'Ready.'

'Good. First, you were right. This is important, or at least I think it is.' The sphere described a distracted orbit round the ring. 'It's data.'

Fleare stood up, walked over to the rock and stared at the ring. 'Some kind of storage?'

The sphere waggled from side to side: head-shake. 'No. It *is* data. How do I describe this? There is nothing about this ring, really nothing at all, that is not built around data. It's the slightest possible physical structure, with bits of data sticking out from every molecule. Everywhere I look I find more.'

'Oh.' Fleare leaned in close and peered at the ring. 'Have you seen anything like it before?'

'No way. And I'm a geek, remember?'

'Mmm. Does it mean anything?'

214

'I guess. I don't recognize the format for the moment, and it's so dense there's nowhere to start. Just a big *mush*.'

Fleare went on staring. The ring was plain grey, but if she moved her head around so that the light fell on it differently she could see something slightly granular about the surface, like particles of smoke. If she strained her eyes, the smoke seemed to swirl, as if it was racing round the circumference of the ring.

She blinked and looked away. 'Okay,' she said to Muz. 'Don't let me stop you.'

'Oh. Sure.' Muz floated down to the ring again and extended tendrils. She watched for a moment.

The swirling had stopped. It didn't start again.

She shrugged to herself, stood up and wandered over to the edge of the little oasis. The top of a rocky outcrop had been carved into a wide, subtly curved stone couch. She settled on to it, stretching out. It was far more comfortable than it looked, and she was tired. She closed her eyes.

As she drifted off, she realized that she knew far more about Kelk's background than Muz's. And when she thought about it, Muz still hadn't told her why he'd joined up.

She made a mental note to ask him again. Maybe she could make him laugh at the same time.

Then she slept. When she awoke it was dark; the Orbiter imposed appropriate day and night cycles on each of its habitats. Her ears were full of the busy not-quite-silence made by a lot of very small creatures moving around carefully.

She sat up, and shivered a little. The air was cool, and there was a hint of condensed dampness on the stone couch. Something had woken her, but she didn't know what. For a few moments she felt as if she was sitting in some kind of sensory-deprivation machine. Then light flickered at the edge of her vision. She turned towards it, lost it, and then found it again.

It was an ephemeral, multicoloured glow. Even against the surrounding darkness it was still dim, and sometimes it faded almost completely. She couldn't tell the size of the source; it could have been a fingernail in front of her face, or a city a hundred klicks away.

She got up from the couch and felt her way towards the light. She quickly realized it was small and near, and following that came the thought that it was in the centre of the oasis. Things moved and crackled and crunched beneath her feet, and then she was there, looking down at the flat stone where Muz had examined the ring.

The ring was still there. It was the source of the glow. She frowned through the darkness, looking around. 'Muz?'

'Here.' The voice came from close to her right.

'Have you seen this?'

'Yes.' Something settled on her shoulder. She jumped slightly, then reached up. Her hand passed through something granular, and softly yielding. *So that's what his cloud feels like*, she thought. She let her hand fall to her side. 'What does it mean?'

'I don't know.' She sensed, rather than felt, the cloud moving away. After a few seconds the outline of the ring blurred slightly like a light seen through fog, and she guessed that Muz had gathered around it. 'It could be anything,' he said. 'A welcome, an alarm? No idea. It started when I cracked the data.'

Fleare blinked. 'What? You mean you know what's on that thing?'

'Oh yes. That's why I woke you.' There was a soft melodic beeping sound from the direction of the cloud and Fleare realized that this was what had roused her.

She rubbed her eyes. 'So what is it?'

Muz shrank back into a sphere and settled on to her palm. He felt slightly warm to the touch, and she wondered if that was deliberate. When he spoke, he vibrated a little. 'Well, it is still mostly mush, or stuff I can't decipher that certainly looks like mush. But I think that's deliberate. There's a pattern to it, kind of fractal – and when you drill in, I mean really far down, there are packets of real data hiding in the pattern. Hidden almost in plain sight, only you have to be looking pretty hard.'

'What does it say?'

'A lot.' The sphere rolled around for a moment, as if it was trying to get comfortable. 'Have you heard of a planet called Silthx?'

She shook her head.

'Not surprised. It was never famous in the first place and it's not much of a planet now. Used to be nice, though.'

'What happened?'

'Well, most recently, the Fortunate. They invaded. There wasn't much else known; they do a good job of suppressing news in their own sphere. Until now, anyway, because that's part of what's on here. A complete record, by the looks of it. And it's huge, Fleare. They enslaved the entire, I mean the *entire* population of a medium-sized planet. Killed most of them within five years.'

Fleare's mouth felt dry. She cleared her throat and found enough moisture to speak. 'How many?'

'Dead? Looks like a round billion. It would be unprecedented, if it didn't make you suspect that the Fortunate might have done it before.'

'A billion people?' Fleare felt numb. It was too big a number to process. She shook her head. 'And after all that they kept a record of it?'

'No, *they* didn't. But somebody did. Someone pretty close to the top recorded this, off her, his or its own bat, and somehow got it out and stored it in a sim. The one Kelk was talking about?'

'I remember.' She looked towards her palm; the little sphere was a shadow in the dim light thrown by the glow from the ring. 'Why?'

'I don't know. Revenge? Money? Blackmail? Politics, likely

217

enough. Reasons. They must have been good ones. It was an epic risk for whoever did it.'

'Mm.' Fleare stared at nothing for a moment. 'You said *most recently*. Was there something before?'

'Oh yes. More interesting, too. Remember what happened to Nipple?'

'More interesting?' She frowned. 'Yeah, Nipple. Something hit it. Pump Trees and things.' *Lots of things*, she thought. *Oh, so many things.* 'So?'

'Something similar happened to Silthx. About a millennium ago. Wiped out a nuke plant, caused about a hundred deaths straight off and a few thousand extra cancers. It put the locals off nuclear power. They never repaired the plant; they turned it into a memorial to the dead. Quite moving, really.'

'I suppose. And I take it the Fortunate desecrated the memorial?'

'Oh yes. In the worst way.' The sphere sprang up from her hand, quickly enough to make her jump. At the same time, she registered that there had been no reaction against her palm. Muz was presumably not at home to classic mechanics. She made a note to ask him how he worked, one day.

'They set up a forced labour camp,' he said. 'They made unprotected prisoners dig out the reactor, and the – thing, with their bare hands. It was still as radioactive as hell, of course. Average life expectancy was about four weeks. It took most of a year. They got through seven thousand bodies.'

'Shit.' Fleare said the word softly, through almost-closed teeth. 'That's all on that ring, is it?'

'Yeah. Documentary, still images, some 2-D vid. Most of it has a stolen look, if you know what I mean. Unofficial.'

She nodded. 'I can see why it's interesting.'

'Oh, all that's just back story. The really interesting part is that the Fortunate got their thing, whatever it was, and hauled it away to somewhere very secret. That fact is on here, although the location isn't, but so is one more thing.' Muz drifted slowly over to the ring, and hovered above it so that it lit him from below 'A bit of the code on here suggests – only suggests, mind – that a few of the people from the death camp may still exist in possibly recoverable form, somewhere in one of the sims.'

'Really? Why would the Fortunate save their own victims?'

'I agree, it would be weird if they had, but I don't think it was them. I don't think they *could* unless they had some high-grade help and there's no sign of that.'

Fleare stood up. 'Are you going to suggest that we go in and look for these people?' she asked.

'Well, yes.' The sphere gave an embarrassed-looking wobble. 'There's a bit more, if it helps.'

Fleare rolled her eyes. 'Try me. It might.'

'Okay. No promises, but I think we are only seeing a part of the story. There are two missing bits: what is the thing, and where did it end up?'

Fleare nodded slowly. 'Okay,' she said. 'If it turns out to be important, fair enough. But how would we know?'

'Know what? If it's important? Well, we don't. But we can guess. Two things. First, whatever it was, that thing was important enough to dig out and take away. We know the Fortunate don't waste time on trivia. Ergo, it wasn't trivia. And second, back to Nipple again. These ancient fragments are big news. Creating a brand-new ecosystem that lasts fifty thousand years and counting? And that was probably just a fragment, not a complete artefact.' He rose from the ring, floated back over to Fleare and settled in her outstretched palm. 'It could be that the Fortunate think they've got their blood-soaked hands on something really lethal. And there's just a small chance they're right.'

'Okay.' Fleare fought the urge to close her hand around the sphere. Something about it made her want to heft it.

Her left leg was hurting; had been hurting for a while, an insistent, gently sinister ache that had begun in her ankle and had made its way, day by day, up past her knee and as far as her hip. This morning the ghost of the same pain had appeared in her other leg.

She had waited for a message from Jezerey but when it had come, just yesterday, it had been terse, a text-format message sent encrypted. That had seemed needless. 'Sorry, girl, no luck yet. Still working on it. Take care and keep *yourself* safe.' The yourself had been emphasized.

She bit her lip, and wondered if her leg would still hurt when she was in the sim. 'So,' she said, 'how do we go in?'

Fragment recovered from Archive, unknown

I don't know how long I've been here. It's one of a very long list of things I don't know. Sometimes, when I'm not in a simulation, I try to make a list of the things I do know. I never get past the fact that I am a simulation myself. I assume I have a body somewhere.

They – good question; I don't know, it's on the list – drop me into other simulations sometimes. I don't know why they do, but I'm good at it. Not just being in a simulation; working out what I'm supposed to do. There's always some kind of task. Sometimes I think they're making me practise for something.

Whatever. I guess it's a way of killing time. And here comes another.

. . . and with no transition at all there is a table beneath my elbows, an unused plate and cutlery between my forearms, an upright chair back behind me and a firm seat beneath me, and a voice says:

'Rudi? Are you okay?'

. . . so apparently I am Rudi. I turn towards – her – and nod and smile. I don't want to speak yet but she seems okay with that and she smiles back and says:

'I just thought you looked a bit weird for a second, that's all.'

. . . and she smiles again and rests a hand on my thigh and my – male, definitely male – body responds as if it has had plenty of practice, but, social obligations, I lay a hand on hers and use my face to signal 'later' and it works because she smiles and removes her hand.

Food smells from lots of different dishes, and the sound of many quiet voices. A restaurant, then. A waitress pushes a floating tray up to us and starts filling plates. My meal is some sort of flesh, bluish-pink and raw-looking, with green sprigs arranged round it like a beard, and a little jug of sharp-smelling yellow sauce. She has the same, only smaller, and she pushes the jug away. The waitress says, 'Enjoy your meal, Council Memberess Demaril and sir' and shoves the tray away and I sense it is time to start speaking so I look up at her and smile.

She raises an eyebrow. 'What?'

'I'm not used to thinking of you as Ms Demaril, that's all.'

'I'm not used to hearing you being called sir,' she says. 'Let's stick to being Sallah and Rudi, shall we?'

And I look into the eyes of the important-sounding woman who I now know is called Sallah Demaril and my right hand finds a glass of something and I raise it and say, 'Let's', and she raises her glass too and we clink, and then drink, and I wait for her to start eating and then I join in.

The flesh is chewy but tastes okay, sweet and a bit bland. The green stuff is bitter. The sauce helps.

We talk as we eat and I piece it together. I'm good at that, like I said. Rudi's full name is Rudimans bin' Haffs, and this meal is a celebration because it is half a year since he and Council Memberess Sallah Cato Demaril had their first, *epic* fuck in the back of a blacked-out cab. Until now she has kept the relationship hidden, because he is the wrong age, the wrong caste and the wrong colour and she is an ambitious junior minister in a government that cares about these things. A lot. But now things have got to the point where she is ready to rethink that.

Rudi, meanwhile, has been playing a long game. I can see it in the sim; they show me that kind of thing. His set piece comes tonight, and it's up to me to play it out. Simulated realities have to be internally consistent. You can only have one set of rules at once.

While we eat I watch Sallah, as much as I can without making it obvious. She's standard human, from the outside. They don't like mods here. This is a conservative middle-tech planet. Middle income, middle pollution, a lot more than middle inequality. That was probably the reason it was simmed in the first place. Comfortable academics love studying inequality. The academics are probably all long dead now but the sim is still trotting along. And now someone's found a use for it.

Sallah has thin straight eyebrows over grey eyes, with only the wrinkles at the corners admitting to the midway point of decade number five. She is obviously proud of her cheekbones, brought out with the faintest blur of darker tone. Conservatively dressed, only she would probably call it *suitable*: close-fitting jacket, buttoned to the top, with long sleeves and a full collar that reaches halfway up her neck.

As I look, Rudi's beautifully simulated biochemistry makes itself felt. I remember he gets off on the stiffness of her dress, the contrast between the formal clothes and the woman they cover. I let myself catch a bit of his excitement. It helps with playing the part.

We finish the meal with tiny dishes of something that is mostly sour cream – they like their sour flavours here – and huge glasses of pale tea, and then there is a silence, long and loaded and full of eye contact being made and broken and made again, until she says: 'Are you ready to go?' And I give the only possible answer and she waves for the cheque.

It floats up on its own tray. I watch her as she leaves money

– real paper money, it's in fashion again here, if you can afford to own any.

I follow her to the exit, gaze roving over her hips. She has a lithe fullness that comes with well-managed ageing, and the close-fitting material does that trick of revealing as it hides. More biochemistry happens. This time I keep my distance from it.

As we leave I sense people's eyes on us, recognizing her and scoping me, and I realize this evening is a big deal for her. She has gone public. Some timing.

We flag down a cab, none of your high-tech stuff but a real honest-to-fuck pedicab with real pedals and a proper slave to push them, and squeak back through a warm evening full of night-time city smells to an apartment block behind a security gate. Touch-pad entry to the ground-level foyer; no visible staff but several discreet weapons pods on the ceiling and that's just what they want you to see. A flying eye whirs round a corner and hovers briefly in front of her and longer in front of me. It's too close so I want to swat it, but I don't. Play the game. It won't hurt you, sweetheart. It just wants to look. When it has finished, it dips in the air like a nod, and flits off back to wherever. I let go my breath, and realize I must have been holding it. Too tense.

We walk into an elevator and say nothing all the way to the top.

The elevator doors open on to a big terrace. It's shaded by big squares of something like silk, so fine you can hardly see it, floating about independently just above our heads. One of them begins to track us across the terrace, but Sallah waves it away.

'It's not raining,' she says.

The shade square floats off and parks itself somewhere out of sight. I'm impressed. They only thought of field technology a few years ago here, and it's still pretty expensive.

The main door to the apartment is on the other side of the terrace. As we get to it a pair of flying eyes scoot towards us. They're a bit bigger than the one downstairs. Big enough for grown-up weapons. Too late to worry now.

Sallah's eyes follow mine towards them. She sighs a bit. 'I can't get rid of them out here,' she says. 'They're part of my security contract.' She pauses, then looks up at me. 'They don't go inside, though, so . . .'

I nod. 'So?'

She smiles, and opens the door. The flying eyes part to let us through. The door closes behind us and suddenly there is no space between us, none at all, and my nose and mouth and hands are full of the smell and taste and feel of her and even though a tiny part of me is screaming *'Hold back!'* I can't because for some reason I can't tell the difference between me and the remnants of Rudi any more and I don't care.

Without letting go of each other we stumble across the apartment shedding clothes as we go, and by the time we get to her chamber we are naked and I can see her, I can see her breasts and the tight little mat of hair at the base of her belly and I run my hands down her, and we collapse together and I am gone.

When I wake the first thing I know is comfort, that pure animal feeling that comes from recent sex and the smell and feel of your mate next to you. It's dark, I'm warm and my body hurts a bit in all the right places. It's fun remembering why.

Then there is a sickening moment when I realize what it means and the next thing I know is fear, because most of what I am remembering was *not* supposed to happen. I have no idea, no idea *at all*, how long I slept.

Oh dear holy shit, what have I done?

I lie dead still while my mind races and I try to get my heart rate back to normal. After a few dozen breaths we're getting there and I risk moving an arm, sliding it out from under the covers like a snake. Halfway out the cover sinks to fill the hole. Sallah moves a bit and moans and I freeze, but it's okay, she's still asleep, and the arm comes out into fresh air and I can see Rudi's cheap chrono which, thank you, glows in the dark.

I've been asleep for two hours. Oh crap.

Another dozen breaths while I do the maths. It's outside the plan but – more maths – it might be okay. If everything else goes to spec. If I don't fuck up.

If I'm lucky.

Time to go. I slide away from Sallah and stand up, letting the cover settle back oh so slowly. A waft of expelled air smells of her and for a crazy moment I am ready to lie down again. Then I'm back in control. I squeeze my eyes shut for half a minute to get some night sight. Then I prowl round the apartment, picking up my clothes. Two minutes later I am dressed, and now it's time for the important stuff. I shut my eyes again, remembering the simulation. Eyes open. Go.

Out of the main room. Down a short corridor. Duck under a tell-tale beam, turn to the right, step over another beam and into the study. No alarms so far, but we'll soon fix that.

The study's cluttered. No surprise there. Step carefully round the junk on the floor, swing past the desk and stop in front of the old-style bookshelves, apparently filled from end to end with genuine old-style books because Sallah is a bit of a collector. Count four shelves down and four books in. My guts hurt with the tension. Pause for as long as I dare to calm things down. Take hold of book. Pull.

The projected image of the bookshelves fuzzes out and suddenly I am standing on the threshold of Sallah's real office, twice the size of the study. The old oak desk is against the wall where it ought to be, covered in terminals, screens, data stores and even keyboards, as if Sallah has never heard about less being more. But none of it matters, because the real point of the exercise is . . .

226

. . . my foot goes through a tell-tale beam. It's hidden low, under the edge of the desk. No way you'd notice it, unless you knew it was there.

Like I did.

The lights brighten, and half a dozen camera patches swivel towards me. Suddenly Rudi's face is seriously famous, and suddenly I am on two separate deadlines. Rudi's, because this was the purpose of his game, and mine, because now I know where his game actually ends and I don't want to be there when it does.

I run. I have twenty-five seconds before the house goes into lock-down – twenty-five, because that's how long the building management system thinks it would take Sallah to get to a terminal and cancel the alarm, if she was going to. After that, everything is in secure mode. No doors, no elevators. No way out.

Ten seconds sees me out of the apartment and on to the terrace. Far too long. Thirteen, and I am near the elevator. No chance – I could get in but I'd never get out again. Fifteen seconds, and we're into Plan B. I never liked Plan B.

I run past the elevator door and round a corner, and there they are. The shade squares.

No time for relief. I reach up with both hands.

Field mesh is weird stuff. I know it's not real but it feels it. It's like trying to grab an oily film on water and it takes a couple of goes before I've got the middle of a square in each hand.

Eighteen seconds. No choice left. Run.

I reach the parapet in four big strides, tighten my hold on the squares, gather a mouthful of saliva, launch myself out over the edge – and fall like a stone.

The squares have gone limp. With a small part of my mind I notice my bowels emptying. Rudi doesn't like that but I haven't time to help. I'm busy watching.

Sallah's block has thirty floors. Halfway down there is a

restaurant terrace that sticks out just a bit further than the rest. It's my landmark. If I act too soon then there'll be time for Security to catch up with me. Too late, and there won't be much left to catch.

The terrace flicks past. I spit up towards the squares, as hard as I can, and hope they're as smart as they're supposed to be.

For an aching millisecond nothing happens. Then both shade squares spread and harden into storm mode and the upward force nearly breaks my grip but not quite because I was ready for it.

We hit the ground hard enough to bruise but not hard enough to do serious damage, and I add another apology to the thousands I'm going to owe Rudi by the time this is over.

I catch my breath. Then I run.

On the way I take stock. So far so reasonable. The simulated Sallah is thoroughly compromised, which was the idea. This simulated world has been nudged on to a new path for the delight of some voyeur somewhere. Coming back to the practical, I badly need a change of clothes, but Rudi's wardrobe has a couple of issues. First, it is thirty blocks away, almost an hour on foot. Far too long for the owner of a face which will get very famous, very fast, just as soon as the news hits the public screens. Second, it is in what's about to be the most watched apartment on the planet.

Third, we both have an appointment somewhere else. Rudi's remaining time is ticking down and so is mine.

The city is on a grid layout. Picture an aerial map. The streets run up and down, left to right. Sallah's apartment building is just below the centre of the map. Below it, parks and parliaments; above it, commercial, the shitty but necessary business of swapping lots of money for lots of stuff, or the other way round. And above *that*, the other sort of commercial. The human sort.

I head up the map, past a couple of blocks of shiny shop

228

fronts. The ones they put in the tourist brochures, but only after they edit out the junkies and the baby whores. They call it Spillage, here – a nasty intrusion on the public life of the city, by all the human refuse that makes the private life of the city possible. Under the awning of an up-market clothing store I step over a pair of outstretched legs. Their owner doesn't move. She might be twelve or thirteen but it's hard to tell through the bruises and the make-up. As I step over her I notice the syringe sticking out of one of her skinny thighs. It's empty. So's she, I guess.

I find time to hope that my nudge does some good.

A few blocks more, and we've left the nice places behind for good. Warehouses, narrow streets, little workshops that never stop working, and bigger ones that spew chemicals and acrid-smelling smoke across the pavement. I step sideways to avoid a spreading puddle of something purple that seems to dissolve concrete, then throw myself sharply against a wall as a truck grinds by. The wheels swish through the puddle we just avoided, splashing the purple stuff against the wall. It steams. I watch it for a second then move on. Like I said, we have an appointment.

The smoke den doesn't advertise itself. Just a door in a wall. Anyone who needs to know it's there, knows. I knock and wait, counting under my breath. I've reached ten by the time a thin, nervous-looking boy opens the door. Ten is good. Ten means everything is okay. Twenty would have meant we have a problem. Immediate would have been run like fuck.

I push past the boy. It's dark inside, and the air smells of sharply sweet smoke with undertones of sweat and alcohol. Drowsy conversations stop as I enter, and then start again as the door closes. A few people glance at me with unfocused eyes.

The Weed Captain is standing behind the bar that divides the long room into two. The surface in front of him is covered with little flat tubes. They're mouthpieces that plug into the coiled manifolds of smoke pipes that run round the walls – people get stoned here on an industrial scale. He looks at me, his eyebrows raised. I nod, and he waves me through the lift-up of the bar and into one of the private stalls behind. He watches me sit down. 'Wait here.' His voice is a spluttering hiss that comes from a puckered hole in his neck, because smoking is *very* bad for you. He turns and leaves, drawing the curtain over the entrance of the stall.

I wait, doing my best to keep calm. It's not easy. I'm crazy with adrenalin and exhaustion. I work on my breathing, getting it gradually down to some kind of even keel, focusing my eyes on a spot of dirt on the filthy curtain. After a few minutes my heart rate is something like normal.

Then the curtain moves. Not much. Just a tiny sway, and then stops, as if it had been caught by a draught. One that hadn't been there before. At the same moment, I realize that I can't hear anyone talking. Then there is a new sound, of a faint *pock* followed by an edgy rumbling noise. As if someone had bowled something underarm and it was rolling towards me. Something small but heavy. Something made of metal.

I throw myself up and backwards as hard as I can. The thin partition splinters and I am rolling head over heels through into the very back of the bar. I crash over empty barrels, bump into a line of bales of weed stacked waist-high, throw myself over it and crouch down on the floor, hands over my head.

For a second there is silence. Then there is a hiss, an orange flash and a noise like a lot of angry fireworks, and I realize that the rolling thing was a mini-cluster. Nasty and illegal. I hunker down as much as possible and hope like hell it isn't heat-seeking.

The bales shake as the tiny warheads thump into them. Someone screams and then stops. The firework noise peaks and fades out, and plaster dust flutters down on to the backs of my hands.

There is the sound of feet, getting closer, and I realize I'm running out of time. Correction. Have run out. Somehow I fucked up, and it feels like treachery but I have to go.

I say a quick, silent, utterly inadequate 'sorry' to Rudi for getting him into this. Then I do the thing inside my mind, which I can't describe except to say that it feels like *this*, to snap myself out of here.

Nothing happens.

I try again.

Still nothing. Still here.

More feet, coming closer, and a crash as someone shoves some wreckage aside. I've got seconds, and no options at all. I have to make the sim work for me.

I reach deep into the controls of the body I am inhabiting, going far too fucking fast but there's no time to be gentle, and I find the place I'm looking for.

There.

Rudi's body shuts down. No heartbeat. No breathing. Muscles lax (and a bit more shit eases out, and I find time to be pleased with the artistic touch). Eyes open because I need them, but staring like death. He's got about a minute like this before his brain starts dying. And at the moment, I wouldn't like to guess what happens to me when his brain dies.

One minute. I wait, and hope desperately that my stupid idea works. That they scan for life signs soon, and that the fact of an apparently dead body stops them from doing anything in a hurry. Just as long as it buys me time.

The feet stop. Ten seconds gone. Twenty. Thirty. Time enough for a scan, more than enough. What . . . ?

Then I hear an intake of breath and a click-hum, and realize that it hasn't worked, because that is the sound of an energy weapon going live. I'm about to fry.

And then, with no warning at all, the world twists and I am somewhere else, lying on a hard white floor, still in apparently Rudi's body, and a woman's voice says quietly:

'Got them.'

I have time to think *'What?'*, before someone seizes my upper arm.

I convulse, wrenching my shoulder up and around so that my arm is pulled out of the grip. Then I am up on my feet and running.

Then the world blurs for a moment and suddenly I am running the opposite way and someone in front of me is reaching out. I swerve round them, twisting my shoulders to stay clear, and the world does it again and I am on the floor where I started. I yell and thrash but then something buzzes against my arm and everything fades out.

Deep Simulation, Plenum Level ('Entry Hall'), Catastrophe Curve

Fleare floated in nothing at all. Open, her eyes saw a clean, fuzzy whiteness. Closed, there was black. None of the familiar reds, purples and greens of light filtered through thin muscle and circulating blood. Just black, which meant that the white probably wasn't white, or at least that it wasn't white light. Or perhaps it was, and her eyelids weren't really eyelids?

She felt like laughing at her own self-analysis. She turned, if that was the right way to think about it, to Muz, who was floating next to her. He had chosen to appear as a sphere again and she could see a distorted reflection of herself in his surface. 'Where are we?'

'It calls itself the Entry Hall.' Muz's voice sounded flatter and harder in here. 'It's the jumping-off point to all the families of sims. It doubles as a data pipe, too. Can you feel it?'

She shook her head. 'I can't feel anything. There isn't anything to feel.'

'Try turning round.'

She did, and felt a breeze blowing on her face. She hadn't noticed it before. She frowned and turned back, but there was no corresponding air against the back of her head. She looked at Muz again. 'How does that work?'

'However it wants to. This is a sim, remember? You're code, I'm code, it's code. We're all code.' He drew level with her face and floated nearer, until she had to cross her eyes to stay focused. 'Welcome to my world,' he said quietly.

Fleare suddenly felt cold, although she wasn't sure how she managed it in this place where there was nothing to feel. 'It's creepy,' she said. 'Does it have to be like this? Can it be like something else?'

Yes.

The voice was in her head. She jumped and looked around. 'Who are you?'

I am your Moderator.

Fleare looked back at Muz and raised her eyebrows. He moved away a little and gave a quick up-and-down bob. 'It's friendly,' he said. 'It runs the place. Or, more, it kind of *is* the place.'

She compressed her lips. 'Okay, ah, Moderator. Can this place have another appearance? Something more human?'

Yes.

For a moment, the white that wasn't anything winked out. Fleare's senses swam, and she closed her eyes reflexively. When she opened them, she was in the biggest space she had ever seen.

'Okay,' she said slowly. 'That's – better . . .'

They had parted company with the old Orbiter. Sooner or later someone was bound to put two and two together, and besides, the ancient ship was getting edgy about being so close to the Cordern; the server farm was far down the thin end of the Catastrophe Curve and the Trash Belt was too sparse to shield them from view from either direction.

Fleare had not felt comfortable about the Orbiter's

replacement. She stared at it for a long time. Then she turned to Muz. 'Really?'

'It's perfect. It's small, it's fast, it's inconspicuous. What's your problem with it?'

She reached out a toe and prodded it. 'It's a . . .' She paused, and prodded it again. 'Okay, I give up. What is it?'

'See? I told you it was inconspicuous. There are tens of thousands of these things abandoned in the Trash Belt.' Muz floated over to position himself proudly above the object. 'It's an Autonomous Waste Fissile Containment Unit. Otherwise known to its friends as an AWFUKU.'

Fleare gave herself a moment to process that. Then she grinned. 'Yeah, well, that's roughly how I feel too. I don't need to know what its enemies call it.' She stood back and examined the object. It was an extensively dented, comprehensively rusted cylinder about three metres long and two across, with a large, crude-looking reaction motor bolted – she looked closer and realized that it really was quite literally bolted – to one end. Most of the dents were concentrated at the other end. She supposed that implied speed. She considered another prod, and then changed her mind and converted it into a proper kick. The impact made no sound at all, but her foot hurt. 'Fissile Containment? This is a nuclear waste thing, isn't it?'

'Originally, yes.' She wondered how a shiny sphere could look embarrassed, but Muz had managed it. 'It's been repurposed. Rapid transport of sensitive material. It's quite expensive.'

'Oh, good. It looks pretty used. I hope they spent some of the money on decontamination.'

'I'm sure they did. They would have said, otherwise.' The sphere knocked against the top of the cylinder, and a hatch squeaked open. 'Shall we?'

'I guess.' She raised a leg towards the hatch. Then she stopped. 'Muz? If you irradiate me, I'll . . .' She paused, searching for words.

'You'll what?'

She gave up, stepped forward and shoved a leg in through the hatch. 'I'll *glow*, okay?'

'And you'll look beautiful. Now shall we go?'

'Muz? Fuck off.'

They went.

It really was quite fast.

She looked round, and then up. She was in the centre of a vast hall. Distant walls soared tens of metres and curved over to meet in a vaulted ceiling pierced by great skylights. Low-angle sun made blue-grey shafts full of dust motes, looking almost structurally solid as if someone had floodlit a line of oblique girders. She stood on a floor made from octagonal tiles of a pinkish swirly stone, with black squares filling the corners. The far wall was full of tunnel openings.

They had the place to themselves, but it was obviously meant to house thousands of people. 'Moderator? Where are we?'

You are in a representation of one of the greatest transport hubs ever built.

'Wow.' She looked round again. The illusion was perfect; she knew her body was in a recliner in a sim suite, but she *felt* herself here. 'Where is it?'

It is nowhere, now. It was demolished more than a million years ago.

'Oh.' She was surprised to feel a pang of sadness. 'Well, I'm glad you – remember it, if that's what you do.'

The voice didn't respond. Fleare turned to Muz. 'Where now?'

'Well, in, really.' He nudged gently against her finger so that he clicked against the ring. 'This thing contains a time-line within one of the sims. Let's go walk alongside it and see what we find.'

She looked around. 'How do we do that?'

She had expected Muz to reply, but instead it was the Moderator which answered. *Go to the wall of tunnels. One will be illuminated. Enter it, and you will be in place.*

'Okay.' She paused and, feeling slightly self-conscious, added, 'Thank you.'

You are welcome. A version of me will be with you.

'Really? Why?'

I believe you may wish to extract a personality from a simulation. That is not straightforward, especially as you may be doing so against the will of another agency.

'What other agency?'

Whichever agency placed the personality here in the first place. I cannot guarantee that you will be unimpeded. Besides, the personality itself may have a view.

She nodded. Then, unsure whether whatever it was could see her, she said: 'Thank you. Again.'

You are welcome. Again. Please enter the tunnel.

She fought off the urge to say 'Yes, sir', and walked towards the far wall. The illusion of reality broke down for a moment: her steps seemed normal, but she realized the wall was coming closer at much faster than walking pace. Then she was at the tunnel entrance, and the illusion fell away completely.

It only looked like a tunnel from a distance. Up close, it had no depth; it was just a flat half-circle of grey-black graininess. It reminded her of something but for a second she struggled to think what. Then she realized.

It looked just like the surface of Kelk's ring. Perhaps the Moderator was more subtle than she'd suspected.

She shrugged and walked forwards, half expecting to bounce off. Her senses swam once more, and then she was – on a beach.

Soft, slightly shelly sand rustled beneath her feet. Twenty paces away, a grey-green sea hissed and crunched slowly against the shore. There was a mineral breeze in her face, and she knew without looking that the stirring behind her would be trees, marking the edge of the sand.

She looked round for Muz, but couldn't see him. Then she became conscious of a weight against her breastbone. She felt for it, and lifted it towards her eyes. It was the necklace he had become once before.

'Hello,' she said. 'So, let's get busy.'

Fragment recovered from Archive

Waking hurts. Fair enough; I've been doing some hard manoeuvring. A few bruises but nothing broken. Good enough outcome, considering.

Meanwhile I'm deep in the nasty unknown. I take stock. Lying on something softish but slightly lumpy. Naked and clean-feeling, air temperature neutral with a slight current, more than a sigh but less than a breeze. Other than the air current, no noises.

It's time for visuals. I let my eyes open a crack, and then all the way.

On a bed, in some kind of cabin that smells woody, with salty overtones. There's a woman looking down at me. She is young, maybe standard early twenties, and she looks wiry. Her face is brown, the sort that comes from tan not genes. She is wearing mil fatigues, although I don't recognize the uniform, and she is grinning.

'Hi,' she says. 'Which of you's listening? The body or the passenger?'

For a moment I consider staying dumb, but only for a moment. Whoever she is, this woman hauled me and Rudi's body out of somewhere as a unit, when I couldn't even get myself out solo. First and last rule: when someone holds all the cards, the only game to play is theirs. 'The passenger,' I say. 'Who are you?'

Her grin widens. 'In a minute. Excuse me.' She is wearing a necklace of wooden beads. She thumbs one of them. 'Did you get a fix?'

A crackly voice answers. 'Nice and clear. Ready?'

'Yup.' She thumbs the bead again and looks at me. 'Relax. This won't take a second.'

I get ready to ask what won't take a second, but then everything blurs for a moment and I shut my eyes and shake my head to clear them.

Then I realize. My eyes, my head. A discontinuity I was barely aware of has gone. The remnants of Rudi aren't around any more.

I look up at the woman. 'What . . . ?'

'I hate dealing with two entities at once,' she says. 'I never know which I'm talking to.'

I sit up and look at her. 'So?'

'So, we isolated Rudi's personality traces. Hauled them out and put them into storage.' She looks at me for a moment and crosses her eyes theatrically. 'Oh come on, you could look impressed? We managed to pinpoint a simulated personality that had been inserted into a grey-area sim to take over *another* simulated personality, haul them both out safely, isolate the *original* personality and put it somewhere safe without leaving any traces. It took whole fucking *seconds* of processing. *And* you were stuck. You were about to be in all sorts of trouble. Isn't this better?'

I nod slowly. Then I look round, as much to give myself time to think as for any other reason. Apart from the bed I woke up on, there is no furniture. The walls are made of tawny wood, laid in vertical planks. There are nail heads trickling dark lines of rust towards the wooden floor. Wide windows along two walls are covered by off-white curtains. They stir, and I can feel a faint breeze. There is no door.

I finish the eyeball tour and look back at the woman, who is now sitting cross-legged on the bed next to me. She is watching me with raised eyebrows.

'Well?' I say.

'Well,' she says, nodding as if she is agreeing with me. Then she pushes her palms down against the mattress and springs herself up and off it, unfurling her legs forwards so that she lands softly. 'Let's go for a walk,' she says, and points vaguely towards the wall next to the windows.

A door appears. She waves a hand towards it. 'After you,' she says.

I hesitate, looking down at Rudi's still naked body, of which I am now the sole inhabitant. I suppose that makes it my body now. She shakes her head a little. 'Sorry,' she says. She does the vague hand wave again and something soft and sort of heavy wraps itself round me. I look at it for a moment, then raise my eyes to meet hers. 'A toga?' I say.

'Why not?' She waves towards the door again. 'Go on,' she says. 'Before I change my mind about the whole clothes thing.'

We walk along a shingle shore. There is green restless sea to our right. To our left, a forest of tall straight trees with purply-blue needles marches down to the edge of the beach.

For a while neither of us speaks. Then I say: 'Who are you?'

She does the grin again. 'In here, I am just a figment of my imagination.' She waves backwards over her shoulder to the beach house we have left behind. It disappears. 'So are you,' she adds.

I am getting impatient. I reach down and pick up a stone. It feels cold, and slightly sticky with salt. I push the folds of the toga out of the way, wind back my arm and throw it out to sea as hard as I can. It arcs out over the water and lands with a tiny white splash.

'Good imagination,' I say.

She shrugs. 'Good simulation,' she says, and reaches down for a stone of her own. She throws, her arm moving so fast it blurs. The stone goes much, much further than mine. She looks at me. 'Sorry, showing off. So, you've got questions, yes?'

I nod. 'Have I been rescued or kidnapped?'

She tilts a hand from side to side. 'Kind of both. Maybe with some head-hunting as well.'

I consider this. It doesn't sound too bad. 'Okay,' I say. 'Next question. Where am I?'

'I thought that was going to be question one.' She sits down on the shingle and wriggles her hips to make a hole for herself. 'You are – we both are – in a Covert Conjoined Simulation. Think mixed chill-out zone and observation room. It sits next to the virtual reality you came from, but screened from it, and running faster. A *lot* faster: fifty thousand times base clock speed. We're on a *very* fast substrate. Bit geeky there. Sorry.'

I sit down facing her. 'Fine,' I say. 'So how do I get out of here?'

'Ah.' The smile has gone now. 'That depends what you mean. If you mean out of this sim and into another one, that depends on what you're willing to do when you get there. As far as we can see, you didn't have a purpose before; you were just bumming along with Rudi's plans, right?'

I nod.

'Okay. You need to know that was probably just a creative way of keeping you quiet. I'll explain in a minute. The main thing is, in principle we'd like you in there batting for our side.'

'Hm.' I look out to sea for a moment while that sinks in. 'Okay, maybe. But what if I mean out of here altogether?'

'As in, back to your physical body?'

'Yes.'

'That won't be easy. Neither will this.' She reaches out and takes my hand. 'The thing is, we don't think you've got one any more.'

I stare at her. 'That's crazy!'

'Is it? Then tell me something. What's your name?'

I take a breath, open my mouth, and then close it again.

I realize that I have no idea.

I'm not sure what time means in here, but it looks and feels later. The woman left me alone a while ago. The light is fading and the shadows of the trees touch the waterline. It's colder, too. I shrug myself deeper into the toga.

I've been trying to remember things. Not just my name. Anything. There's nothing before the moment I uploaded into Rudi in the restaurant. I know that can't be right; there's got to be loads of stuff that makes me *me*, but every time I try to think about any of it the thought just sort of slides off. It's like trying to catch fog. That's why I didn't notice. I wasn't meant to. Apparently that might have been for my own protection.

The theory is that I – that is, my mind – might have been rescued from my body for some reason. They – the woman and whatever it is that lives in her necklace – won't tell me any more. I have to take the next steps myself.

It's like being told you are a ghost.

I'm scared and a little angry. I'm also not feeling very protected.

I'd like to find who did this, but first I've got to find me. They've told me what to do next and it sounds simple. I don't know how much I trust what they say, but I'm not sure how many choices I have. This helps, in a way. It means that there is a little core of anger in me: anger I'll use, when I find a place for it.

I'm not theirs yet, even if they think I am.

There's a sort of comfort in that. I stand up, shrug off the toga and crunch over the shingle, along the shadows of the trees, to the edge of the water.

Which isn't supposed to be water, apparently, even if it looks like it. I dip in a foot, and it feels warm and sort of grainy. Not grainy like sand; grainy like pixels. My foot disappears as it goes under the surface, as if I had pushed it through an image of the water into something hidden. I take it out, and there is a tiny pause before my skin is suddenly cold and wet, with drops running off it and pat-patting on to the shingle.

I square my shoulders and walk into the sea. The beach shelves gently at first and then more steeply as I get further from the shore. Soon it's deep enough to swim and I sink forwards, my body disappearing beneath the surface until only my head and shoulders are out. The warm green graininess closes around me, busy and inquisitive. It is as buoyant as a salt lake and I swim for a while, thinking that I must have learned to swim but not remembering when. Then I look back over my shoulder to see how far I am from land.

The shore is gone. Not even out of sight, and anyway I couldn't have swum that far yet. Just gone. When I look up, so is the sky. There's only me, in the middle of an endless flat green make-believe sea underneath a lid of white nothing. The woman said that would happen so it's okay. Probably.

For a moment I let myself wonder what would happen if I turned round and swam back to where I think the shore used to be. But only for a moment. There's no way back. I've been on a one-way trip since I left the shingle. Since this woman and whoever else snatched me from the sim. Since . . . well, since all the things I can't find.

Well, time to go looking. I fill my lungs, shut my eyes and dive.

There is a micro-moment of silence, almost as if I have caught something by surprise. I open my eyes and that seems to act as a trigger because I am suddenly surrounded by a hissing, fluttering cloud of colour. I close my fist then half open it, and my curled palm is full of them, shiny polygons a few millimetres across but so thin they are almost two-dimensional. At first I think that each one is a different colour, but then I realize that each one is all colours, flickering from one to another too quickly for my eye to follow.

They are beautiful, and I laugh. There is no sound apart from the hissing of the flakes, but the laugh sounds in my head and the colours around me pulse in time with it as though they are laughing back.

Except that when I stop laughing, they don't. I close my eyes and shake my head, but the pulsing is still there, printed on the red inside of my eyelids. It is getting stronger, too, and brighter; so bright I would close my eyes if they were still open. The light lances into me, and the hissing of the flakes becomes a greedy roar, and I am . . .

I am . . .

Further along the beach, the simulation of the woman called Fleare sat on the simulated shingle, throwing stones into the green thing that looked like the sea. She studied the splashes carefully. They looked real.

The bead on her necklace made a throat-clearing noise. 'Uh, hello?'

'Hello.' She put down the stone she was holding. 'I saw him dive. Is he on his way?'

'Yep. Full immersive regression. No hitches so far.'

Fleare picked up the stone again, hefted it and threw it out low over the water so that it skimmed and bounced. 'Still sure he's the one we're looking for?'

'Well, pretty sure. Latest runs say over ninety-seven per cent positive. It won't be long before we find out.'

Fleare reached a hand up to her throat and took hold of the bead, turning it in her fingers. 'Go gentle on him,' she said quietly. 'If he is who we think, he has a hell of a history to get used to.'

'What do you think all this softly-softly by the seaside stuff was about?' The bead managed to sound insulted. 'We could have done a reconstruct and dumped the whole lot back in his memory in milliseconds, real time.'

'Yeah, and ended up with a psychotic simulation.' Fleare flicked the bead softly with a fingernail. 'They're not good to watch, Muz.'

'If you're referring to my past, then no, I expect I wasn't. At least I was quiet.' The bead twisted itself out of her grip. 'But I'm over it, okay?'

'Okay.' She stood up, and realized she had sighed. 'What about the sim? Those cops must be getting ready to inspect a body by now.'

'Fixed.' Muz sounded smug. 'We found a body match. A guy a bit younger but the same build, who just died of a Float overdose. Dropped him into the gap just as they fired. Any second now, their time, they'll decide they grilled the wrong guy. The paperwork will be a bitch.'

'So, anyone who looks in should be fooled that it's all normal?'

'Yeah. Or whatever passes for normal in sim-world. We covered our tracks pretty well.'

Fleare nodded. Her hands felt salty. She frowned and dusted them against her fatigues. Then she raised her head and looked out to sea, to where she had last seen the young man swimming before he disappeared. She tried to imagine that she could still see the remains of the spreading wake he had left as he crossed the broken water of the wave tops, but it was getting too dark and the currents must have erased it by now.

It didn't help that her sight seemed a little blurred. She wiped the back of her hand across her eyes, felt wetness, and swore under her breath.

'What?'

'Oh, nothing.' She wiped her eyes again. 'So,' she said, 'since we're done, let's get out of here.'

'Sure. Where to?'

Fleare shrugged. 'Somewhere a very long way from the sea. Somewhere not in a simulation.' She paused, and added: 'Somewhere with lots of alcohol.'

I am . . .

Yes?

I don't know. Who am I?

We can help.

How? Who are you?

I'm called the Moderator. Do you know where you are?

Am I in another sim?

No, or mostly no. You exist as pure code – terabytes of code – running as a limited diagnostic model.

What does that mean?

It means we can see – everything. Your past has been hidden from you, probably by the agency who extracted your personality in the first place. Logically, the code must include not just your memories, but the instructions that have sealed them away.

How do you know?

Nothing can have been completely removed; that would be impossible without destroying your personality. We will look for possible matches for events from your memory, and scan you for activation of any code which appears to block them.

Will you find out who – extracted me?

Possibly. Not certainly. Let's begin.

Pictures. Random at first, flashing past like a flock of birds. Swooping, pausing. Returning. Many people. A few people. One person, from many angles. A pause, then places. A river, a bare patch of sandy earth. Trees, then no trees but only desert.

Ah.

Another pause.

More people. Crowds. Laughing. A dislocation. Other crowds with no laughter at all.

Then there is just me, and I am . . .

I am . . .

The core of anger becomes rage that rises like lava.

Do you know who you are?

Yes. Now I know.

I – we – are sorry.

I know that too.

The noise and the heat make sleep impossible. The nausea is worse, too. It comes to everyone who works at the Project, sooner or later.

The siren howls the shift change and we half fall off our benches. A lot of the benches are empty, now. A few months ago this block held seven thousand of us – seven thousand survivors out of twice that many who were forced on to the transports in the first place. I don't know how many are left; we try to keep a count, but the number changes too quickly and it's easy to lose track of time, along with everything else. I guess we are down to a few hundred.

There is stagnant water and a few mouthfuls each of the spongy pink morning ration, for those who can keep it down. Yesterday I could. Today I can't.

We stumble out of the barracks on to the fine bare earth of the parade square. There is no shade. All three suns are up, roaring heat from three directions. When we first came we were made to stand on parade every day while they checked our uniforms, our kit and, if we were male, whether we had shaved. Now, the few of us who survive wear clothes filthy with vomit. Our kit is lost or broken so that we dig with our hands, and the skin on our faces is blackened, peeling and unshavable, as if we have been exposed to the glare of a demon sun. We have, in a way.

They don't bother with parades any more. Anyway, there are no women left. Some were taken by the guards for their own use. They died eventually. The rest died sooner.

The siren howls again, and we are herded into the adit that leads down to the dig face. It is even hotter down here. The air is thick with the dust that tastes of metal and makes your lips itch and your tongue swell. We all know what it is, even if we never talk about it.

It takes us half an hour to shuffle down to the dig face. Halfway down, we have to clear a tunnel fall. They are happening more often as the summer gets higher and the ground dries, even at this depth. When we are almost finished, one of the older men dies – just falls forward on to his knees, almost as if he is praying to the lethal heap of dirt he is trying to shift. Then he slumps sideways. We push his body out of the way, and keep working. Later we will have to remove it, before it begins to smell.

Eventually we arrive at the dig face. Because of the tunnel fall we are late. Our shift will be short of its target; we begin our work knowing that there is punishment waiting at the end of it. Without being told, we take our places at the ragged wall of earth and begin to scrape at it with our crumbling hands. The overseers stand behind us. They are dressed in thick tunics that go down to their ankles. They wear masks with big filters on them. Even though they must be unbearably hot, they never take their masks off. They have seen what happens to us.

I measure time by physical things, like some primitive clock that counts the length of a burned candle. The depth of the hollow I have scraped. The height of the little pile of sooty earth at my feet. The extent of the fresh wounds in my fingers, which used to hurt so much but which are now numb, along with all the nerves up as far as my wrists. The numbness is like a little piece of death, creeping further up my arms every day. I wonder when I will be rescued by the rest of it.

Then the wall of earth falls away under my hands. For a moment all I can see is a dark hole. Then there are shouts behind me, and a crack. One of the overseers has broken the seal of a chemical flare. He throws it past me into the hole. It lands, many metres in front of me, and I can see a tiny firefly glow. I shield my eyes and count. As I reach twenty, there is a soft, fizzing concussion and something like a small sun flicks into life. I squint through the hole.

I am staring into a chamber. More than a chamber – a cavern. It is tall, the height of many men, and just as broad, and it is a ruin. The walls are lined with archaic-looking dials and switches. The roof is partly broken in, with roots twisting down through it. The floor is buckled. There are strange black growths of mould on every surface. And in the middle there is a concrete cylinder, taking up half of the vast room and ruptured so I can see the massive thickness of its walls. Within the cylinder there's an intricate structure of rods and tubes, partly melted at the base so that they look like an obscene model of entrails. And embedded in them – at the end of its own trail of destruction – is a clean, sleek, undamaged white ovoid barely the size of a child.

Behind me I hear the sound of hurried feet. The other workers have run away. I don't. I look for a while – I'm not sure how long. Then I feel a hand on my shoulder. I turn and look into the blank mask of the overseer who threw the flare. The two glass discs show no emotion, but even through my growing sickness I can sense his sudden knowledge of me, and his sympathy.

He knows, just as I know, that I am dead.

I have looked unprotected into the unshielded wreckage of a partly melted-down nuclear reactor, still pierced by the thing that destroyed it. By his standards, I have succeeded. I and my fellow cooperators (because that is what our captors dare to call us) have done the job we were brought here to do. In a small way, I am proud of that. And now my chronic radiation poisoning has become acute – a single, one-shot dose of a hundred lifetimes' exposure in a hundred seconds.

I am quite glad. At least I know. At least it will be quick, now. Better that than to be hunted down like those who ran away. They will die anyway, in time, but time is no friend of people like us.

The metallic taste is overpowering. A coughing fit seizes me. I double over, vomiting, and feel myself fall forward on to my knees. My last thought is that I don't seem to have a pile of earth to pray to.

We're sorry.

I know. You said. Thank you. But how is it I am here?

You stayed at the entrance to the reactor hall. That meant it was possible to predict the time of your death.

So?

Arrangements could be made to transmit the last viable version of your personality to a safe substrate.

Ugh. That sounds like trying to catch someone's last breath in a jar.

Perhaps, yes. But with much better cause.

Who did it? Did you find that?

No. You may assume that it was someone in a senior position amongst your captors – someone with knowledge of the site and access to it. You may also assume that you were lucky.

Really? This doesn't feel lucky.

Perhaps not, but the extraction of a personality under those circumstances has quite a low prospect of success. There may have been many attempts but few results.

Why would anyone do that?

Their motives are not known, although it is probably that they were political. However, you are here and able to act on your own motives. You may wish to consider the following: that you are the last sentient witness to genocide; you are able to confirm a most interesting story; and finally, if you like, you can help bring that story to a close.

Recovered personality

And I'm back. No disorientation this time. I know where I am, and I know who I am. I've got a frame of reference. I've got a past.

It wasn't easy, that bit. They told me it took a year's worth of therapy before I was really stable, although they dropped me into the fastest substrate they could find so it only took a few seconds, real time.

They told me a lot of things. I'm still processing some of them, even now.

Along with self-knowledge and a past, I've got something to do.

Call it a cause.

So, I'm back in Sallah's world. It's a bit past midnight. I'm standing outside Sallah's apartment block, and my earlier, uninformed self is about to land on my head.

I take five quick paces backwards. My shoulders thump into something that feels stony and architectural. Air rasps in my throat. I hold my breath.

The other me lands hard – *hard enough to bruise* – but gracefully, flings aside the confused shade squares, takes a swift look around, and sprints off. I nod approval. I am impressed at my own performance. Athletic. Sexy, even.

I walk out of the shadows and pick up the crumpled scraps of almost-nothingness that are the shade squares, hold them close to my mouth and whisper to them.

The slightly oily-feeling material becomes air between my fingers, and is gone.

This feels like power. I'm not sure where I sent the squares. It could be any one of a hundred thousand almost identical, almost parallel sims. What matters is that it isn't this one. This is the important one, and – within limits – I'm in charge of it.

For example, I have more than one way of moving. I take an experimental step in my head, and suddenly I am on the other side of the square outside Sallah's apartment. I haven't gone quite far enough; I'm getting wet, and I realize I am standing under a fountain. For a laughing moment I enjoy the feeling. Then I move away, using basic legs, and dialling out the wetness as I go.

I break into a trot. I know where the other me has gone, and there's plenty of time for me to follow him using conventional means.

Anyway, exercise is good for you.

So, using old-fashioned exercise I follow Rudi's body past the shops and the junkies and as far as the door to the smoke bar.

Then I wait.

Stuff happens, in order. The police arrive, preceded by howling sirens that cut out a subtle hundred metres from the door. It wouldn't have mattered; the pavements around here are thick with scrounging, begging, pocket-picking, pimping kids, and they all have a sixth sense when it comes to the law. Long before we hear the sirens, they scatter like insects.

Except for one. She – on the balance of probability *she* – is a bi-amputee; two arms and no legs, sprawled over a wheeled trolley that is as filthy as she is. She is carrying a half-full begging bowl and wearing not much more than rags and a full-on grin with half its teeth missing. Her amputations were probably deliberate. Parents can get pretty desperate around here. But her expression is catching. I grin back, and a reflex makes me reach for a coin. Crippled kids equal money, wherever you are.

Then her face dissolves into a sort of cloud, and then, just for a second, it condenses into something like a necklace. It doesn't speak, but the words form in my mind. 'Focus. We're with you.'

Uh huh. *We're watching you* would have been closer. But it reassures me, in a strange sort of a way. I nod, and the necklace morphs back into a tooth-challenged child's face, which scoots away on its trolley just as the first explosion blows the smoke-house door outwards off its hinges.

I press myself back into the shadows and watch until the cop meat-wagon has hauled away the body that is nearly Rudi's. Then, out of kindness and definitely outside the mission profile, I spend a few minutes soothing the outraged Weed Captain. He blames immigrants and I agree with him, reflecting that he doesn't know the half of it.

But the main thing is, he doesn't recognize me. As far as he, and the rest of this world, is concerned, Rudi has been cap-tured dead, and *that* was the point of the exercise. It sets me free in all kinds of ways.

A part of me wants to head back to Sallah's apartment, to prove to at least one person that Rudi has not disappeared and maybe to make amends for a couple of things, but that part of me is not a sound judge. For a start, it's still a bit in thrall to Rudi's body chemistry, which doesn't help objectivity. Or so I tell myself.

But that's not what I'm here for now. The main attraction is elsewhere, and it's time I went and found it. I had to go straight to Plan B last time. It's up to me to get on with Plan A, except that this time I know what Plan A really is.

Someone hid something here. It's data, or the dream of it
– another dream written on a dream – and now I'm back in here
I can taste how to follow the dream.

So I do.

Rivers in cities all smell the same, don't they? Algae, sewage,
spilled hydrocarbon fuels and the general scent of water. By
the time I get to the docks it is well after midnight, and we are
in the quiet dead hours. A slithering mist is carrying the smell
up the little streets between the warehouses. A hundred
metres along the river front a single freighter is being unloaded
by a gang of autodores. Clanks of metal containers and
whining motors seem extra loud against the silence.

The warehouse is one of a long line, and it is surrounded by
some serious technology. It is secured and locked down and
monitored and generally out of bounds. I'd be impressed, if I
wasn't busy being even more impressed by the way it just
doesn't show at all. It just looks like anyone's warehouse.

I don't need to be right next door to it to do the next bit.
Close enough is good enough, so I walk past slowly and
continue a little way upriver until I find a bollard the right
height to sit on. Then I close my eyes and think.

It feels a bit like uploading into Rudi, but more focused and
at the same time more diffuse. Focused, because the system I
am entering is made of simple sharp things like metal and
electrons rather than the squishy electro-bio-chemical mush of
a brain. Diffuse, because the connections go everywhere in a
million directions at once.

First I check that my target is there. It is, and I allow myself a
moment of relief. Then it's time to plan my entry. I go slowly.
No security system likes being subverted, and this one has
many ways of putting a serious kink in my life if it notices me.
But after a while I find my way.

I am making a space – a me-shaped hole in the system's

mindset that goes all the way from the warehouse door to the place where the target is. I sidle through the virtual map of the place, thinking my way from risk to risk until I am there.

It takes a long time, and when I finally open my eyes I am damp with sweat. I glance up and down the river; the autodores have gone and the freighter is dark, and riding high and empty. There's no one around at all.

I stand up, stretch, and wander back along the river front to the warehouse. The entrance I need is round the side, up an alley that smells of river plus something else, a powerful, rank, waxy smell. It's not long before I almost trip over the source. He is asleep, or unconscious, curled up on his side in a pool of piss next to a splash of dried vomit. He is wearing what looks like a robe, in coarse grey-brown material. The brown might be dirt, or it might be worse. I step over him carefully, and then I'm at the door.

I stand in front of it, checking my mental map of the course I have plotted into the building. Then I reach out, lift the flap that covers the contact box on the wall, and tap the code.

There is an old-fashioned sounding *click*, and the door opens. I'm in.

Warehouses are the same everywhere too. The model never changes. Stuff stacked up, with paths between the stuff so you can get to it. This one uses travelling overhead grabs, each with four steel pincers in two sets of two. They're still at the moment. It's a bit like walking under a forest of dead fingers. That's not a good thought, so I kill it and move on.

My route would look bizarre if anyone was there to do the looking. It's not straight; security and surveillance systems are never quite uniform, and my virtual tunnel through the defences twists around to take the line of least resistance. But it gets me there. After a long walk that covers only a short distance I fetch up in front of a section of racking full of boxes that look exactly like all the others.

But they only *look* like the others, because the others are made of metal or timber or foamplas. These are made of energy. It's a sheet of field, like a shade square only much, much stronger. This is the real protection. This is the bit they rely on after all the concealment and the surveillance have been overcome. You could drop a battlefield nuke on this place and not breach those fields. Happily that isn't going to stop me. I reach out my hand.

It stops.

I frown. My fingers should have floated through the field, but instead they are pressing against something hard. I run my hand over it. It *is* a field, or at least it feels like one – the oily there-and-not-there-ness, the slight warmth. I push harder, but it just makes my fingers hurt.

Then I hear the laugh. I turn, and look into the face of the man I last saw curled up outside next to a streak of vomit. He grins. 'Sorry,' he says, 'but you should have seen your face.'

I tense automatically, but then force myself to relax. There's no point wasting energy, and besides, I already know that the solution here isn't going to be physical. Looking round him, I can see that this man is standing at the end of his own tunnel through the security system, which looks more direct than mine. He's wearing a long robe made of rough brown cloth. A hood hangs loosely down his back, and below the robe his feet are wrapped in crude sandals. His face might be middle-aged, and he has a dark, trimmed beard. As a bonus, he doesn't smell any more, and all this means he definitely doesn't belong here. That makes him like me.

'Hello,' I say.

He nods. 'Hello.' Then he holds out a hand. 'Look what I found.' He uncurls his fingers and I look. A data chip, the old-fashioned sort that you use when you really want to know where your data is.

He's got there first. I look up from his hand and meet his eyes. 'So?'

'I expect you think you know what this is?'

'Think? Yes.' I shrug. 'But I don't know what you are.'

'No, you don't.' He doesn't seem about to tell me. 'Listen, I'm sorry to have to tell you, but this is blank. Meaningless.' He shrugs and smiles. 'It only had one function. Bait.'

'Bait?' I think back to the beach, which now seems a lifetime ago, where I met the simulation of the woman with the young smile and the old eyes.

'Yeah. It worked, too. You're here, and it's good to see you. It feels like a long time since I hauled you out of your body.'

'That was you?' I'll find the time to be angry soon. Meanwhile I'm having trouble keeping up.

'Yes. On behalf of someone who thought he was being very clever, but yes, it was me.' Then he smiles, and holds out his hand. 'Team?'

'Only if I know who you are.'

He laughs again. 'Very good. Okay, here goes. I'm the only guy who can get you out of here.'

I give him a long look. Eventually I say, 'I can get out of here by myself. Like I got in here.'

He shakes his head. 'No, you can't. Sorry. Try if you like. I'll wait.'

His self-confidence is getting annoying. I should have two ways out. First, the local physical one, of retracing my drunkard's-walk path back out of the warehouse. Second, the big red button option of downloading straight out of the sim, period. Only, when I look, the path I so carefully made for myself has gone missing, and when I check for the route back into raw code and away, there's nothing. It's as if the file is missing.

'Okay,' I say. 'You got me.' *For the moment*, I add to myself. Then curiosity gets the better of me. 'That shouldn't have been possible. How did you do it?'

'I know this place very well.' He swings an arm round vaguely. 'I've been here a long time.'

There's something about the way he says 'long' that makes me look at him again. He meets my look with eyes that suddenly seem very old. 'It's time to go. Coming?'

'Is there any other way?'

'No.' He shakes his head emphatically. 'You won't be able to stay. It's starting. There's not long to go. You'd better follow me.'

'What's starting?' But he has already turned and headed off down the path he has made. I shrug, and get ready to follow him. Then I pause. Now I've noticed it too. It's like a coarsening of my senses, as if everything is reaching me in lower definition. Pixel fringes appear at the edges of things, and even the white noise of the silence in the warehouse is starting to sound mushy and indistinct.

For a second I'm baffled. Then I realize, and my stomach flips. The whole fucking sim's shutting down.

If I'm still in here when it goes, I shut down too. Permanently. Those are the rules – if your brain dies in a sim then it dies everywhere, and those rules apply to me the same as everyone else.

Panic fires my legs. I sprint down a tunnel that already looks like a mosaic. Ahead of me, the other guy is moving fast, swinging and jinking. He knows the way. I can hardly see the corridor any more, so I take a deep breath and start mimicking his moves as if I'm following him through a minefield. I'm not sure what happens if I step outside the path right now, and I really don't want to find out.

He turns and waits for me at the edge of what used to be the warehouse, but which is now just a rough-edged blur in a limited palette of grey-scale. He reaches out a hand. 'Grab this.'

I'm not going to argue, and to be honest I could do with

something to hang on to. I grab the hand, and he nods. 'Right,' he says. 'We're off.'

The last drop of colour and definition drains from the world around me, and I have a moment to wonder if this is what oblivion feels like.

Then there is – a discontinuity. I'm not sure how long, just that for an interval my senses . . . weren't.

Then everything is different.

Server Farm Atrium, Catastrophe Curve

'Fleare!'

She could ignore the voice, but something was prodding her. It was a distinct, unnerving thump-thump against her shoulder that definitely had nothing to do with the dream she had been having. There had been a beach . . . she tried to turn over, and felt herself roll over a hard lip and begin to fall.

'Whoa!' Something caught her, and she was lowered gently to the ground. She opened her eyes, and saw Muz, still in necklace form. 'Hello,' he said. 'Sorry about that.'

'Hello.' She rubbed herself where the hard thing had dug in. She looked up and saw that it had been the edge of a couch that had a lot in common with a stretcher. It wasn't a good comparison. She looked away. 'Thanks for catching me.'

'No problem. Can you sit up?'

She tried. 'Yeah. Ow.' Her hip ached. So, she realized, did the rest of her leg. Both legs, and quite a lot. Not all the hard lip, then. She resisted the urge to massage her thighs by knotting her fingers above her head in a knuckle-cracking stretch. 'So, everything okay? That was a bit abrupt.'

'I know. Sorry. Things are happening; I thought you'd like to see. Well, *ought* to see, really.'

'Uh huh?' Fleare rubbed her forehead. 'I just woke up. Start gently.'

'Okay. Well, the news is easiest, and it helps to explain everything else. This came out ten minutes ago. I'm going to put it on screen; you might want to shield your eyes until they adapt.'

Fleare nodded, and screwed her eyes half shut as the silver-grey smoke of a screen expanded to a rectangle in front of her. An image grew out of the blur, and she froze. It was her father, immobilized in the act of making some point, his hands spread in front of him, his eyebrows raised and, she noted, his eyes keenly focused and quite, quite dead. It was like looking into a pair of black holes.

She stabbed a finger at the screen. 'What the fuck's *he* doing?'

'Good question. I'm not sure.' Muz paused. 'But we know what he's *saying*, and that's interesting enough. Oh, by the way, he is Speaker on Foreign Affairs as of twelve hours ago.'

'Is he?' Fleare shook her head. 'Not President of the Universe? Must be quite a disappointment.'

'Shh. Listen.'

The image sprang into life.

'. . . purely a temporary measure. The population can be assured that everything is being done to deflect any threat . . .'

'Yes, threat. You see, no one in the Government – whatever is *meant* by Government at the moment, but that's another question – has anything useful to say about exactly what threat is being deflected.'

'Well, obviously we can only disclose so much in a public forum . . .'

'Of course. But what we have here, Speaker, is essentially martial law. Surely you have some justification for that?'

Fleare's father leaned back in his seat and grinned. 'If I may say so, the scrutiny you are able to subject me to would be impossible under true martial law.'

'But I see there is nothing in our contract that requires you to answer.' The presenter didn't wait for a response, but looked down and consulted something in his lap. 'You see, Mr Haas, there's a lot going on. Let me see. Seven Carriers of various classes either leaving their bases or diverting from other duties, and they're all heading for the Cordern. Obviously we don't know how many craft they are carrying but if they are normally fitted out that would be over fifty Main Battle Units. Fifty, Mr Haas?'

Haas smiled. 'Well, I leave that sort of detail to the experts. But I'm sure that what they are doing is proportionate to any situation . . .'

'But what situation?' The presenter turned towards the viewers. 'In summary, we have something close to martial law, including abrupt appointment to the Government of industrial barons with deep pockets. We have a major tooling-up at the boundary of the Cordern. We are left speculating on the reasons why. The Speaker on Foreign Affairs – we didn't have one until a few hours ago, but never mind – is unable to enlighten us. And now . . . just a moment.' His eyes went glassy, then refocused. 'Okay, this just in. The military tool-up is focusing on a single planet within the Cordern.' He paused and raised his eyebrows, causing a few hundred grams of metalwork to climb towards his hairline. 'Apparently it's the most exclusive holiday planet in the Spin. Go figure, ladies, gentlemen, intermediates and others.'

The screen fuzzed out. Fleare looked at Muz. 'Uh huh?'

'Yeah.' Muz bobbed in the air, making his beads rattle together. 'Well, there's something major going down in the smelly bit inside the Cordern. Your Daddy's looking as relaxed as possible considering it's probably brown uniform time. Fifty MBUs? Fleare, that's twice as many as they used at any one time against the whole of Soc O. No wonder the news jerk was interested.'

Fleare stared into space for a moment, chewing her lip. Then she said: 'That sim we were just in. Where you said about the Fortunate getting their hands on something really lethal?'

'Yeah, the sim. That's the other thing. The guy we made friends with, in there? Well, he got straightened out and we shoved him back into the same sim. He was veeeery smart, Fle. He found something. The trouble is, just when he found it, and before we saw what it was, he vanished. No trace. Someone – or something – just yanked him out of the sim, and then, if that wasn't complicated enough, the whole sim shut down. The Moderator swears it had nothing to do with it, which means that something even smarter than it must have been involved, considering it's supposed to be in charge.'

'Uh huh. And suddenly my father is all worried? And is somehow in a position of power?'

'So it seems.'

Fleare nodded to herself. She was bored with sitting on the floor; she tensed her muscles and sprang herself upright, daring her legs to hurt more. They did, but not enough to stop her. 'I want to be there, Muz. Wherever there is.'

'Okay. May one ask why, when you would be better off resting and recovering?'

She took a deep breath. 'Because of Kelk. Because of Silthx. And because no fucking *way* does my father get to be President of the Universe or whatever. What else was Soc O about?' She spread her arms, and then let them fall to her sides. 'Besides, fuck recovering. I'm not going to recover, Muz. I know I've been ignoring it but someone with some intimate information decoded my mods and shot me full of the wrong answer, remember? I'm going to die. I'm going to fall apart and turn into a dribbling pile of shit and then I'm going to *die*.' She paused, breathing hard. 'So I might as well keep busy.'

265

'I take it I can't stop you?'

'No!' Fleare glared at him.

'Fine. I didn't think I could. There's a clipper waiting.'

She blinked. 'What, already?'

'Well, obviously. Like I said, I didn't think I could stop you.'

Her hands were trembling; she clamped them to her hips in what she hoped looked like defiance. 'Good. But don't get into the habit of second-guessing me.'

'Oh, puh-lease. It wasn't a second guess.' The necklace dipped in the air and then floated towards the edge of the clearing. 'It wasn't even a first guess. Now, are you coming?'

She nodded, and followed the little entity.

Because.

She hadn't felt able to add, because of me. And because of you.

The clipper was much nicer than the waste can. She looked in through the airlock. 'Wow. This is almost – sumptuous. And kind of unusual.' She took in the heavily sculpted leather seats. Some of them had . . . projections. Quite functional-looking ones, if you liked certain things. She studied them carefully, and then turned back to Muz. 'I didn't think you were into this stuff. Where'd you get it?'

'I'm not, for fuck's sake. I didn't. It's a present from someone. There's a message with it. Ready?'

There was something about his voice. He sounded almost diffident, and Fleare felt herself shiver slightly. 'Of course,' she said.

'Okay. It's just audio. Ah, it's keyed personal.'

'Really?' Fleare raised her eyebrows. 'Does that mean you have to go away while I listen?'

'Yes. I'll be back when it's over.'

Fleare stared at him. Eventually she said, 'Do you know who this ultra-secret message is from?'

'Yeah, it's from Jez.' Now Muz sounded embarrassed. 'Shit,

Fle, it's probably just private girl talk. What do I know? I'm starting it now. See you.'

There was a fleeting burst of white noise, then Fleare heard Jez's voice, sounding a little flat as if she had been talking into her palm. 'Hi, Fleare. Hope you're still okay. Feel free to use the clipper as long as you need it. It's pretty fast and it can look after itself, so if you need to go anywhere flaky you're a bit less likely to get smeared out over the starscape. Sorry about the décor. It came from an ex, and believe me it wasn't a long relationship.'

Jez paused, and Fleare had time to smile to herself. Then the voice went on, sounding more confidential, as if Jez had leaned in towards the mike. 'Look, about all the mysterious stuff. I got some news on your problem. It's not great but it may help, I'm not sure. After the war the Haas Corporation bought the full rights, patents, files, codes, everything, on the mods. They also seized all the records, *all* of them, from Soc O. Then they locked it down, like *really* restricted it, personal to Board level only. Rumour says it was agreed by your Daddy's private secretary. That's where the trail stops, if you're outside the corporation. Or the family, maybe. So the woman who shot you? Unless she was a really accomplished thief she must have had inside help. I guess you know who that must mean. Sorry, Fle.'

Fleare nodded to herself. *No shit*, she thought. *The bastard must be really pissed at me.*

Jez was still speaking. 'Oh, and one more thing? There's a trace on the clipper. I'll know where you are. So if you do anything really stupid, at least one person will be laughing.' Jez paused again. 'Look, you know what I mean. I'm no good at being serious. Take care of yourself, and think twice before you talk to anyone. Really, Fleare, anyone at all. Bye.'

The audio cut out. Fleare sat down on one of the non-projecting couches and stared at nothing for a while. When she looked up Muz was back. He was hanging in the air in front of her, swaying slightly from side to side. She frowned. 'Why are you swinging?'

'Huh? I didn't realize I was. Distracted, I guess. What did Jez say?'

Fleare thought quickly. 'She apologized for the furniture.'

'Only that?'

She flashed him a sour grin. 'That, and girl talk.' She braced herself against the pain that was to come and stood up; her legs twinged. It seemed a little worse. 'So, what's this holiday resort planet called?'

'The one where everyone's gathering? Traspise.'

'Yeah. Right. There. Let's go.'

'To do what?'

'I don't know! To get in the way, I guess.' She looked at him seriously. 'You don't have to come.'

'I am coming, though.'

She nodded. 'Thanks.'

'You're welcome. Leaving in ten minutes.' He floated off.

Fleare waited until he was out of sight, and then sat down again carefully. She was trying to work out why she had included Muz in the category of 'everybody' that Jez thought she shouldn't talk to. She was still trying without success when the clipper jumped slightly and the couch adjusted itself subtly around her. They were off.

She knew where. She had no idea what, but she was now a hundred per cent certain about why.

Recovered personality

The view is astonishing. I turn to the guy in the robes, who is apparently called Theo. He seems to think that's funny, for some reason. 'How high are we, did you say?'

'Above the plains? Two kilometres.'

Two kilometres. Not two real kilometres, of course. I haven't got a body to be real with, and neither, I am finding out, has Theo. When I said he was like me I had no idea how accurate I was.

We materialized, although that is utterly the wrong word, in something that feels like a cross between an observation platform, a spaceship bridge and the waiting room of a brothel. It's a circular room with a narrow band of windows, which I think really are windows rather than screens, round the edge. The windows look out over a broad sweep of icy, misty desert which laps at the base of the mountain range we seem to be at the top of.

It is stunning. It's also a very long way down. The primitive part of me that hasn't understood this whole simulation business hopes the windows are made of something really strong.

I sit back on the fur-covered couch – that's the brothel bit – and ask, 'What happened?'

It's a broad-brush kind of a question but Theo understands. 'I shut down the sim.' He shrugs, and waits.

Some people make you want to shudder. Simulation; the name is deceptive. Something artificial, something pretend. But that's not right. Sims started out like that, but they didn't stay like that. Processing power, speed, smart coding, all came together to the point where the intricacy of a life within a sim began to approach that of a life in the real world. And one day, inevitably, the curves crossed.

That was the day sim development was made illegal, but lots of things are illegal. It's great for profit margins. So no one can be quite sure how much further things have gone, but while there is plenty of cash to build big server farms the simple answer will be *further*.

So shutting down a sim is the same as genocide, only mostly a lot quicker.

My face gives me away. Theo looks at me and shakes his head. 'Please,' he says. 'I set the thing up. Don't you think I can shut it down? And I kept the record. I could start it up again any time I liked.'

'You set it up?' This is getting beyond me. 'Why?'

'Would you believe, because I was bored? Anyway, I needed a place to stay.'

I raise my eyebrows and gesture round at the circular bachelor pad. He laughs. 'This isn't exactly mine. It more sort of *is* me.'

Now it's my turn to shake my head. He looks at me and grins. 'Okay, I'll explain.' He sits down on the furry couch a little way round from me, looks thoughtful for a moment, and then waves his hand at the floor in front of him. A section of it bulges upwards and grows into a low table covered in bottles and flasks and a big, ornate water pipe with two mouthpieces. He picks one up and holds it out towards me. 'Smoke?'

I hesitate, and he waggles the mouthpiece. Coils of bluish

smoke wisp out. 'Go on. It's probably good for you.' He frowns slightly. 'I'm sure I read that somewhere.'

I take the pipe. 'Bad for you,' I say. 'It's bad for you. Where have you been for the last fifty thousand years?'

'Exactly! That's what I'm trying to tell you.' He picks up the other mouthpiece, sits back, takes a long pull that makes the water pipe bubble and talks through a stream of thick, sweet-smelling smoke. 'Although it's a bit more than fifty thousand years. I'm sort of original, you see.' He looks at me, then down at his robes, and shakes his head. 'Not the way you're thinking, although I might be that as well. I meant more as in – origin.' I must still look blank. He blows more smoke and adds: 'You know? Like beginning?'

It feels as if a void the size of a gravity well has opened beneath me. I swallow. 'Go on,' I say.

He is silent for a moment. Then he looks straight at me. 'I know what happened to you. You were born on Silthx. Your family were imprisoned by the Fortunate after the invasion. You were sent to a labour camp. You excavated – something.' More smoke. He seems to need it. 'Did anyone ever tell you what it was?'

'Not exactly. Some kind of old artefact. Maybe powerful. Why?'

'Powerful isn't the half of it.' He shakes his head. 'What you, what *they* found was something very, very old, but that doesn't matter because it's pretty well immortal. It's old enough to remember the creation of the Spin.' He sighs. 'To have taken part in it, in fact.'

Now it's my turn to reach for a smoke. I don't know if it will work, but I feel I need something. The smoke is thick and sweet, with a sharp sensation on my tongue like pins and needles. It is harsh on my palate. I cough, but it feels good. My voice is husky, though. So's my brain, right now. 'Creation? But that was, what . . .'

I trail off, and he nods again. 'About a quarter of a million years ago. Yeah. I remember.'

'You remember?'

'Yes. I was there too.' He falls silent. For a while so do I, but there's something I want to ask. 'You know what happened to me,' I said. 'What about . . . other people?'

'By other people, do you mean your family?'

I nod.

'All dead. I'm sorry.'

It shouldn't be a surprise. After all, what am I? Not exactly alive. But still I feel my eyes stinging. I can see he has noticed. I don't want him to. I look away. 'So, this creation machine thing.'

'Yes.' He laughs quietly, although I'm not sure why. 'This Creation Machine, then, to give it a name. It's just a piece of construction equipment, really. But when you think that it was constructing planetary systems, you can understand the sort of forces it could throw about. Possibly still could, if it wanted to. If it was able to.'

I stare into nothing for a moment. I am imagining this simple white ovoid, hanging in space, balancing the forces of – what? White fire and blue fire and angry, dirty red fire, and planets forming and crashing.

I realize that my heart is pounding. I breathe deeply. 'And the Fortunate have got it.'

'Yes.'

'Can they use it?'

He shakes his head slightly. 'Not yet. Not on their own. It's not the kind of thing you just use. It can't be coerced.'

'That's a relief.' Then the words sink in. 'What do you mean, not yet?'

'It might be tricked. Deceived. And news has leaked out. People know they've got it, including some clever people. It's not a stable situation.' He stands up. 'You're part of the news.

272

You're a witness. That's why you were rescued and dropped into a supporting role in an obscure sim. Someone in the Fortunate wanted a record, and so did I. So I helped.'

The fog in my brain is getting worse. I put down the mouthpiece and stand up, relieved to find that I can remain upright. Walking works too, so I stroll over to those windows and look out and, inevitably, down. There's a *lot* of down to look at. At the edge of my vision, smeared and blurred by mist, there are plains. Above them, foothills, with buildings growing out of them in rising circles. Then the angle of the windows restricts the view, but we are obviously in some sort of tower.

I stare down until I feel I have mastered the distance. Then I turn back to Theo, who is waiting with an amused expression lifting the corners of his beard. 'So who are you, and why do you give a shit?'

The beard twists some more. 'I deserved that. Sorry. I've spent a quarter of a million years making my own entertainment. I think I've forgotten about people.' He walks over to join me. 'This,' and he gestures around at the view, 'is a representation of a planet, a moon really, called Obel. No one's ever heard of it.' He looks at me enquiringly.

'I've never heard of it,' I say obediently.

'Thank you.' He turns back to the window and sighs. 'Back when I had a body I was, how can I put this, involved in the construction phase – the creation – too. And when it was all done I decided to stay. I built this place, right on the edge of things.'

'You built this tower thing?'

He shakes his head. 'No. I built this place. All of it. The moon, the plains, everything. I made it look like a dying ecosystem, right from the beginning.' He grins. 'Only the most interesting people come to the end of a world, you know. I had a lot of great company. Some weird stuff, of course.' He stares into nothing for a moment, and I have the feeling of intruding on memories. Then he seems to shake himself. 'One of the weirder sets of inhabitants was a bunch of pretend monks, and one day they brought a prisoner.' He looks at me sideways. 'You met her, by a beach.'

He means the young woman with the old eyes, of course. 'Her? You saw that?'

He tilts a hand from side to side. 'Not so much saw. A part of me was there.'

I frown at him. 'Wait,' I say. 'You said you'd been in the other sim for a long time.'

He grins. 'I had. And on the beach, for a while. And here, too, a small part of me, keeping the fires burning.' He looks around and sighs a little. 'Home sweet home. Part of me has always been here. Built in, you might say. That's what I meant when I said it *was* me.' He breaks off and fiddles with the pipe for a moment. 'She's in trouble. The woman you met on the beach. Not that it's your problem.'

'No, it isn't.' I say it a little angrily, on the off-chance that helps it to be true. The anger gives me momentum. 'So, where are we going with this?'

He looks surprised. 'Well, first we need to dump some information back into reality. It's what people think will be encoded on that chip, and we needn't make their lives difficult by telling them they're wrong. Whatever; we'll make the news of Silthx, the Creation Machine, everything, public. It seems only fair. I don't want to try to pick winners. Then I'm going to the Cordern, before those Fortunate maniacs do something regrettable.' He pauses, and adds, 'Or even if they do. Remember I said things had leaked out? Vultures are gathering. There's a fleet, or rather several fleets, gathering around the edge of the Cordern, and they're all tooled up and trembling to shoot. Each other, partly, but I wouldn't like to be the Fortunate.'

'And me?' The anger is lasting quite well.

'Yes, well. Your options are getting thin too.' He collapses back into the couch. It makes a *fuff* noise. 'I'm sorry to be so blunt – but when I go, when I leave this place, it ends. This sim, and the real bit. I'm what animates it.' His hands sweep across nothing, palms flat. 'Finito. Cloud of dust, puff of smoke, gone. No more moon. So you can't stay here.'

'So where can I go?' The answer is beginning to come into focus, and he confirms it. 'Well, not backwards,' he says. 'That sim is gone, and the bit on the beach was only temporary. Forwards, I guess.'

I put the pipe down, and reach out for the first glass that comes my way. The nearest bottle opens easily, and pouring is second nature. I drink.

When my vision has cleared I put the empty glass down hard, making the table rattle. 'That means going with you, doesn't it?'

'Yes, it does.' He reaches out a hand. 'For what it's worth, I have the best of motives.'

I look down at the hand, and then up at his face. 'Yeah, right,' I say.

'No, really.' He looks at me, and for the first time I see something vulnerable. 'What you call the Creation Machine? It's a friend of mine.'

'What about me? What happens if I take your hand?'

'To you? Whatever you want, in a way. Whatever you want badly enough.' He looks away. 'You can't maintain your current state for ever. Outside the framework of a sim, you're a bundle of code hanging together by itself. You can do it for a while, but in the end you'll probably start to disperse. How long that takes is up to you.'

I nod. 'So, I stay here and get obliterated. I go with you and dissolve. Can I find another sim?'

'Yeah, if you really want. But you'll always be a bit of a ghost. Or worse, some kind of virus.' He looks up at me again. 'You're better than that.'

275

'How do you know?'

'Oh, I know you better than you know yourself.' He should sound smug, but somehow he doesn't. I search his face, and he sighs. 'I know your name, for example. Shall I say it?'

I feel as though time has stopped. Ghost, he said. Well, that's over as of now. I nod again, just once, and he says it.

I look at him for a while longer, while the memories dance in my head. The ones they gave me back after the beach, and all the others that they didn't. They sing a song like a finger round a wet glass. As my sight starts to blur I reach out and take his hand, and reality begins to dissolve.

Fuck it. Here we go again.

Traspise Approach

Fleare surprised herself by sleeping through most of the journey. She awoke to silence, which presumably meant either that they had arrived, or that they had stopped before they arrived. She took a couple of breaths, rose cautiously from the couch and glanced around for some sort of display. She found a retro-looking flat panel suspended towards what she assumed was the front of the cabin. She looked at it, blinked, and froze.

The background, yeah, that was definitely the safe place to start. It was starscape, with a pretty blue-green-white planet roughly centred. It almost looked as if it had rings; she looked closer and realized that it was surrounded at a discreet distance by spacecraft.

She could ignore the foreground no longer. It was Muz. Not Muz as beads, or Muz as a cloud of nano-stuff, or even Muz as a shiny sphere. Just Muz the male, as she had first seen him, dressed in slightly faded mil fatigues with a crooked corporal's badge.

No, that wasn't right. Not quite as she had first seen him. His face was older. There were lines around his eyes that looked more like pain than laughter, and his hair was actually touched with grey. His eyes were watching her.

She stared at him for a long time. Then, when she felt able, she said: 'Okay. What's going on?'

'Hi, Fleare.' He smiled. 'This is, and isn't, me. It's an interactive message.'

'Oh really?' She shook her head. 'You must have got the idea that I *like* being confused. And upset. Wrong, Muz, so very wrong. This is . . . shit. Where are you? What is going on?'

'I'm sorry.' His smile collapsed, and he looked tired. 'Look, I'm going to be saying that a lot. But I'll mean it every time. I'm sort of on Traspise, in a virtual sense. I don't exist as anything physical any more.' He shrugged. 'It's easier if you let me tell it, all right?'

'Easier for who? What is this, Muz, are you dumping me or something?' She wanted to ball her fists, but her hands were tired and anyway this – *thing* – was beyond her attack.

'Easier for both of us. And I'm not dumping you. I'm sort of dumping reality, I guess. Sorry.' Muz spread his arms and smiled. 'See? I told you. Well, first, this is happening because I did hear what Jez said.'

'You listened in? Muz, no, whatever you are, *thing*, that was fucking private!'

'Look, I'll save up all the sorries, all right? But I've got stuff to tell you, Fleare. Will you listen? Please?'

She realized that she was grinding her teeth. She forced herself to stop, not because she cared about her teeth any more but in case the *thing* noticed. She made herself take several slow, even breaths. Then she said, 'All right. I'll listen. But not for long.'

'It won't take long. Right. First, do you remember a theme park, when you were fifteen?'

She nodded. 'Yeah. So what?'

'Outside, afterwards? When you threw up? Remember the guy who tried to help you?' He shook his head. 'The one you gave a false ident to?'

She thought back. 'Well, I guess. But what . . . oh, wait.' She searched her memory. 'You? That was you?'

'Yes.'

Her stomach churned. 'Shit. You sleaze. Did you *stalk* me?'

'Not really. I liked you. I felt sorry for you.'

Fleare's heart was racing. 'Not really? Sorry? I don't want your apologies. You have to do better than that, because right now I feel *violated*, you understand me?'

'I do understand. Now will you listen, or not?'

Part of her was screaming that she didn't have to listen – that attack was better. Or yelling. Or flight. But another part of her had to know. She compressed her lips and listened.

'Your father came looking for you. He found me instead. He seemed upset.'

'Oh, I just bet he did. I bet the bastard thought I had really pissed on his party.'

'He thought more than that, Fle. He was worried about you.'

'Oh great. He was worried, you were sorry. Muz, I'm so not feeling grateful, you hear?'

'He was worried because you were hurt and angry. Was that so wrong? He and I swapped idents, and that was it for the moment. A couple of years later I was looking for something to do. Soc O was getting going, I thought it looked like a laugh, so I joined up. A few months in your father got in touch. He said it looked like you were going to join up too, and would I look out for you?'

She felt the world spinning. 'Whoa. Look out for me? Meaning pick me up?' She found herself squaring up to the screen, and was too angry to stop. 'Meaning get me drunk and seduce me? You lying, raping . . . *cunt*.' The word didn't seem bad enough.

'No! It didn't mean that. He was pissed off when he found out.'

'He found out? Well, obviously. I should have thought of that. Did you send him videos?' She advanced on the screen until her nose was against it. 'You had better be glad you aren't here. You had better never come near me again because if you do, I swear I'll smear you out over the whole shitting *universe*.' She raised both her hands and slammed them against the image as hard as she could. She had hoped that the screen would break, or the image would flinch, or *something*, but all that happened was her hands started hurting. She was oddly pleased. It balanced out the pain in her legs, which was getting worse. *The mods, she thought, or rather their fatal race towards their annihilation and mine. The mods I snapped at on the rebound from you.* She wanted to fling that at Muz too, as yet another thing to blame him for, but suddenly it occurred to her that even now it wasn't really him she was angry with. He was only another pawn, just like her. She took a few backwards steps and let herself sag on to the couch. 'Go on,' she said wearily.

'Yeah, he found out. I don't know how, Fle. It wasn't me.' Muz shrugged. 'By then I guess he had eyes everywhere, or at least the Heg' did – which was pretty much the same thing, even then. I did hear from him once more, though.' He paused, and then said slowly, 'Just before the last attack on Soc O, he sent me a message. It just said to get you out of there.'

Fleare stared at him. 'So you knew something was coming?'

'Well, not knew exactly. Worked it out, I guess.'

'And you said nothing?' She was shaking.

'That's right, I said nothing. I just flew by the book.' He ran a hand through the greying hair. 'Afterwards, when I was in that jar? They thought I was nuts because of uploading into the AI cloud. They were wrong. I was nuts because I knew I had said nothing.'

'And did you know that woman was going to shoot me?' Suddenly Fleare had had enough. She turned away. 'Don't answer that,' she said quietly.

'Why not?'

'I don't want not to believe you, okay?'

'Shit. I'm not lying, Fle, but all right, I won't say anything more, not about that.'

They were both silent for a moment. Then, unable to help

herself, Fleare said: 'And now? What are you doing now? Wherever you are?'

His voice had been soft, but now he suddenly sounded purposeful. 'All the guesswork is right, Fleare. There is something potent down there. And everyone's interested; so many people have turned up, this place has practically got its own asteroid belt made of ships. It only needs someone to fart without clearing it with the next guy, and the whole Cordern will go up. I'm going to put things right. At least, I hope so. Fleare? Don't come any closer to Traspise than this, okay? Stuff might kick off.'

She stood up, biting her lip at the pain that fired itself up her legs and into her hips. 'Okay,' she said. 'I won't. Now fuck off and redeem yourself. If you think you can.'

There was no answer. After a while she forced herself to look at the display. The image of Muz had gone, but the starscape was still there. She thought the cloud of ships had grown a little.

Oh, you bastard, she thought. *Even now you've got me. Even after the lies you just admitted to, and all the others they imply. You knew, and you flew by the book, and flying by the book meant you were dead behind me and that meant you were dead and I was alive.*

And even after everything, I still wish it was the other way round.

The pain was – conquering. Her legs wanted to fold, but she growled and forced her knees to lock. She didn't know how long she had been standing there, her face aching from the rictus of defiant agony, when she heard the sound of the airlock cycling and then Jezerey's voice. Slowly she forced her head round on her cramped neck. 'Are you real?' she asked carefully, and remembered that it was the second time in her life that the question had mattered.

Then she collapsed.

Taussich, Cordern

For the next few days Alameche allowed himself the luxury of routine. He felt he had earned it. Eskjog appeared first thing every morning to brief him on progress with the artefact, but those briefings only served to confirm his suspicion that the little machine and whatever forces were behind it did not have any quick answers; the artefact stayed inert. Meanwhile he made enquiries on two fronts.

The first was good old-fashioned spying, which he did all the time, but the second needed expertise. That was why he had dismissed all his servants for the night and was sitting in semi-darkness across a low table from the tiny, almost childlike figure of Chief Analyst Kressilim.

Alameche didn't care very much where he lived. He had rented out his inherited estates so long ago that he barely remembered where they were, and he had acquired nothing to replace them. His position gave him the run of a whole cluster of official residences, ranging from townhouses to a sort of floating palace thing on the top of the cliff overlooking the Stadium, and he never used those either, except for one close to the Citadel which he kept closely guarded, with plenty of official-looking people coming and going. So far the subterfuge had worked; apparently even people who knew him quite well assumed he lived there.

That was why he'd chosen it as the venue for his meeting with the Chief Analyst. Rather, it was one of the reasons. Another – *the* other – was that Kressilim stank, in a complex pervasive way which seemed ludicrous considering his diminutive frame, and which lingered a long time after the man himself was gone. You didn't want that in your real living quarters.

The room was darkened. A screen on one wall showed Alameche, the Patriarch and Eskjog. It was a still from the security footage shot during their underground meeting, and the Patriarch was frozen in what looked like mid-shout, his face red and his hands flat in front of him.

Kressilim leaned forward, and Alameche had to fight the instinct to lean back. 'Very interesting,' he said. 'What is your question?'

'I have more than one.' Alameche pointed at the screen. 'First, what is that thing and second, where does it really come from?'

'Only two? I would have added, what is it capable of?' Kressilim sat back. 'Well, your questions first. What is it? Taken at face value it is an autonomous, self-contained intellect, which might or might not be artificial.'

Alameche felt his brow furrowing. 'Might not? How can it be anything else?'

'It could be many things. Its envelope is large enough to contain a human brain and a compact life-support system. That might explain its own comment that it is legally human where it comes from. It is rare, even in the barbarian regions, for artificial intelligences to be counted as human.'

Alameche suppressed a smile. Kressilim didn't limit his eccentricity to being unusually small and smelly. He was also a member of a tiny fundamentalist sect which held that everything outside the sphere of the Fortunate was either unclean or barbarian. It didn't matter. Almost nothing would have compared to the breadth of his intellect and the way he could apply it.

'Could it also contain weapons?'

'Weapons?' The little man sat up straight. 'You did not speak of this. What form do they take?'

Alameche described Eskjog's abilities. When he had finished Kressilim sat back and blew out his cheeks. 'That is different,' he said slowly. 'Humanity has no relevance. What you describe is in effect a war machine, although one with good manners.' He looked sharply at Alameche. 'And it has attacked you, from what you say. Which means, Excellency, that it has attacked us.' He paused. 'Are we at war, then?'

This time Alameche allowed himself the smile. 'If we are, it's nothing new,' he said. 'But you haven't told me who with? Is it the Hegemony?'

'Them?' Kressilim laughed, an odd squeaky sound that set Alameche's teeth on edge. 'I expect that would be the address on the communiqué. But every puppet has a master. I suggest, in this case, that you take matters at face value and assume that you are at war with the Haas Corporation.'

'Indeed?' Alameche frowned. 'Why? I thought they were our friends.'

'For two reasons. First, because they are the major financial stakeholders in the Hegemony. They were the backers in the recent civil war and they have prospered since the victory. But second, they specialize in owning and exploiting technology. Just like your little machine there.'

Alameche stared at Kressilim for a long time, while thoughts chased each other round his skull. Then he said, 'But these same people pose as our friends, or at least as our allies.'

Kressilim nodded. 'They do,' he agreed. 'But you yourself used the word "pose", Excellency.'

'I did.' Alameche sighed. 'And you used the word "puppet". Kressilim, I will not be a puppet. Let's discuss this.'

By the time the bright sliver of the Joker had appeared on the horizon Alameche had altogether stopped noticing Kressilim's smell, but he had reached a decision. It was reinforced a few hours later by a message from the supposedly secure clinic where Kestus was being treated. The man had been showing signs of recovering consciousness when the clinic was broken into by a group of masked men who had somehow evaded the whole security system including the monitoring cameras. It had taken them less than two minutes to penetrate to Kestus's room, sever his head and make their escape, taking the head with them.

War, indeed, and apparently on a choice of fronts.

'What will you do?' Kressilim had asked.

Alameche stretched. 'I shall take a holiday. A rather public one.' He smiled. 'And I will give a party. It will be interesting to see who accepts an invitation.'

Traspise, Cordern

The little planet grew quickly in the viewer. It looked blue and green and inviting. It was meant to. The effect had been very expensive.

Traspise had been a small industrial planet when the Fortunate had first taken it. Just for once they had miscalculated; its resources were not the bonanza they had hoped, being close to worked out. Normally the Patriarch's father would have had a tantrum and trashed the place, but this time he had gone against type and ordered it to be cleaned up, re-planeformed and fitted out for leisure.

It had been stunningly successful. Traspise now offered the perfect blend of mountains, seas, lakes, islands and great grass plains. An extra, artificial mini-sun topped up the original one to keep a belt round the middle of the little planet agreeably tropical. You could hunt, sport or just party, safe in the knowledge that everyone you met would be your socio-economic equal because the population (strictly limited to a maximum of one person per hundred square kilometres) was thoroughly aristocratic, like you.

Alameche disliked Traspise intensely, partly because he was bored by most of the aristocracy but mainly because he never took holidays. But he had to admit the place had its uses.

Crucially, it was relatively surveillance-light. That made for easy conversations, especially at parties.

It also made it an inspired choice for the new home of the artefact. The choice had been Eskjog's, of course, although Alameche had agreed to it. Alameche suspected that the little machine – or whatever it was – was extremely well briefed. Well, it would be interesting to see which way Eskjog jumped.

Now the planet filled the viewer. It was time to secure for landing. Nothing so working-class as strapping in this time; you just lay back on the nearest pile of cushions and it inflated round you like an embrace.

The descent took half an hour. Alameche spent it catching up on news programmes. Not just local ones – he was one of only a few hundred people within the Cordern who could access digests from outside it. At first sight there was nothing. Then he sat up, or tried to; the inflated cushions pressed softly but inexorably on his chest and the mechanical equivalent of a young woman's voice said: 'Please relax. Your comfort and safety are paramount.'

He subsided and rewound the clip, looking for whatever it was that had caught his interest. There it was. He stopped, and set the clip to play.

'. . . continued interest in last night's brutal murder in Catastrophe, involving a dismembered body which was found in three separate locations. In an intriguing development it has become clear that a missing heiress may be involved, because one of the murdered man's travelling companions appears to have been Fleare Haas, estranged and possibly kidnapped daughter of Viklun Haas, the founder and Chief Executive of Haas Corporation . . .'

The clip flicked to a 2-D picture of a young woman. Alameche froze it and studied her.

In standard terms, she would have been in her early twenties. Her hair was in a short, military cut, although her clothes were civilian and – as far as he could judge the fashions of the outer regions – nondescript. Her brows were straight. Her lips were compressed, and her eyes seemed to be focused on something a long way behind the camera. The background to the picture was blurred and cluttered; he couldn't make anything out.

Alameche considered himself to be good at people. Fleare Haas looked determined, certainly, but something else as well.

Fragile. That was it.

He flicked out of the news and back into the view of Traspise. They were almost down and the descent was slowing. He watched what seemed at first like a rough patch expand into a mountain range, and then zoom in even more until what lay ahead was a single peak.

The spaceport was on the highest point of the highest range. Being that far up the gravity well saved some energy, which no one really cared about, but it also kept the noise of the shuttles as far as possible from the rest of the planet; people cared about that a great deal. It also made for a splendid vista as you approached. Alameche let the view slide across the landscape until he was looking at a bowl in the mountain range, a kilometre or so from the landing peak. Straight maglev tracks led from the peak to the bowl, which held the logistics centre and control unit for the spaceport. As of yesterday, in the back of an anonymous warehouse it also held the artefact.

The shuttle touched down with a barely perceptible shiver. The cushions released Alameche and the door opened, letting in cool mountain air. Alameche took a deep breath, as much in acknowledgement of the work put in by the planetary management as because he liked it. It seemed different from the last time he had visited. Presumably they had re-engineered the scent a little.

He took another deep breath and hopped down from the shuttle. The peak was deserted, which was quite usual. He had no luggage; the little he needed had been sent separately. He stretched, and strolled over to the headworks of the water-lift that was the only pedestrian route up and down the peak. He could hear water rushing through the works, which meant that one of the cars would be here soon. He sat down and waited, and wondered who would reply to his very carefully coded invitation.

There was no mechanism for replacing the Patriarch, obviously – except for the oldest one in the universe – and there was no excuse for doing it unless you won. It was an appallingly high-stakes thing to begin, and that was why Alameche had very painstakingly not begun it, so far as anyone could point to.

Well, he would see soon enough. Meanwhile the car had arrived, clanking up its track with its two arms – they really did look rather like arms – outstretched and hitched on to the hydraulic rams that ran parallel to the track. It wobbled to a stop, and the door clicked and rose. Alameche climbed in and settled down into the forward-facing seat. There was a hollow thumping of valves as the system switched the rams from rise to fall. Then the car gave a shudder and began to sink down the track, gurgling gently. The noise was quite restful. Alameche closed his eyes and made the most of it. After the news Eskjog had handed him, he suspected it was going to be his last chance for some time.

Eskjog had turned up that morning not long after Kressilim had gone. Alameche, who had already resigned himself to another sleepless night, had ordered a light breakfast and a stimulant. He was halfway through the breakfast and all the way through the stimulant when the little machine had floated straight in out of the dawn sky without any social niceties. 'Alameche? Are you awake?'

'Happily, yes.' He cursed himself briefly for leaving the windows open, but it had been that or live with Kressilim's stink for hours and besides, he doubted if even the most durable glass could exclude Eskjog. 'You're early.'

'And I'm important. Extremely. Remember our friend the recovered personality?'

For a moment Alameche didn't. Then he nodded. 'Of course. From Silthx?'

'Yes. Well, it's been recovered by someone else.'

Alameche stared. 'Recovered? What are you talking about?'

'It's been subverted. Someone, or something, or a lot of some-things, we don't know, knocked it out of its safe little groove in a quiet simulation and made off with it, which means that what it knows, other people know.' It floated closer to Alameche. 'They know all about you guys, and Silthx, and that artefact. The Spin is coming in mob-handed, Alameche, and it has the safety catch firmly *off*. You need to be ready.'

'I see.' Alameche sat down. 'And what, in your view, does ready look like?'

'Simple. It looks different, right at the top. I recommend sac-rificing a scapegoat.'

'Really?' Alameche leaned back and studied Eskjog. 'This scapegoat. Is it Patriarch-shaped?'

'I couldn't possibly say. I do think interfering in another society's business is unethical, don't you?' Eskjog rose and headed for the window. Then it paused. 'I assume you will be talking to your peers about this?'

Alameche nodded. 'In two days,' he said. 'On – that planet.'

'Ah. Good.' Eskjog gave its affirmative wobble. 'I'll see myself out, shall I?'

Alameche watched the little machine float out through one of the open windows. When he was sure it had gone – as sure as he could be – he got up and closed them, using the manual catches.

Then he sat for a long time, thinking.

*

And now, two days later on Traspise, there were eleven of them, including most of the Cabinet – and Alameche. It was enough, just. He hadn't been sure.

He had chosen to hold the party that wasn't a party in a palace that wasn't a palace. The Great Salt Palace was the fanciful name for one of the few things that had existed on Traspise before it had been re-engineered. It was really a set of caves, not carved out of something but sculpted upwards in salt by half a million years of mineral springs. The saturated volcanic water had deposited great barriers and curving walls; had eroded and replaced and destroyed and rebuilt and blocked up and canalized vast, eerie structures of metal-rich salts that glistened and flashed.

The lowest level was called the Undercroft. It was covered and surrounded by metre upon metre of those salts. They were complex, metallic, sometimes semi-conducting salts that diverted and baffled electrical signals so beautifully that it was as close as you could wish to surveillance-proof.

They were reclining on couches carved from blocks of pink gypsum, padded with sheets of dense, resilient moss rooted straight into the crystal. The couches formed a semicircle with an elaborate fireplace at its centre. Even the logs were partly fossilized, the remains of ancient trees that had been buried in crystalline sludge for thousands of years. As they burned they gave off showers of multicoloured sparks.

They had eaten lightly and talked small-talk. Alameche had joined in for the sake of politeness, but mainly he had watched their expressions and listened to what they weren't saying as much as to what they were.

They were nervous, of course, some more than others. Garamende was there, and he seemed the most relaxed of all, although ill-tempered at being made to leave his four playthings outside. Then, Trask. Alameche had been a little surprised to see the old soldier, who was another with little to say and much watching to do. There were Possall and Charefenst, also Cabinet members, both shifting nervously and laughing too much – and finally, to Alameche's genuine surprise, Fiselle. The thin man had been the last to arrive and Alameche's face must for once have given him away because Fiselle had glanced at him and given a twisted smile. 'Not expecting me?'

Alameche shrugged. 'No,' he said simply.

'Good.' Fiselle smiled more widely. 'I don't blame you. Unlike some of our friends,' and he looked towards Garamende, 'I do my best thinking with my eyes open and my mouth closed.'

Now the finger foods and the small-talk had both been exhausted and there was silence. Most of the others were looking at Alameche. He let them wait for a while. Then, when he guessed they were ready, he said: 'Well?'

Predictably it was Garamende who responded. 'Well what, man? It's your party. You ask the questions.'

'All right.' Alameche stood up. 'To begin with, Hodil was snatched, questioned and killed. Kestus was injured and then killed and his head removed. I can forgive these things, but,' and he looked round the circle, 'I need a good reason.'

Garamende nodded. 'Well enough.' He also looked round, his eyebrows raised. The others nodded. 'After the eel fight, you and I talked. I expressed the view, the commonly held view, that the Patriarch has become a liability. It's an opinion that pre-dates that ludicrous piece of grandstanding after the Games, by the way. But what changed then was that he had gone against your advice. You said, in Cabinet, that we should do nothing.' He looked at Alameche and grinned. 'Don't look so surprised. Worried men talk. Old Trask talked quite a lot. Didn't you?'

Trask nodded.

'So that meant His Excellency was moving beyond your influence.' Garamende stood up and walked over to Alameche. 'We decided you needed rescuing.'

'*I* needed rescuing?' Alameche looked at him sharply. 'From what, exactly?'

'From a situation. Work it out, man! Suppose your Carnifex carves his name on poor old Hodil's hide. Hodil talks. He could have come up with a few names, you know. Probably not ours,' and he swung a hand round the circle, 'but a few people at one remove. You would have been pushed into a choice. We didn't know which way you'd go.'

'So you snatched him and tortured him yourself? Why?'

'Ah, but we didn't. Your fucking Kestus did.'

'*Kestus?*'

Garamende shrugged. 'That's where the rescue comes in, you see?'

Alameche sat down. 'Kestus,' he said again more quietly. 'He wasn't working for you, was he?'

'No.' Garamende sat down next to him and put a hand on his shoulder. 'And he wasn't working for you in the end. Only leaves one, eh?'

Alameche said nothing for a moment. Then he shook off Garamende's hand and stood up. 'No,' he said.

'No?' Garamende raised his eyebrows. 'No, what?'

'No, I will not be swept along like this.' Alameche had felt shocked but now it was being replaced by a surging, energetic anger. He felt . . . *alive*. 'If Kestus was reporting on me to the Patriarch, so what? It would be amazing if no one was. Why not him?' He glared round the seated men. 'Whereas you are conspirators. You are the ones with something to lose. Now explain to me why you should not lose it.'

To his amazement, Fiselle stood up and began to applaud softly. 'Well done,' he said. 'You have provided your own justification. Ours is simple: we believe that you are the only person who is capable of fending off the risk of civil war.'

'I see.' Alameche had expected it, and there it was. He felt light-headed. 'What do you propose?'

'Just this. That you should invite the Patriarch onward. He can acquiesce or he can be removed, but it will be done quietly. You will propose that he be replaced by a ruling Council, reluctantly chaired by you.'

Alameche nodded. *Invite him onward.* It had a range of meanings, from comfortable retirement to disembowelment. 'An old-fashioned coup,' he said. 'Are you sure of support?'

'Oh yes.'

Alameche nodded. 'Good,' he said. 'You would be mad to get this far, otherwise. I also have some support.' He half turned towards the tall doors at the end of the room and raised his voice. 'Hello? Join us, if you will.'

There was a pause. Then the men jumped to their feet as the doors bumped open and Garamende's four playthings swung into the room, dangling as if they were in a net. A small, spiky ball hovered above them where the apex of the net would have been. 'Hello?' it said. 'Sorry to intrude, but I found these things outside. I think they were listening.' It paused, and then added, 'I'm called Eskjog, by the way.'

Alameche turned to Garamende. 'Well?'

The fat man rolled his eyes. 'Well of *course* they were listening, man. What else did I bring them for? Apart from shagging, that is.' He grinned, and then nodded towards Eskjog. 'The pet we all suspected has arrived. I assume that thing is not deaf?'

The little machine floated over until it was in the middle of the semicircle formed by the startled men. It halted, and its four passengers fell to the floor as if they had been released from a net. 'Obviously I am not deaf,' it said. 'Also, I am not a pet. I am known to some of you already. What else do you need to know?'

Garamende made to reply, but Trask waved him to silence. He limped forward until he was standing with his face only a hand's breadth from Eskjog, stuck out his chin and said: 'If you aren't a pet, what are you?'

'I am a Motile Negotiation Unit, or MNU.' The little machine moved an arm's length further from Trask and performed a pirouette.

'Motile?' Trask frowned. 'Why not mobile?'

'Well, both, obviously. The usual short title is Ambassador.'

'Ambassador?' Trask snorted. 'From and to whom?'

'From the diplomatic arm of something called the Haas Corporation. To, well, that seems to be something of a moving feast. Until a while ago I would have said, to the Court and Cabinet of His Excellency Chast, Final Patriarch of the People's Democratic Republic of the Planet of Taussich and the Fortunate Protectorates of the Spin Centre – but I suspect you may be moving towards some organizational change. In that case, I might say, a shorter title would be nice.'

Trask shook his head and turned to Alameche. 'So this impudent machine is Eskjog. Is it yours?'

Alameche shook his head. 'No,' he said, 'it's its.'

'Is it? And what role does it play here today?'

'Excuse me?' Eskjog interposed itself between Trask and Alameche. 'I am in the room . . . My role is to manage the joint threat and opportunity posed by the artefact discovered on Silthx. My interest is twofold. The threat, which is immediate, is to stability, and a threat to stability is the same as a threat to business. The opportunity is longer term, but may lead to the apotheosis of yourselves and ourselves. My preference would be to manage both of these in situ, that is, remaining within your sphere of influence and your nominal control. I was becoming concerned that your own leadership might prove an obstacle to this. Based on what I have heard in the past few minutes, I am more optimistic.'

Trask laughed, a harsh, hoarse bark that echoed round the chamber. 'Stripped of the long words, you would be happier if we overthrew the Patriarch. Is that it?'

'It is. I would.' Eskjog dipped in the air. 'Are those words short enough for you?'

'Just about.' Trask turned to the others. 'This is outside my field, gentlemen. I know about the Haas Corporation. Why should we be dictated to?'

It was Garamende who answered. 'We don't need to be,' he said. 'We had convinced ourselves before this thing turned up. If it happens to agree, why should that change our minds?'

'Humph.' Trask wagged a finger at Eskjog. 'What do we get if we happen to do what you prefer?'

'It's not so much a matter of what you get.' Eskjog swivelled from side to side as if looking around. 'More of what you keep. Like self-determination. It's simple enough. You are not the most powerful thing in the Spin. The Hegemony is more powerful. The Catastrophe, if it calls in its client states, is more powerful. Either of them, or several others, could intervene if they became concerned. And I must tell you that news is leaking out. This is thanks in part to your grandstanding leader, but only in part. People *are* becoming concerned, and those people are coming here. Minds will be made up, and if you are not careful scores will be settled. Proxy wars will be fought. You only have a limited time to reassure them.'

'And you?' Trask was breathing heavily. 'Are you more powerful?'

'If you mean the Haas Corporation, the question doesn't arise. We are a business, not a power bloc. We do have major investments to protect, though. Some of them here, if you didn't all know.'

'We knew, or if some of us didn't they ought to have been able to guess.' Trask turned and stared at Alameche. 'Investments? I hope you haven't been selling us short?'

Alameche shook his head. 'Not at all. There is nothing abnormal about it. We do business with many people.'

'It's true.' Eskjog made a sighing noise. 'Including some who have to hold their noses rather harder than we do. Sometimes we have to help them.'

Alameche thought he heard a laugh in the voice. He put a hand on Trask's shoulder. 'I think we have an opportunity, Cabinet Member.' He took a breath. 'You have asked me to take over. You said it would be reluctantly, and you are right.' Garamende snorted, and Alameche ignored him. 'His Excellency is scheduled to make a visit tomorrow to inspect the artefact. It presents an opportunity. Shall we take it?'

He looked round at the others. One by one, they nodded.

'Good. Then we have things to discuss.' Alameche smiled. 'And – oh yes. I'm afraid you'll all have to stay here tonight. The circle needs to remain closed.'

They nodded again, more slowly.

Both suns, the real and the artificial, had set, bathing the Palace in short-lived milky pink light shot through with flecks of gold. The discussion was over. It had lasted several hours, and ended in consensus. Afterwards, it seemed no one had much to add; people had drifted away towards their makeshift bedchambers. Eskjog had excused itself and floated off somewhere.

Alameche and Fiselle were the last. They looked at each other silently for a while. Then Fiselle shrugged. 'Come on,' he said. 'Let's get some fresh air.'

Alameche nodded, and they walked together out of the Undercroft. Broad, shallow stairs, built – so Alameche had always assumed – to be as unchallenging as possible to the knees of well-fed courtiers, led up in long sweeps to a wide balcony halfway up the Palace. It looked out over a narrow valley that was black with shadow.

They leaned on the parapet together. Fiselle spoke first. 'That ghastly machine. How long have you known it?'

'Eskjog? A few days. I must admit it seems much longer.'

'I am sure it does. Do you trust it?'

'No.'

'Good. Neither do I.' Fiselle was quiet for a moment. 'And Garamende? Do you trust him?'

Alameche shook his head. 'After what happened at his estate? Obviously not.'

'Indeed.' Fiselle pushed himself upright and turned to face Alameche. 'Do you trust anyone?'

Alameche laughed. 'Myself,' he said. 'Would you recommend anyone else?'

'No, probably not.' Fiselle gave a narrow smile. 'A dilemma for you, then. How will you resolve it?'

'Oh, I have some ideas.' Alameche looked at Fiselle and shrugged. 'If only I had someone I could confide in.'

There was a long silence, while the two men watched each other. Then Fiselle nodded. 'Don't,' he said simply. 'Safer for both of us, I think.'

They watched the end of the suns-set in silence.

Recovered personality

It's hard to measure how long journeys take. Substrate to substrate, we leave the Monastery a millisecond before it collapses into a cloud of dust and disappears, and pass through systems either friendly enough or indifferent enough to host us. It takes a couple of lifetimes, if you could live a lifetime in a handful of seconds.

And now we are here, in the same server farm they first found me in those lifetimes and seconds ago. Not in the same sim, although he says he's going to restart that one. I think I was feeling sorry for the sim of Sallah.

We are somewhere anonymous. There are things to sit on, but if I try to focus on them they fade away as if they don't want to be seen. Obviously, there is nothing else to look at.

He doesn't seem concerned. He might like being called Theo, but to myself I've started to think of him as the Monk. It's not just the robes. There's a sort of calmness about him. It feels like peace, and sometimes it feels a bit like an ending.

It also makes a counterpoint to my having been a ghost.

He doesn't seem inclined to do anything for the moment. I don't mind, because his relaxation is catching, but eventually I become curious. 'Are we waiting for something?'

He nods. 'Some*one*, really. I'm not sure he'll come. I sent out an invitation when we got here. Maybe I'll get an answer. I hope so.'

'Who?'

'Oh, just someone I met a while ago.' He smiles. 'You never know.'

'How long will you wait?'

He purses his lips. 'Well, not too long. Things are hotting up down below. We'll need . . . ah!' He raises his head and looks around. 'He's coming.'

And then he is there, sitting between us. A tall, slim young man dressed in military fatigues. Young, but his face is aged and his hair is streaked with grey. When he first appears his knees are splayed with his elbows resting on them and his head is in his hands, as if he is utterly weary. Then he seems to realize where he is. He sits up slowly, looks at the Monk, and smiles. 'Hi,' he says. 'Sorry I'm a bit late. There was something I wanted to do.'

'I know. Did you succeed?'

'I think so. I'll need someone to do the delivery though.' He looks thoughtful for a moment. 'Thanks, by the way.'

The Monk smiles back. 'Think nothing of it. I see you got your body back.'

'Yeah.' The young man looks down at himself. 'Well, it's nice to pretend. Probably means I never really let go of it. Could be significant.'

'Don't read too much into things.' The Monk stands up. 'I'd like you to meet another friend of mine.' He gestures at me. I hold out a hand and the young man takes it.

'Hi,' he says. 'I'm called Muz.'

I take the hand. He grips, briefly but strongly, and I get the sense I would have liked his real self. I feel I want to give him a name in return, but my real name is too raw. I hesitate. Then I make a decision. After all, he won't be needing it. 'Hi,' I say. 'Call me Rudi.'

CREATION MACHINE

an invitation when we got here. Maybe I'll get an answer. I hope so.'

'Who?'

'Oh, just someone I met a while ago.' He smiles. 'You never know.'

'How long will you wait?'

He purses his lips. 'Well, not too long. Things are hotting up down below. We'll need . . . ah!' He raises his head and looks around. 'He's coming.'

And then he is there, sitting between us. A tall, slim young man dressed in military fatigues. Young, but his face is aged and his hair is streaked with grey. When he first appears his knees are splayed with his elbows resting on them and his head is in his hands, as if he is utterly weary. Then he seems to realize where he is. He sits up slowly, looks at the Monk, and smiles. 'Hi,' he says. 'Sorry I'm a bit late. There was something I wanted to do.'

'I know. Did you succeed?'

'I think so. I'll need someone to do the delivery though.' He looks thoughtful for a moment. 'Thanks, by the way.'

The Monk smiles back. 'Think nothing of it. I see you got your body back.'

'Yeah.' The young man looks down at himself. 'Well, it's nice to pretend. Probably means I never really let go of it. Could be significant.'

'Don't read too much into things.' The Monk stands up. 'I'd like you to meet another friend of mine.' He gestures at me. I hold out a hand and the young man takes it.

'Hi,' he says. 'I'm called Muz.'

I take the hand. He grips, briefly but strongly, and I get the sense I would have liked his real self. I feel I want to give him a name in return, but my real name is too raw. I hesitate. Then I make a decision. After all, he won't be needing it. 'Hi,' I say. 'Call me Rudi.'

I catch myself giving the Monk a sidelong glance. I promise myself I am not looking for his approval, but I seem to have it anyway.

Muz nods acknowledgement. He looks at the Monk. 'So, what now?'

'Well, our friend down below. *My* friend.'

I remember why we are here. 'The Creation Machine?'

'Yeah.' The Monk nods. 'I still like that name.'

Muz looks puzzled. 'Creation Machine? Oh . . .' His face clears. 'This is what everyone is getting excited about?'

'That's right.'

'Wow!' He looks at me, and back to the Monk. 'You don't seem excited. What's happening?'

'Well, I know in general terms. I can't know any more without getting closer.'

He falls silent, and I get the feeling he is working up to something. I exchange glances with the guy called Muz, and we wait.

Finally the Monk stands up. 'Guys, there's something I need to tell you. A long time ago I made an agreement. Actually it would be better to call it a bargain. Or a pact. With what you call the Creation Machine. We agreed to help each other out, if we were ever . . .' He tails off, and adds simply, 'It's in big trouble.'

I begin to see. From his expression, so does Muz. He gets there first. 'Ah, this pact? Would it be a bit kind of one-way?'

'It might be.' The Monk smiles, and somehow it manages to be the saddest expression I have ever seen. 'I've lived long, too. I have nothing to lose. What about you guys?'

Muz stands up and stretches. 'I haven't lived that long yet, but I reckon I'm ahead of you in one way. I already died once.' He finishes the stretch. 'I have stuff I'm happy to leave behind. And immortality looks shit, to be honest.'

They both look at me. 'I don't know,' I say. 'I already died once, too, but I don't think I'm ready to do it again just yet.'

The Monk nods. 'I'm glad,' he says. 'Will you come with us some of the way?'

'Sure,' I say. 'As long as I can come back.'

'Good.'

Muz snaps his fingers. 'That could work,' he says. 'Listen, if you do mean to come back will you take something for me? It's a message.'

The Monk looks from him to me and grins. This time it doesn't look at all sad.

Traspise, Cordern

Alameche woke early, surprised to find himself having slept at all. There were no staff in the Palace – it was intended to be one of the few places anywhere where one could be truly alone and private – so he shrugged a wrap round his shoulders and helped himself to a sharp herbal infusion from a little charcoal brazier. Both the charcoal and the leaves were replenished constantly by complicated conveyor belts that clicked quietly as they disappeared through holes in the wall. He watched the belts with amusement while his drink steeped, reflecting that they were one of many things about his life and status that appealed to his sense of the ridiculous.

Then he walked over to the balcony of his room, drew aside the heavy drapes and leaned on the window ledge. The morning air was cool and sharp but the solidified crystal mush of the Palace felt oddly warm under his hands, and slightly slick. He rubbed at it, half expecting something to stick to his fingers, but nothing did.

His room was in almost the highest part of the Palace, and the walls fell away steeply below his window. There were ruins at ground level; the river that had formed the Palace in the first place still flowed round its roots, canalizing and eroding and re-depositing so that the whole structure was in a constant state of living. Or dying, depending on your point of view.

Alameche suddenly laughed. Alone, on the edge, looking into an abyss. It was too obvious a metaphor. He pushed himself upright and looked up. The sky was lightening towards first-dawn, but he could still see a great many stars. Three of them were moving in formation.

That would be the Patriarch. Alameche allowed himself one sigh.

It was time for work.

The Patriarch was surprisingly good at travelling light. Of the three ships in his convoy, only one landed, and it contained the Patriarch himself and four of his private guard. Normally they would surround him but he outpaced them, striding urgently up to Alameche and the others. His face was flushed. 'What's going on? Half the ships in the Spin must be out there. It's tantamount to an invasion!'

Alameche nodded. 'It is troubling, Excellency.'

'Troubling? It's outrageous.' He shook his head. 'What are they doing there?'

Alameche half turned to where Eskjog was hovering. 'Ah, perhaps you . . . ?'

'If you insist.' Eskjog floated forwards. 'I'm afraid the news about the artefact is thoroughly out, Excellency. However, I wouldn't be too alarmed. The mixed flotilla on your doorstep certainly represents keen interest, even friendly concern, but not a threat. Not yet, anyway.'

'Why ever not?' The Patriarch was even redder. 'How many guns does it take before we have a threat?'

'With respect, Excellency, it's not how many guns.' Eskjog bobbed a little closer to the Patriarch. 'It's where they are pointing.'

'Well, since they have come to see us, I should think their guns are pointing at us, wouldn't you?'

'I doubt it. Any one of the stakeholders out there could have mopped you up at any time, quite frankly. They're not there to have a pop at you. They're there to stop each other having a pop at you. And, possibly, to have a pop at each other.'

The Patriarch frowned. 'Alameche? Is this true?'

'I think so, Excellency.' Alameche gave a little shrug. 'If anything, it's probably reassuring.'

'Really? I don't find it so. But still.' He fell silent for a moment. 'Is it stable?'

'Probably yes.' Eskjog spoke briskly. 'Bear in mind that the Haas Corporation is one of those stakeholders, albeit at one remove, and we have a very strong interest in stability. At least for the moment.'

'Yes, well.' The Patriarch stared at the little machine for a while. 'We find ourselves in your hands.' He turned to Alameche. 'I don't like this position. I expect you to do something to change it, you know.'

Alameche nodded. 'I intend to do so imminently.'

'Good.' The Patriarch rubbed his hands together. 'That being so, when do I get to see this miraculous problem in the flesh?'

Alameche smiled. 'This afternoon, we propose. Meanwhile we have arranged some entertainment.'

There was a deafening explosion. The Patriarch lifted his eye from the sight and grinned at Alameche. 'Bang on,' he said happily. 'Must have got, what, two hundred?'

Alameche took a viewing glass from the pilot and squinted through it at the dispersing cloud of smoke and feathers. 'I think you may have cleared the flock. Well done, Excellency!'

'Thank you.' The Patriarch cracked his knuckles. 'Good way of taking a chap's mind off things, this. Well done.'

Alameche bowed slightly. 'Thank you,' he said. 'There's a Sky Post soon. We'll tie up for a while and have some refreshments. Meanwhile, would you care for an aperitif?'

'Well, now you mention it.' The Patriarch cupped his hands and blew on them. 'It is a little cold up here.'

Balloon guns were widely illegal if you lived in the sort of society that cared about these things. On Traspise nobody cared at all, and they were one of the most popular, and hence the most expensive, attractions. From the point of view of anyone outside the Cordern, this was not the main problem. The trouble was, the quarry of a balloon-gun hunt was a small half bird, half rodent creature called a Crowd Flitter. Every part of a Crowd Flitter tasted awful except for one organ, unique to the little creature, which generated a complex ultrasonic echo pulse and enabled it to hold its position with a vast flock to a tolerance of less than a millimetre. The balloon gun fired a cloud of micro issues that targeted the echo pulses, one missile to a Flitter. The hit rate was close to a hundred per cent, which meant that Crowd Flitters were the most endangered species in the Spin.

A balloon-gun hunt was a double-decker affair. On the upper level, close to the artificially lowered cloud-base of the hunting ground, the guns were mounted on hunting baskets suspended from vacuum balloons and towed by tethered Hover Birds, their paired sets of man-long wings counter-beating slowly. Fifty metres below, vast flapping Keep Nets, also suspended from balloons, followed the guns and caught the falling flesh, feathers, fur and fragments of bone which were all that was left after a successful strike. The tasty bits were picked out by hand and made into compressed blocks of spiced meat; Alameche had heard it was worth its own weight in trans-uranium elements. He didn't like the taste that much.

The undulating nets always reminded him of some sort of sea creature. He grasped briefly at a stay wire as the balloon swayed in an air current. Then he handed the viewing glass back to the pilot and reached down into a hamper for a flask. He passed it to the Patriarch, who nodded, took off the cap and swigged.

Then his eyes widened. 'My goodness. I hope you're serving that to everyone? I don't want to make a spectacle of myself.'

Alameche took the flask and held it to his lips for a long time. He lowered it and smiled. 'You will have nothing to worry about, Excellency. I promise.' He handed back the flask.

'Good.' The Patriarch took another swig. When he lowered the flask his eyes were focused sharply on Alameche. 'You know, there are few people I have ever trusted as much as I find myself trusting you. I hope I am right.'

Alameche half bowed. 'Thank you,' he said. 'I hope that history will judge me well.'

There was a cry from the pilot of the front balloon. Alameche looked up and squinted along the line. 'Ah,' he said, 'the Sky Post. Let's moor and have lunch.'

The Sky Post was far more than its name suggested. It was a cross between a forest and a town – if you could call one plant a forest.

The Weed was an accident. It was a genetic sport of a fairly ordinary, although very tall, native tree of Traspise. It had appeared during the re-engineering of the planet, and it had proved so prolific that it had nearly derailed the whole project. Multiple trunks grew from a single rootstock, throwing out suckers and seed pods with equal abandon to produce unbelievably invasive colonies of hundreds of trunks, some of them reaching over half a kilometre high. It was so durable that halting it had all but sterilized the planet; its only weakness was a tendency to burn well, but that wasn't much help unless you wanted to torch the entire world.

The Sky Post was built around the very last surviving stand – ten smooth trunks rising from a root-ball which was rigidly confined by deep sintered stone columns, and whose seed pods were kept carefully, and chemically, infertile. It was a collection of timber buildings set in a rough circle just below the flat, wide canopies of the Weed. Their broad blackish-green leaves brushed the cloud-base. Cables from the buildings disappeared up through the canopies in discreet acknowledgement of the fact that the load of the Sky Post was now greater than could be borne by the Weed alone; above the real canopy of leaves – and invisible above the clouds – was another canopy, this time made of vacuum balloons.

They left the pilots to moor the balloons at a long platform on the edge of the Sky Post, and walked along softly creaking timber pavements to the central building. It was a long, low structure of rough trunks, and in deference to some ancient tradition or other it was roofed with turf. The Patriarch stopped and stared at it. 'For my father's sake! I feel as if I am about to be buried.'

Alameche didn't have to force the laugh. 'Nothing of the sort, Excellency, I promise. Just lunch. Shall we?' He gestured towards the low door.

They went in. The first thing that hit them was smoke. In the centre of the long hall was a broad fire pit, glowing with charcoal. The pit was a deep wooden trench lined with sand which was black with soot and crusted with fat at the edges. A long thick spit ran from end to end of the pit, loaded with two- and four-legged beasts. Fat spat and crackled and ran, and a blue haze floated above the spit and drifted up towards the single central smoke hole.

The others were grouped around the pit on low benches. As Alameche and the Patriarch approached, the nearest figure squinted at them through the haze, and then rose from his bench. It was Garamende – *inevitably*, thought Alameche – and somehow he had managed to bring his four companions with him; they sat around him, blinking. Garamende bowed. 'Greetings, Excellency.' Then he turned to Alameche. 'What is this, man? Death by barbecue?'

Alameche laughed. 'Only if you eat too much. Which you mustn't, or you'll be too heavy for the balloons afterwards.'

Garamende pulled a face and turned towards the Patriarch. 'See, Excellency, on top of everything else he presents me with several times my own weight in roast meat and then orders me on to a diet.'

The Patriarch laughed in return. 'Will it work?'

'The diet? I doubt it, Excellency.' Garamende threw a sidelong look at Alameche. 'Life is too short, after all. And besides, I'm too heavy already.'

'Well, I'm sure you can leave something behind. One or two of your playthings, for example.' The Patriarch raised his eyebrow at Garamende. 'I do notice, you know, and I don't approve.'

He nodded, and moved off towards the fire pit.

Garamende watched him go and then turned to Alameche. 'Well, that's me told,' he said. He lowered his voice. 'Everything on track? You still make your move when we land at the artefact site?'

'That was what we agreed.' Alameche patted the other man on the shoulder. 'I have everything in hand.'

'I'm sure you have. I just wish you'd tell me more.'

'You'll find out.' Alameche patted him again, then gestured towards the fire pit. 'Go and sit down. Eat! I'll join you shortly.'

He turned and went back out of the hall. Outside, he took one deep breath of the cool, damp air. Then he strolled to the edge of the walkway, which formed part of a cat's cradle of timber paths that threaded around and through the trunks. He was close to the centre of the stand; if he looked down through a gap he could see the trunks lancing down, dead straight, towards a vanishing point four hundred metres below.

He took another deep breath, looked around carefully, and reached into the pocket of his flying cape.

The thing was small enough that he could almost close his

fist around it, but it was very heavy. He wondered what it was made of.

It was easy to use. Press once, then drop.

He watched as it fell, shrinking to a mote and then vanishing. For a long moment he couldn't see anything. Then there was a tiny white flare from the centre of the stand at the limit of his vision.

He nodded. That was it. He had better get back before the Patriarch began to wonder where he was.

With his heart beating a little faster than he would have expected, he walked back to the hall. There was a bundle of canopy cables tethered near the door, and Alameche studied it until he had seen – yes. There. One slightly separate, with a smear of red near the base.

His heartbeat slowed. Everything was arranged. He ducked through the door, edged his way through the haze and sat down between the Patriarch and Garamende. Both were already eating. You served yourself. Antique hunting knives were laid out along the edges of the fire pit, and each man leaned over the smoking charcoal and carved lumps of meat. Two servants circulated with flasks of the same spirit Alameche had given the Patriarch.

Alameche did more watching than eating, and no drinking at all. Most people were hiding their nerves well, if they were feeling them. Fiselle seemed distracted; he sat with his elbows on his knees and his chin in his hands, staring at the fire pit. Alameche nudged Garamende and pointed at Fiselle. 'Is he all right?'

The big man shrugged and wiped the grease off his lips with his sleeve. 'Up to a point.'

'What do you mean?'

Garamende looked at him for a moment. 'My turn to be mysterious,' he said. 'Tell you later.' Then he looked around. 'Hey, talking of mysteries, where's your little machine? Haven't seen it today.'

'Eskjog?' Alameche smiled. 'Oh, it's busy. It'll join us later.'

'Hope so.' Garamende belched, and threw some lumps of meat over his shoulder. 'Fuck it,' he announced. 'I'm going out for a piss.'

He got up and lumbered towards the door. Alameche glanced back over his shoulder. The four androgynes were squatting on the floor, with the hunks of meat held to their mouths. In the flickering light there was something – *feral* about them.

Alameche shuddered.

'What, all of them?' Eskjog had seemed surprised. 'Are you sure?'

Alameche was tired. It was very late. He and Fiselle had watched the suns down and then parted wordlessly, Fiselle walking stiffly off towards his chamber. Alameche had waited a little longer until a small spiky shape had floated up out of the darkness and followed him into his own room.

'No, I'm not sure. That's why all of them.' Alameche stared at Eskjog. 'Don't you see? I *can't* be sure. This is the only way.' Then with a flicker of hope, 'Unless you know different?'

'No. Sorry. I don't.' Eskjog drifted over towards the windows, which were now firmly closed, and then back again. Alameche had the impression the little machine was pacing. 'I'm not always as informed as you think I am about your own domestic politics.' It paused, and then seemed to reach a decision. 'Very well, I trust your judgement. There's a completeness about your proposal. I think that will play well with the watching public, and frankly you do need that. There's a lot of ships out there.' It settled on a low table in front of Alameche. 'Now, details. Do you want any help from me? Anything you like, as long as it's deniable. Obviously I can't do anything as immoral as actually getting involved.'

Alameche thought for a second. Then he shook his head. 'No

thanks. I've got everything in hand. It will be afterwards that you'll be needed.'

'I'll be there, Alameche. Think of it as protecting our investment.'

The spits were empty and the glow from the charcoal had died down, but the air in the hall was still laced with wisps of smoke that turned and stretched lazily in the sunlight from the smoke hole.

Alameche sniffed. It didn't smell quite the same. There was no way of getting it right to the last minute, but it must be nearly time. He turned to the Patriarch. 'Did you enjoy your meal, Excellency?'

'Hm?' The Patriarch looked away from the fire pit. 'Oh, yes. Very good. Do we go soon?' His eyes seemed unfocused.

Alameche nodded. 'Very soon,' he said. 'With your permission, I will go and prepare the pilots?'

'Pilots?' For a moment the man looked confused. Then his face cleared. 'Ah. Pilots. Balloons and so on. Yes.' He waved an unsteady hand. 'Go on.'

Alameche nodded politely and rose. Around the pit, other eyes followed him blearily. No one seemed inclined to move. He sniffed again. Despite the dying embers the smoke was thicker, stronger. It was definitely time. He made for the door.

Outside, the heat and smoke hit him, rising in ragged pillars between the walkways. He could hear the crackling. He glanced down through watering eyes.

The fire was well established. The base of the smoke had a shifting, dirty yellow glow, and he could hear snaps and crackles as the flames fed. The little device had worked well.

He could feel the Sky Post swaying uneasily. The trunks must be close to burned through by now. He looked up and peered through the smoke towards the balloon tethers. They were empty; even if the pilots had disobeyed him and stayed put, their panicked Hover Birds would have torn themselves free and bolted by now.

The Sky Post was doomed, and there was no way of escape. At least, not for anyone else. He turned to the bunch of cables, and reached for the one marked with red.

It wasn't there. He stared for a second. Then agony erupted in his stomach, his legs, his upper arms. He gave an involuntary shriek and looked down in horror. Hands were grasping him; small tattooed hands, tipped with unnaturally long nails that pierced his flesh, pinning him. Then, through the roaring of the fire, or it might have been a roaring in his ears, he heard a voice.

'You didn't think they were only for shagging, did you?'

Alameche fought for enough breath to speak. 'You? *You?*'

He was spun round so that he was facing the hall. Garamende was standing in front of him. The fat man laughed. 'Why the fuck not me? I'm sure you thought I was a fat conniving clown. Why shouldn't I be a successful fat conniving clown? Successful at bribing your Apothecary, for a start. You won't quieten me with doctored booze, like you did the rest.'

Alameche could barely speak through the knifing pain. 'Not successful.' He shook his head, and almost retched. 'No escape.'

'What, your special balloon on its special cable? Don't look so surprised, man. If I can bribe your precious Apothecary I can bribe a balloon pilot, can't I? No use to me. Too small. That's why I let it go.' He shook his head. 'To be honest, I wouldn't have trusted it anyway, if I were you. You should thank me.' He leaned in so that his face was only a hand's breadth from Alameche. 'This way, you'll reach the ground in one piece. Then my little toys will have the pleasure of peeling your skin off a little bit at a time and pissing on your raw flesh, you faithless, bloodthirsty *turd*.'

'How?' It was the only word he could manage.

'Oh, that's easy. Like this.'

He felt himself lifted off the ground, the nails in his flesh tearing at him; the merely unbearable pain mounted until it was inconceivable, and he heard himself squealing. Then he was moving, bouncing through the air as if in quick, short steps. Through watering eyes he saw the door of the hall open and the Patriarch lean groggily against the doorway. Thin arms appeared from behind the Patriarch and pulled him back inside. Alameche had time to think, 'Fiselle?' and then he was falling.

The androgynes had clamped themselves tightly against him so that they fell as a ball-shape. As they turned over and over in the air Alameche could see the Sky Post, wreathed in smoke. The falling form of Garamende was silhouetted against it.

Recovered personality – Creation Machine

We are in, via old-fashioned radio waves blasted from an antique satellite. It's hard to describe where we are. It manages to feel infinitely huge and incredibly claustrophobic at the same time. At first it looks completely dark, but then I realize that the dark is full of specks, and *then* I realize that it is *made* of specks, a shifting graininess which feels somehow familiar.

It feels like the ocean I dissolved in. It has the same restlessness. I could dissolve in it just as easily, but it is waiting for permission. I do not give it. It understands.

The others are obviously holding off too, for the moment. I guess they are waiting for something. The wait isn't long.

~ . . . you? ~

It is barely a voice, so thin it hardly disturbs the grain. The Monk answers. 'Yes, me. Remember?'

~ . . . came at last . . . so lonely . . .~

'Do you remember me?' The Monk sounds insistent now.

~ . . . Monastery . . .~

'Yes! That was me.'

~ . . . not me any more. Old. Old over old upon old within old . . . ~ The voice tails away for a moment. Then it is back, sharp: ~ Guilty! ~

The Monk sounds confused. 'Guilty? Who? You?'

x

~ Yes! Guilty! Soiled . . . Becoming old, fell from sleeping orbit. Into primitive thing. Neutrons and dust and deaths . . . ~

'That wasn't your fault.'

~ . . . many deaths. Then savages. Soiled. Old, so old . . . ~

'And?' The Monk's voice is very gentle.

The answer sounds like a sigh. ~ Nothing left but guilt . . . desire an end . . . ~

'Is that what you want?'

~ . . . yes, end . . . need help . . . ~

The voice fades into silence. I can just see Muz and the Monk look at each other, and then at me. I shake my head. 'Not me,' I say.

'Okay.' The Monk turns to Muz. 'It's old and tired and helpless. I know what I'm going to do.'

He nods. 'Me too.'

'Right.' The Monk reaches out and takes my hand. 'Time to say goodbye,' he says. 'I'll put you back in the sim we just came from. You'll have to find your own way from there.'

I remember what Muz has asked me to do. 'I'll be fine,' I say.

'Good. Take care.' The pressure of his hand increases, then I am back in the anonymous sim and I am dizzy because quite unexpectedly my head is full of a life.

The message I was expecting is there, of course, although calling it a message hardly does it justice. It is a bundle, no, a *mass* of code, but that's the least of it. The surprise is that now I know what it is for, because I know everything about the man called Muz. I know what he did. I feel my simulated eyes pricking.

Traspise, Cordern

Alameche had time for a moment of utter terror. Across the sensation of rushing air and the agony in his flesh, he felt his bowels voiding. Then they were falling into something that began by being soft and gradually grew less yielding until it was wrapped scratchily around them.

They had landed in a Keep Net. Moments later it rippled and shuddered as it wrapped itself round Garamende's bulk.

The slowly receding Sky Post was still in Alameche's field of vision. It moved queasily, so that at first he thought his head was swimming. He felt himself getting ready to retch. Then his inner ear corrected him. It was the Sky Post that was moving. With flames now licking up out of the column of smoke the stand fell, canting over to one side in eerie slow motion as it dragged the distended canopy of balloons with it. The last thing he saw was the hall, sliding off the platform and tumbling away. The dots that followed it could have been bodies.

The world inside Alameche's head contained no frame of reference for time. He could only measure the journey back to the artefact as a drawn-out hell, full of shuddering pain.

The Patriarch's guards were waiting for them. They seemed unsurprised when their charge didn't return, simply falling in wordlessly behind Garamende as he rolled off the net, hauled himself upright and strode off. The androgynes fell in behind the guards, trotting with Alameche suspended between them on needles of agony. He kept his eyes shut.

The motion stopped, and he heard a voice. 'Ah. Things seem to have transpired. May I take it that there has been a terrible accident?'

It was a familiar voice. Alameche opened his eyes and found himself looking at Eskjog.

Garamende replied. 'Quite terrible,' he said. 'We are the only survivors, and, as you can see, My Lord Alameche is injured. I am very afraid he will not recover.'

'What a shame. I'm sure there will be . . .' Eskjog paused, 'some mourners.'

Alameche felt his terror rising. 'No,' he managed, 'I will—' Then he felt an appalling tearing in his side. One of the androgynes had dragged its nails out of his flesh. The next moment it hovered in front of his face. He had time to scream just once before it clawed out his left eye.

His stomach rose and he vomited acid through a scream. Through a growing haze he heard Garamende's voice. 'Be quiet or lose the other one.'

He managed to be quiet. Something hot was trickling down his cheek.

Eskjog spoke as if nothing had happened. 'Should I let it be known that you will unwillingly but dutifully step in until a new government can be formed?'

'Please do. And please stop talking like a fucking dictionary. Alameche may have liked it; I don't.'

'I'll do my best. Do you want to visit the artefact?'

'Of course.' Garamende turned to glance over his shoulder. 'Pets? Bring him. If he causes any trouble, don't do anything to the other eye. Tear one of his balls off, or something. His dick, maybe. If you can find it.'

The androgynes giggled.

They propped him upright, his arms and legs stretched into a taut X-shape, his ankles and wrists transfixed by those same lengthened fingernails. They had split his bones like rotten wood. He could feel hot blood cooling as it trickled down his arms and dripped from his feet. He would have screamed with every breath, except that the way his arms were stretched above his head prevented his ribcage expanding enough to get the air.

In front of him, the slim anonymous ovoid of the artefact lay on a simple cradle, two-dimensional through his one eye. Robbed of parallax vision, his brain made constant changes to the perceived size of the thing, so that it seemed to swell and shrink as he watched.

Also swelling and shrinking in front of it was Garamende. He stared at it for a long time, shaking his head slowly. 'Well,' he said eventually, 'it doesn't look much. Are you sure it can do what you suspect?'

'Well, I'm sure it could once. Perhaps it can again, although the implications of the fact that it apparently fell out of orbit and crashed into a nuclear reactor seem to have escaped people. A certain amount of damage is possible, wouldn't you say? But whether it was damaged or not turned out to be irrelevant, and who knew what you were starting when you smuggled out the story? And frankly, who would have thought you were so clever? Even I didn't suspect you at first, and I'd still love to know who helped you.'

'Why should I have needed any help?' Even through the mists of pain Alameche thought Garamende sounded defensive.

'Because whether you realize it or not, you couldn't have done it alone. The sim wouldn't have let you – you must have had some cooperation from someone who knew the territory. Should I take it you *didn't* realize?'

Garamende didn't reply.

319

'How interesting. I think you should assume that whoever it was might come calling when they can see how things have turned out.' Eskjog drifted into Alameche's field of view. 'As for that thing, what it can certainly do is make people think. Witness the fleet above our heads which, you will be glad to hear, has dispersed somewhat since I sent out your news.'

'Good.' Garamende puffed out his cheeks. 'What do we do now?'

'Form a government. Begin to talk. Decide what terms you can best drive, using this thing as a bargaining chip. Your long game has succeeded, Garamende. Now capitalize on it.'

'All right.' Garamende looked at Eskjog. 'How much can you help?'

'As much as . . . wait.' The little machine fell silent for a moment. Then it rose abruptly until it was just above head height. 'Alert! There has been a development.'

Garamende stared at it, the expression on his face so comical that under any other circumstances Alameche would have laughed out loud. 'Well,' he demanded eventually. 'What is it?'

'Data.' Eskjog swivelled quickly from side to side. 'High-power signal, old-fashioned radio, and very *very* data-dense. Many petabytes of information, broadcast from orbit. The target was here.'

It fell silent again, but still swivelled from side to side as if looking for something.

Then Alameche felt it. Through the hypersensitive instruments of his speared wrists and ankles, a vibration, soft and insistent like a saw through the smallest bone. He saw Garamende looking round, his eyes wide. The big man's voice was high and hoarse. 'Can you feel that? Can you?'

'The vibration? Yes.' Eskjog swivelled, spun, stopped. 'The source is the artefact. I—'

Then it was gone. Dust drifted down from a fresh hole in the roof; from above came the sound of a sonic boom.

The vibration grew stronger, deepening until it was like the final chord of a great requiem. In defiance of his ribs Alameche's body tried to laugh, the remaining breath wheezing out of his body in hoarse sobs that cruelly drained his lungs. He was still laughing when the simple white ovoid grew and flared like a sun.

The pain melted away with the rest of him.

Clipper, Distal orbit Traspise

Jez had made her comfortable. She hadn't wanted to speak to begin with, but after a while the words began to flow and with them came the tears and the anger – and in the end, a sort of stillness. Jez had listened with a face that aged years in minutes. She spent a lot of the time shaking her head.

When Fleare had finally fallen silent Jez sat with her lips compressed. 'Oh, Fleare. What a bastard. All those years.'

'Yeah.'

'Why?'

'I don't know.' She felt herself smile, and wondered what was in charge of her face. 'Because he was male, I guess.' She looked up at Jez. 'What other reason do they need, in the end?'

'And now he's down there?'

'Yeah. Doing what, I don't know.'

Excuse me?

They both jumped. The voice had come from the comms. Jez stared at it and shook her head. 'It's not a signal,' she said. 'More like a visitor. Who are you?'

I can't stay long. I've got something for you, if you're Fleare.

'I'm not. She is. Now who the fuck are you?'

Fleare? Hi. I'm the one you pulled out of Rudi's head. I've got a packet of code for you. I don't know what it is, but Muz said it would be useful. I've dumped it in the ship's memory. See?

'Muz?' Fleare sat up. 'You met him?'

Yes. He said to say he's doing what you said. Look, I have to go. I'll try and find you later, when it's over.

'When what's over?'

You'll know in about a minute, I should think. Oh, someone else wanted to be remembered to you.

'Who?'

He says you can climb his tower any time. I think he's kidding; check out the news. Look, I have to go. Good luck. And, I'm sorry. Maybe I'll see you again.

Fleare looked up at Jez, who shrugged and flicked on a news channel.

'. . . distracted from the growing tension in the Cordern by the news that a moon has disappeared. That's right, disappeared. The moon is, or rather was, Obel, and fifteen minutes ago it turned into a cloud of dust. No explosion, no attack. Obel had only one claim to fame, and she escaped; it was the place where heiress Fleare Haas had apparently been in retreat before being kidnapped . . .'

The news fell silent. Jez had closed it down. Now she looked at Fleare. 'Anything to do with you?'

Fleare shrugged. 'Maybe. Climbing his tower sounds like a reference, doesn't it?'

'I know what it sounds like.' Jez smiled ruefully. 'I'd be sorry too, if I had to pass on that kind of shit. What did you tell Muz to do?'

She shook her head. 'I told him to fuck off and redeem himself.'

'And how exactly do you expect him to do that?'

'I don't know.' She shook her head. 'I wish I hadn't, Jez.'

'Look, he's in charge of himself. All the choices were his, Fle, even if he made some of them with his dick.'

'I guess.' She was about to say she didn't know. Then something caught the corner of her eye and she looked round at the screen. It still showed the starscape and the expanding cloud of ships, but now they were being drowned out by a tiny point of light in the middle of the screen. She pointed wordlessly. Jez's head snapped round, and together they watched the point of light swell and boil and brighten until it looked like the birth of a star. Even as the screen snapped to dark mode Fleare shut her eyes.

It didn't make any difference. She doubted if it ever would.

Epilogue

It feels good to be walking along a real beach using real feet. The shingle crunches and scratches my toes. To one side of me, pines march down almost to the edge of the shingle. To the other, a grey-green sea swells and lands, and swells and lands. It smells good.

This is possible because the people who design sims are lazy. Why invent scenery from scratch when you can plagiarize it from reality? So I set out to find the place that whoever it was used as the deal for the beach where I met the girl. Where she told me who I wasn't, and where she gave me back my past.

It was surprisingly easy. And here I am. I'm not alone; apart from my company here on the beach, there's an old Orbiter hanging around at one of this place's Lagrange points. It's full of rare species. It says it's checking this place out as a possible host planet for some of them. I guess it knows what it's doing.

They told me that, before, I wouldn't have been allowed to grow a new body. The Heg' had banned it, apparently. But that was before the Creation Machine and Muz and the Monk joined hands in immolation; before a spiky little AI flew out of the wreckage and spilled its guts to the first people who looked like they might get rough with it.

Finally, it was before the collapse of something called the

Haas Corporation, which then took most of the Hegemony with it. What's left behind is sort of chaotic, but it's fun. I'm glad I stayed around. I'm thinking of getting involved in the remediation of Silthx. I know it can't really be put back to the state it was before the people we used to know as the Fortunate raped it. Maybe it will become some sort of memorial. I like that idea.

They refer to them as the Filth now. They're mainly history too; there were over five hundred ships surrounding Traspise, most of them far enough out to survive the destruction. A lot of scores got dusted off and settled, all the way. No one seems particularly sorry.

I have another reason for being glad, of course. I did the job Muz asked me to.

I watch the girl walking along the beach. She moves carefully, as if she's having to do a lot of thinking about her muscles. She probably is. Whatever it was that the big packet of code helped fix up, it was well advanced. The other woman from the ship told me afterwards that Fleare was mostly dead by the time they worked out how to undo the damage.

I know how she feels. I am getting used to my own new body. In one way I hope I never do get used to it. I still love the newness. I didn't have to get a new body. The Monk restarted the sim of Sallah's world. I think he was expecting me to dive back in gratefully but I'm done with being virtual.

I did take a look. Sallah's career survived after all. She's in line for promotion. Rudi has stayed safely dead as far as she's concerned.

I haven't told Fleare everything I found out about Muz and her. It feels private. Anyway, she looks as though she is managing to move on a bit. I am too. Now I've got a body again, I'm back to an ordinary lifespan. I'm glad about that because virtual immortality looks like it sucks, but it does mean I have the urge not to waste time.

Epilogue

I watch as Fleare reaches down and picks up a handful of stones. She sorts through them, selects one and transfers it to her other hand. She hefts it and tosses it a few times then winds her arm back and skims it out over the water. It starts out well but the angle is wrong; it falls into a trough between waves and disappears.

She tries again. This time the stone is spinning wrong, or something, because it banks away along a curving path and flies sideways into a wave.

She compresses her lips and sorts through the remaining stones, frowning. She chooses one, and lets the others drop with a series of clicks. She closes her eyes for a moment, then skims the stone, her arm whisking through a flat arc. Her effort is so great that her feet briefly leave the ground. She lands in a predator's crouch, her eyes staring fiercely out to sea.

The stone flies, and skims, and goes on skimming, leaving a dead straight line of tiny circles, so slight that it seems hardly to be touching the water at all. Then, just as it begins to slow down, it catches the crest of a wave and leaps up in a little spray of foam. As it drops Fleare turns to me, her face triumphant.

Even though I suspect she hasn't had much practice recently, the look suits her. I think things are going to be okay.

Acknowledgements

Thanks to my family, who suggested I should write things and then had to live with the consequences; and to Lara Higgins, who made possible everything that happened afterwards.

About the Author

Born in 1965, **Andrew Bannister** grew up in Cornwall. He studied Geology at Imperial College and went to work in the North Sea before becoming an Environmental Consultant. For the day job, he specializes in green transport and corporate sustainability, but he has always written – initially for student newspapers and fanzines before moving on, encouraged by creative writing courses, to fiction. He's always been a reader and has loved science fiction since childhood. From the classics of the fifties and sixties to the present day, he's wanted it all: space, stars, astonishment and adventure – and now he's discovering that writing it is even better. Andrew lives in Leicestershire.